Praise for Joseph Connolly

'Connolly unfolds a rich and compelling drama of life that is anything but everyday, with Dickensian attention to detail, trademark black humour and a genuine love for his creations' *Daily Mail*

'Connolly specialises in sardonic period melodramas whose characters he either harshly cherishes or affectionately despises – it's hard to resolve the nuance, which is part of the sour fun of reading him . . . He knows exactly what he's doing, in an immensely contrived, sophisticated and satisfying game' *Observer*

'Connolly remorselessly points up social pretensions with the eye of Dostoevsky . . . this satire on human behaviour is timeless' *Independent*

'A writer of considerable power and subtlety' *Guardian*

'Connolly has a keen sense of the hushed emotional tenderness of English life and our silent shattering pain' *Sunday Telegraph*

'It is Connolly's skill to get the reader to laugh at what should make you cry or at least wince' *Times Literary Supplement*

'A virtuoso performance' *Sunday Times*

'Connolly creates a sense of intimacy and collusion with his reader that is rare in contemporary fiction' *Financial Times*

'With brilliant execution Connolly plunges the reader into each of his characters' heads . . . keeps the reader hooked through it all' *Mail on Sunday*

'Connolly has an extraordinary prose style. It's jaw-dropping. Shocking. Mesmerising. It's desperately and excruciatingly funny' *Ham&High*

'He remains essentially a comic novelist but one whose work has its dark, even sinister side . . . other novelist today who writes qui

By Joseph Connolly

BOYS
AND
GIRLS

JOSEPH CONNOLLY

Quercus

First published in Great Britain in 2014 by Quercus Editions Ltd
This paperback edition published in Great Britain in 2015 by

Quercus Editions Ltd
55 Baker Street
7th Floor, South Block
London
W1U 8EW

A CIP catalogue record for this book is available
from the British Library

ISBN 978 1 78429 346 8
EBOOK ISBN 978 1 78087 724 2

10 9 8 7 6 5 4 3 2 1

Typeset by Ellipsis Books Limited, Glasgow

Printed and bound in Great Britain by Clays Ltd, St Ives plc

To the boy and girl
Charles and Victoria

Boys and girls come out to play,
The moon doth shine as bright as day.
Come with a whoop and come with a call,
Come with good will or not at all.

(Traditional nursery rhyme)

PART ONE

CHAPTER ONE

I got up at the crack of noon – show a bit willing, make a kind of effort – but it seemed to be far too late for, oh – just everything. I was still in my pyjamas, had them bunched up at the scruff of the waist – no slippers on, or anything – and then she just hit me with it. I was stunned, and I had to look down, trying to avoid any sight of my feet. Hate them in general, feet, and my two especially. I have to say I was stunned, though: stunned.

'Why are you leaving me? I thought we were happy.'

'It isn't really a question of happy, though, is it Alan? Really.'

'Is it not? I thought it was. Oh God I'm so miserable. Don't leave me, Susan. Please don't leave me. I never thought you would, just walk out and leave me.'

'I want another husband. It's simple, really.'

I think I must have been pinkly blinking – maybe a true white innocence suddenly awake and crawling all over me.

'Oh God. Oh God. You're leaving me. You're really going to do it . . .'

'You're not listening to me, are you Alan my sweet? My sugar. I've not even mentioned it, have I? I said nothing about leaving you. Did I? Mm? All I said is, I want another husband.

You see? Yes? No. You don't, do you? Just look at your face: total blank. Well let me explain it to you, yes? Shall I, Alan?'

'That would be . . . nice . . .'

'Well listen, then. I want another husband. With me so far? Good, Alan: good. But not instead of, Alan – no. Not instead. As *well* as . . . You see? Oh do shut your mouth, Alan, for heaven's sake do. You look just like a fish. Gaping like that. And don't for goodness sake start worrying about having to *do* anything, or anything – I'll take care of all the details, just as I always do. I'll arrange it all. You could give me away, if you liked. Would you like that, Alan my sweet? And of course you wouldn't *really* be giving me away, would you? Because I'll still be here. And so will he.'

'He . . . ?'

'He. Whoever he may be. Don't know yet. Must be rich, of course. I'm rather fed up with being the breadwinner, now. It's really a bit late for breakfast, anything proper. Why don't you just have some cereal, or something? Apple, maybe.'

Mm. So that, I suppose, was the start of it all. That, I think, must surely have been the moment. And I tried to think that she's joking maybe, is she? But she didn't much – joke, my Susan. Can it be, then, that she's merely mad? She certainly could seem so, at times, my Susan, and never more so than just lately. It was my being out of work that could have triggered it. I think that's what it must have been. The nub of it. I used to be in advertising, you know.

'It's a shame, I think Alan, that you had to go and be one of the creatives. Because you aren't really, are you my sweet? Creative. My sugar.'

'McVitie's Bake a Better Biscuit didn't just tumble out of an actor's mouth, you know . . .'

4

'Mm yes of *course* I know that, Alan – of course I do. It was terribly clever of you to think of it, terribly terribly clever. But it was rather a long time ago, wasn't it? That one. And the agency, well . . . they can't really have thought you were, can they? Very. Creative, I mean. Because it's hardly the way, is it? Generally speaking. To reward a valued creative by giving him the sack. It's roundabout, isn't it? Oblique. Praise-wise.'

'They were downshifting . . .'

'Yes. That's what you said at the time. Well they certainly shifted you anyway, didn't they Alan? Out if not down.'

'I think you said that at the time also, you know. More than once, as I recall.'

'Well it's no help at all if you're just going to get into one of your *sulks* now, is it Alan? Really. And it's not as if your next endeavour was exactly a runaway success now, is it? If we're being honest. Writing the things in Christmas crackers. Didn't scoop you the Nobel Prize, did it? Wasn't the great novel, was it, that we were always hearing about.'

'Cookies . . .'

'I beg your pardon, Alan? What did you say?'

'Fortune cookies. They weren't for Christmas crackers, as well you know. They were for fortune cookies.'

'Oh yes of course they were – they were, they were, of *course* they were. How could I be forgetting a simple thing like that? Because we got them, didn't we? Boxes and boxes of them. Crates of the things. Maybe in lieu of a fee, were they Alan? I never did ask. Did you think those little crackers were better than money, did you Alan my sweet? But of course the electricity people, the gas people, all the rest of them – they're terribly old-fashioned when it comes right down to it, aren't they really? Will insist on *money*, won't they? No matter how sweetly you offer them a box of cookies, they still seem to prefer hard cash. Yes . . . those little cookies . . . our life seemed rather to depend on them, didn't it? For a long while. Biscuits, of one sort or another. Poor Amanda, she practically had to live off them – took nothing else to school with her for months on end. She said she wouldn't mind, but the mottoes, jokes inside, were just so very awful. Were they jokes, Alan? That you wrote? Were they meant to be funny?'

'Not especially . . .'

'Oh good. Well this is good to know. I maybe should tell her, Amanda, should I? Amanda, dearest – they weren't actually *meant* to be funny, all those little things your father put into the biscuits. They were in fact meant to be . . . um, what were they meant to be in fact, Alan my sweet? Wise, were they? Were they meant to be wise, do you suppose? Alan? My sugar?'

On and on. Then I got into hardware – don't ask me how. I don't mean computers, or anything. Just, you know – hardware. Simple things. Tools, and so on. I quite like them, respond to them, simple things, if I'm honest. Yearn for the days, really, when the only thing that was the size of a cigarette packet was a bloody packet of cigarettes. That wouldn't up and rattle you with a nursery jingle, when you least expected it. But it's what they say about the genie, isn't it? When it's out of the thing – bottle, is it? Or was it a lamp? Anyway – when it's out of the thing. Can't go back, can you? No matter how much you'd like to. Just can't do it. I don't think it can have been a lamp though, you know. Not what they came in, is it? Genies. Can't think it can be. Anyway. Hardware. There was this shop going, you see, just off the high street. Cheap. Scruffy. Had a bit of money left over from the agency, borrowed the rest at a quite startling rate of interest – the reason for its so being, it

6

was patiently and even rather cruelly explained to me, was the fact that I did not actually own anything as collateral – something, say, in the way of the sort of business I was seeking to acquire. I didn't decide that here I would found a hardware shop – it already was one.

'But did you never pause for even just the most fleeting of milliseconds, Alan my sweet, to ask yourself frankly why it should be that the owner was selling? Could the fact that it was tiny and dingy and at the end of a perfectly filthy little alleyway off the high street and a large new branch of Robert Dyas poised upon opening at the very epicentre of the high street itself – could these facts have had the merest scintilla of *bearing*, do you imagine Alan? Or that the local paper was just full to bursting with the likelihood of a Homebase being built on the old airfield not five minutes drive away? Do you think that Mr Greasy thought he would dearly love to call it a day, if only some complete and utter dunderhead would appear from out of a fairy tale and actually give him *money* for the dump?'

'Greasby was his name. His name was Greasby . . .'

'But notwithstanding, Alan my sweet, does the thrust of my proposition still not stand?'

'It wasn't the best thing I could have done. I'm not all sure, you know, that a thrust can *stand* . . .'

'Not your finest hour, you think on reflection? How very generous-spirited of you, Alan. How noble in defeat. It was the proposition I was referring to. Not the thrust. And what element of your daring foray into the fabulous world of hardware would you imagine became the very nadir? The lowest ebb. The rock bottom, the ultimate in ridiculous, would you say? Because me, I have long cherished my personal

7

favourite, and it would be just so wonderful if it were yours as well. Shall I go first? Shall I, Alan my sweet? Well all right, then. Now leaving aside the moment, of course, when you managed to sell what was remaining on the lease for a pitiful fraction of what you were sagacious enough to pay for the thing – to a wily developer who had the wisdom to raze the little hole to the ground, and sell on the land for a fortune—'

'Nor am I convinced, Susan, that you can raze a hole to the ground . . .'

'Alan. Do you wish me to lose my temper? Do you, my sweet? Because I am, I promise you, just this close. Now where were we? Oh yes. The low point of your seemingly unfathomable incompetence. And do please know that if you dare to suggest to me, that a state of unfathomability can be possessed of no low point, then I think I might be moved to terminate this discussion by the simple expedient of just killing you with a knife. Is that clear? I do very much hope so. Now then. To my way of thinking, I think the point must have been reached when the local paper picked up on the story that you were attempting to sell these sad little packets upon which you had written: screws, 3 approx. Too sad. Too too sad. I ask you, Alan: 3 approx!'

It was worse than she knows. On some of the packets I had written Longish Nails, Several, And Other Things Too. The problems arose when the shelves that had borne these vast open tins of all the bits and pieces for centuries just simply gave way the very day I came to own them – rot *and* woodworm, said the chippie I had to bring in, near enough crying with laughter – and there was no way at all I could bring myself to sort them all out. I had attempted to buy some little transparent bags, but these, apparently, have yet to be invented, and so all in the end I could latch on to were hundreds upon hundreds of small manila envelopes. I had no idea in those days that woodscrews, say, were classified in girth by means of a simple number – one to eight, I think it is. My sizes ranged from Really Teeny Weeny to Very Big Indeed, but mostly tended to be labelled Assorted. And things like 3 approx. Oh dear me. But she's right though, Susan – of course she is. It wasn't brilliant. Nothing I touch ever seems to be. Or never mind brilliant, for Christ's sake – adequate would easily do, but these days even that seems surely to elude me. So it's not too surprising, is it? Really. On the whole. That she wants another husband. The only mystery, if I'm being honest with myself, is why she should want me as *well*, and not instead of . . . What good am I to her, after all? Oh well. But she's set on doing it – I know her, Susan. Some way or another, she'll do it, I just know she will. So we'll just have to wait, I suppose: see how it all works out.

I am a sensualist. Not at all, you see, how Alan I suppose must now have come to regard me. He may remember how it was I used to be, how he once saw me, though I somehow doubt it. And he has to be spoken to like that, you know, however unkind it might appear. I very rarely, of course, would subject him to anything like it in public – on extreme occasions, well yes, but only quite mildly. With him not having worked for so terribly long, you see (not in the proper sense, not in the sense of actually bringing in some bloody money) he has more than been given his proverbial inch, wouldn't you say? Really? And I cannot – not just for my sake, no, because there is always Amanda to be considered, if Alan only knew it – still just fourteen, but seeing everything before her, and I am sure quite horribly clearly – and so as I say, I cannot, can I? Simply can't. Sit idly by and watch him take the yard. Because in common with many men, I suspect, he is at base quite thoroughly idle. He will do what he is permitted to get away with. But Alan, you see, as with all the very most pitiable cases, he is not, as you might say, the idler par excellence, in the sense of just loafing about. I mean he drinks too much, obviously – maybe even more than I am aware of – and he staggers out of his bed ever later and later in the . . . well, I was going to say *morning*, but so often now it can easily be lunchtime, and especially at the weekends. In many ways I don't really mind it, to be truthful, because then he's not constantly under my feet. This is part of what I was saying, you see, about his own quite particular brand of idleness (it is peculiar to him) – he's a bustler, Alan, always active, some fool thing on the go, but never actually getting around to achieving an *end*. Either because he quickly loses interest (you can actually see it die, behind his eyes) or else the task in hand – whatever little thing it might be – will have simply, and yet once again, proved to be utterly beyond him.

I should love to be able to say that on the day I first met him, I was breathless and slammed by the wall of his charm, the wit and dazzle in the eyes, his savage good looks that made me pulsate. Sometimes, indeed – during my cold and older moments, alone, so often in the night, when I have needed not just a lustful comforting but the grain of an explanation as to why I have actually or ever gone through or along with anything at all in the whole of my life – I have wilfully and falsely remembered, almost inveigling myself into unquestioningly swallowing all of this as truth. But here is mere embroidery, for decoration's sake – more than that, in truth, for no embroidery, no matter how gaudy nor intricate, could ever be so ornate as my own imaginings, their contrasts picked out sharply. For I am a sensualist – a sensualist, yes: I love the *feel* of things, you see, and not just deeply.

He was not, of course, a man without qualities. Alan was always then and still I suppose is, a perfectly reasonably handsome man – as Maria, my very oldest friend (who I almost know is also quite dear to me), will sometimes rather swinishly indicate, if ever she senses a chink in my composure, a hairline that she can agitate with a cold and fine-gauged needle. He is intelligent (I could not have lived with a fool) though not, we don't think (do we?) in any way – *intellectual*: even to whisper the word into Alan's atmosphere, the soft breath catches within you and the moment seems immediately to me to be one of regret, but also quite giddily humorous. A rich man? Powerful? Oh no – but I did detect the bare bones of a prospect, you see. I was completely prepared to have faith, wanting it to devour me. To faith though, I have found, there is most certainly a very closely proscribed perimeter – the limit, my boundaries. Beyond them it becomes almost Catholic and hysterical in its purposeful blindness; in order to remain yourself, the demands of faith must not encompass your leaving behind all reason. So I could go on believing in Alan, you see, only up until the moment when he faltered and doubted himself – then, I think, we both of us felt immediately rather stupid, for having wandered, wide-eyed and parallel in a dream of our own concoction, and for quite so long. We should all know, really, shouldn't we, that the defining features of dreams are that they are not real and that one does wake up, and out of them. And yet their warm and languorous embrace (the harlot promise of a ready bliss)

11

is so very headily seductive that we are tricked every time into believing the illusion – then comes the plummet, and we are grasping blindly and with such desperation, at the scattering spangles of a now dowdy mirage, mocking us and fading before our very eyes. There can be few crueller moments than a rough and reluctant awakening. I would never say this, or anything like it, if Alan were around. I always do, though, think it.

In a way, it might be said that I rescued him. We both of us pretended otherwise at the time, of course (if we were already pretending, then . . . it maybe hadn't yet come to it: no, I have to suppose that right at the very beginning it wouldn't have, really). I had this small but terribly attractive flat in the very best part of Chelsea, thanks to my darling father (heaven knows I miss it, and I miss him too). I never had a job, not really, never really wanted one. I knew that I always had needed a man to look after me (cherish, spoil, adore and ravish me would all have been lovely, but just looking after, I could have coped with that). Because I am so beautiful and clever – and no, there is no point at all in talking down or gigglingly blushing over the very evident truth of the matter: I have always possessed this luscious and almost liquid ability to raise or reduce any man at all to the level at which he clearly belongs. And so because of this, I suppose that my Daddy was simply assuming that someone maybe even as wonderful as he would some day come along (not possible, as we both of us knew) and that until that day he'd be happy to keep me warm and safe, and gently ticking over. And there were men, of course there were – I soon grew weary of their constant and really quite overwhelming attentions. If I had ever to slip out quickly to a supermarket for some soup cartons or a quiche, say, I took to consciously making myself as hideous as a beauty can ever be – headscarf, flats, no make-up – simply to avoid some or other hopeful, oh God – *boulevardier* utterly revelling in his own ready wit, in his cool audacity – and canvassing my views on this or that bouillon, asking me constantly if I lived around here, suggesting that we could do worse than to pool the fruits of our trolley and basket, add much burgundy and hie away to rustle up something impromptu, somewhere nearby. Always they thought their approach so original – either brash and very cocksure, which I hate, just hate (unlike assurance and a true and manly confidence, which I am not sure I have ever encountered, except in my father), or else there would be a coy and stuttering attempt at boyishness, so pink and appealing in a puppydog way, and this of course I loathe even more – as I do puppydogs, as a matter of fact. Kittens too – they make me squirm. It is not that I wish any animal harm – and nor, I suppose, was I ever moved to react with violence to the endless strings of young and old men who perpetually were annoying me; I just never wanted to touch, that's all, not have them brushing against me, neither licking nor purring. And then suddenly – and how and why on earth in the world do these things happen? – suddenly, there was Alan. Who for reasons now very much lost to me, I evidently imagined would do.

He lived at the time in a . . . what shall we call it? Run-down apartment in a not very nice part of London? No – it hardly does it justice: hellhole is what we were dealing with here (it's always just as well to be frank about things). I invited him remarkably swiftly to share my beautiful little Chelsea home – part one of the rescue, I suppose, though I am sure that at the time I was unaware of being party to the launch of any such

13

thing. At first I did not notice the ugliness of his shoes, say, one of them on its side on my pale-pink Chinese rug. Did not gag at the hair in the washbasin. I even chipped away gamely at the caked-on cornflakes in a long-abandoned bowl. I must have loved him, or else why would I? I did love him, of course I did – I remember the fact of it, if even the merest tingle of engulfment has utterly departed. And I still do, really – love him, if only in a rather residual sort of a way. But I am done with trying to boost and reinforce him: his battlements are stormed, he has no longer any defences. And this is why he must now be supplemented – I am helping him by bringing in another strength (and one day, my Alan, my sweet, he will see it).

He was sort of a jobbing journalist at the time I first met him: of course, he had failed at a clutch of other quite airy occupations prior to failing at jobbing journalism – and this was before he came to fail in advertising and close on a decade away from his ultimate and staining failure amid all the silliness of hardware. Some or other paper you will by no means have heard of had given him an agony column, which neither of us considered to be even a little bit comical, rather bewilderingly. At the outset, he made a sort of an effort with the solving of all these personal problems (at the outset, he generally will – and the Lord only knows how many utterly blameless lives he devastated as a consequence), but soon he was had up by the editor for replying in print to every single letter with something along the lines of 'It rather depends, really' or 'Well yes and no, if you see what I mean'. He was moved to a 'handy hints' sort of a column – I seem to recall, you know, that its title might have been actually Handy Hints – though of course because my poor dear Alan has not an iota

14

of practical knowledge of any single thing on God's earth, this was never going to be the most dizzying success. He grew angry, I think, with his ignorance, his own incapability – this was some time before the internet, you see, so there were so few ways even to cheat at it effectively. They finally fired him when he printed the following . . . I saved it . . . it's rather wonderful, in its way . . . I'm just now calling it up . . . yes yes – this is it: 'Here's a hot tip for the winter months ahead – get hold of an old pair of tights, and then just ram your bloody old legs into them!' Dear dear. But you see, where others abandon him, my inclination is always to keep him on, help him where I can. I have to admit, of course, that we have now reached the point where I am no longer willing or capable of doing it on my own – I need a big strong man to help me. But I would never just let him *go* . . . how could I? And marriage, it is after all a *contract*, you know: so many seem to forget that.

When Amanda was still a little girl, Alan, believe it or not, he was actually faring really rather well. He had just pulled off his McVitie's thing for the agency, and we had moved to a rather larger, quite fine, but not nearly so pretty new home – still in Chelsea though – and more or less solely on the strength of it. The trouble, of course – as it always is with him, I'm afraid to say – was that here was no sort of a launching pad for a new and soaring lucrative career, but rather its acme. He came up with a new slogan for a very fashionable spirit of the time, white rum it might well have been (please listen to this): 'It's Intoxicating!' They thought he was joking, so he just barely got away with it. Ho ho Alan, they went: highly amusing. But now seriously, mate – what have you got . . . ? Poor Alan, poor sugar: he had nothing, did he? Nothing at all. In order to have come up with this slogan, he had stayed up for nights on end, endlessly downing just pints of the damn white rum, if white rum it was (maybe for inspiration, more likely because it was free), and had been, he told me, juggling concepts concerning its clarity, utter purity – its heavenly grace, I'm afraid is what he said to me. This, I think, led him to choirs and angels and then the thin and rarefied air, way up amid a clouded sunlight in Paradise. 'It's Intoxicating!' became his eureka moment: it assailed him at 4.15 in the morning of a Tuesday – he passed out on the floor, the crashing of bottles awakening Amanda.

They gave him another chance, though – working on the premise, I think, that no one could really be quite so sincerely idiotic. They put him on to something less contentious, and far lower-profile – some sort of dog biscuit, I seem to recall. 'Dogs like to eat it' was the gist of his proposal, so irresistible a pitch made to the background of hugely expensive and animated storyboards, not to say a barbershop quintet; it was received into a sea of unwavering eyes. Then, of course, the anger took over: they tried him on an uplift bra whose manufacturers were seeking to break the stranglehold of the unquestioned market leader. 'Makes Your Tits Stick Out' was Alan's nearly spat-out response, and well – that was the end of things, really. Rather oddly (and I've often thought this), just maybe five or so years later, they might actually have used it: it could have been huge.

Sex. That sort of rather quietly expired, you know. According to these terribly forthright magazine articles that are forced into all our faces these days – Sunday supplements and so on (things that used to be for all the family) – this is hardly unusual, a number of years on. I can't say I even remarked upon it at the time. I just didn't seem to care for it any more, as simple as that . . . though it had never been a priority with me – all the touching, the licking, and then any purring. I did not care any more to be a supine receptacle – and not just the intake either, but the outlet for an appetite. Alan said I was spurning him because he was no longer an employed and productive member of society – he said I was unmanning him; I told him to stop at once being quite so utterly ridiculous, and that he had achieved all that under his own volition, needing no sort of help from me – which may, I suppose, have been unkind, but look: we cannot, can we, squander the allotted time remaining to us just in scanning and analysing all our past remarks, assessing each one of them for sensitivity, or else an unnatural bluntness. I doubt anyway he even remembers. It is just as well though, really, that Amanda came along very early in what we might quite happily term the proceedings; Alan had been predictably amazed (mouth open, gaping like a fish) – he imagined, I think, that it was quite unplanned, as so many men, I'm told, will do. She's sweet, Amanda – so very beautiful, and nearly a young lady, as I simply can't ignore. She has a way of looking, though, you know – at me, I mean: I couldn't even begin to tell you, whenever she does it, what it is she might be thinking. I ask her outright, from time to time: Amanda, my darling – whatever are you thinking? What is going on behind those dark and big blue eyes of yours? Well – you put it to a child like that, you can't expect it, can you? An answer. No, not really.

And then he started going rather funny. Little things, you know, that only I would notice (for who else, please tell me, would even frankly care?). One day, for instance – not really long ago – I went into the kitchen after work, and there he was at the table, quietly shelling peas. He likes, you see, to be seen to be helping me out – having a sort of dinner (he is, though, no maestro of cuisine) at least in preparation if not actually on the table, for whenever it is I can get in from my work. Sweet, really – as well as, on the other hand, the very least he could do. Anyway – there he is in the kitchen, and wearing a pinny that had Come And Get It written across the bib part of it in signal red (heaven only knows where such things come from) – shelling his peas and dropping them singly into a Pyrex bowl. I said to him gaily . . . oh, I don't know – something or other, and he was most irate. What on earth has got into you this time, Alan, I asked him then – and I suppose quite petulantly. It's *you*! It's *you*! – he was seething (and his eyes were white with an unaccustomed fury): You've gone and made me lose *count* now! And so I'll have to start *again* . . . ! Well – not normal, is it? Not by any standards, I shouldn't have said. And then there was the time he spent the better part of an evening attempting to fold a napkin into six – I think it was six – because he had read somewhere that it couldn't be done. I became just slightly more concerned, though, when I found him in the spare bedroom, which we had decided to redecorate. The dust sheets were down, the room was stripped and there was Alan with an open can of paint (Apricot Blush, I think – although it might have been Aurora Dawn) and in his hand was a brand-new paintbrush, at which he was staring very warily, as if it were a rattlesnake that could at any moment strike. What, Alan, I gently enquired, do you imagine you are doing, in fact? He slowly emerged from what could have been the very deepest of trances, as he revolved his hooded eyes to meet me. I have to be *sure*, he said quite steadily, of just which end of this thing it is that I should actually be submerging into the depths of this rather thick and heady paint – and then I must have flinched, I think, as he suddenly barked out at me: Because if I get it *wrong*, then what we have on our hands here is very little better than a bloody dog's breakfast! If . . . he added more quietly, you take my meaning, Susan. Mm, yes well, I was thinking. And soon after that I thought I had to have him seen to. He still goes once a week – I think the analysis calms him. I do so hope. Heaven knows it costs enough. And the spare room now he's decided isn't, in fact, the spare room at all – not any longer, no no no: it is formally now his private, um – 'den', I think is currently the favoured term. He dallied with 'lair' for a considerable while, our both having rejected 'study' as frankly just too laughable for words. I suggested all sorts of variations on the theme of bunker, burrow, sett or even simple hole, none of which he appeared to care for. The Lord knows what he gets up to in there – there's seldom any noise, and the door, he always keeps it locked. If he were a normal man, Alan, I would imagine it had something to do with a murky obsession with on-line filth of some colour or other (though in Alan's case, heaven knows what) – but he isn't, is he? Normal. I shouldn't have said so. It keeps him out of the way, though – and it must be plain that I don't frankly care. If I do come to, however – mind what it is, what is going in there – well then I'll fetch up one day with an axe and just bloody break the door down, I suppose.

It's complicated, our relationship – which is strange in a way because we are, the two of us, really very simple people, though in markedly different ways. I am simple in the sense of knowing who I am and what I want and feeling comfortable about it. Alan, well – I think he's maybe just a little bit simple, really. My discontentment springs from knowing that I am currently being forced to behave in a way that just isn't *me*. I never wanted a job, and now I have one – because all I needed was a big strong man to take good care of me, and all that I'm left with is Alan. I have to say, though, I quite like the job, the job I have now – not the job I started out with, but the job I have now – and of course I excel at it, just as I told them I would (when still I had the job I didn't like). It's *having* to do it, that's what I object to – but then of course without it, I never would have run into him, would I? Black. It was getting to know Black that gave me the idea. Of course, he had ideas, other ideas, quite of his own – but then they will, won't they? Men. They always will. I let him go on – it was amusing to to see him imagining himself to be so very suave, so flirtily seductive, but to me such butterfly tactics were no more than oafish and predictable (because I've seen it all before, so very many times). But he's almost quite acceptable to look at, Black: no Adonis. Old, though. But better than any of that, he owns nearly all of the company. There are a few shares, not many, in trust for the son and daughter from his fairly brief and firmly obliterated marriage, and 11 per cent, oddly, seems to be held by some sort of transport union, or a pension fund, something of that kind. I know, because I looked it all up. As far as I was concerned, throughout our initial dalliances, Black was no more than my interviewee. I simply sat there, seriously considering him as a candidate for bigamy – and yes, he might well have been a good deal less twinkly, had he had the merest notion. Well I'm pleased to say that he passed the audition, but in truth there was never another even in the running. His actual name is Martin Leather, and Black, I can only suppose, has evolved over the years into a whimsical nickname. Black Leather, you see – which is, yes I agree, just a little puerile. You can see how much it pleases him, though – because men, you see, they're all like that. Some are docile, endearing up to a point, and incapable of holding down a job – even one so simple as selling nuts and bolts – while others are, if a mite overbearing, able and willing to spend on you the money they have accumulated. There are slight and rarely interesting variations along the way, but all of these creatures are united by a cord – the rope of manliness, they would love to hear it called, but in reality it is sadly no more than a childish thread, over the years grown plump.

And later, this very evening as a matter of fact, I have decided that the moment has come for me to put it to him. It is not before time, because Black, he has already made it quite cringingly clear to me that over the course of this dinner, somewhere divine, he is to put to me a proposition himself. But that is not the way it must be. A proposition – and I know that's how he sees me (for how else should we have come this far?) – is, to a woman such as I, altogether different from a proposal of marriage, the heart of my pledge, my offering to him. Which I know (of course I know) will never be utterly *legal*, exactly – but I have conjured an avenue whereby the bonding might be marked and made formal. For it is a waste, you know, and a mark of foolishness, to be a beautiful woman and fail to have realised that you can so very easily, with persistence and by means of the carefully eked out bestowal of precious and intimate gifts, be far more than merely the mistress; why settle for that, when you can be lord and master? The level and balance is all, of course – the timing and warmth of one's favours – or else you risk the danger of his anger or his cooling (I know all this because I am a sensualist). But even if ultimately you do just everything for a man, he

21

can and will find another who is willing to do anything at all, the distinction being clear. And so tonight I shall ask him the question – wondering, of course, that when there can no longer be truth, whether it is folly even to look for an honest answer.

This psychiatrist that Susan sent me to, he really is a piece of work. Needn't actually even be a psychiatrist, now I come to . . . psycho-something, anyway, so who the hell cares? They're all of them bats as they come, just everybody knows it. The joke is, he actually seems to believe that I'm a simpleton or something, so I really must be doing rather well. It's the way that he nods when I'm speaking that really just does it for me – and he'll half close his eyes and tap his upper lip with the pommel of a shiny black and gold and fucking expensive pen unwittingly paid for by how many legions of loonies who have all clubbed together over so many years in order to furnish this sententious bastard with, oh – Christ knows what else. He wears glasses, it need hardly be said (thick, black) and don't, just please don't, all right? Get me on to his bleeding moustache. I am given to understand that seated beside me (because I do, I lie on a couch) is the omniscient sage, and whenever he nods – and he's always nodding – I am not meant in any way to take succour in the spirit of encouragement, no no, but rather the intention is to signal his intense absorption, his wisdom in drinking it in. His name is Doctor Atherby, and he's the sort of person that you really ought to be able to damage, or even slay at will, but they just won't let you, you know. Well you *can*, of course, but you're going to get yourself into all the sort of bother that'll follow.

'We'll come back to Susan in just one moment, Alan. But if we could just for now talk a little bit more about your father, yes?'

I know: barely credible, but that's the sort of man we're dealing with, you see. My father – has to be, doesn't it? The root of it all.

'Mm. Yes well, Doctor Atherby, I'm not really sure that there's a great deal I can usefully, um – add, as it were. I mean, I would of course genuinely love to recall for you all of a sudden the flood of instances where he thrashed me – buckle end of the belt – abused me – hush hush, not a word to anyone – locked me in a cupboard – and you won't come out until you're sorry for your sins – came home drunk, bashed up his old lady . . . that would be Mummy, of course . . . but I'm afraid it's just not there, you see. I'm awfully sorry. Pain, I know. We played Scrabble a good deal. That help at all . . . ?'

'Rage. Resentment. Take many forms . . .'

'Yes, I'm sure that's so. But not *Scrabble*, surely? Monopoly I could understand . . .'

'You did say, however Alan, that he was away a good deal? Your father.'

'Well – he went to work, if that's what you mean.'

'Come, Alan – you really must help me if I am to help you. That is why we are here, after all. I have said this before.'

'You have – you have, Doctor Atherby. You've said everything before. And God – I must have said everything about a thousand times over, but still we go round and round, don't we?'

'Maybe here is the nub. Maybe here, Alan, is the nub. Round and round – but never penetrate.'

'Am I to understand that we are now on to sex again? Or

23

would that be a word association too far? Could I, Doctor Atherby, have altogether failed to grasp the *nub*?'

I silently laughed myself silly while he did his half-blind impersonation and set to nodding his head off like a very superior toy in the back of a limousine – and none the less irritating for that. Then he battered blue murder out of his bristly bloody upper lip with that very ostentatious fucking pen he's got.

'You don't, do you Alan . . . ? Take drugs at all? I do ask from time to time.'

'Drugs? No, Doctor Atherby. Not drugs, no. Alcohol – yes. Great deal of that. Nicotine, naturally: fine cigars. Caffeine – well of course. Oh – and the little blue ones that you give me, the pink of course. Susan, she gives me white ones, whenever she thinks of it. And didn't you just briefly prescribe those rather jolly red ones? Might have been Christmas time. I well remember telling you that you really shouldn't have. But apart from that, no. No drugs. Why do you ask, Doctor Atherby?'

'You never feel the need to . . . escape? You never maybe felt it as a child?'

'Oh God *yes*! Why didn't you say? Escape – oh Jesus yes. I've wanted to *escape* since the day I was born. Well actually – that's not quite true. On the day I was born, and I'll never forget it – not a day you would forget, is it really? It was a Wednesday, half-closing round our way, glorious sunshine, unseasonal for the time of year, everyone said so – on that day I terribly wanted to *de*-escape. Took one swift look around me and thought to myself oh dear me no – don't at all like the look of this lot, not one little bit: think I'll go back where I came from. Had a quick chat about it with my Mummy – the first of many of our little tête-à-têtes – and I could see it at once – perceptive child – that she wasn't all that red hot on the idea, which was wholly understandable in the circumstances. Wouldn't you say? She'd had a hell of a day, after all. Because childbirth, well – never easy, is it? No sort of picnic. But apart from that one instance, from that day forward – oh God yes: escape, became my middle name. So there, Doctor Atherby: an early – post-natal, indeed – and deep desire to regress to the womb. We've that, at least. Something to go on, surely? Meat on the bone there, I should have said.'

'Let's wind it up for today, Alan, shall we?'

'Oh really? Oh blow. And just when the nub was looming.'

I could write a book about my parents, as a matter of simple fact, but I'm damned if he'll get to know even any little part of it. Not his business, is it? I don't honestly know why I still go on seeing him, bloody Doctor Atherby, except for the fact that it can be quite diverting. But all this digging around about one's *parents* – totally absurd. I mean to say, my father – just a fairly all-round average sort of chap, I'd say. In insurance. And no he didn't really, well – talk to me, so to say. Take me to the park, kick a ball around; read to me at bedtime. Men didn't, not in those days, not really. Unless they were pretending to be enlightened – cravenly desperate to divert at least the worst of the animosity from a wild-eyed woman who was frightening them. And my mother? Normal, completely everyday. Never quite sure how she did fill in all the hours, to be perfectly honest with you. And Dad, he's dead now of course, though I couldn't even begin to tell you, really, what it was that he got up to while he was still alive. Didn't play golf, do the garden, collect things. No interest in travel, apart from hearing about it on the television. Never went in for sport of any kind – and nor was he a one for the pub or the ladies, only inasmuch as he wasn't really a one for just anything at all – nothing I can put a finger on, anyway. Mystery, in truth – though hardly a beguiling one. So I couldn't, now I think of it, write a book about them at all – not unless publishers are suddenly in the market for very short and dull ones. No no – never mind them: it's Susan we ought to be talking about, if we're forced into discussing anyone at all. I mean – how did the two of us ever get together in the first place? Astonishing, really. I never paid her a lot of heed – thought she was out of my class, and of course she was: she is. On the plus side, I remember thinking (and all of this, it's just on fifteen years ago now – fifteen years, dear oh dear) . . . yes, what I did observe about her was that she hated, absolutely abhorred, chocolate, cats, soft toys and lip balm (didn't even have a thing about shoes) – and that, as far as women went, made her quite utterly unique, in my admittedly very limited experience. And that's a lie. My experience, I mean: wasn't very limited – hardly more than non-existent, it has to be faced. When we first met . . . and how on earth did we? *Where* did we? I expect she knows, Susan; I'm sure she remembers every single detail. Blank to me, though. Suddenly she was just sort of *there*, that's all, and she didn't go away. Anyway, I had this tiny little boxed-off room in the iffiest part of Kentish Town, over a kebab shop and a grimy old pub next door. There were a couple of tarts just along the landing, Zizi and Pearl, and up in the attic was Toe, a one-eyed Taiwanese drug dealer who spoke not one word of English and had a lucrative sideline in deviant porn . . . and so I just can't tell you how blissfully convenient it all was, having these long-standing and easily elastic arrangements with everyone concerned. But Susan, she dragged me away from all of that – had me installed in her cute little lavender

26

doll's house just off the very best stretch of the King's bloody Road. I was doing rather well in journalism at the time, which I've often thought I maybe ought to have persevered with, who's to say? Might by now be editing *The Times*. (And I do this, time to time – go thinking or saying something perfectly ridiculous like that: because I wouldn't, would I? Be editing *The Times*. Lucky to be cleaning their lavatories. Oh God – I really have to keep it in check, you know, all that sort of thing; get a tight grip.) But anyway – at the time, I wasn't doing badly. *North London Gazette & Mercury* – they gave me every sort of column and feature and story to work on. My finest hour, in retrospect, was probably the agony page – I eschewed the customarily dogmatic and absolute responses of my peers in favour of a more liberal and open-minded approach, one where all the given angles and perspectives could be viewed simultaneously, the better to see that no cut-and-dried solution easily presented itself. The current feeling upon high, though, was that dogma should very much be the order of the day: they had to be sure they could foretell that predictability would soon and definitely be coming. But there were many more strings to my particular bow: I gave the readers advice and tips on any number of things – including (Susan laughed, but Susan would) interior design. And not just that, but gardens too – even what to look for when investing in a property. Many pointers were a given, of course – obviously one avoided anything described as 'architect-designed' (and as opposed to designed by what, exactly? Greengrocer? Cocker fucking spaniel?) – unless of course one wished to inhabit a glass-walled refrigerator the size of a football field with nothing even approaching a curtain, with a 'poured concrete floor' (I am not kidding), the damned Eames chair, the Corbusier long bloody thing, a weirdo Noguchi table and a giant glass and spherical vase with an orange in it. Oh yes – and thick white candles where any normal human being might be more inclined to either a decent log fire or even an electric light. They weren't always five shades of white and glass though, these arrogant nightmares flung in your face by self-serving maniacs who all lived happily ever after in their eighteenth-century rectories. Once I remember I received a press release from some po-faced and deluded 'wall-covering consultancy' (I tell you, I tell you: I am not horsing around here – this is gospel) which confided breathlessly that this season the new and must-have shades were to be 'Noir and Cohiba'. In short, if you were fed up being blinded by the white and thinking of dickying up the old homestead, why not obliterate it under a bucketful of soot and crap? Well I took it upon myself to steer my readers away from all this nonsense: gave them the facts about three-piece suites, wall sconces, nests of tables, fireside rugs – things you want to live with. I got no sort of backing from the editor, though – I think I was too avant-garde for the times: he just wouldn't take the risk. (Yes: I know. Again, of course, I'm fooling myself. No – not fooling, just trying for my own sorry sake to cushion the blow. I know I didn't understand the first thing about it – I just thought, write about the obvious comforts, the unassuming reality, and you will sweep all before you. Well not, apparently. I wasn't, in truth, doing at all well in journalism. Was I?)

Ah well. Maybe a bit of all that has rubbed off on me, though, because I do quite like it – decorating, a little bit of home improvement, whatever they like to call it these days. DIY. Oh yes – here's a memory, here's a little something for Doctor bleeding Atherby: it's about my father. One time – I must still have been a schoolboy – he came home from work on a Friday evening with a saw in his hand. What's that, my mother said. This? It's a saw, my father replied, perfectly reasonably (and certainly I was with him so far). And that, my mother said – what's that thing there? That, my father assured her, that, my dear, is in fact a hammer. Moreover, in the car there is timber: I have decided to fashion for us all a three-legged stool. My mother blinked: a three-legged stool? Had she heard him correctly? My father was nodding quite vigorously (he could have given Doctor Atherby a very good run for his money in the nodding department, my father could – always nodding away with the best of them, he was). Indeed, he averred: a three-legged stool. Why, my mother wanted to know now, must its legs number three, exactly? For the simple reason, she was told – and I remember his solemnity, whether genuine or feigned – that were there but two, it would surely topple over. Ye-e-es . . . came my mother's quite measured agreement – but I was thinking, you see, rather more on the lines of, well – four, you know (not to put too fine a point on it). I see, said my father quite coldly: well in the light of this barrage of quite ceaseless criticism I consider it the better part of valour to withdraw wholeheartedly from the entire proceedings; the subject is closed forthwith. And neither saw nor hammer was ever seen again. Strange though, isn't it? These small and silly things that you remember.

Anyway – I've done up the spare room. *Not* the spare room, though – not any more: it is now my oasis of peace. I humoured Susan – I do it a lot, much more than I care for, because I have to, I have to – and I just let her get on with it, extracting huge amusement from the singular inaptness of my referring to it ever as my 'study' (because of course you *don't*, do you Alan my sweet? Study? You never ever really have. Studied. Have you? Alan? My sugar). It is of no matter – she can call the damn room whatever she pleases. But for me it is now my very Valhalla: a place of bliss. And when, very annoyingly, she barged right in, and just at the very moment I had decided that of course all this dreadful and peachy paint simply wouldn't do at all, I had the brainwave of covering the thought by worrying her more than slightly – making her wonder if I am now truly on the verge of becoming quite unhinged. I do it from time to time – it amuses me to witness the quick light of fright leap up into her eyes – I am maybe a little more interesting, then – and anyway, it keeps her on her toes, as well as making for a degree of distance. I later on bought a couple of cans of deep French blue, very thick and luscious: this went all across the walls and ceiling and doors and skirting – all is now a Mediterranean blue. I have in there a powerful patio heater and a huge umbrella with a raffia fringe. When Susan was at work and Amanda still at school, I sneaked into the room a structural surveyor who assured me that the floor could support with ease the fourteen sacks of fine and golden sand that were due to be delivered the following morning, along with the smooth round pebbles (he gave me a look, of course, but I'm used to looks: I get them all the time). The deckchair is the traditional stripey kind – canvas, though, not a clammy vinyl – and I have a little fridge, for alcohol and ice cream (you can still buy the cones, I was gratified to discover). I was pleased too to be able to download from some strange website or other the most spectacular and evocative sounds – the wheeling and mewling of gulls overhead, the gentle rush of the incoming sea. A fan is there to supply a gentle breeze. And I am in there too, whenever I can be: my secret life – at last, it's a beach!

And when I'm in there, what do I think of? Slumped into the sling of the deckchair, I squint behind my shades, the soft warm sand oozing so very nicely between the toes of one foot, the other quite happy to be plashing idly in a shallowish paddling pool of cool, fresh water (and I am most assiduous in changing it daily). Well now there's a question. I simply am able to luxuriate in the moment: black-out thought, or try to – it's hard, of course, it's tricky to achieve, but I have to suspect that I am so much better at it than many more sentient beings. Susan, say – or practically anyone, really. And then I come to remember all of the things I have striven to forget . . . the time I was on a real beach, in Eastbourne, I couldn't have been more than ten years old (I think I might even have been seven or eight) and the donkey I was geeing up and so gleeful to be on top of, simply died beneath me. Sighed so curiously through his two great nostrils, and folded heavily on to the sand: briefly he sounded disgruntled, and then he made no sound at all. My mother was screaming at my father for letting me go on such a thing, and now look! Now look! Now look what's happened! I was quivering behind her skirts, afraid that the owner would have me up for murder. I then sat down and cried. Children were swarming and they prodded the dead donkey, the furious owner swatting and flicking them back with the flail of a bamboo goad. My father roared at the man quite briefly, and then he turned and stamped away. I sensed that my mother, she wanted to move us away from the scene of the disaster, but was worried that then my father would fail to find us. And so we waited, my Mummy and I, until it was dusk, but he did not come back. They tied all these ropes around him, and then they hauled him away (the donkey, I mean). That night in the boarding house, I shared my

Mummy's bed and he came in late, my father, and we heard him stumbling and banging about in the room next door that used to be mine. Something tinkled and then it tumbled, and then there was quiet. My Mummy told me that everything was all right – she hugged me closely, and I loved it.

At other times I will remember that I never have forgotten that hot and sunlit August afternoon when Susan had slung from a distance and into my face the splat of information that she had got herself a job – a good job, did I hear her, a better job than I had ever dreamed of or had even the merest hope of achieving. Painful, yes, but I was pleased for her – more, though, I think, I was pleased for me. Can't explain. But the sex then, well – it just sort of expired. We had never remotely been party to any form of fantasia, this is true (of course it is, of course this is true), but nevertheless I just had to confess to a wince of regret at its summary and final extinction. It was all of it so very much easier in the days when little Zizi was mine, just across the landing. Not to say Pearl. Even through the rosiness of retrospection, of course, one cannot pretend to glamour (there was always, it could hardly be ignored, the underlying and lardy haze of overfried onions, fortified by a staleness in the sheeting and a dead dog dampness that none of their enthusiastic squirtings of Shalimar, Opium or Coco ever did manage to thoroughly dispel). But leaving aside one's finer sensibilities – by God, could they do the business. Professionals, you see: knew what they were up to (like everything in life, isn't it really? You get what you pay for). Although with me, of course, more often than not all they would require (and they asked me so sweetly) was a little bit of bookkeeping – a reassuring endorsement with regard to just how little they could get away with declaring to the Revenue in the form of a feasible income from 'casual cleaning', sufficient to stay the trigger of investigation, to lull the suspicions of a judicious inspector. Or maybe it could be that their suntan bed had overloaded the circuit, and would you mind, Alan, taking a little look at it (ooh ta – we'll be ever so grateful). Young, you see – so terribly young they both were: had not the slightest knowledge of DIY. Fifteen years on now, the two of them: hard to think of it. I doubt they're still, you know – doing it all . . . or at least no longer, one hopes, in the same old rathole in the iffiest part of Kentish Town. Zizi, she really was possessed of the most perfectly lovely face – oval and wide-eyed, so very pale and trusting: truly the face of an angel. Pearl though, it has to be said (oh God yes: Pearl) – she had by far the better body. It went in, and then it went out in the best way imaginable, and so utterly resilient she was. Her trick, her party piece, was to take you in her mouth and then keep on saying Gina Lollobrigida, repeatedly. Happy days. Zizi, she was always convinced – bit of a dreamer, Zizi – that she would one day run into a rich and handsome man (young and tall and preferably a film star) who would be smitten by love, whisk her away and set her up royally as a lady, and a wife. They were thin on the ground though, that type, over a kebab shop in the iffiest part of Kentish Town. The men who did trudge up those rickety steps with her, they weren't like that at all. Pearl, she was much more of a realist: saw things square on. She just wanted to earn enough to buy herself a chain of florists by the time she was thirty, seal away the past in a lead-lined trunk and begin to behave in the way she imagined a normal girl would. The trouble was, a great deal of her sometimes really quite startling income ended up in the hands of Toe upstairs, who would unsmilingly dispense to

33

her powders and pills, pungent and unctuous phials with thin and dangerous needles. She could even still be living there, Pearl – she could well still be doing it all, if the body's held up, if her mind's not gone: no flowers yet, not for Pearl, I daresay. The women I use these days, they're not nearly so good as she was, though. They tend to be very clean, which of course can be good and bad – and Christ, do they cost me. Just as well that Susan's earning a fairly decent salary, on the whole, else I'd find it harder to keep up than I already do.

But now, apparently – and it does seem strange, however often I come to mull it over (I sometimes feel I've dreamed it all) . . . but it surely does appear as if there is soon to be a brand-new breadwinner in the family, in the unlikely and really quite laughable form of yet another husband for Susan. Not just some fancy man with a bit of money whom she may screw at will – literally, yes, and metaphorically too, and all on the q.t., somewhere cosy, oh no no no no *no*. But a husband. New one. Not instead of, but as well as. I, she just assumed would go along with the thing, no matter how bizarre or distasteful, not to say quite utterly castrating I might have found it (I go weak, and I pine . . .) – but how does she imagine the candidate might be feeling about the whole idea? The new boy. If he is to get selected. Well more than likely, he'll think her mad (and I could back him up on that one, if he felt he could do with some support) and then he'll just tell her to get lost, I shouldn't wonder. As any sane man would, let's for God's sake face it. Taking on a fourteen-year-old daughter, well that's one thing – but to include in the package a husband not much shy of fifty? Not the same, is it? Not the usual run of the thing. And Susan, has she I wonder troubled herself to go into all of the detail? Or do we have here merely the

34

bones? You never really know with Susan, you see – she can happily go either way. Sometimes she'll work out a scheme to so very fine a degree – foreseeing and countering every conceivable hitch or setback – that your head will be spinning with it all; other times, all you get is the broad and slapping brushstroke of the latest big idea, left there boldly to drip and then congeal, the assumption being that all will come together quite beautifully for the blissfully simple reason that she *wants* it to, you see. So what, I wonder, has she got in store for me this time? Are we all to pay a visit, a happy little trio, to Furniture Village and spurn with disdain the must-end-soon-once-in-a-lifetime offer on the king-size divan for being altogether far too puny in girth, on account of, do you see – and Susan will smilingly and patiently explain all of this to the goggle-eyed sales assistant – there are to be *three* in our bed (though I would hold no hope whatever of anything in the way of a *romp*, of course – or not, at least, where I'm concerned). Or will he, the new man, simply be expected to subsume my own, if erstwhile, position, while I shall be relegated to my private shoreline, and the life of a permanent beachcomber? There are worse places, I admit (I do, after all, get year-round summers).

She reads a lot of books, Susan – and proper things too. Well, working in publishing, I suppose she has to really – but to give her her due, she always was, Susan, a bit of a reader. Novels mainly, largely the better sort. I wonder if it's these that give her all her strange ideas . . . ? Work away on her subconscious. You know – some crackpot writer in his bloody garret, stunned by booze and crazed by debt, censoring no mad wheeze as at all too wild: just bung it down and for God's sake give me the money. And then some innocent, some ingénue, some open-eyed and naïve young girl (or even an

35

unchained loony the likes of Susan) – they will happen upon all of this tosh in passing and then they might go thinking, hm – damn good idea, that: take a second husband (think I'll try it). They've a hell of a lot to answer for, writers, were they not all too smashed and up their own backsides to know it. God. I can't, you know . . . really bear to think of it: Susan, with another man. Just the thought, the mere idea, is just so indescribably painful; the reality – when she comes to do it – well it could come near to closing me down. Even if, as once she told me (and how can I ever forget it?) I am no longer in her eyes even a man at all. And it's odd, though . . . little bit of a tangent, this, but how can it really matter? In context. Let's face it: I've got nothing but time. So yes – I was just thinking that it's odd in a way that I hardly ever read, because writing, if I'm being really and for once deep and downright honest with myself – writing, you know, is the only thing I've ever really wanted to do. I've started a novel, matter of fact. Which doesn't mean a thing. Well it's the easiest thing in the world, starting a novel, course it is. And I should know: I've started dozens of the fucking things. It's going on with them, that's the bugger. It's going on that's hard: that's when the problems arise. In my more self-castigating, if still marshmallowy moods, I decide that all in fact that I want is to see my name in print, plain and simple – a sort of stark and incontrovertible evidence that I do in fact exist. And there is undeniably more than a grain of truth in this – I have, more than once, looked myself up in the phonebook, you know, just in order to see it. But of course it's the wrong way round in there: Peacock, Alan. Alan Peacock, that's the way round I want to see it (fair bit bigger, of course). There was a famous author once, you know (dead now) name of Peacock. Thomas Love. It always made me giggle – I really am so very incurably shallow and juvenile, I can't help admitting it – wondering whether his mates used to maybe slap him across the shoulders and say to him: 'How are you feeling this morning, Thomas Love?' or: 'You really are a sensitive and delicate artist, aren't you Thomas Love? I love roast chicken – but Thomas Love Peacock.' I do, I get ambushed – waylaid and bushwhacked – by all these stupidities, and then I'm gone, I'm utterly lost in them. But I do really believe that it's more than that – got to be, hasn't it? More than just the glory of seeing my name up there, and in bold. But God knows if I'll ever achieve it, more than just a beginning. I never really know, after a certain point, what the devil more I can possibly *say* – where I should go from there. You're always hearing, aren't you, that you should write about what you know, draw from your own experiences of life. Well in my case, very obviously, no use whatsoever: no one's going to believe in a single word of it, are they? My life. Jesus – look at me, will you? I can hardly believe it myself. Oh God. Enough – enough of all this. Because whichever way you look at it – in life as in art – it's going on that's hard: that's when the problems arise. I think now . . . I've got to get back to the beach. Listen to the gulls and the lapping of the waves – have myself a paddle and a nice big cornet (restore a bit of sanity, God alone knows).

I so like worry about them loads of times, my mum and dad. I think this is a sign of growing up, because all I used to ever worry about was me, but now it's not like that any more. It's them I have to worry about, and if you had a mum and dad like mine, then I think you would as well: you'd worry too. When I was little, I didn't notice they were weird. I've talked to Jennifer and Tara about it all, parents, and they say to me oh but you're just so like really really lucky, Amanda – at least your parents are still together: at least they don't always throw things. Because Jennifer's mum and dad are divorced and they really like hate one another now, apparently – which yeh, that must be bad, although Jennifer's dad, he gives her piles of stuff whenever she sees him. Tara's dad is a children's entertainer, which is so totally worse than anything I can think of. He does clowns and magicians and balloons and stuff for all the ickle kiddies – we all used to think he was just so fucking cool when we were younger, but now it's lame and just so embarrassing. And Tara's mum, she throws things at him, Tara says. The minute he walks through the door – whap, he gets it in the head. Teacups mainly – Tara says her mum, she gets them wholesale like by the gross so she's always got loads just for chucking at his head. I used to think she was just like . . . joking? But she always looks dead serious whenever she says it. Well OK, yeh – my two are still together, which I suppose is fine, and nobody throws stuff, yeh that's true, but still though, they really are, the two of them, you know: just so like weird? Like my mum – she goes to work, yeh? Publisher, I've never read any of the books or anything, never even opened one: they all look so totally boring. Anyway, my mum, she makes this really big deal of getting back from work as early as she can so she can like talk to me about my *day*? 'How I got on at school', oh yuck. I just always used to say fine, yeh fine Mum, but it was never enough. So now she kicks in with all her questions: So did you have English today, she'll go. And I'm like yeh Mum, we have English every day, don't we? And are you still doing well at it? Yeh. And Miss Brunson – that is the name of your teacher, isn't it? Yeh. Are you still getting along well with her, are you? Yeh. Because I recall that at the beginning of term you had a little misunderstanding with her, didn't you? Yeh. But that's all right now, is it? All cleared up? Yeh. Well look, Amanda – I daresay you've got homework to get on with, have you? Yeh. Well off you go then – and don't spend the whole evening playing those awful computer games, will you Amanda? Promise me you won't: do you promise me, Amanda? Yeh. I like these little talks of ours – I think they're important; so many mothers and daughters just seem to lose touch, simply drift apart – and I like to think that you get something out of them as well: you do, don't you Amanda? Yeh.

So you see what I mean – I worry she's losing it, really. My dad is nuts, that's obvious, but at least he doesn't go around annoying me all the time. Not nuts, I don't mean, in a wacky off-the-wall and like good old lovable Dad sort of a way – just like mental, basically. He doesn't work or anything. He used to, but my mum says he kept on getting the sack, so maybe he just went off it all, I don't know. He had like this little shop once – I used to go there sometimes when I was small. Apart from him, though, it was always like – empty? Everything in it was either sharp or dirty. There was a bell above the door which never jangled because nobody ever came in. But I'd stop, if I could – I'd stop going to school. It's just such a fucking like great waste of time: bloody *Henry IV* and adverbial clauses or whatever? Yeh, like I so care. They should teach you cool stuff like make-up and driving a car and how to run like credit cards and things you're really going to need. Estuaries? The Continental Shelf? *The Canterbury Tales*? Oh *please*.

Anyway, it's dinner time now. That's the other thing my mum always says: it's important that we all of us sit down together around the table as a *family*. Dad cooks, usually – well always, really, unless we get like a takeaway: Chinese, because Mum says that Indian always stinks the house out. And she sets the table because she says my dad couldn't set a table if his life depended on it, and she makes the napkins like stars and ponced-up like angels and stuff. Anyway, that's now. (And this evening, I suppose, will be pretty much the same as all the others.)

'Mm. Shepherd's pie. Oh yes of *course* it's shepherd's pie, how very foolish you must think me, Alan. It's Tuesday, isn't it? So of *course* it's shepherd's pie. Tuck in your napkin Amanda, there's a good girl. Why have you opened two bottles of wine tonight, Alan?'

'Well actually, my cherished one, I have opened four. But two are now empty, you see, and so the two you see before you are all that remain. Cottage.'

'Is there any Coke, Dad?'

'What did you say, Alan? There's Coke in the fridge, Amanda. You know where the Coke is – just get it, can't you?'

'I said cottage. It's cottage pie, not shepherd's. I know what a stickler you are for having things just so, Susan, so I thought we might really as well get the whole meal off and away on the proper footing, so to say. Beef, you see: not lamb. It's as well to know.'

'The top looks a bit burned . . . Pass the Evian, would you Amanda?'

'People at school, they all say bottled water is like just one big rip-off.'

'*Browned* it is, Susan. Not burned, no – just rather nicely *browned*, you see. And be careful of your tongue, Amanda – it'll be awfully hot.'

'More than last night's was then, Alan my sweet. If you knew where tap water came from, Amanda, you wouldn't say such things. It's been through *people*, that's what I read. Can you imagine such a thing? Through *people*. This isn't the usual wine, is it Alan? It seems a bit, I don't know . . .'

'Well spotted, Susan – well done indeed. It is a different label from the usual – and as a matter of simple fact, now I come to regard it afresh, I see that it is also a different *colour*, well well well. So yes, I commend your perspicacity. But do you *like* it? That's the thing.'

'Can I taste it, Dad?'

'If you like. It's nothing special.'

'Amanda! Put down that glass at once. What are you *thinking* of, Alan? She's a child. You can't have a child drinking *wine* . . . And anyway, it's not very nice, not very nice at all. It was cheap, was it? I expect it was cheap. I do so hope it was cheap, Alan. Or did they maybe start rubbing their hands when they saw you coming? My sweet.'

'They do in France, Mum. And like Italy? Drink wine. Young people.'

'This is surely the moment, Amanda, when your mother says to you quite solemnly and defiantly that while that may well be the case, we are not *in* France, are we Amanda? Or Italy. And of course, you could hardly fault her logic . . .'

'I was going to say nothing of the kind. I was not even intending to bestow upon so very crass a non-sequitur the merest response. Is there anything else we could drink? To go with this oh-so-luscious pie of yours.'

'Hear that, Amanda? You are the author of a very crass non-sequitur. It's an education, isn't it? Living here. More peas?'

'They're bigger than usual, aren't they Dad?'

41

'My my. The powers of observation in the two of you tonight come close to overwhelming. Yes – these are what Messrs Birds Eye are pleased to call "garden peas", no doubt in order to distinguish them from, say, "railway peas" or "drawing-room peas", it's quite hard to fathom. We can only assume that Messrs Birds Eye have a jolly big garden. I have hitherto always patronised the "petit pois", it is true, but I was told by a very great man in the pea world that the garden variety is possessed of considerably more flavour – as would seem to be the case, if my palate is any judge. Though they are, of course, "*moins petit*". Or "*plus grand*", if you prefer. Do they mean the same, those two? Hard to say. There is some very good Chablis under the stairs, if you can run to opening it, Susan. You may or may not think it will go with the meal.'

'Well I hardly think we have to be *too* sensitive, do we Alan? Matching a wine with a rather burned shepherd's pie. My sugar.'

'Amanda – would you be so good as to fetch the Chablis from under the stairs? It will not be chilled, of course, but it doesn't do to be over-sensitive, does it? When matching a wine to a quite perfectly browned cottage pie.'

'Don't trouble, Amanda. I've eaten all of this that I'm going to anyway. And listen – I've something to tell you.'

'Oh *man* . . .'

'Why did you say that? Oh *man* . . . What's oh *man* . . . ? What meaning does it have? Did you hear her, Alan? Oh *man* . . . !'

'I expect, Susan, that it was intended to convey a spirit of foreboding – of impending doom. Something along the lines of, Oh Christ – what's she going to come out with this time?

And the creeping certainty that whatever it is, it will hardly be fun. Broadly correct, Amanda?'

'Yeh.'

'See? Yeh. As for myself, I can barely wait. I am agog. Do tell, Susan. We are in your thrall. Teasing out the moment would be simply too cruel.'

'Oh *do* shut up, Alan, there's a good and gentle idiot. Anyway – you already know, don't you? I've already told you. About our new little forthcoming arrangement. It's Amanda I have to tell now.'

'Tell me what? What arrangement?'

'Oh now steady on, Susan. This isn't . . . the time, surely? You can't just . . . No no Susan: this just isn't the time.'

'And when would be? You – you'd put it off for just ever, wouldn't you Alan? Till doomsday. As you do with everything. Amanda – could you take my plate away please? I just can't bear *looking* at it any more . . . Now listen to me, Amanda. We're all going to have a grown-up talk.'

'Susan . . . !'

'Quiet, Alan. If you do not wish to be a party to this, you are excused from table and have my full permission to scuttle away to your secret little, oh God – *study*, and play with your trains and soldiers or whatever it is you get up to in there. On the other hand, I want no accusations later of any bias or pressure on my part, and so I really do believe it to be in the interests of all concerned if you could bring yourself to remain seated. Yes? Good Alan: good, my sweet. Now then, Amanda—'

'Oh *man* . . .'

'*Now* then, Amanda—'

'Be careful, Susan . . . be very careful . . .'

'Oh for goodness sake will you just please shut *up*, the pair of you, and just let me say what it is I have to say! Do me, please, the *goodness*. Thank you. Now, Amanda, as you know, for quite some time now Mummy has been going off to work in the mornings, and Daddy hasn't. Now I've never complained about what is after all a . . . well, rather unjust, I should have said, um – situation, but now it's become frankly rather tiresome, and it's time for a change. I might go on working part-time, I haven't finally decided. I rather think I will, you know – don't really want to be at home all day, do I? With your father. I don't know how he sticks it, quite candidly – I don't Alan, I really don't. I just fail to comprehend how you stick it, just being here all the time. Day in day out. Still – not your fault, I suppose. Is it? If no one will give you a job, well then that's rather that, isn't it really? Anyway Amanda, my darling – the point is money, you see. I have had to put my thinking cap on. And what I have decided is—'

'Susan. I really don't think—'

'*Alan*. I shan't tell you again. And so, Amanda, what I have decided is, I have to have a new husband.'

'*Christ* . . . !'

'Saying "Christ", Alan, doesn't really help now, does it? One way or the other. All right, Amanda?'

'Ex-*cuse* me?! All *right*? What do you mean all *right*? You're like telling me you and Daddy are getting divorced like Jennifer's parents, right?'

'No no. Quite wrong. Silly girl. What ideas you have. No no. We would never do that – would we Alan? To you. No no – what I'll be doing is having another husband as a sort of, um – little *extra*, if you like. And you – well you, Amanda, you'll be in a perfectly lovely position really, because instead

44

of having just the one old Daddy knocking around the house like normal people do, well – you'll have two! Won't you? Hm? Be nice. Won't it? Hm? It's not instead of, you see? It's as *well* as. Tell her, Alan. Say something. No? Apparently no. Silence from Alan. Well there. Is there a pudding at all, my sweet? My sugar? To round off this utterly delightful little snackette of yours?'

So yeh – I was just so like totally wrong: wasn't the same as every other evening, was it? No it fucking wasn't. Except for the dumb way they're always talking. I had a gun when I was little that shot out all these like ping-pong balls? And that's the way they're always talking. So right – what exactly's been dumped on me here? What have I got to get my head around? Mum, she went on a lot after about this mad and stupid idea – I think she's even more nuts than Dad is now. He wouldn't say anything to me – he just like went off, the way he does. He said we'd have a proper talk later – tomorrow, maybe; at the weekend, possibly. Yeh – as if. We've never had a proper talk in the whole of our lives, so like – why now? And she went on and on about how so cool it's going to be with this new shit who she's presumably fucking, oh God what a totally gross idea! She's old and she's my *mother*: I feel sick. And she kept on saying that he's going to be a proper *husband* and I said but listen he *can't* be, how can he be? It's illegal unless you're a Moron or something. And do you know what she said? Tell you. She said they'd make it as legal as they could. Mad talk, right? Like, it's either legal or it isn't – there's nothing in between. It's like when she told me she was being 'very honest' with me – it's crap, isn't it? It's just so totally crap. You can't be *slightly* honest, can you? Or very honest either: you're either like straight, or else you're not. And how can you be straight, right, if you're a complete fucking lunatic? And I'll tell you what else she said: she said that all this, she was doing it out of love. Out of love. Yeh right. And then when I walked past my dad's little hideaway, the room he always keeps like locked, I thought of knocking, maybe see he wasn't too upset or anything. But he was singing. He was singing Oh I Do Like to Be Beside the Seaside at the top of his fucking voice. God. So you can see now, can't you? I think now you must be able to see it. Why it is I like worry? About them? It's like that movie was called: *Secrets and Lies*? Well I've got secrets too – yes I bloody well have. And lies? I've been lying to them for ages now. And the only good thing is I feel better about it all, because now I think they deserve it. And I'm not even sure now I will. Worry any more – not about them, no way. I'll just go back to worrying about me. Because I like have to now, a bit.

Harry – he's a poet. He wrote for me in my special book: 'You can seek out softness, even in the hardest of places.' Beautiful, isn't it? He's like a real and proper poet, Harry is, I think – the only good thing that's around me now. And I haven't told anyone – not even like Jennifer or Tara, about him – how totally cool he is. And. I love him.

CHAPTER TWO

Well certainly – it's perfectly obvious, that little Susie, she's in this solely for the ride, that's what I've decided. It's just the good things she's after – and well, who can actually blame her? Wasn't it just the same for me when I was thirty, forty years younger? An eye on the main chance. That what they say? Because this, all this, it was clear to me from the outset – from the very day when we first took her on. Publicity Cyril was the one who had initially interviewed her – she'll do well, Black, I reckon, is what he afterwards said to me: she doesn't know too much – out of the loop, I have to say – but by Christ she does look good ... half the battle, isn't it really? And also, he said to me, there's a, she's got a ... I don't know: presence, maybe; determination about her, you know? Well I wouldn't even have bothered giving her the once-over had it not been for that, or anyway some of it. I usually, if it's a junior position we're talking about, just let the department heads get on with it – hire who you think you can work with, basically. But this one, she sounded interesting. I asked Jane to set up an appointment with her – tell her she's on the longlist, shortlist, I said ... tell her it's all very informal: tell her I'd just like to have a little chat, will you? Good, Jane: good.

'Cyril, he tells me he's just slightly concerned about the level of your, er – computer skills, Susan. It says here. Do you mind if I smoke? Will you have one?'

Susan adjusted her posture in the too-low chair across from this Mr Leather's great cliff of a desk – which, she was not at all surprised to observe, he very much enjoyed being safe and smugly the other side of (sprawling a bit, tip-tapping up and down the odd little thing on its quite clear surface, suddenly hunching forward in his too-tall chair, his face assuming a spurious interest, and then relaxing to emphasise a thrust in the direction of light-heartedness – or even, she noted with a lowering calm, the throwaway quip). She placed her large handbag on to the floor beside her (a rucked-up and quite good rug over a flattened, grey and ancient carpet) and prepared her cocked and elegant hand for the flick-back of the hair at just the moment – this moment – when it fell across her eyes.

'Well I can *use* a computer. I do have one. So I don't know what you mean. Please do have a cigarette if you'd care to. I shan't.'

Martin Leather nodded, and knocked one out of the pack.

'You don't?'

'Don't what? Mind? I told you not.'

'No. I mean smoke. You don't?'

'I don't, no. Otherwise I should have, you see.'

'Right then. Well now. So you do *use* a computer, then. Well that's good. But it's all to do with, I don't know – formatting, and so on. I myself do not. Use one. Never have. Last of the, um . . .'

'Dinosaurs?'

'Well no. Well yes, if you like. Yes, I suppose I am. But I was actually going to say, er – well I can't actually remember what it was I was going to say, as a matter of simple fact. Book. Book title, conceivably. And yes, talking of which – what was it, Susan, that drew you to publishing? All of a sudden. You haven't worked for any other house, I notice.'

'I wasn't. Not actually.'

'You weren't? You weren't what, in fact? Mohicans – that's what I . . . well there, never mind. You weren't what, Susan?'

'Drawn, as you put it. To publishing. Not drawn a bit. It's just really that this job I saw advertised. The fact that you are a publisher is by the bye. Or that, at least was my first thought. And then I considered it. I could be very good indeed, you know, at bringing people together. Sparking ideas. Making things happen. People sit up. I would be great as a publisher, if not in publishing, if you see the distinction.'

Martin Leather exhaled, long and reflectively. He pursed his lips and narrowed his eyes, the better to evaluate this lady before him.

'You do know . . .' he said quite slowly, 'that the post is that of a junior publicity assistant? You are aware?'

'Oh well yes of *course* I know – of course I know that, else why should I be here? As I say, that was the job on offer, and so I applied. I have not the slightest interest in being a junior publicity assistant – which means what, precisely? You concentrate upon obtaining very minor puffs indeed. Conceivably. Anyway – no. No interest whatever. And I don't frankly suppose, Mr Leather—'

'Oh Martin. Do please call me Martin, Susan.'

'As you like. All I was about to say then, Martin, is that I can hardly imagine I'd even be very good at it. Or any use at all. I do not excel in a junior capacity. My idea is that I could demonstrate as the weeks go by my real and evident talents, and you would come to feel foolish for having failed to exploit them. Is that a Braque over there?'

'Hm? Oh yes. Reproduction, of course. Can't bear it. But just let me recap for a moment, can I Susan?'

'I think, that had it not been for the impossibly long shadow of Picasso, you know, then Braque might now be hailed as the greatest twentieth-century innovator of them all. Debatable, obviously . . .'

'You like art, do you Susan?'

And rather to Martin Leather's quite startled surprise, Susan threw back her head, as people are said to, when the laughter is both glottal and unstoppable.

'Oh but it isn't a *question*, surely, of liking or disliking. Is it really? It is more in the nature of *response*. I am a sensualist, you see. It is all a matter,' she said now darkly, and leaning forward, and looking quite hard at the man, 'of *feeling* . . .'

Martin Leather ceased to fool with the knot of his tie the very instant he realised he was doing it. He folded over the rest of his cigarette into a large glass ashtray and shifted it around, only then looking over to her.

'Shall we . . . ?' he suggested.

'Shall we what?'

'Recap? Just briefly? On the situation so far. You have never before worked in publishing – oh, and incidentally, had you done so you would know that even with a position like junior publicity assistant, we and every other house in London are simply inundated with applications. Hundreds. Literally. The lure of publishing is a very strong one. But not, it seems, in your case. So. The job on offer you consider yourself unequal to—'

'Unequal, yes. In a particular sense.'

'Quite. Yes quite. You have basic PC skills, but no more. You would not, I imagine, take at all kindly to being subordinate to people – women, largely, rather younger than yourself, if you will permit . . . and your sole intention is to one day more or less run the company and possibly and incidentally put me out of a job. Have I missed something? Oh yes – and if I stand in your way, fail to perceive your talents, I am made to feel foolish. It is hardly, Susan, compelling . . .'

'Except for the fact that I am sitting here now. I have already been interviewed by Cyril, have I not? Who has spoken to you. And now I am here. Something, surely?'

Martin Leather smiled, and quite expansively, as he had been simply yearning to do for just bloody ages now. Such cool audacity, raised to this level – it was energising, yes, to the point of high excitement.

'Well, Susan. You know what they say, don't you? At this juncture.'

Susan stooped to pick up her bag, her slender fingers knocking back the thick block of hair that momentarily covered her eyes, their lashes now flickering.

'What, Mr Leather, do they say? At this juncture.'

'Martin, I told you. Please call me Martin. They say, Susan, that we'll let you know.'

'Aha. I see. And you will then, will you? Let me know.'

Martin Leather closed his eyes and flattened his lips and nodded briefly.

'Will, yes. Indeed. Actually, Susan . . . my friends, they all call me, um – Black.'

'Really? How innovative. And why do you suppose they do that? Your friends. Because you're not, are you? Black.'

Martin Leather laughed, enjoying this whole morning more than he could say.

'Not, no. No I'm not.'

'No. I thought not. I perceived as much. Well now – you'll take up no more of my time. For the present, of course. I shall leave you, shall I, to let down lightly the literally hundreds of disappointed young women whose hopes and dreams of becoming your junior publicity assistant now lie just dashed and broken. Poor Black: so much to see to.'

And when she had gone, I lit another cigarette. Well now. Well now. And Cyril had been right: she'll do well. She's got a, I don't know . . . presence, maybe. Determination about her, you know? And I have to say, by God she does look good (half the battle – isn't it, really?). And do you know what I just have to do now? Jesus, Jesus – it kills me, this thing. I've got to pull it out. There. That's a whole lot better. I wish in a way that I'd never even got the damn thing, but I couldn't go on wearing the old one. That's the trouble, you see, if you've gone a bit . . . if you find it harder to hear things. You either have this unsightly great beige sort of lump thing sticking out of your ear with a bloody curly wire hanging down and out of it (and then everyone talks at you not just too loudly, and then you have to turn the volume down, but also quite achingly slowly, because they have seen you advertise the fact that of course you're little more now than a complete and fucking imbecile) – or if not, if you don't wear it, then you're saying what, I'm sorry, say again, run that past me one more time (but not bleeding *pardon*: there is such a thing as a limit) – raising an eyebrow, cocking your head – and people, well, they soon lose patience with all that sort of caper, I can tell you that as a certain fact. Or else you take to nodding serenely while not in fact having the smallest clue as to even the nature of what is being said to you (changing the nod, stopping it in its tracks, if the wince of bewilderment should shadow their eyes) – and look let's face it, it's no way at all to be carrying on now really: is it? Not if you're supposed to be running the bloody company. So. I got this new damn thing after it was brought home to me by an outraged author that I had okayed a sadomasochistic jacket under pressure from Sales for his pretty milk-and-water so-called damned novel, if you really want the truth of it (but he sells: what are you supposed to do?), and I had had not even the slightest idea that I was ever being pressured at all (and nor, if I'm honest, that the design of the jacket was even under discussion). That was, admittedly, one of my worse days. Sometimes, I genuinely can barely hear a thing; normally, though, it's just a bit faint and then quite boomingly distorted. So I saw an ad, some magazine or other. Virtually undetectable, it said it was. No wires, nothing. And it is, I have to agree. I have these quite thick sideburns that I brush back over a good half of the ears (I know, I know – last of the dinosaurs, sixties hangover, pick which one you want) and you really can't spot it at all. But God it hurts: you feel invaded – almost as if your ear is going to breathe in sharply, gulp and swallow the thing whole, and then it will stop your heart. And I think I am particularly sensitive in matters of the heart, and I do not speak of romance. Since the last palpitation, I have to be careful: remember, Black, the medico said – you're not as young as you used to be, so try to take it easy, yes? Well I do now – of course I do. No bloody choice in the matter. What chances do I get these days for a bit of a roister, for a rollicking ride? It's mostly early to bed with a DVD, and I'm even quite chary about the rude ones, now (excitation and all the rest of it: God, it's no sort of a life at all really, is it?).

And all this time, while I assumed I had just been sitting here and mulling it all over, I find that I have in fact been scratching

53

away at the inside of my elbow, right into the crook of that tender little fold. Because if ever I am stimulated (and how rare is that?) then the old eczema starts to needle me to death – I've never quite wholly shaken it off, you see, not since my childhood. Lot better than it was in those days, of course (my I was a pitiable sight, wrapped in gauze, my hands in cotton mittens, and all of me under there, alive and livid with it) but still though it can fire me right up. And then I have to take a puffer, used to be Ventolin, now it's something else, which I always have to carry about with me. Because they're linked, you see, there's a truly unholy alliance – eczema and the asthma. One can quite often trigger the other, twin and cruel goblins, one on each shoulder. And yes of *course* I know I shouldn't be a smoker – how many decades have I been aware of that? And after all the years of pounding I've given it, the old liver is starting to rebel on me as well. Stick to spritzers, the other medic says – if, that is, you have to drink at all. Well yes I *do*, as a matter of fact – it's the job. It's how it runs, publishing: part and parcel, the oiling of the wheels, not to say the personnel. Smoking, though – yes, I know it's a mug's game, of course I do, and every morning, every single morning when I wake up and I'm parched and strained and wheezing from the last day's fags and the first little rasp of asthma I think OK well right then – that's it. No more. But how could I go down and make coffee? How could I even get myself into the bathroom, if I couldn't light up that first and blissful cigarette? And then I go mauve and hack up my guts in the time-honoured way and then I drag deep down into me another purple lungful, and then I'm OK, and then I'm calm and smiling, and then I'm off into another couple of packets, as the day wears on. I did manage it once, just the once, to give it up. Go cold turkey. Well Jesus. Worst afternoon of my entire life on earth.

So that's how my mornings begin – first the fag, then the coffee, and after that, all of the pills. Not nearly as many as I used to have to take, but still quite a colourful array. There was a time when it got completely out of hand. Go and ask him, Mylene said – this is when we were still married, of course, when she was still around. Go and see him and ask him, this bloody quack doctor of yours – lay out on his desk all the pills you take every morning noon and night, and ask him explain to you what each of them is, and why you take it: what does it suppress or promote, counteract or stimulate? And so, rather remarkably, I did that (never listened, in the normal run of things; half the time, of course, I didn't even hear her). Well, he made a mighty great stab at it, give him his due, silly old sod (Damn, he's even older than I am, David is – been my doctor since God knows when. And few are, you know, these days – or at least in my world, anyway. Older, I mean. Than I am). There were three or four that stumped him completely (he was man enough to admit it) but the gist of what he said to me then was that the majority of the others seemed to be a succession of fail-safe antidotes to the potential and deviant side effects of a good deal of those remaining, whose purpose still lay shrouded in pharmaceutical mystery. So I just stopped – stopped the lot. Next morning, and the one after, I didn't swallow a single pill – very liberating, I remember the feeling. And do you know what? Shall I tell you? Within an extraordinarily short while, I was feeling close to death. So I resumed with a motley selection, which more or less restored a form of equilibrium, or at least kept me blanketed from the wilder excesses of behaviour, while still saving me from slumping into a virtual coma. The official diagnosis of (very) mild schizophrenia, of course – they call it something else now: the illness, it now has dual identity – that came later. I personally am of the opinion that they are lying or mad: Jesus, if anyone knows their own mind it's me. I *never* see the other point of view, let alone go changing my mind – so how that mind can be schizoid . . . ! Well I ask you. Meanwhile, I receive the diagnosis, and I nod. And since then, oh dear Lord, what can I not have ingested? Risperidone, Haloperidol, Carbamazepine, Lofepramine – they all sound like wizards or knights errant, don't you think? Maybe? Magical crusaders. Of some quite ancient and arcane order. Or maybe not. Sodium valproate and Sertraline. Prozac – oh God yes, but of course: does anyone escape it? There may be one or two out there. Olanzapine and Clozapine (ugly sisters?). I think of them all as this collective of not at all chums but possibly aliens I was once at school with. Anyway. It comes and goes – and what, I ask you, doesn't? I'm completely fine at the moment: not at all frenzied, nor sunk down into the depths. I can always tell when I'm on a fairly even keel because then I find myself dwelling on all of the other and lesser ailments – because there are many more, I do assure you: unlike with the eczema, I've barely scratched the surface. And I do seem to add to them on an almost weekly basis. The arches, my arches – that's the latest thing, apparently. In danger of falling, is what yet another of these thirteen-year-old doctors is telling me now. How odd, I thought, that the very thing beneath your feet can come to fall. He couldn't explain the condition, how it came about, but I can. It's down to the shoes I wear with the hidden lifts – elevators in America, they call them. And in common with this tiny little hearing thing I have to suffer, they are virtually undetectable. There's this company in the West End that custom makes them for me – expensive, of course, but worth it, I think. I've never liked it, being short: even the word, even the word. And to this day, you know, I wonder if that's the real reason why Mylene, she was always so rude to me – because she had this thing, you see, about heels: five-inch stilettos, a lot of women like them, and let's thank God for that at least. I said I didn't mind – I didn't have a complex, I explained to her. I would *like* to be taller, of course I would – in common with the way that everyone really would like to be more *something*: rich, young, beautiful, powerful – famous, talented or immortal. But I didn't have a *complex* about it: I quite lost track of the number of times I insisted upon that. She said I was missing the point. She said that while I might not mind walking alongside a willowy woman who teetered and towered above me, she bloody well *did* – and that not the least of it was to risk a twisted ankle in all the time ducking her head down to hear what I was talking about (while I of course quite routinely never heard whatever it was she might have said in reply). Because all of this, it was before the tiny miracle hearing aid that seems to be eating its way well into my brain, and before the secret and uplifting shoes, which are causing my feet to break and decompose. I hadn't even yet had all those hundreds of little fleshy divots of tufty healthy hair punched into my skull: they came from the back of the neck, largely, the trichologist was explaining – is that all right with you? Oh yes, I assured him – that's quite all right with me: a bald neck I can live with. It bloody well hurt, of course, the entire procedure – eternally ongoing, needless to say – but when you're spending a fucking fortune, what can you expect? I couldn't really say if it's virtually undetectable (I'm never high enough to see). I can certainly tell you, though, that if you fail to brush it with care immediately after a shampoo, it can come to resemble pond growth. It takes someone new to be a judge, I suppose: someone like Sue, that cute little Susie Q. Did she see across the desk from her a mature and debonair publisher, rich and suave and maybe just a little bit attractive? Or just an old deaf dwarf with clunky shoes and a scalp quite recently grazed upon by a passing herd of fallow deer, and all the while scratching at his elbow, in the manner of a simian forebear? Time, I suppose will hold the answer. And if I had gone ahead with all of these body repairs just, say, five years sooner . . . would she still have been rude to me, Mylene? Would she still be here now? And maybe even loving me? You can't ever know. Can you? What might have been. The marriage, I just must put it aside – try now never to remember: make it a forgotten atrocity. She came to hate me, though, that's for sure. And whether she fed them, the children, with sly and malicious morsels of it – force-fed them, conceivably, with great big gobbets of it, this hate that she had for me . . . I'll never really know that either. And of course they're *not* children, are they? That's what one has to remember. Tim, now – he's got to be, what? Christ – not much shy of thirty, I suppose. Jesus – that's a thought, isn't it? That's a thought in itself. And little Millie, my sweet and pretty little baby girl – twenty-five? Could be. Maybe twenty-four. No younger, though. You lose all track, don't you really? Tim, he's been married himself now for . . . must be three years. Got to be. Warned him against it: didn't listen. But she's quite a nice girl – never really got to know her. Got a little boy, name of Adam. And yes I do know, thank you, exactly what that makes me – I don't need reminding, believe me.

And now – big sigh – here I am, here I do find myself, in yet one more relationship. I think it's a relationship – it's hard to tell. Because I'm really a bit old school, you know, when it comes right down to all this sort of thing. Always a bit wary of hurrying things along – don't want to be in any way pushy, you know: don't want to be seen to pounce, as it were. Mainly, of course, I need to be absolutely positive that there is no danger whatever of any sort of a rebuff, any single whiff of rejection, you see. As was the case with, um . . . good Lord, you know – I can't even remember her name. How awful. No come on – I *must* be able to remember her . . . but I can't, you know. Gone. Completely vanished. Annette, it might have been. No, not Annette. I can see her face, I am picturing it now, and Annette . . . no, it doesn't seem to fit. I mean yes, admittedly, I only really knew her for a month or so (until the day I pounced, until the day she rejected me) but still you really would think, wouldn't you, that I could remember her bloody *name*, at least. Well there you are – there you have it. David, my doctor – he'd say well you just have to *understand*, Black: as you get older, the brain cells, they're not what they were. Well now look: there's not one single part of me, is there, that's even remotely the way it was. I sometimes think that all the bits of my body have secret meetings in the middle of the night when at last I have achieved a partial oblivion – gang up and cackle over which one of them next is going to down tools and pack up on me, which is to be the new and eager recruit into all this deeply damaging and covert sabotage. But Jesus – if the brain goes too . . . if I start to lose my *mind* . . . ! But then of course I already have in a way, haven't I? I sometimes forget. I am after all, they tell me, a schizophrenic. Very mildly, it's true. I have yet to be committed. Restrained. But clearly all is far from well. Which makes me aware of the time that is ticking away. We all know what's in store, the inevitable end: because I can never forget that I am latently late. But bloody hell, in the meantime, I can't just cease to be a man, can I? I mean, Jesus – I'm not *ancient*. Am I? I just don't happen to be one of these thirty-year-old Masters of the

Fucking Universe, that's all. No crime, surely. Marianne. That was her name. Stupid bitch she turned out to be. Lovely name though, Marianne. She didn't deserve it.

But Sue, though – little Susie Q . . . I suppose I must have known it really, right from the beginning. All during the course of that ludicrous pantomime of a so-called interview, God save me. Or why else would I have taken her on? At an admittedly shamingly low salary – but then that's publishing for you: nobody comes into this game for the money alone. Why I had to make sure I got myself into a position to take over the company: always wanted money, always did. Wasn't too worried about the means: just had to have it. And of course it turns out now to be the only power that's left to me. And with Susie . . . I surely didn't believe for a single moment that she would grow into a more demanding and positive role: I assumed that all of that was merely a rather brazen display of feminist arrogance, or else just so much flirtatious banter (not to say a way of getting her quite gorgeous hair to flop across her wholly spectacular face). But I think she has amazed us all, and in really a remarkably short time. She has blossomed into a quite excellent managing editor, you know, and I couldn't now afford to be without her: I do so hope she never leaves the firm. Which is why, for a while, I resisted. It's true what they say about relationships in the workplace – no matter how crafty you imagine you are being, no matter how sly and devious and thoroughly in control, it will get out, and it will get messy. Like that awful awful time with Yvonne – never forget *her* name, that's for bloody sure. I was a fitter man in those days – I used to have her across my desk, when everyone else had gone home. Once in the Xerox room, if memory serves. Then she started asking me for trinkets – this in addition to all our expensive

60

lunches and so on. Little Tiffany things, and the shoes and bags and so forth. Rather a good watch, on one occasion – might it have been a Longines? Anyway, her girly and giggled-out requests, they soon became rather more insistent in their nature and culminated in a barely camouflaged case of blackmail. Ten grand it cost me – to keep her mouth shut, to get her to leave. Ten bloody grand. I only later found out from Publicity Cyril that old Bob in the postroom and Jonathan, the homosexualist in Sales, they were about the only men in the building she hadn't been screwing. But I, of course – who thought myself so very wily and magnetic – I was the one who got *really* screwed – and right bloody royally. Oh well. Only money, isn't it? And another great fistful of shame. I used always to say to myself well now look here, Black old son – so long as you've got your health, hey? I don't any more.

But Sue, with Susie, all we've really done is go out for lunch a few times. She seems to be ready for more, but really you know these days I can hardly dare to trust my own judgement. There was one time she was working late, and I popped my head around the door. Was looking over her shoulder at some sort of a spreadsheet, green on her screen, much of it beyond me. Trailed a few fingers in and among that sweet-smelling hair. She didn't leap up and stick me with a sabre. Sort of stroked the side of her neck . . . didn't recoil, wasn't being sick into the wastepaper basket. Then I kind of slid my hand downwards, you know, and over the swell of a breast, and without even so much as glancing away from her computer, she calmly removed it. Which was a hell of a relief, one way and another. Because you see I rather *like* it in a woman, to have reserve, a degree of dignity: morality, it used to be called, if anyone still can remember such a thing. Disappointed in another way, well naturally – it was a mighty fine breast, I can assure you of that. Firm, but soft – just yielding enough, if you know what I mean, and so very lovely and warm, beneath the cashmere. Because it's feeling, and so on – that's what I really like best. Undercover cuddles. The sort of thing one used to do as a teenager, when everyone knew that it would go no further. Whispered rustlings and exploring secret places – and then when she touched you! The intake of breath, and then the swelling: marvellous, that. But as to the whole, you know – *thing* . . . the utter nakedness and high expectation – the assumption of a mature and experienced woman that you actually, damn it, know what you are *doing* . . . oh God, oh God. Off-putting, very, and also quite starkly terrifying, I'm afraid I find it. And so after this dinner I'm having with her this evening, little Susie Q – our first real (Jesus) *date*, I suppose – I would be very happy, if I'm honest, with a generous and protracted series of fumblings in the back of the car, somewhere dark and silent. And if she could maybe ease my tension . . . well then I would be ready, I think, to lay down my life for her, such as it is. But she'll be expecting more, I just bloody know she will. Women do, these days – you read about it everywhere. And then she'll see all the gaps between the tufts of my hair, and the bits of scalp that have been dyed to match. And then I'll be expected to take off my shoes, causing me to vanish from her sight completely – and don't even get me on to the corset and the padded underwear. And even if still she's willing (and she won't be, of course she won't be – well ask yourself: would *you* be?) – but even if she were to go suddenly blind and then I gagged her with a scarf to stop up all of her laughter – even if we made it as far as the goddam bed, well then with the exertion, in my condition, I could well just peg out on the top of her. Or (worse) underneath. It would be so nice, really, just to be like a teenager again. Oh well. Just about time to go now. I'll change my shirt and tie. I know that most men these days – certainly all of those thirty-year-old Masters of the Fucking Universe – they go out in the evening, they never think of wearing a tie. Well I do. Always have, and I always will. It's the right thing to do, and it conveys a certain respect – for the venue, for the lady. Right then . . . just deal with this nicotine patch, get that thing out of the way at least (they're highly addictive) and then I'll have a puff from my inhaler and then a very swift fag. I'm wearing lenses: they sting, and I lose them all the time. OK: nearly ready now. Damn, you know – it's really giving me gyp tonight, this bloody old knee of mine. I think what I must do now is anticipate a triumph, pray that my hand is not too bold, nor stuck up the skirt of calamity.

'Where's Mum tonight, Dad?'

'She's, um – out. Tonight. Didn't she tell you? How's the linguine? To your taste? Not too much pesto, you don't think?'

'She never said anything to me. Where is she, then?'

'Well I told you, Amanda. She's out. Maybe do with a touch more pepper . . . What do you think?'

'I think she's with him.'

'No – I meant about the food. Could you go another spoonful, do you imagine? There's a bit more in the pot if you'd like it, my cherub.'

'So, you know – *what*, Dad? We just like don't talk about it, is that it?'

'I think then maybe I'll have some, if you're really sure you won't.'

'You're like that bird in the sand, you are Dad. What's that bird that like – puts his head in the sand?'

'Well you're meaning the ostrich, though apparently it's a myth. There is no known record of an ostrich actually doing any such thing. Certainly no photograph, anyway . . .'

'Yeah well. You know what I mean. Look, Dad – you can't like just *ignore* this.'

'You'd be surprised. What did you get up to at school today, Amanda?'

'Usual. *Talk* to me, Dad.'

'I was under the impression—'

'Yeh yeh. You were under the impression that you *were* talking to me. Yeh yeh yeh. Look, Dad – can't you . . . you know – like, talk her out of it? I mean it's *crazy*, isn't it? She can't really mean it, can she? It's so like – dumb.'

'You know your mother, Amanda. She'll do what she wants. There's an apple pie. I didn't make it. It's bought. Good, though. And cream.'

'Well I think you're just being so *pathetic*. How can you just sit there? Knowing she's with *him*? How can you, Dad? And per-*lease* don't ask me if I'd prefer it if you stood *up*, OK?'

'Am I really as dull and predictable as all that? Well well.'

'OK. You don't want to talk? Fine. Have it your way. I'm going out.'

'Out? No pie, then? Where?'

'Tara's. She's asked me to help out. Her dad, he's got this man coming round with no arms.'

'Really? Of all the things you might have come out with, Amanda, that one I must say was quite a surprise.'

'He does this, Tara's dad. It's sort of like – charity work? Deserving causes. Sometimes it's one of those kids with the moony eyes – he did a bunch of gaga old women or some-

64

thing, last weekend. He entertains them and gives them their tea. Like – conjuring tricks? All that. You know what he does.'

'I see. And tonight it's a man without any arms.'

'Yeh. Apparently. I don't really want to see it. Gross. But I promised Tara I would.'

'Well – sounds armless enough.'

'Oh *God*, Dad . . . ! You had to, didn't you? You just had to.'

'So long as he doesn't ask him to pick a card, any card . . . Sorry. Tara's father – isn't he the one you said was a wallaby? But you're perfectly correct, of course – I did, I did just have to. Do you want me to drive you over? Pick you up?'

'That'd be cool actually – yeh Dad. Thanks. *Wannabe* I said he was – reckons he's like going to be on the telly or something, one day. Yeh right. Hospital, more like, if Tara's mum goes on pelting him with crockery and stuff.'

'Crockery? She throws crockery at him?'

'Teacups, mainly. He makes her angry, Tara says, and once she's chucked like a whole load of dishes or whatever at his head, she says she gets calmer.'

'Hm. Women do seem to get angry and calm in the weirdest of ways. And also for the oddest of reasons. Oh Christ – I've just remembered. Your mother – she's got the car. Oh well. Not too far, is it? I'll walk you over. So now. Pie? No pie? What do you reckon?'

'I don't know how you can just like sit there and take it . . .'

'Pie? Take pie? Quite like it.'

'I wouldn't. If I were a husband, I wouldn't. I just so know I wouldn't.'

'Well. At least you have the comfort, Amanda, of knowing you will never in your life be called upon to be one of those little things. Well look – let's just go then, shall we? If you don't want pudding. Then you can have more time with Tamara.'

'Tara, Dad. Her name's Tara. Jesus.'

'Oh Tara, is it? I thought it was Tamara. Who was Tamara, then? You knew a Tamara though, didn't you once? Friends with her?'

'*Duh* . . . ! About like eight centuries ago, yeh . . .'

'Really. Time does fly. Well well. Right. Let's be off then, will we? Yes? Fit?'

And as they trudged out of the house, both Alan and Amanda found themselves more or less bonded into silent agreement as to its all being very sad but true that you get no sort of conversation, no contact, no matter how much effort you care to put into it. Just plain rude, youngsters, aren't they? As Alan had gone through the whole of his going-out routine, Amanda was just slumped against the door, the droop of her suggesting that she might have been there all night, knocking with her knuckle on the shiny hall tallboy as if frantically requiring admission. He had checked both windows, scooped up the big fob of keys from the delftware bowl that he'd hurriedly overpaid for at Schiphol one time – a carelessly selected and black and guilty gift, cover for some or other murky misdemeanour, real or imagined . . . a bowl that Susan, oh Christ how predictably, had fingered and sneered at and pronounced quite vulgar. She must like it really though, he had long ago decided, or else it would never have been allowed to remain: soon it would have become smithereens (could maybe have given it to Tara's mother, by way of emergency ammunition). And even as Alan had shrugged on the old Harris tweed that he habitually wore to go nowhere much, there still was Amanda, sighing, nearly wailing, lolling and hanging about, doing all of her goggle-eyed moony-faced

66

and loony-looking, and then glaring at him, projecting the loopiness of her expression on to and into the depths of his cranium. And as the strain of Amanda's interminable waiting plucked and then was strumming maniacally the very highest notes on the strings of her nerves, still her bloody father just went on bloody doing all the bloody bloody things he bloody did. And that stinky old jacket – just, like – oh my God: *look* at it, will you? Twice, two times – yeh no really, if you can possibly believe it – Mum has lugged it down to Oxfam, and twice, two fucking times, the dopey old sod has bought it back again. I mean: *Jesus*, right?

Quite early in the evening, and already it's practically dark. I used, thought Alan, to hate that, the season's change, when one seemed to be robbed of the value of the day, the bright goodness wrung out of the thing. But I suppose that really it could hardly matter less: I am inured to making my own sunshine now. Tara though, Amanda has just now informed him, her house was more towards the Fulham end of things, and fortunately he knew of a short-cut. And when he took it, he very much wished he hadn't. The narrow back road was barely lit at all, and the feeling of nauseous unease was thumped within him the moment he first caught sight of them – sort of just hanging around, like that. And as he and Amanda walked on, the glutinous mass of it expanded inside him and became just harder, much more set, throbbing like a heartburn.

'Maybe we shouldn't have come this way, Amanda. We might go back . . .'

'Why? What's wrong? Is it the wrong way? Seems right.'

'Well yeh but um. Let's cross the road, then.'

'Why? What's wrong?'

Christ. Why does she keep on *saying* that? Is she blind, or simply stupid? Why can't she *see* what's wrong? Staring her in the . . . Jesus, we're nearly right up to the pack of them, now – and that one, that one there . . . because there are four, I thought at first it was three, but no, I was wrong, because it's four, as I now can see so clearly – and one of them, that one, that one there, tall he is, big hands – he's detached the leg he had bent and cocked behind him, the flat of his trainer against the wall, and now he has turned about to face us and he's looking so intently: black, deep liquid and somehow imploring, his eyes are, in a blacker and shrouded face, and yet they seem as white as a searchlight to me now, no longer so huge, but narrow as a laser.

'Oh God Jesus don't worry about *them*, Dad. Just ignore them.'

Right. OK. I'll do that. Yes yes – I'll do that, then. Ignore them. Just ignore them. She's quite right, Amanda. Of course she's right, course she is. Because it's what you learn to do, isn't it? In London. Ignore. Very early on. Should be second nature. A staring into the yonder – never the overt or sudden aversion of the head, no no, never that – that could so easily be construed as distaste or aloofness, could so very quickly strike the tinder of offence; don't look down or behind you – this is not just a manifest humbling, this, it betrays white fear, pure and at its simplest, heady aphrodisia to a thug or a lout (a footpad or a brigand) – and positively not one scintilla of eye contact, oh God Christ Jesus no, and every Londoner who walks the streets or rides the Underground, they should know this and feel it in their blood and water – a fixed and non-committal gazing into a blurred and unspecific distance, here is the only way. Ignore. Just ignore, and sail on through. Bland and unseeing, radiating the certainty that you are in fact currently in quite another borough (projecting like a streamer a sure sense of elsewhere).

'All right?'

At the shock of the sound, Alan flicked up his eyes to the man as their paths now merged in the shadows – contact there, oh Christ, oh damn, for only the merest split millisecond, oh yes that's true, but the steady bore and dullness at the back of the man's pupils just flickered with a spark, I'd swear it unto God.

'Fine, thank you.'

Oh Christ oh Jesus oh shit shit shit – what did I have to go and open my mouth for? Now he thinks I'm a right posh bastard – worse, he could now think I'm a right posh *rich* bastard, oh Christ oh Jesus oh shit shit shit . . . ! And the other three, now, they've gathered around and they're looking – glancing over to Amanda, but looking, quite evidently, straight at me. And I would – I would just sail through, sail on past them, but collectively they do not appear to have left me the space to: the leeway, as it were (the simple means to get around this thing).

Tall. Did I say he was tall? Said that, have I? Well he is – he's tall, very – much, oh Christ yes, much much taller than I am: you only have to compare us. Seems bigger than the wall behind him, and a sight more looming. He doesn't smile, no no, but nor is the dart of challenge sharp and alive in him, not so far as I can . . . Amanda now, she just said something, pretty damn sure she did anyway. Can't quite seem to, um . . . shaking a bit, you see. 'Come on', think is what I heard. And I will. I'll do that. I'll come on now – sail right through. Have a bit of gumption and ignore them.

'Light, yeh?'

Blinking quite hard, is what I seem to be up to now. Fair bit of swallowing I'm also rather aware of.

'What . . . ?'

'Come on, Dad. We'll be late. Come on.'

'Light. You got one, yeh?'

'What . . . ?'

I said what, yes, but of course I'd heard him. Heard Amanda too. Just couldn't seem to say or do anything at all, is the essence of it. That would appear to be the heart of the matter.

'No – he hasn't got a light, have you Dad? Come on.'

Mouth open. Mine is. And now she's tugging at me, pulling at my sleeve – and she's grinning, look at her, the silly little girl, for all the world as if she's really very *happy*. And then suddenly somehow we're around and beyond them, back into the bliss of a wide and open pavement, just the rumble of a muted sort of chuckling momentarily afloat from somewhere in the hell behind us (the slapping of could-be victorious palms).

'It's down here we go now, isn't it Dad?'

And I nod automatically, twisting my face, as I glance at her askance. It truly does seem as if nothing now has happened. Or no – it truly does seem as if she's merely unaware. So young, then, and so very enviably untender. And I no longer seem to be padding along (in that old, accustomed manner of mine) – shambling then, that would be, according to Susan – but strutting quite sharply, as if once frozen, but now wound up tight and sent on my way. And I tell you something else: never mind 'light', never mind anything about wanting a bloody 'light' – he didn't even have a fag out. That big black bloke back there. Didn't even have a fag out. Well now look: this is what I'm thinking now, striding with a set determination down Lord knows which street it is we're in now because I've frankly lost every shred of sense to it . . . alongside a blanked-out and carefree Amanda . . . what I'm thinking now, as the shadows

70

all around sidle up to me for maybe just a kiss, but still they go on getting just darker and darker . . . what I'm thinking is simply this: what, in fact, am I to make of this? What am I to make of it all . . . ?

It's just so like *rubbish*, having a dad like mine. I mean, yeh, OK – most dads seem to be not that great, is what all my friends say, except for Arianna's, obviously, because he's just like so totally rich . . . but Dad, my dad, Christ – it's like it's sometimes *he's* the kid and I'm like, don't know, some kind of *nanny*, or something. I mean like right now, we finally got to Tara's – not actually *really* at Tara's, cos I got him to leave me at the corner – and it was like I ought to be walking him back home again, or something. Like – holding his *hand*? He gets really freaked, see, when there's anything around he doesn't *know* about – so he's freaked like a lot, yeh? Anyway, he got a taxi. I know. It's only, what? Ten-minute walk? Anyway, he got a taxi. Reckon he would've spent the night on the pavement rather than walk past those black guys again. They were OK – having a laugh. I think they're pretty cool, actually, black guys, some of them. I've never known one properly or anything. Harry, my Harry the poet, he couldn't be whiter. His skin, his face – it's sometimes like transparent, he's just so white and pale. People think he's ill all the time, but he isn't. It's not that. It's because he's like – sensitive? Anyway – I just can't wait to see him. His parents, yeh? They're like gone for the weekend so we got the whole house, and I'm meeting him in a minute. Got other clothes in my bag, quite sexy. Because I was going to see Tara and like watch her dad make a right bloody prat of himself with all of the *freaks* . . . ? Yeh right. No – that was just to get out of the house. It's Harry I'm going to see. Harry the

71

poet. Can't wait. Can't wait. He's just so totally cool. And. I love him.

Embarrassing, really. Having no money for the taxi. Well all of it – the whole thing was rather embarrassing, I suppose, because when I hailed him and told him (and I was breathlessly eager) where I wanted to go . . . he was one of the old ones, the ones with not much ochre hair and in a muffler, the ones that never retire and tell you how long they've been doing it and whose cabs are always squeaking and the doors, they yawn and then clang shut . . . and I told him where I wanted to go (my face was red with the need to be there) and he said Just round the corner, mate – and made then, I think, to just flick me away, but I frantically laid hands upon his tugged-down window and implored him never to leave me. Did Amanda see? Witness to any of this? Hard to say: wasn't aware. Matter if she had? Do me any damage, would it? Hard to say: how could I be diminished further? In those censorious eyes of hers. So he gave me a look, could have been pitying, more likely openly scornful (fuckin' 'ell – people in this area, people what live round 'ere – more money than bleedin' sense, the lot of them) – more likely still, white indifference just tainted by loathing – and so I clambered in and clanged shut the door and he spun the cab round in a sweet little circle, my heart going out to its innards – nearly shrieking and from really deep within (the machine and me) and before I could even sit well back for both comfort and safety, there we were, back to the chill of hearth and home. And so it was embarrassing, really, having no money for the taxi – so I said to him Look, you just hang on here for a minute, will you? Shan't be a jiffy, be back in a mo. Christ knows this time what crawled all over his face: sometimes you just *can't* know, can

72

you? Can't bear to think, because (Christ Jesus) it could break you. Anyway: no money in the delftware bowl, where there usually is (and God alone knows where it ever comes from: not from me, that's for bleeding sure). Bugger all in my wallet because I remembered now – I'd spent the whole lot in a funny little shop in Putney I'd never come across before: bought a couple of rather nice starfish and a good length of fishing net . . . anyway, that's not the point, how could it be. And Susan's money was wherever she keeps it: on her, shouldn't wonder, day and night and even in the bath. So there was a jumble of coins on Amanda's little pink dressing table, the one she wants to paint black (and Christ, by now I was panting like a bloody animal, heaving up and down the stairs, horsing in and out of every room in need of lucre) – and we're five pence short, it transpires: the taxi driver, though – he said he'd let it ride. Yep, let it ride: that's exactly what he said. And this time I didn't – couldn't, really – look him in the face (well Jesus, there's got to be a limit).

I don't really feel I can go to the seaside. Not right now, no not really. It's a shame, it's a pity, but my light and secret stupendous oasis – it cannot, maybe by the very jauntiness of its nature (cocking a snook) always come through for me. Sometimes – most times, thank Jesus – when I'm frazzled, I am sucking down the ozone even as the key so very reassuringly clunks open the door; already I am heady with the blousy charge to come. By the time I am slung into the deckchair, my mind's eye crimson against the sun, dizzily tracing the wheel and swooping of a single seagull . . . then the deadweight of care – or jagged angst, or flashing terror, or the plunging of misery, or bilious self-disgust or merely the stark blank wall of boredom (for there are shock-few gamuts that can be so ingloriously extensive) – that care, that stone, has plummeted from me like a rusted anchor on the heft of its thundering chain, fathoming down to the bed of the sea where it rests in peace, and then I can too. But on other occasions – and wouldn't this just have to be a white and luminous example of just such a terrible thing – I feel too salty to mingle with the brine of my imagination, too gritty inside to be coping with a warm swathe of sand, cosseting my toes. I never dare go in at times like these, for fear that then I shall associate this fragile harbour wholly and solely with its innocent failure just that one earlier time to jolt and then restore me. If I went in now (and I cannot tell you how very strong the yearning) I would only mooch – joylessly finger a casual barnacle, allow my sullen cornet to glossily slump: observe through hot and barely sucked back tears the warm and sticky rivulets coursing on down and over my panicked and bright-taut knuckles. Even the thought of the potential for sadness – in there, in my little maritime hideaway – it makes me so brimful of the sort of despair from which (I cringe at my knowing) there can be no exit. Yes. So no. Alcohol, then . . . and maybe just a touch of something else: a hit of the aroma, the memory of then, when times were finer.

There is a chest, always locked, that reeks of the essence of Susan's femininity. I would never have come across the key had I not, during the course of a routine and periodic rummage, found this other key to a particularly pretty little limewood and ebony jewellery box, which could easily be French and art nouveau (or, of course, from some other age and nation altogether). And so now I sit here, on the sheeny slide of her rose and satin deep-quilted counterpane, hot and dirty tang of whisky on my breath, as the pads of my fingertips are gliding

74

just touchingly over the planes and yielding layers of chiffon and of silk. The scent, as ever, is Guerlain, though naturally I could hardly be expected to recall quite which of them. She has three (three, she has often declared, is the perfect number) – there they are on her dressing table, the bottles and phials, large and handsome, comforting in their seeming oldness, their unchanging stability, proud and quite effortlessly dominant amid the much less than salubrious wash and clutter, the clatter and gumminess of all of the rest of it. I cannot from here read the labels, and I'm damned now if I'll be making the walk, giving up my seat in the very front row of this so very rich and glittering revival (if just for one night only) of the way it used to be, with Susan and me. Chiffon, satin, silk – and here now comes the bulbous crunch of something lacy, and I feel its contour in the cup of my hand. It is not all just black and white (it never is, or rarely); there is turquoise too, and coral – a deep champagne and powder pink. The whisky bites because I need it to, now: the burn down the throat is pleasingly painful. She still must wear such stockings, then (gloss and gossamer, and all the gear is here), though I could never remember when last I was aware of it.

I get distracted. I have been conscious now for quite some while of the noise, a fracture in the room, though only now have I registered that it is no more than the drone of the telephone (though behind that monotone I am sensing muted anger).

'Dad? That you?'

'I suppose so . . .'

'Can you ring me back?'

'Ring you . . . ? But you've just . . .'

'Credit's like really low, Dad. Can you?'

And I must have, I imagine: she's talking again, anyway.

'Look listen, yeh? Tara, she's like asked me to stay over. Kay? Kay? Can you tell Mum when she . . . ? Dad? You there?'

'Oh yes.'

'So you got that, yeh? Back like – sometime tomorrow? Not sure when.'

'Well . . . I suppose so. But won't you need—?'

'No. She's got. Tara's got. Don't need anything. Bye, Dad.'

Didn't say bye, because the phone now had clicked and was purring at me softly. Well there. That's the young, and this is me. She doesn't need anything, you see: she said so. That is what she said. I do. Christ. I do. Yes. Well there. And so. The curtain, now, it must ring down on this suddenly hushed and singular charade . . . and oh but if only, as I give something peachy (and creamy to the touch) one last and gentle caress . . . if only I hadn't wondered what it was now that could be next to her skin.

I shall go downstairs and drink until I can feel things shrinking; then I can give myself up to it and spreadeagle my mind. The last I shall see tonight is the light wink out, just as I am shuddering into my mortification.

CHAPTER THREE

Black, who had been leaning with attention across the table and idly stroking the joint on the middle finger of Susan's soft and outstretched hand flat against the weave of the deep-red cloth, now pulled away sharply and stared at her hard. He dabbed at his lips with a napkin and held it up there, consciously willing a glinting of amusement to pepper and invade the confusion in his eyes.

'I'm . . . sorry, so sorry, I must have—'

'Misheard? No no, I assure you. That is exactly what I said.'

Her composure, thought Black, was really quite remarkable.

'Indeed?' he said. 'Indeed? Well. Well well.'

And what else, pray, could he decently say? Thrown, really, is what he was feeling. Evening had gone really very straightforwardly up till now – and straightforwardness in any sort of venture of this sort, well I ask you: what more is there to wish for? But this, now. Well I don't know what to think, tell you the truth . . . I don't know – missed something? Have I? Somewhere along the way? Sign, of some kind? God knows it's possible: so very out of practice, you see. Rusty is the word: the *mot juste*, as it were. Seemed all perfectly normal when I met her in the bar. She was already there, which I hadn't intended (Lord: I had had to spray the crown of my head with some of the darkening stuff that they give you with the thickening agent that they give you after again you've been freshly plugged, and damn me if it hadn't dribbled down and over the rim of the collar of my shirt – and so then I had to go through all the business of . . . well now look, good God – I don't want to go *in* to it all, God's sake. Let's just say I was unavoidably delayed, shall we? And leave it at that). Anyway, there she was, little Susie Q, perched up on a bar stool, and in the pink soft lighting and amid the tinkle of piano looking very fetching indeed, to my eye. Elegant cream sort of wraparound dress, it looked like – certainly it fell away over one knee, revealing a good deal there to be savoured. Around her waist – and I've looked at it since – the most remarkably broad black patent belt I have ever laid eyes on. Stretches from just under her very amply projected breasts all the way down to the swell of her hips, and there must be half a dozen vertically stacked-up and cinched-in buckles along the way. Her heels are high, I could not help but notice, as she swung a leg gently, by way of a wave (raising her flute, and then an eyebrow). Fine when we're sitting up on a bar stool, but not too good while we're walking to our table. I could've worn the shoes with the tallest stacks of all, had I but thought, though not only do they weigh an absolute ton, but they always do make me feel as if I am giddily teetering on the very brink of a soaring tower (peeking over the edge, eager to leap, and shaking with fear at the very thought of it). My doctor, one of the many, he says it's impossible to suffer from vertigo as a result of wearing a pair of shoes – but me: I'm not so sure.

'Good evening, sir. Mr Leather, sir. A glass of champagne can I get for you?'

'Evening, Smales. Yes that would be lovely, thank you.'

'Carlo, sir, it's my name.'

'Really? Hello Susie, my dear. Damn they're tall, aren't they? Bloody stools. Carlo, hey? Really? And another glass for the lady, if you'd be so . . . How are you, Susie? You're looking absolutely, um . . . well what happened to *Smales*, then? Lovely, my dear: quite lovely.'

'Mr Smales has not been with us for quite some time, sir. May I help you up, sir? Mr Leather?'

'No no, quite all right. Haven't kept you, I hope? Dear Susie. Smales not here . . . well I never. Ah! Bubbles: splendid.'

'Have you been bleeding . . . ?'

'My dear Susan: what an opening remark! No no – not bleeding. *Bleeding*? No, not at all. Cheers, my dear. So good to see you. Let's clink glasses.'

Of course that would, wouldn't it, just have to be the very first thing she notices about me. Anyway – haven't been bleeding, have I? It's just that there's this red and viscous fluid, don't ask me what it is – I have to take it if I'm anticipating a bit of a night on the toot, if you get my drift (coats the stomach, simmers down the liver, keeps the heart from more or less exploding) and because I was already running so late due to all the sodding shirt business I went and slopped some over my cuff and I'd only just come through the whole damn malarkey of changing my . . . so I just thought oh to hell with it: who's going to notice a tiny speck of red? Well there you are – it's just sod's, um . . . thing, isn't it really? Can't get over old *Smales* not being here, though . . . Presumably I knew. Presumably they told me. It's a worry in itself.

'Lovely restaurant, Black. Oh God: *Black*. Do I really have to call you that? It's just so . . .'

'Oh it's not. Not *so* . . . do you think it is? It's maybe a *bit* . . .'

'It's more than a bit.'

'More than a bit? You'd say so?'

'I've said so. It's a lot. I'd much prefer to call you Martin.'

Black was shifting about in the bar stool; there was this sharp little half-back to it that somehow forced his stomach way up into his ribs, and already his corset was giving him gyp.

'You'd be one of the very few who does. My son does, Tim does. But only, I think, because he doesn't at all care for me. Can't blame him, I suppose. Although I *do*, of course. Of course I do.'

Susan looked at him reflectively, tapping a long and aubergine fingernail at the rim of her flute (waiting for the ping until she did the thing again).

'You're a singular man, Martin.'

'Martin. Black. That's two men already. Oh look – I don't want to make a, you know – big sort of deal of this, or anything, Susie . . . but I'd be awfully pleased if you'd drop all of this "Martin" business, you know. It's my instinct to look over my shoulder to see who you're talking to. That, or duck.'

Susan laughed, low and throatily, showing him her neck and the glimpse of white in the pink of her mouth and letting her eyes glimmer with secrets. He felt caught short by a wave of something, sort of inner convulsion – a reminder, he supposed, of what in Christ's name he was even doing here in the first place.

'Duck? Why on earth *duck*?'

'Oh. Wife. Ex-wife. She said it in such a way . . . Well. There it is. Don't really want to, um . . .'

'No of course. Of course not. What's her name? Your ex-wife. I've often wondered.'

'Name? Well like I say, Susie – if it's all the same with you, I'd really rather not, um . . . and particularly this evening – the very first evening I, er – have you all to myself, so to speak. Mylene. Actually. Is her name. Shall we go to our table? Hungry, Susie? Are you?'

'Mylene. Odd name.'

'Yes well. Odd goes nowhere in describing the woman, believe me. Let's go and eat now, shall we? I really don't wish to spend these valuable moments together with you discussing all the—'

'So it was acrimonious, I'm assuming. The split.'

'Ha. It would be fair, I think, yes, to term it acrimonious. Let's not talk about it, hey?'

No. Let's bloody not. How many times have I said it? What's wrong with the woman at all? What are you supposed to *do*, exactly, when people go on and on about a thing that you've repeatedly made perfectly plain to them that you don't, you really *really* don't want to fucking talk about?! Because what is there to say? That she beat me senseless, Mylene, laughed as I bled on the floor? Slept with a knife beneath her pillow? Attempted to poison me, and not just the once? All this is true, all this and more. So forgive me *please* if I choose not to dwell. I have buried it. It is a mound. I lay on it not fresh flowers, but just another shovelful of brown and stinking loam. Let it rot. The forgotten atrocity.

'The table is perfect . . .'

'Thank you, my dear. I'm glad it, um . . . Yes, I always sit here. My table, you know. Pretty sure it is, anyway . . . Now do listen, Susie – I don't want to tell you what to eat, or anything of that kind, but there is this one thing they do here which is just perfectly *sublime*. Quite wonderful. But do please look at the menu, won't you? Scan it thoroughly. I assure you you won't be disappointed. Never had a bad meal here. No no. Not ever. Not once.'

Susan was genuinely pleased with the table and its setting – not too far removed from the warm and throbbing heart of the thing, but secluded enough for her to feel easy in putting everything she had into doing and saying all that she intended. It was, of course, one of the old-school restaurants with carpet and burnished mahogany, small brass sconces with speckled glass shades – large silver wagons, stiff and proper linen. Black had told her on more than one occasion how he could not abide these stark white and wood-floored clattery places with paper cloths, if any at all, and cheery Australasians who announced their names as if they were clever to have one and quizzed you as to whether or not you fully comprehended the *concept*.

'What is it?'

'Now, dear Susie, I myself always tend to have red wine with a meal, but if that doesn't suit you – and please do be frank – then naturally we can opt for white. Or both, of course. We could always have both, of course we could. No reason why not. What, um . . . what is *what*, my dear?'

'The thing.'

'Thing? What thing would that be now, Susie?'

'The thing. The absolutely sublime *thing* that they do here. What is it?'

'Ah. Oh yes. *That* thing. Yes of course. So: red all right with you then, is it? Claret, I tend to. Burgundy, if you prefer.'

'But what *is* it then, Black? I really want to know.'

'Yes . . .'

Susan sat back and just gazed at him.

82

'You do *remember*, don't you? It was the first thing you said to me the moment we sat down.'

Black now chucked down his napkin, and just anyhow.

'Oh well now *really*, Susie – what a thing to . . . ! Of *course* I remember saying it to you, of course I remember. I'm not *completely*, um . . . whatever it is. Of course I remember. *Gaga*, that's it. Not *completely* gaga, you know. I mean Jesus . . .'

Susan was doing her laugh again now, which immediately cheered him.

'Well what *is* it then, God's sake?'

'Mm yes well that's just the point. Just for the moment, it seems to have slipped my mind. But it will come back to me, I have no doubt, as soon as we cease to *talk* about it. That's the key.'

'Maybe if you looked at the menu . . . ?'

'Ah well no – it's not *on* the menu, you see. That's the whole point of it. That's what makes it special. That's what makes it sublime.'

'Well anyway . . . I'm having oysters to start.'

'Ah. Excellent choice.'

'Do you eat oysters?'

'Hard to say . . .'

'You don't remember?'

'Of course I—! It's just that I had a duff one once – ooh, you don't want to know, believe me: you really don't want to know. Woof. And I've had them since, pretty sure, but I can't quite recall whether I enjoyed them or not. Maybe time to find out. Maybe not, though. I'm actually having the whitebait. Always do.'

'You can have one of mine.'

'Well we'll see how we go, shall we? You know – it occurs to me, Susie . . . don't want to hark back to what we were talking about earlier – you know, the past, my ex and all that. No no. But it occurs to me – apart from what you, you know – do at the office, I really don't know the first thing about you.'

Susan smiled and lowered her eyelids: now she could begin.

'The truth is,' she said, 'I'm – lonely . . .'

She swiftly bit her lower lip, looked up and full at him with the very largest eyes, was abashed as she half-smirked at her own girlish foolishness, and then she glanced away from him. But . . . he did not seem to be there yet: she didn't seem to quite have him.

'I expect,' she rushed, 'I'm being so silly . . . it's just that – it *hurts* . . . !'

And then from one quite pained and helpless eye, the big fat tear, it bloomed and rolled on down. Black leaned quickly across the table and grasped her hand in his, his eyes and eyebrows very busy with concern.

'My dear! A woman such as yourself! Lonely? That will never do. Won't do at all. Believe me – you shall never be lonely again. I shall personally see to it.'

Still so demure, she nevertheless allowed herself the merest quick peek at him.

'You will . . . ? You really mean that? You . . . *promise*?'

Black just smiled with huge and avuncular reassurance – and felt pretty damn good about it until the sheer relentlessness of her gushed-out gratitude and spasms of relief – the breathless gasps of could-be newly let-loose rapture (the Lord knew he was no expert) left him, yes – still just heady with gratification, but also there was the thrum there of uneasiness alive in his ears (still a tinge, though more was lurking). He was on the whole rather saved, now that the waiter was suddenly here and half-bent at the waist, notebook eager, his head keenly cocked as if to eavesdrop upon an insider tip.

'Ah – Smales, good man. So. The lady is having oysters. Natives I'm assuming, Susie? Six? The dozen? Yes a dozen? Really? Good Lord. Well that then, Smales – and then the whitebait for me, as per. And after, the, um . . . have we actually decided about mains, Susie? I can't, um . . .'

'We're sharing the Chateaubriand.'

'Are we? Are we really? Oh splendid. Well that suits me very well, I must say. And we decided that, did we? Now the only thing is – I expect you like it rather rare, do you?'

'Very. Not quite blue, but yes – very rare.'

'Mm. Yes. Why did I know that. Whereas I, you see, I tend towards medium rare to medium, so we might have a bit of a . . .'

'No no, sir, Mr Leather – chef, he can do this.'

'Really. Well that's very clever, isn't it? Thank you, Smales. And then the usual, I'm assuming? Sauté? Chips, conceivably? Few beans. That sort of thing. Béarnaise, of course. Best bit. What are you laughing at, my dear? Said something, have I . . . ?'

'I was just thinking,' giggled Susan, 'that all this will maybe be quite as sublime as the thing you couldn't remember.'

The light and concentration in the glittering smile she now splattered across the waiter was of a force that could render him helpless with love; his eyes tipped down and he was visibly weakened.

'*Thank* you, Carlo . . .'

'Yes,' added Black quite quickly, 'thank you indeed. And send over the wine chappie, would you? So much.'

Black now tore apart bread.

'I did know, you know. I hadn't forgotten. That his name was . . .'

'Carlo.'

'Carlo, yes Carlo. I hadn't forgotten. Just so used to old *Smales* being about the place, that's all. Well. This is all very jolly. You're laughing again, Susie . . . Obviously I am being highly amusing.'

'That's a bad thing?'

'It . . . depends. Depends upon the nature of your delight. Anyway – enough. Tell me – talk to me. Tell me about your life.'

Susan sipped water, and glanced about her. There was a big red bald man, two tables down, laughing as if relieved at having relinquished all of his control: his eyes had retreated into black and fleshy creases and the light from one of the sconces overhead made his skull a luminous pink, and seemingly irradiated. The much younger woman opposite was smiling just tentatively and in sympathy, as if struggling to keep up with an increasingly involved and arcane deconstruction.

'I have a nice house in Chelsea. I have a little girl.'

'Ah. Little girl. How lovely. I have one myself. Well – I say little, she's hardly little now. Must be twenty . . . three. Four. But they're nice when they're little, aren't they? How old is she? What's her name?'

'Fourteen. Nearly fifteen. Amanda.'

'Amanda. That's a very nice name. I think. I used to know an Amanda. Pretty sure. Maybe not. Could've been Alison. Fourteen – not a baby, then. If what you read is any guide, they're quite grown up these days, are they? That age? Ah – wine man. Excellent.'

'Mr Leather. Always a pleasure. You well, sir?'

'Couldn't be, um . . . Bottle of the Gruaud, I think. Better. Couldn't be, um . . .'

'It is already open for you, sir. Good evening, madam.'

Black was watching him swagger away.

'Good fellow, that. Been here for ever.'

'Not *Smales*, is it . . . ?'

'No no! *That*'s not . . . Ah I see. We're having a little joke at Mr Leather's expense. Well well. Highly amusing. *Must* be, apparently – you're laughing again, anyway . . .'

'I'm not – I'm not laughing, Black. Honestly. I'm just enjoying the evening. What's that you're taking?'

'Mm? Oh. Pill. Take it before eating, this one.'

'What's it for?'

'What's it for? Oh, something allied to what they're all for, I imagine. Or else to counteract some or other ghastly side effect of what one of the others goes and does to me, I really couldn't tell you. Just swallow them, you know . . .'

'The thing is – she needs a father. Amanda.'

'Really? Oh so you're not, um . . . There isn't a, er . . . ?'

'Guidance. She's at the age she needs stability and guidance. I mean, me, I do what I can of course, but one always feels it's never quite enough. I think, Black . . . the man is waiting for you to taste the, er . . .'

'What? Ah. Yes – hello. Didn't see you standing there. Well look I shan't trouble with a taste – and shall I tell you why, Susie? Shall I tell you why? Because he will already have done so – am I right? Am I? I thought so. Yes yes. They think of everything here. Pour on then, Smales. Oh no – you're *not*, are you . . . ?'

'Chester, sir. Wine for you, madam?'

'Chester, Chester, yes of course. I knew that. So where were we? Ah yes – your little Alison. No other children? I have a son. Tim. Told you that, have I? Grown man. Thirty whatever. Got a son himself. And yes I *do* know what that makes me, thank you very much.'

'You're very lucky. The wine is divine.'

'Is it? Haven't tasted it. Am I? Suppose I am. Some ways.'

Susan's face was now a spotlight, white and narrow, and it had him between the eyes. As he felt its bore – flinching, eyes flickering to pin down its source – she cranked it up full into a flood, and he was quite now in a dazzle.

'Black. There's something I want to ask you. Put to you. Look at me, Black. It's really so important. I feel with you . . . a bond. Yes I do. I would not say this to any other man alive.'

Black's eyes were wide. He gulped some wine. Swallowed it down.

'Uh-huh . . .' he said, as if on tiptoe.

'Are you . . . all right? Black? What's wrong with you? Why are you—?'

'Perfectly. Quite all right, thank you.'

'—*squirming* like that? What on earth's wrong with you?'

'Nothing whatever.'

'Well then why are you—?'

'I just have to go to the lavatory, that's all. Comes upon me rather of a sudden. Nature. Not a lot to be done about it. Apart from the obvious, obviously. Anyway – carry on. Something important, you said.'

Susan bit her lip and sighed; the lamp was fizzing, growing dim now.

'No, Black. You go.'

'No honestly, Susie. You say whatever it is you have to say. I'm perfectly fine. Well – minute or two, anyway . . .'

'No, Black. Go. It'll keep. I'll tell you when you come back.'

'No, Susie – I wouldn't hear of it. You get it off your chest. All ears, promise.'

The light was dead: it cut dead into darkness.

'No, Black . . . It's not . . . no. You go.'

'No *really*, Susie, I'm—'

'Fuck's sake *go*, will you, or I might have to bloody *kill* you.'

And during the silence, Black could easily have gaped at her for a much longer time, but what with things being the way they were, he just simply had to *go* (fuck's sake). And it's no sort of a picnic, please let me assure you, this whole business of going to the sodding lavatory, Lord no, not in the state I'm in. Particularly as now when it's been left just that smidgen too long – all the bloody argy-bargy with Susie there, doing my best to be bloody polite – and so I'm blundering past the tables (although I'm only small, this always makes me feel like a runaway bison, can't explain it) – and at least one bread roll I'm aware of has gone skittering away into the unknown and I'm snapping on my instant and elastic smile at the vaguely familiar darkish waiters who are cringing away from the full-rigged bluster of this vast and lumbering approach (no doubt a blend of dinned-in deference and a deeply comprehensible and full-throated revulsion) and finally into the blasted Gents, a place I belong, and only momentarily aware that on my way back out I'll have to chuck a lump of money at the black chap there with all the white hair in an effort to stop him annoying me with brushes and cologne – and now I'm bundling a good deal of myself into one of the airless and quite ridiculously cramped cubicles (hauling in the rest of me by the clammy sweaty handful) and now there's the jacket and the waistcoat and the braces and the corset (oh Christ yes, the corset – sit on the pan, blow out your cheeks and put your back into the charged and mighty burden of evacuation and the whole contraption is liable to be ripped asunder and hit the opposite wall, if you don't undo the bloody laces) . . . and then after it all falls out of me, the weight of the world, with just so disgusting a slither, thud and then attendant spatter, there's the truly foul aspect of a rudimentary clean-up to be attended to now – and more and more, you know, I am so really revolted by this, the wiping, the wiping, but look, let's face it: who else is going to do it for me, eh? You just answer me that. And now I'm as done as I ever will be (the one side effect of a drug that forces me to gallop in a panic is soon overcome by that of another, which seals me up with a trowelful of mortar) I have to bang my elbows and huff like a bull in the wrestle to grapple it all together again, and Jesus I'm tempted to let the corset go hang, but if I do that I've lost all hope of getting the waistcoat buttoned up and then the bloody stomach is going to go flopping out all over my waistband and everyone will remark upon this singular vision of the red-faced old man soon to be delivered of triplets . . . and now I'm trussed up and sort of prepared for my evil-tempered and blood-hot exit, so light up a fag now, suck on it as if I'm being paid to – revel in the hit and suck on it again – hear it sizzle in the bowl as I barge my way out and I chuck a lump of money at the black man there with all the white hair and I bat away the brush and nearly evade the squirt – though the corner of my left eye caught the hissy dregs of it, I can feel the wince, and now the bite (don't want to wash – you only get germs) . . . and bingo! Here I am now back in the gravy-scented hubbub of the restaurant's guts and thundering back over to what I'm nearly quite positive is my regular table and I collapse like a spavined old carthorse into my chair, sending just the one dessert fork up and over into an arching somersault and clattered descent, and there is a frankly startled Susie, oh what joy – and so now we can resume at the point whereat we left off, although I'm damned, but of course, if I can recall what it was. Woof. On the whole though, I think, that went not too badly.

Susan blinked, and poured more claret into her glass.

'All right? Yes? Everything . . . ?'

'Mm? Oh yes. Course. Tip-top. Never better.'

Yeah well: you bloody don't look it. I've had a little time to think, and I really do hate that, once I've made a decision. Once the die is . . . you know. It's just that I can't help thinking . . . he's not young, is he? Leather. Not in the first full flush, shall we say. Yes: laughably, let's say that. And I know, I know – of course I know (it's my plan, isn't it?) – of course I know that youth and beauty are not of the essence. Not in this particular case. I just sometimes cannot help but wish . . . that they were. Then I could go and marry Carlo, who I'm sure now would quite gladly lie down and die for me. His eyelashes are like those of some long-eyelashed thing, you've seen the pictures, I don't recall the names of them. Maybe camels or giraffes, but they're both stupid-looking, and Carlo, he isn't. A firm strong chest and the sleeves of his jacket are so well-filled. But alas, it is not a waiter I need (although every man on earth, to a larger or lesser degree, is certainly one of those . . . and if he isn't, one can easily train him to be). But how very wonderful to have a young and beautiful husband who is not just rich and talented . . . but one could actually *respect* him. Just think of that: *respect* him (up to, of course, a point). And look at Carlo's hair in the lamplight – thick chestnut, with an elegant wave. I know just how it would feel – my fingertips ache and tingle with the certain knowledge: I know this, oh yes, because I am a sensualist. Black's hair, though – oh God. It looks as if his pale and gluey scalp has been bombarded by the matted evisceration of an old and fetid mattress, the resultant unlikelihood having then been given a thorough going-over with a ragful of blacking. But the point is, he has the money, and he can be formed. Carlo, for all his loveliness, is, by definition, a loser. And if it's a loser I was wanting . . . well, I can get that at home.

Carlo was smiling wildly at Susan as he told Mr Leather that his whitebait was cold.

'Let me get you fresh plateful, sir. Take no time.'

'No no – I shan't bother. Let's just have the beef now, shall we? Oh – Susie: your oysters . . . ?'

'Eaten.'

'Really? What – whole dozen?'

'Yup.'

'Ah. Good, were they? Enjoy them?'

'Yup.'

'Good. Very good. Serve the beef then, would you? Oh – and tell the wine chappie: another bottle of the, ah – Gruaud, yes? Good. So much.'

Carlo and Susan did a swift and private eyebrow thing, and then he jerked his shoulders and set himself to jiggling away, and really rather bummily, to Black's eye, like the smuggest and most insufferable sort of Greek or something dancer. (God Almighty, the way things are now: bring back Smales, that's what I say.) But the Chateaubriand, it arrived in a twinkling, this leading Black to murkily suspect that it had been hanging around a bit under one of those fearsomely hot and sci-fi downlights, the ones they have in rows in those carveries, should such things as carveries still be in existence. But no – it was quite perfect: just as I like it at either end, and disturbingly burgundy at its glistening core, the slices thick and fleshy (wetly ripe for the Amazon). There's a bald fellow, you know, couple of tables away, just caught my eye – distinguished he looks, I'd say: makes me wonder about all this hair of mine (because who, in fact, do I imagine I'm kidding? Would any foolhardy fingers tempted to run through it ever be the same again?). Amusing man, he seems, with weight and intelligence. The rather dim-looking child who's with him, though – she seems way below, to my mind: lucky to have him.

'Here, Black – let me give you some Béarnaise. All looks lovely . . .'

Mm – conciliatory tone, seeping into sweet: not about to tell me to fuck off again then, by the sounds of things: a renaissance of sorts. And no immediate signs that she's going to resume her Pronouncement of Importance. And I have no idea whatever of what it could be, I have to tell you – never do, never know what in blue blazes people are thinking, hinting at, pussyfooting around; even if things are made as plain as a tower block to everyone within hearing – even as I see their eyes narrow into understanding, watch the new and veiled prudence, the sapient pursing of so subtle lips, still I am blinking amid the gloaming, blind to what is evidently unmistakable to all (it's maybe my shelter, this – a flimsy form of defence, could it be? Though to shield me from the barrage of what imagined onslaught, I really couldn't say).

There was of course far too much of the tenderly yielding fillet of beef, but I've eaten all of my better-done slices, while she's left quite a fair proportion of her carefully specified butcher's slab. Feminine, is it? To do that? Or simply rude and wasteful? Leaving room for pudding, she could be, although I might be out of date. In the old days, you took a woman to any

93

halfway decent sort of nosherie and her eyes were scanning the puddings before she'd even started fooling with her napkin. It's maybe different now, I'm hardly the person to ask. Heard a line the other day from someone or other, God knows who – this doctor, do you see, he says to his female patient: Tell me, do you drink at lunch and dinner? And she – young thing – she replies wide-eyed Oh good heavens *no*, doctor – I don't even *eat* at lunch and dinner. Modern way, I expect. Don't find it particularly amusing.

'Pudding, Susie? Squeeze something in?'

'I might just have a crème brûlée.'

Well at least she's human: quite mannish in her appetites, some ways. I think it's something I've sensed before. Nearly half a bottle of wine left: mm, let's drink it. I've offered her some, to top up the glass, but no, she says no I shan't, thank you: she's too intent upon cracking into that sugary crust, scooping up the cool and creamy custard and into her really quite remarkable mouth. Which . . . Damn, oh God: sigh – *sigh*! Brings me to sex. I mean . . . I *want* to, yes – of course I *want* to (what in Christ's name I'm even doing here in the first place: well isn't it?). I mean . . . you've just got to look at her: she's mesmerising, captivating, all the weak-inducing and mind-swimmingly enslaving things you ever could dream of. But you see . . . well there are two things, really, that are worrying me now. Two, yes, just for the present, but doubtless many more will assail me as I plod along this leaden way. The first thing is the looming actuality . . . the point at which all the really enjoyable bits – the undercover and lacy rustling, the good and weighty fumble, squirming one's fingers into tight and giving spaces – the caught throat and the short hot breath of a single just audible gasp against one's cheek . . . well, time must have a stop – and then it's a question of actually, oh my good God – *disrobing*, not to put too fine a point on it . . . and well look – am I really compelled to illuminate this? *Look* at me, can't you? Hm? Yes? You see? And revolve, if you please: mm, and now look at her. Yes? Well quite. And it's here that the other thing moans and stirs and heaves into view: why me? Hey? I mean, point one: how can she be lonely? Actually? Not possible, is it? Woman like that. Not even conceivable. And say, just say for the sake of, um . . . you know: thing. Argument. Just say for the sake of argument (and how feeble and wheezing, how visibly collapsed and broken-backed it is, this putative argument, to be sure) – but let's just all agree though, shall we, that this sultry, elegant, quite breathtaking woman (whose body warmth can hit you from across the table) is – hah! – *lonely* . . . well then go on – ask yourself, as I have: why me? See? Makes no sense. No sense at all. I mean, I don't even think I'm particularly amusing. I have no fame. Money? Well – a bit . . . but nothing, surely, to light up the eyes or kindle the dreams of one such as this. So what on earth can be going on here at all? Unless, of course . . . oh God, here's a thought, and I can't say I'm liking it, no not a bit, but here's a thought – listen to this: what if I am merely the boss at the office, the (much) older man, a mature and safe acquaintance? What if, when I lay upon her a finger, maybe eventually even more (who can ever say?) – she screams? Or is sick. Or pityingly shuns me. Or takes out a whistle and blows for the police. Or stabs me with a knife, as Mylene might so very easily have done that sourly muggy August Bank Holiday, had I not so deftly parried her demented lunge with the first thing that came to hand, which turned out to be an early hardback copy of the ghosted autobiography of a callow and talentless proto-punk named Gideon, which I had recently undergone

95

the extreme displeasure of having to publish. Yes. What if. So all things considered, I can't say I'm not concerned.

But distance, logic, coherent thought – they have left me now, for she is touching my skin; the tiny espresso cup jingled in its saucer as her white long fingers and the gloss of their aubergine tines shimmied past it, just glancingly. And she speaks. I am leaning with attention across the table and idly stroking the joint on the middle finger of Susie's soft and outstretched hand flat against the weave of the deep-red cloth. I now pull away sharply and stare at her hard. I dab at my lips with a napkin and hold it up there, consciously willing a glinting of amusement to pepper and invade the confusion in my eyes.

'I'm . . . sorry, so sorry, I must have—'

'Misheard? No no, I assure you. That is exactly what I said.'

Her composure, I am thinking, is really quite remarkable.

'Indeed? Indeed? Well well.'

'And would you like to? Think about it, at least?'

'Well I mean . . . well Susie, Susie – I am quite . . . I mean – this is all so very sudden. So unexpected. I mean – we barely even know one another . . .'

Susan laughed quite delightedly (the teeth, that hint of pink) pressing her nails into the flesh of his palm with just sufficient force as to leave so white, already fading traces, soon to be the trail of memory.

'Oh Black, you sound like a virgin girl!'

'Who has just been proposed to . . . ! Susie: are you serious? I mean – you're not just—?'

'No. I'm not just. I'm serious. Very. Yes I am. I think we would be marvellous together. Don't you? I can't believe that you don't. Tell you what – come to dinner. Yes? At my house. We'll have . . . anything you like. What is it you like, Black? Tell me.'

Black looked about him. It was terribly warm, rather suddenly: really very close. The bald man – tall, I see now, as he gets up to leave – he puts his arm across the young girl's shoulder quite as easily as a spellbinding vampire in a floor-skimming cloak.

'Well – I like . . . anything, really. Dinner, you say? Well – dinner's always very nice, of course . . . But Susie—!'

'Let's go now, shall we? Get the bill, will you? Yes? Let's go now, and think of the future.'

Black was aware of very little (he realised this later, as again and again he went over and over it) until the cool of the evening air smacked him across both cheeks. He just about remembered gulping down the blue pill and the whitish capsule with the dregs of his claret (these drugs together, they were reputed to valiantly join forces in the battle to vanquish all of the evil that dinner had done him) and then briefly tipping Smales for holding open the door . . . and now he was out here in the street then, was he? And Susie seems to have flagged down a taxi and she's saying something to me rapidly with bright eyes and a great deal of gesture and . . . all of a sudden a blackened and toothless old woman is beside me and imploring that I buy from her a long-stemmed rose, for the beautiful lady. And I seem now to have done just this, because Susie's face is alive and aglow with more angelic laughter as I slither now all of its cellophaned meanness into both of her hands, and her lips on mine as she stoops now to kiss me . . . the warm and pillowy jamminess of her mouth, heavy there and lingering, it has me close to tears and fainting. Before the slamming of the taxi door, before it pulls away and just leaves me here, she says she will call me – she says she will call me and that it'll be such fun, the dinner, our dinner – it'll be fun, she tells and tells me, our very special dinner, for only just the three of us. At which I am puzzled – the taxi now just a melting blur of shivering raindrops (and soon it is gone) . . . but I then realised later (as again and again I went over and over it) that she is including in our oh-so-special dinner, the daughter, Alison – could be Annette – who needs, lest we might forget, not only a father, but stability, yes, not to say guidance. At the time, though, it was just that kiss that had wafted me home. My own daughter, Millie (and why do I think of this now?) she has to my face and jeeringly dubbed me a 'dodosexual'. Oh I know – so silly, and quite utterly baffling it always seemed to me. But at a time such as this, I nearly come close to seeing what she means.

Tara, OK? I wasn't like going to tell her anything at all about Harry – even that I knew him – but then I just had to, had to, because I was just bursting. So I just told her his name and that he was like just gorgeous and what he did and everything and then I so wished I hadn't, because she got it all wrong.

'Working in a garage doesn't sound too great, Amanda. What's he want to work in a, like – garage for? How old is he anyway?'

'Shit, Tara – I *told* you – he doesn't *work* in a garage . . . well yeh OK – he does, yeh he does, OK, he works in a garage, but that's just to get money for the meantime, yeh? It's not what he *is*. He's like a poet. Told you. It's only temporary, the garage thing. Just till he gets started.'

'Well how old is he, Amanda? I mean – he sounds like really old. When did he leave school? Is he going to uni?'

'He's not *that* old. He's a lot more mature than anyone you know, though. He's different. He's not, like – a *boy*. You know? And he went to an ordinary school, if you must know, state school, and he's not going to university because it's a middle-class thing to do and everyone's got degrees now and it's all just meaningless and it's got nothing to do with art and life.'

'Is that what he said?'

'More or less. And I believe him. He's right. Isn't he? Everyone like us, everyone we know, we're going to be at school for what? Like three more years, and then uni for another three, and it's all just a waste of time because it's got nothing to do with art and *life*.'

'Well how old is he?'

'Oh *crap*, Tara – why do you keep on and on about that?'

'Because you won't tell me, will you? Jesus – it's not a difficult question, Amanda. How bloody *old* is he?'

'Well . . . eighteen, nearly.'

'Eigh-*teen*?! Jesus, you're *joking*! Eigh-*teen*. Man – that's bloody *ancient*.'

'Nearly – he's nearly eighteen. He's seventeen and a bit.'

'But Amanda, you're like – fourteen? Remember? It's illegal.'

'Fifteen, nearly. And what do you mean *illegal*? There's nothing, Jesus, illegal about it. We're not – God, Tara: what the hell do you think I'm doing? I'm not like *stupid*, you know. You think I'm stupid? Well I'm not. And I'm not a slag either, so fuck you.'

'I didn't say—'

'Yeh well. I just wish I hadn't said anything now. I should have known you just like wouldn't get it. You don't, do you Tara? Do you? You just so don't *get* it.'

Well of course she doesn't – nobody would. How could they? Because Harry, yeh? He's like an enigma? He's not like anyone I've ever met in my entire life on earth. He's a million miles off all the boys you get like on the bus and in the newsagent after

99

school – all those pathetic little dickheads from St Vincent's up the road, just laughing and hitting each other and saying like really sick stuff and basically they're still into toys and all those games that are about sawing people up or running them over at like a hundred miles an hour. It was in that poxy little newsagent that I met him, actually. He was looking at a magazine and that old miserable fucker called Mahal or whatever with the creepy moustache who sort of guards all his crappy magazines as if they're like valuable or something, and he comes over and he says in that voice he's got that Harry – I didn't know he was called Harry, right, because it was the first time I'd ever set eyes on him – but Mahal, he says to Harry that he is not to be looking at the magazine, sir, because this is not a lending library, no no no, and you please put down magazine, sir, unless you are intending to buy – and Harry (the mag, it was called Guitar Something or Something Guitar and it had this CD on the front?) – Harry, he stuffs a fiver into Mahal's little hand, and he tells him to keep the change! Well wow – how cool is that? And then a couple of minutes later, there's that old loony Mahal chasing after him down the street because it turns out the magazine, it's some sort of special issue or something and it costs like five pounds ninety-five? I nearly pissed myself with laughing – and after, next day and after, I kind of waited around for him. It wasn't till Friday that he was in there again though, and I looked at him and then stopped looking at him and then I sort of like looked at him again until I just knew he'd have to say hi – and yeh, he did. God, I nearly died. And this time he just bought some Tic-Tacs and I kind of like bumped into him in the doorway going out? And he was going to walk away so I said So what – you a guitarist, yeh? My heart was really going like crazy and I'd

100

gone all red and everything because I could feel it. And he looked at me with his eyes – which sounds like just so stupid, yeh I know, but what I mean is I really saw his eyes for the very first time and they're really dark brown and artistic. And what he said was Well yeh, kind of – I put my poems to music, is what I do: you want to get a coffee or something? And I just shrugged and sort of looked at my watch and then I said Sure: cool.

And that's all we've been able to do ever since, really, apart from that one time in the Everyman. In the coffee shop – it's called Franco's – we've got our special table away from the window and under this neon little clock they've got and he has a frappé and I have a smoothie. I hated that he'd only ever seen me in uniform with my hair like all back in a scrunchy and no jewellery on, but he said he was fine with it and it wasn't that long since he'd been wearing uniform himself – but not like a scrunchy! And that was really funny, when he said that, and I laughed a lot. His hair is long enough for one, though, a scrunchy – it's really like long and beautiful. Turned out he didn't, actually – wear uniform at the school he went to, I don't know why he said he did. He knows about everything, Harry – he doesn't just go on about like football and drinking and the internet and crap and he said he was currently really into Dylan and I said oh yeh do you mean Dylan Thomas because we've got him as a set book, and he said no. So I googled Dylan later and downloaded some tracks and yeh I see now why he's so like into it because of all the poetry and stuff and I said it's a shame he can't sing though and Harry, he went kind of quiet? I don't know nearly as much as Harry does and so I don't just come out with crap now, but I listen to him, so I'll learn. And I have done – more than I ever do at school.

It was me who suggested we go out in the evening – movie or something – but he said he still lived with his parents and he was saving every penny he got at the garage for like a place of his own because he couldn't stand it any more, living with his parents, on account of his parents knew jack shit. And I said OK yeh sure, I'm cool, I can empathise with that (cool?) and how about I pay for the both of us? And he said Cool, which was great. So I got the money off Dad – said it was for some like really important software for a project at school which has got to be in next week, which always works because I don't think he even knows what software is, he's so totally useless at all that: he goes all glassy when you say anything computery, and just gives me the cash. Mum says any money Dad's got he got from her, I don't know if it's meant to make me feel guilty or something, but it so like doesn't. I never get how the money or anything works in our house, and I just so don't care. Harry said we should go to the Everyman, which I'd never heard of but it's up in like Hampstead which I don't think I've ever been to since I was really like little and Jesus, we all used to go to the *fair*? My mum always took me on the rides because Dad wouldn't go and then I'd say to him Oh Dad, Dad, look! Look at the, God – like dollies or whatever – because I was so totally into, like, softies yeh? I had hundreds: *so* embarrassing. They're all up in the attic now except for Ralph the cat, obviously, who is totally special. Tara's bed, though – you should see it: all covered in like teddies and ponies and heart-shaped cushions which I just think is gross, and boys I know really hate all that. Anyway – at the fair, right? I used to go on and on at Dad to win me one of these really like naff sort of, I don't know – Teletubbies or something, and he'd shoot this gun and just miss everything, he was so completely hopeless – must've spent like pounds and he didn't even get close. And so I'd throw this like giant strop OK? Hissy, really heavy, and next day he'd go to like Hamleys or somewhere and get me the real thing and by then I'd forgotten all about it and I'd just go Oh yeh, cool, just put it wherever, yeh? You should've like seen his face. Anyway: Hampstead. There's this little cinema, really cool actually, and Harry likes it because they sometimes show these like really old movies he's into like wrecks like Tara's dad watch on TV in the afternoons before *Countdown*. Harry doesn't seem to like any movies that are in colour, or even in English. But the movie we saw that time was English, though – *Brighton Rock*, which I'd never heard of. It's a novel by Graham Greene, who I'd never heard of, but I googled him and I started to read *Our Man in Havana* which I got from the library at school but I found it like really hard going so I stopped. Anyway, Harry was really into *Brighton Rock* because he said that the guy in it – Pinkie, yeh? He was only young, but he was doing things his way and not being dictated to by all of the crumblies. And I said yeh Harry but what he's doing is like slicing people up and trying to kill his girlfriend which isn't very nice, and he said that's not the point and so I said well what is the point then, and he just went like quiet again, like he does quite a lot. But it's really comfy in the Everyman and we sat at the back and I had a Magnum which made me a bit sick actually, and he kissed me when the credits came on and it was really like soft, you know? Really sensitive. And that's when I so like fell in love with him – and I've just been waiting ages and ages for my dream to come true, being like alone with him, which may sound pathetic but it isn't because I really really mean it. See, sitting in Franco's with a frappé and a smoothie, it's not like romantic and there's just been nowhere else to go because cinemas are really expensive

103

(I can't go too heavy on the software thing) and Harry has been promising for ages that his parents were going to go away for a weekend to visit his aunt and uncle in Lincolnshire (like I give a fuck) and I kept on saying to him yeh but *when*, Harry – *when* are they going? Because you've been saying all this for like a hundred *years*, yeh? And then just yesterday when I was paying in Franco's, he goes: it's tomorrow! And I'm going, what's tomorrow, what? And then he tells me and I'm like, Jesus Harry – you could've given me a bit more notice! What the fuck am I going to tell my parents? And he goes yeh I know, but I only just found out myself, they only told me this morning. And I was really really pleased – and I said just think how great it'll be when you've got a place of your own. Then we can go there and be alone together whenever we want and then the whole like rest of the world can just go fuck itself. He said yeh, I know, but have you seen what flats cost? And never mind flats – even a room. And I went no, because I haven't, but I bet they're like a lot, particularly in Fulham and Chelsea. And he laughed at that, but not like it was funny or anything, and he said oh Jesus Amanda you can completely forget Fulham and Chelsea – I'm talking about shitholes, bits of London you've never even heard of, just miles and miles from here, and still they cost a fucking bomb. Well he's right – I don't know anywhere that isn't round here except for Oxford Street and all of that, course. He maybe means Hampstead, which is like just ages on the Tube. Anyway – I decided I wouldn't go and tell Mum and Dad some great all sort of carefully worked-out story, because they'd only go on and on asking and asking about it – or Mum would, anyway – so I just like did this Tara thing pretty much without thinking – and I've got her to back me up if Dad rings to check, which he so won't – and Mum being out was a kind of bonus, really, even if I am like so just sick at what it is she's *doing* tonight. Anyway – fuck that. I'm here now. I've phoned Dad, given him the story – he sounded just fucked and so out of it, as per bloody usual (it could be the whisky, or maybe it's just everything else in his crappy little life – and Mum, she's not exactly helping, is she?) and now – wow! – I'm here. It's a small house, Harry's got – a lot smaller than ours and no colour anywhere, all just grubby white and sort of brown. Tara would say it's really naff and common – she'd laugh at all the video boxes on the shelves, and the like dolphins in the loo? But I don't care. Harry's here – that's all that matters. And so am I. We're alone. My dream come true.

'You want a drink or something, Amanda? Something to eat?'

'I've eaten. Had dinner at home. What's this . . . ? Is it a vase, or something?'

'Christ knows what it is. Some crap my mum brought back from somewhere – Spain or Mexico or somewhere. Horrible bloody thing. She buys all this shit-type pottery. It's all over the house. I break a few whenever I can. Drink, then?'

'Don't mind. What've you got?'

'Don't know what's left. There's vodka, probably, unless my mum has drunk it all. Beer in the fridge.'

'Haven't you got anything like, I don't know – Diet Coke or something?'

'Yeh – probably something. Steering clear of the hard stuff, are you? What you want to do?'

'I hate it. Don't like the taste. Well wine I do. You got any wine?'

'Should think so. What you like? White? Yeh? Won't be cold, though. I'll have a look. So what you want to do then, Amanda?'

'Don't know. What you want to do?'

'Not bothered. I'll see if they got anything under the stairs.'

Amanda watched his easy amble as he left the room, his shoulders bonily shrugging up and down beneath his khaki T-shirt, a truckload of denim rucked up and over his chucked-out feet. His hair, she thought, it looks really nice tonight, all long and wavy like he only just washed it. She followed him into the hall and watched his jeans grip tight on his thighs as he crouched down low in the cupboard.

'There's . . . what is this? Oh no – that's red. Chilean. Instant headache material. Oh here's one – Chardonnay. Chardonnay, that do you?'

'Don't know. Expect so. Yeh. Great.'

'Stick it in the freezer for a bit . . . Think I'll have a beer. So OK – decided what you want to do, then?'

'Don't know. Don't mind. What you want to do?'

'Don't know. We could watch a film, or something. Play some music . . .'

'Oh I know! You could play to me on your guitar.'

'Nah. Let's watch a film.'

'Oh why not? Oh please do, Harry – I'd really love it. Where is it? Upstairs? Is it upstairs? Oh do go and get it, Harry – please do. Go on.'

Harry closed his eyes and shook his head.

'I'll just stick this in the freezer . . .'

'Oh but *why*, Harry? Why won't you?'

'Because I don't bloody *want* to, all right? Now what bloody film you want to see? The good ones are in my room. It's all crap, stuff they got down here. Carry Ons and *Pretty Woman* and David bloody Attenborough. How about *Belle de Jour*?

Classic, that is.'

'Builder Jaw? Never heard of it. Not foreign, is it?'

'Got subtitles.'

'So it's foreign, right?'

'Well of course it's bloody foreign if it's got subtitles – what's wrong with you? It's French. Sixties. Catherine Deneuve. Classic. Buñuel.'

'Can't we just, I don't know – sit and talk . . . ?'

'What you want to talk about?'

'Well I don't know, do I? Anything. You. You and me. Let's sit on the sofa, yeh? Put on some music. What you got?'

'Dylan?'

'Oh Jesus. I mean I know you're like really into him and everything – but does it have to be? I mean – haven't you got anything a bit more, I don't know – just not quite so . . . ?'

'You'd probably like all my parents' shit. What they like is Rodgers & Hammerstein and Tony Bennett and bloody *techno*, if you can believe it. Don't know how they stand it.'

'Haven't you got any Kylie, or something? Or Madonna – what about Madonna? I like the old ones.'

Harry just looked at her.

'Let's just forget the music, OK? We'll talk. You start.'

Amanda flopped down into the brown velour sofa and heard something funny going wrong with the springs; with the added weight of Harry, the cushions took a plunge. She rootled around for his fingers and gave them a squeeze as her shoulders and eyebrows rose up in delight.

'This is really nice. Isn't it Harry? It's so really nice, this. Just sitting. Just like being here with you. Really really nice. But I so wish you would, though . . .'

'Would what?'

'Play to me. Your guitar.'

'Man, you don't give up do you? Hey? I said no, didn't I? Just bloody leave it, can't you? Anyway – string's broken.'

'Well can't you just play on the others?'

'That's the most stupid thing I ever heard.'

Amanda quickly plucked back her hand.

'That's not very nice. You're not being very nice to me, Harry.'

'Man . . . Look – just don't go giving me a hard time, OK Amanda?'

'What do you mean? I'm not. What do you *mean*? All I said was I—'

'Yeh well just don't, OK? I'll get you a drink.'

'Don't want a drink.'

'Yeh well I'm going to get you one anyway, OK? *Jesus* . . . !'

'Well don't do me any favours, will you?'

'I'm not. I've got to get my beer anyway, haven't I? *Jesus* . . . !'

Harry's head was hung low and wagging from side to side at all the bloody hell of it – but then he stopped all that when he saw her face.

'Oh look . . . come on. Don't . . . cry, Jesus. Nothing to cry about, is there? I didn't mean . . . Come on, Amanda – cheer up, hey? Get you a drink.'

Amanda clutched at his fingers as he made to get by her.

'I've been so really really looking forward to this . . . !'

Harry held her hand, and crouched down beside her.

'Yeh yeh. I know. Me too. I have too. Look – tell you what. I'll get us a drink . . . and then I'll read you one of my poems. OK? Like that?'

Amanda's wet eyes went up to him, and now there was a glistening and brightness amid their pleading.

'Oh *yeh*, Harry – I'd really like that. Really really. And then will you play to me?'

Harry grinned and made to joshingly cuff her about the jaw.

'You're a right little schemer you are – aren't you? Hey? I'm going to have to watch you, I can see that. OK. OK. I'll read you a poem, I'll get you a glass of wine and I'll play the bloody guitar for you. Happy? Satisfied?'

Amanda was beaming as she nodded her head and then shook it quite rapidly as she sucked in her breath, simpering at the absurdity of even her gestures. She drew up her knees and hugged them tightly while he was gone (keeping close within her all this secret pleasure) and then she idly glanced about her. There were two big squareish armchairs that matched the caved-in sofa which every so often seemed to tip and lurch as if in an attempt to swallow and digest her. One of them was over by the bay window in front of the not-quite-meeting flimsy and orange curtains and looking relatively spry and resilient, though piled up with what seemed like just hundreds and hundreds of old newspapers that looked as if they had been there for years. The other one was drawn up close to an old gas fire, tiny and mean under the overscaled mantelpiece. The pockmarked and chalky elements were sporadically blackened and tinged with a singeing of tan. This chair was misshapen and looked truly on the very verge of complete disintegration, the back cushion's velour quite shiny and balding and creased into a permanent depression. On one of its arms was what looked like a tin lid, thick with cigarette ends and carefully crafted spirals and cups of silver paper. On the mantelpiece itself was a wooden clock that was wrong by about five-and-a-half hours and a large blue pottery pig, or an ox it could have been, with pink and yellow daisies painted on its back, and one of its hefty legs snapped off and just lying alongside.

'I won't keep the bottle in the freezer any more,' said Harry as he sauntered back into the room. 'I think it could explode. Wine glasses are all dirty, so . . .'

Amanda hunched forward, away from the maw of the rapacious sofa, and smiling warmly as she grasped the tumbler that said Hofmeister in both of her hands. Her nose quickly wrinkled as she bobbed it down to have a sniff. Harry fell into the sofa beside her, swigged a bottle of Bud that he held in just the tips of two fingers at the top of its neck – spread his legs wide and set to rootling around in the pocket of his jeans for the sheet of paper that he now drew out and set to passing the chop of his hand repeatedly over it, failing to smooth out the worst of the crinkles.

'Oh my *God*, Harry—! You had it on you all the time, your poem. You had it ready all the time!'

Harry smirked and gulped more beer.

'Always as well to be prepared. Boy Scouts.'

'You were a Scout? I so don't believe it.'

'No – wasn't actually. But it's just what they say, isn't it? Be Prepared. Now listen – this one I wrote just yesterday. I was up all night composing it. Listening?'

'I was a Brownie . . . hated it. Really like loved the uniform, though. Little scarf. Woggle . . .'

'Yeh. OK. Ready? Listening?'

'My mum wanted me to go on and be a like – Guide? But I said no way.'

'Right. Now look – you want me to read this poem, or don't you?'

'You know I do.'

'OK, then. OK, right. Well listen. Here goes.'

'This wine . . . it's quite, I don't know – bitter, maybe.'

'Oh bloody hell . . .'

'Do you mind if I don't drink it? I mean I know you've just like opened the bottle and everything, but it really does taste a bit . . .'

'Leave it. Don't drink it. I don't care. Now listen – it's quite short.'

'Because I would've been just as happy with like a Diet Coke, or something . . .'

'Well we might have some – I'll look in a minute. Now do you or don't you want to hear this bloody poem?'

'Course I do – I can't wait. I mean it doesn't *have* to be Diet Coke – I mean, Tango or even like Ribena, don't really mind.'

Harry slapped the paper with finality.

'OK. That's it. Forget it. I'm not going to read it. You clearly don't want to hear it, so to hell with it, OK?'

Amanda was all big eyes and indignation.

'What do you *mean* I don't want to hear it? I've *said* I want to hear it – I *keep* saying I want to hear it. What's wrong with you?'

'What's wrong with *me*! Oh that's good, that is. I've been *saying* I'm going to read you a fucking poem and all you do is keep on *talking* . . . !'

'I haven't said a single word! I'm just waiting, that's all. Why don't *you* stop talking and get on with it?'

'Man . . . OK. Jesus. Last chance: poem – yes or no?'

'Yes! Yes! I *told* you yes . . . !'

'Right then. Shut up and listen. It's free verse, OK? You know what free verse is?'

'Yeh. No, not really.'

'No formal metre. Not, like, a sonnet. No strict rhyme. You know the Beats?'

'Yeh. Beatles, you mean? My Dad loves them.'

'No! Not the—! The *Beats* – Ginsberg, Corso, those guys.'

'Oh yeh. No, not really.'

'OK. Well this is a sort of . . . *hommage*, but not an *actual* one. It's not, you know – *like* them or anything. It's all me. I have found my voice. See?'

'Yeh. If you say so.'

'OK then. Right. This is it. It's called "The Awakening With A Plum".'

'Plum. OK. Go on, then.'

'A perfect poem, right, is when nothing can be added and, um, nothing can be like, you know – taken away. Keep that in your head. OK? Right. Here we go. Ready? OK. The night was cold and I looked up at the stars. I was bright like them. Then it was dark. I slept. I must have. Then it was morning. The awakening. And next to me a bowl of fruit. There was a plum. And I ate it. It filled me up with light and knowledge. Now I rest content. Right – that's it. What do you think?'

'Mm. Yeh. Was "Right – that's it" the last line of it? Or was that you just saying "Right – that's it"?'

'That wasn't . . . that was . . . I just said "Right – that's it", because that was it. Over. The poem ended with . . . *fulfilment*. See? "Now I rest content." Fulfilment. It's quite deep, if you think about it.'

Amanda was gazing at his profile – he just looked so artistic, and he just knew all this stuff!

'Do you want to like – kiss me?' she said.

Harry put the bottle and the paper down on the floor.

'Yeh.'

'Yeh? Well go on, then. If you want to.'

'I do.'

'Yeh? Well go on, then. If you want to, do it.'

Harry put the flat of his hands lightly on her shoulders, twisted his head sideways and gently laid his lips on hers – Amanda's were pouted, and rushing forward to meet him. After it had been savoured, Harry drew back, licking at the taste.

'You're lovely . . .' he murmured. 'You know that?'

'I only feel lovely when I'm with you . . .'

Harry then suddenly threw himself back into the sofa, his head now lolling cockily in a cradle made up of his intertwined fingers.

'Naughty little skirt you got on.'

Amanda smirked, and looked down at it.

'It's actually my netball one, but I double the waistband over. The top I got in Topshop.'

'Yeh?'

Amanda nodded eagerly, and fingered the neckline.

'Viscose. It was in the sale. Really cheap.'

'Yeh? So listen, Amanda – what you want to, er, you know, like – do?'

'Less than half the original price . . .'

'Yeh? So, Amanda? What you reckon you want to do?'

Amanda just looked at him imploringly – begging him or anyone alive to let her in on the secret: to tell her loud and plainly what she reckoned she wanted to do.

'And I really liked the colour . . . so I bought it. I've got some shoes that nearly match it, not quite but nearly. Really close. But I didn't wear them . . .'

Harry sat forward now and leaned his elbows across his knees, hanging his head low, and letting his hair fall over his eyes.

'So listen, Amanda. I really like you, yeh? And you trust me, don't you? Don't you?'

113

Amanda was taut and uneasy, and so all she could do was put everything she had into sounding as careless, as breezily casual as she thought she could get away with.

'Yeh. Course. Course I do, yeh.'

Harry nodded slowly and brought up his eyes to meet hers.

'So . . . why don't we go upstairs, then? You like that?'

Amanda just looked at him, blinking once.

'What – for your guitar, you mean?'

'No I don't mean—! No. No, Amanda – listen. Let's go upstairs. To my room, yeh? Or another room, if you like. My parents, they got this really big bed . . .'

Amanda now was standing, and smoothing her skirt and pulling at the hem of it.

'No, Harry. I can't. What about this movie you wanted to watch? Boonwell. Let's watch that, yeh?'

Harry stood up too and softly touched her shoulders. He peered into her eyes as if attempting to detect there a strain of something that really shouldn't be.

'Yeh you can. Course you can. Why can't you? Hey? Why can't you?'

Amanda bit her lip and looked up at him frankly.

'Because.'

'Yeh? Because? Because what? What? Why can't you?'

'Because I can't, that's all. I maybe ought to go.'

'Go? Don't be stupid, Amanda. You can't go. Can you? Where you going to go? Can't go home, can you? Not now. Not at this time. And anyway – you don't even want to. I know you don't. So come on, Amanda. Let's stop messing about, yeh? Let's go upstairs now, hey?'

Amanda's arms were straight at her sides and she shook her head vehemently, detaching Harry's finger that had begun to describe a series of arcs under her eye and then over the cheek.

'No, Harry. Please. I said no, didn't I?'

'Yeh I know – but why? Tell me why. I know you want to.'

'Not the point. I just can't, that's all.'

'Yeh well let's talk about it upstairs then, hey? Who knows? You might change your mind.'

'Harry – no. I'm not. I can't.'

Harry drew back his head and hissed out his exasperation – bringing up his two rigid arms and letting them clap down against the sides of his legs. He stared at her now.

'OK. Fine. You can't. But just tell me why. That's all. Think I'm entitled. I mean, what – I'm repulsive, that it? Can't stand the sight of me?'

'*Silly*, Harry . . . Course not. I think you look great. It's nothing like that.'

And Harry's face reddened.

'Well bloody *why* then, fuck's sake?'

Amanda's eyes were full and wet and she had begun to snuffle quite badly.

'Because! Because! Because, Christ – I'm only fourteen—!'

Harry looked as if he had been hit, and she ached at the sight of it. And then a sly and creeping grin was working its way all over his face.

'Yeh *right* . . . ! Fourteen. *Course* you are – and I'm still, what – in kindergarten, am I? You're never *fourteen* – what you take me for? You're my age – older, if anything. What's all this fourteen crap? Hey? Because I tell you one thing, Amanda – if I'd ever thought you were fourteen or anything bloody near it, I never would've talked to you in the first fucking place. And you don't really think I would've asked you here, do you? Hey? I

115

mean – why are you jerking me around like this? Hey? No look – it's no good bloody *crying*, Amanda – you got to answer me, OK? You get off on this, or what? Like, what the fuck do you reckon you're *doing* here, Amanda? Hey? What – we going to play cards now, are we? Pass the fucking Parcel? Now I don't know what this new little game of yours is all about, right – but if you're going on with it, if you're going to stand there and tell me that what I got here is a bloody fourteen-year-old *kid* . . . well then you can walk right now. Got it? Out the bloody door. And I don't *care*, all right? Where you bloody go. But you ain't bloody staying here, I tell you that now.' And the light of fury was up and blazing in his eyes. 'I mean Jesus fucking *Christ* . . . ! First you're telling me to like *kiss* you, and then you turn round and say your fucking nappy's needing changing! I mean what the fuck is going *on* here . . . ?!'

The flicker of indecision before she knew she had to turn and run away and somehow stop making this awful and pitiful mewling noise had now just sizzled an instant too long, and she was shocked and then speared by the agony of still and helplessly standing there, her mouth hanging open, sensing that she would be screwed by all that was about to fall out of it. The pained smile, as she tried to assume it, hurt her whole face, though still it felt as if it were someone else's. She forcibly brightened – she attempted to sound quite light and delighted.

'Yeh . . . OK, Harry. Yeh yeh. *Fourteen* . . . ! Ha! As if.'

Harry first stared, and now let his limbs go easy as he laughed out loud, and jubilantly.

'You're quite the little *bitch*, that's what you are Amanda! Oh my God – you really had me going there, with all that load of shit! You nearly had me believing you, you know that? Jesus – you're really dangerous, you are.' And then his eyes were narrow, and aiming right at her. 'Come here, you *bad* girl . . .'

And she hadn't liked it when he just pulled her towards him, forced his face right into hers, his mouth so hard and dry and attacking her, this time – hadn't liked it, no, as so many hot and unaccustomed hands were quite suddenly juddering over her, uncomfortable and helpless as bits of her clothing were half tugged out and dragged aside. And so she said things like Wait – she said Don't Be So . . . ! She even said and yearned for Gentle, because she distantly remembered that it somehow might belong – and although her stomach was walled with tension her mind was resigned then to what she had invited, but she did now urgently say to him Have You Got A . . . ? But he just grunted, and there was spittle on his face. The old brown sofa, the smell was really bad and stale when your face was deep down and into it, and that was maybe now the thing that made her feel the sickest. She didn't know if he was trying at words or if they were just more animal noises as her mauled and bruised discomfort gave way to outright pain – and equally suddenly, when things were apparently done and she was abruptly left alone, clammy and quaking, her eyes struck wide with shock, the whole of her heaving with a billow of nausea, lurching into illness – as she unseeingly pulled her lumped-up and twisted-about clothes from under and around her, she shivered and nearly cried, but just a little cough came – wishing she was back at home and warm in bed and then her mum would come in from wherever she had been to and ask Amanda what she had done today, what she had learned at school, and then she could make up something nice.

She had been amazed – and how much later? – when she knew by her soft and then so very lowering awakening that she must have been asleep, the aroma of unease and severe displacement wafting around and then into her, gripping amid the darkness, making her sad and filled with something she had no word for. And he hadn't even used a . . . no. Huh. Be Prepared, he'd said, but he wasn't, was he? No, and nor was she, in any way at all. She saw in the lamplight a folded piece of paper that said Amanda in red capitals, with a heart underneath. She awkwardly reached across for it – the main pain now was a crick in the side of her neck – and flapped it open, incuriously.

Wow! I didn't like to wake you cos you looked so peaceful. I'm upstairs, first floor, second door on the left, just opposite the radiator and I've left it a bit open. I wrote you this: I have picked of the finest. Not for me, a blushing peach. In the Cornucopia of Life, I have got the plum.

Amanda languorously cast it aside, and wondered what to do. I think just stay where I am, until it gets light. And then go. I don't know if I can sleep again – I would quite like to. (I hate this room – I hate it here.) And dream I am at home and warm in bed and my mum comes in and asks me what I did today, yeh, and what I learned at school, but I can't at the moment think of anything nice, not even to make up. I don't think this is a very good poem. And why is he, the creep, so like fucking nuts about plums?

CHAPTER FOUR

'So you do see, don't you Doctor Atherby? I'm sure you do, you must do – man possessed of all your insight and such capability. What with one thing and another it has been what we in the trade call a rather hellish week. And while making oneself out to be no sort of a soothsayer, all the portents are, it can only get hellisher.'

'The turn of events is, I confess Alan, something of a surprise to me.'

'Well quite. Bit of a bolt between the eyes for me as well, I assure you of that. I mean to say – not every day, is it, that your wife of how many years just ups and tells you she wants to be married in tandem, as it were. As the senior party, do you suppose I'll be promoted to Husband Major? Or will the new chap be parachuted in over my head, so to speak, condemning me for ever to the I admit rather comfortingly familiar role of Minor? Quite apart from the mental turmoil and any of the more telling ramifications, it's going to be one hell of a scrum in the bathroom, of a morning.'

'And all this came . . . without warning?'

'Not Susan's way, you see. Warning. She just hits you with

it, fair and square. The only warning tends to come afterwards when she outlines what will befall you should you contemplate argument. In the realm of the fait accompli, she is the doer, and I am the thing unto which it is done. It's as well to know one's place, how things stand.'

'You seem . . . less than, um – fraught, shall we say, Alan.'

'Ah but am I, Doctor Atherby? Could this be but the brave face? The plucky Tommy joshing in the trenches. Or could I still be in a state of shock? Is the full and murky horror yet to filter through? Or maybe this is a classic and textbook case of outright denial? Amanda, she called me an ostrich, you know. She has, in truth, called me many things just lately, but this one sticks in the mind. She also said I should strive to become an Alpha Male, but me, I've always been more at the Omega end of things, really.'

'And tell me, Alan – what do you *feel* . . . ?'

'Feel. Well. What do I *feel* . . . ? Hm. Sad. Amazed. Frightened. Oddly excited, some ways – can't really even begin to explain that one. Useless, of course – goes without saying. And a little bit hungry – overslept, didn't want to be late for our appointment, so I just sucked on a teabag, glanced into the bread bin and ended up just crunching a handful of Golden Grahams on the Tube.'

'Alan . . . do try to *address* the situation. Your time is nearly up, and we haven't really progressed – would you say we have?'

'Mm. No. Take your point. The nub seems as slippery a fellow as usual.'

'Now you mentioned Amanda. How is she taking all this?'

'Hm. Well she's sad. Amazed. Frightened. Maybe even oddly excited, in some ways, though I couldn't even begin to explain that one. Do you know, I had no idea we had quite so much in common . . .'

'When you meet this man, what do you imagine your reaction will be?'

'Well now yes – that's a good one. I have asked myself this. I would like to say that I would attack him with a club, beat my breast and yodel like a wild man, one jaunty foot atop his broken and vanquished body . . . but you know if I'm honest, I think it unlikely. I expect I'll treat him much as I treat everyone else. Polite, I hope – make a bloody fool of myself without even realising it. Probably attempt a joke or two, before Susan instructs me to fetch something and stop trying to be funny. We'll know soon enough, though – because oh yes, I forgot to tell you this, Doctor Atherby, but Susan, this morning, just before I dashed off here, she said to me Oh Alan, she said to me, we're having a dinner party tonight. And I said Really? Dinner party? Did I know this? And she said No Alan my sweet, you did not know this: this is why I am telling you: had you known, I should hardly have bothered. And then she says Actually, it's not a dinner party. Oh, I say – *not* a dinner party. I see. Did I know this? And Susan, she tells me not to be tedious. Anyway, Doctor Atherby, it turns out that it's going to be just the three of us. Me, Susan and the new boy. Tonight. Can you believe it? I can't. Well. There you are.'

'Alan – I regret: your time is up.'

'Do you know what, Doctor Atherby? I think you could be right.'

Yes. So I left him to his next appointment – man I've seen before, quaking in the waiting room. Always wears the same just-held-together and so exhausted suit and never quite manages to get the whole of his face shaved – always at least just a lozenge of stubble, or else quite bristly thickets. Christ knows how much more of Doctor Atherby's infuriating cocktail of indifference and disdain the poor man will be able to tolerate or afford. I do get angry. Why do we do it? Pay these people to ask us how we feel and what we're going to do? I mean to say, we, the desperate, we're always the last to know (and no of course it doesn't stand to reason). I have, in truth, an urgent hangover – it is, believe me, rather pressing. Got really into it, the Scotch, last night. Was tormented this morning by the spinily tortured memory of having spoken to Amanda on the telephone, some point, and then it oozed further into me (and my throat was stopped and clutched by fear – for myself, for myself: of course for myself) that I had nodded soddenly through a vague and airy go-ahead to her staying the night at Tara's – whereas Susan, sober and parentally responsible, would surely have subjected the child to a pumped-up inquisition of the customary intensity. And I hadn't heard her come in – Susan, I mean, though I had fully intended to be so distracted as to be laughably incapable of sleeping or even repose (on the qui vive as well as, yes, the usual tenterhooks). But Scotch in quantity, it tends to not just drive a roaring and runaway train through the flimsiness of every good intention, but to rot away and then just devastate even a basic sentience. Susan, in the squint of seemingly dawn, as I smiled dementedly – it blazed away, my smiling, to gorgeously display to her how utterly grand I was feeling – she had coyly accused me of feigning sleep when just before midnight she had slipped into the bedroom and told me she was home. No no, I protested – no honestly, truly, it was real, the sleep was real, I do assure you it was real. What – when I accidentally knocked all the books off the bedside table? When I slammed shut the window? When I ran the shower and the boiler started banging? You are telling me you slept throughout? Well she had me there, you see – because of course I *did*, I had slept throughout, but if I'd persisted with the point then she would have known that I'd been drunk (and look at me! I'm beaming! Are you not a living witness to just how grand I'm feeling?) so I barely whimpered when she put it to me that I had in fact just been a teeny bit hurt and sulkily jealous, if only a smidgen – this tacit acquiescence of mine perversely (oh God will I ever come close to understanding?) appearing to please her, and then send her teetering on the verge of outright delight.

Anyway, I was up and roughly dressed and had no wish at all to hang around because of this Amanda thing, which is why I decided to pass up on breakfast – even the coffee, which Jesus was needed – and of all things in the world staggered off to keep my appointment with the blight that is Atherby, the condescending prat. And just when I thought I was gone (she does this, Susan – she's silent and amenable until your hand is on the doorknob) she had called to me casually, the lightness in her tone, even a lilt of music, a melodic rise and fall – the closest I can remember to, Jesus, practically pleasant.

'Alan, my sweet – I am really very happy.'

'Oh? How perfectly extraordinary. But I mean that's *good*, of course. Of course it is.'

'And do you know why?'

'No, but I have an inkling that I shall before long.'

'Because . . . shall I tell you why?'

'It would be a beginning.'

'Well I will, then. It's because I just know – I just know, really deep down, that the two of you are going to get on.'

'Uh-huh. The two of us. So we're talking now about, um ...?'

'Yes. Which wasn't necessarily the point, of course. I mean you do see, don't you Alan, that this is for me? This is about me, yes my sweet? What I need. But this – it's by way of being something of a little *bonus*. That you'll get on, the two of you. And it makes me very happy. Oh and Alan – we're having a little dinner party. Tonight, as a matter of fact. So do look to the wine and so on, will you? Actually it *isn't* a dinner party, no it isn't, it's really just a dinner. The three of us. Yes? And then we can begin.'

I hadn't interjected at all. The way I told it to bloody Doctor Atherby, that was just to fill in the time. My head was clanging, though, and I felt a bit sick – not just, I think, on account of this and that, but because of, well, just everything really. But still and beneath it there was this very faint tremor of I think excitement, the merest thrum; maybe just the coming of the new.

'Bit, um – quick, isn't it?'

Susan smiled with indulgent glee at my blind and disarming stupidity.

'"Twere well 'twere done quickly. Yes no?'

I momentarily wished that I could have been Amanda, so that then I could have slung a withering and weighty contempt across the slump of my eyelids and just drawled out to her Oh yeh right: *whaddever* ... Failing that, I turned to go ... but you know there was one thing I just had to ask her.

'What does *he*, er ... think of it? Hm? All this. This masterplan of yours. And what's his name, actually? Bloody hell, I can't really believe that I'm saying all this ...'

'He is not aware of the ins and outs. Detail. The brushstrokes

124

are broad at this stage. Just the one bold coat of vivid colour. His name is Black.'

'His name is what?'

'Well it isn't really his name. His actual name is . . . well, doesn't really matter, because what people call him is Black.'

'Do they. Yes I see. But he isn't though, is he?'

'Isn't what?'

'Black.'

'Oh what – you mean black as in *black*, do you? Oh no. He's not. Well of course he's not – don't be absolutely ridiculous, Alan.'

'I'm sorry. I shall try to remember not to be ridiculous. I really have to go now, Susan. Mustn't be late, you know.'

'I've never seen you so eager before to get to Doctor Atherby.'

'No well you know – 'twere well 'twere done quickly. Yes no?'

Susan was sour again, which was strangely reassuring.

'Never stop, do you? Just won't let things lie.'

'Can't think what you mean. Dinner, then. I'll look to the wine. You said, did you, the three of us? What – Amanda not invited then?'

'A step at a time, I think. Don't you?'

'Oh absolutely. Oh quite. It's not the sort of thing, is it, you want to rush into.'

'Always the same. You just won't let things lie . . .'

'But you're wrong Susan, aren't you? That, if anything, is my ultimate forte. I look at any given thing, and let it lie is just what I do. It is you, unless I am mistaken, who are driving a digger through our manicured lawn.'

'You'd better go. You'll be late. I hate that phrase. I always

125

have. Manicured *lawn* . . . you never hear talk of fingernails being *mown* – well do you?'

'We've strayed now, have we? From the point?'

And then I just left, because it could've gone on till doomsday, all this. Christ knows it has in the past. And still no coffee, and still no toast – what a waste of bloody time. And I didn't suck a teabag – didn't go munching cereal on the Tube. Didn't even *take* the Tube. It's all for Doctor Atherby, all of that junk that drips and drops out of me: I make it up as I go along, the way I do everything else. It's all just lights and mirrors, serving well to dazzle and obliterate. There is no plan, there is no detail: just the one bold coat of vivid colour.

I was so bloody freezing when I got back home. I was still just in my top and netball skirt and these really pretty lacy tights I had on in what Mum says is taupe and she got for me from Selfridge's and now they're torn all down one side because of bloody Harry, the so-called poet. I didn't bother changing into all my other stuff which I still had rammed into my shoulder bag because I just so wanted to be out of that like creepy and so smelly house as soon as it got light and I thought well look it's not much of a walk so it's not really worth it. I only really knew I was as cold as I was though when I got into the hall and the heating was on and it was really good to just like be there – Dad's lump of keys in the horrible blue bowl, and everything. Because it had been good, actually, just walking through the streets when it was all just grey and empty. I'd never been awake this early before – you feel like the whole of the city, that it's kind of just yours, when you're all on your own and you can hear your shoes on the pavement and there aren't any cars, or anything.

I still wasn't tired – I didn't feel anything much because I'd been thinking about all what I had to do at school – the English essay and the history download – and these great new albums I got from Jennifer and what Mum would say if I woke her up when I got in and if she'd checked me out with Tara's mum and yeh, just like anything really except for what I'd done. I mean, I never really thought that when it happened to me it was going to be all like golden and romantic because things aren't ever like you really want them to be. I remember when I was really little and I had this thing about, oh God – animals, and I was going to be a vet and go to where it is that gorillas and stuff live, can't remember, and talk to them and get really close to them and maybe, I don't know, even live with them, because I was really like nuts and thought people were cruel and stupid and animals had these really big eyes and were all furry and stuff, and I used to drive my mum like so just *mad* because I wouldn't eat anything with meat in, even spaghetti bolognese, which was always my favourite. Anyway, I went on and on at Mum and Dad to take me to London Zoo, right, where I'd never been – and the night before we were going to go I just couldn't get to sleep and I got so really excited and I just looked at all these posters I had of wildlife on my walls and still I was in Mum and Dad's bedroom before dawn and going Can we go now can we go now can we go now . . . ?! You know what kids are like – Jesus. It's like Christmas Eve, which I still do go for big-time, actually: still really like it, don't care if it's babyish, because Dad, he always does me this stocking and he writes on a label that it's from Santa and his little elves and I like pretend it's true and everything and there's the crumbs from the shortbread I left out and the Drambuie's all gone. So sweet. Anyway – we go to the Zoo, yeh? And Mum's going Oh *look*, Amanda – look at the lions, look at the zebra – ooh, look at the horrible old crocodile, look at whatever . . . and I'm like, yeh: *so* . . . ? It just didn't do it, you know? All that really looking forward and going like crazy, and when I was there I just thought OK, great – bunch of animals: like I *so* don't care. Didn't want to hug them, like I thought I would (they smelled really bad); didn't want to let them all out of their cages because oh boo-hoo it's just so like unfair to keep them locked up because they hadn't done anything wrong and they were so like innocent and it was mankind that was wicked and all the other like total, you know – crap I'd been going on and on about. I just didn't *care*, right? And I remember – quite funny, really: that night we had spaghetti bolognese and it was, like – the best food I ever tasted? So yeh – I don't expect things now to be as great as you want it . . . but still I didn't think my, you know – first time, it would be just so totally shitty. Like dirty and it hurt and everything smelled as bad as the fucking Zoo. But when you mature, yeh? You get to learn, that's just how it is.

So look, I was in the hall and the paper hadn't even come and it was all so like really still and quiet and everything – and yeh, that was good because I could get up to my room and no one was going to start asking me like a million questions but at the same time I would quite like to have heard just talking, you know? The silence and no people around, it was all getting to me a bit. And in my room I wanted to play music and really like loud but I knew that was stupid so what I did was I put on all the lights including the pink fluffy bally one I've got by my bed, and that made me feel a lot better – and then I took off all of my clothes (and the tights, I'm going to have to like wrap them up in a carrier bag or something and dump them, shit, because look – there's blood and other muck as well as holes). So I'm standing under the shower now and I raise my head up to the silver thing, yeh, that the water shoots out of – and I'm like imagining that it's the sun in the desert or something, and I know I saw this in some movie, American probably, don't know what it was called, and the woman who had great boobs, fake yeh sure, but a whole load better than mine which are actually a bit pathetic but apparently they can go like completely nuts when you're about sixteen or something so I'm not too like worried about it (I'd never have a boob job or anything though, oh yuck, because it's just so gross) . . . and anyway, the woman, this woman – could've been Demi Moore – she then sort of smooths back all of her wet hair and she just lets the foamy water kind of go all over her like it's more than just a shower and it's a symbol, probably, for something like getting all pure again, and so I thought cool and I did all that but I don't think the heating can have been on that long because it soon got pretty tepid and anyway there were no bubbles left in the squirty thing and so I thought oh fuck this and I had to go out on to the landing all like dripping to get a towel from the airing cupboard which I'd forgotten to do and when I got back into my room I was all just like totally freezing again, and I don't think I felt like any purer.

I put on a dressing gown – the towelling one, not the baby one that I keep telling Mum I've grown out of and I wish she'd just give away or like dump or set fire to or whatever (little bunnies all over it? I don't think so) and I lay on my bed and tried to work it all out, what I was going to do next. And I suddenly had this thought and I jumped up and went to the drawer I keep really like old stuff in. And yeh – here it is: two tubs of ancient Play-Doh from about a hundred years ago when I used to make all armchairs for my Sylvanian Families and even teeny ones for Polly in My Pocket and then I did like all this fruit and cakes for them to eat? Still probably got them somewhere. And what I'm doing, right, is I'm making a model of the fucking shit whose name I don't actually want to say any more – he's blue and podgy, and I make a hole in him right in the middle like where his legs stick out, and I fill that with a lump of yellow and then I pick him up and fix back one of the arms which just dropped off and then I put him in this box with Marilyn Monroe on the lid which used to have thank-you cards in and then I get the needles out of the sewing kit that I kept from the hotel room in the Lake District which we went to whenever and I stick them all like straight into the yellow bit and I do quite laugh at the thought of him rolling about in real like agony in that stinky old house of his, shouting out one of his so crap poems and clutching his balls, the bastard. That would be really really funny, I think.

And then suddenly I just like freaked. You know? Lost it. Cried and cried and cried.

My ears. Giving them a well-earned rest for the whole of today. Saturday, after all – don't *have* to listen to anyone, do I? Because all last evening – throughout that perfectly extraordinary dinner with Susan, I had the thing I sometimes, er – you know: put in, hearing thing, tiny little bugger it is – had the damned thing right up to the maximum it'd go. Eerie sensations, I can tell you that. Um – that's rather comical, isn't it? Eerie? No? Well maybe not. So anyway, yes, right up to the maximum it was. I mean, granted, I could hear everything she was saying, no complaints on that score, clear as a bell – but when that wine chappie, what's his name, not Smales, no, not

130

him, the other one – well whatever his blasted name is, when he took the cork out of the claret with his little waiter's friend . . . well bloody hell, is all I can say. Sounded like the boom of a depth charge detonated in the Underworld. Someone dropped a spoon, some point – felt like my head had been strapped around the business end of Big bloody Ben, I am not joking. And all of this morning, my ears, they've been zinging, you know – bit of a hiss, and then all this zinging, only word for it. How can an honest attempt to not be as deaf as a thing so bloody thoroughly destroy one's hearing? Can't be right, can it really? Post. Deaf as a . . . And I suppose I'll have to have the little sod plugged into me again tonight, won't I? At this cosy little dinner of hers. Couldn't believe it when she phoned me this morning. Was only aware of the thing ringing when I happened to pass it – thought I detected the merest tinkle.

'Christ Black, at long bloody last. Where've you *been* . . . ?'

'You're very faint. Who is this, please?'

'It's *me*, Black – Susan. Am I really not at the forefront of your mind? I simply can't believe it. I would have hoped that after last night, your brain would've been in a fevered tangle, a swirl of delight, concerning only me. Your heart no more than a Susan-shaped and smouldering hole.'

'. . . what?'

'Never mind. Listen. That dinner I talked about, yes? Well we're having it tonight. I woke up this morning and I just thought well why not? You will come, won't you? You've got my address and everything.'

'. . . what?'

'Black. Why do you keep on saying that? Is it a bad connection? I can hear you perfectly well. Shall I hang up and ring you right back?'

131

Black just stared at the phone and then idly glanced about him in childish wonder.

'. . . what?'

And then the line went dead, he rather thought – faint murmur had gone away, anyway. Supposed that he really ought to ring her back then, should he (fairly sure it was Susie, you know – something in the tone), and that the bloody sodding hearing aid would have to go back in, then – because obviously we were getting nowhere at all without it . . . and so he found it more or less where it had been hurled with impatience and he jammed it into his ear just as the phone rang again – and to Black it sounded as if twelve old fire engines were in a state of high emergency and rammed into his drawing room . . . and he fiddled quite frantically with the bloody control while consciously willing this seizure to subside, or at least his heart to cease its beating like a set of bongos approaching the spurtingly gory climax to a voodoo sacrifice . . . long enough anyway for him to at least just snatch up the receiver with the one hand while the other chucked into his mouth a fairly small gathering of the biggish speckled capsules that he rather suspected might be for the subduing or anyway postponement of the onset of any sort of debilitating stress.

'Can you hear me now? Yes?'

'Perfectly, dear Susie. It must have been a bad connection. The only sensible thing to do in such circumstances is, well – just hang up and ring right back. Jolly good. So how are we, my dear? Sleep well?'

'Oh for goodness sake. I'll have to start all over again, it seems. You remember last night when I said . . . you do *remember* last night, don't you Black? Restaurant? With me? Who is called Susan?'

'Droll, my dear. Very droll. You were saying?'

'The dinner I mentioned. My house, yes? Well I thought it would be lovely to do it tonight. You see – I can't be parted from you! Every minute seems an eternity. You getting all this, are you . . . ?'

'Mm. Yes. Tonight. Well actually, tonight is just a bit, um . . .'

'Why? Are you already doing something?'

'Um – not *doing* something exactly, no. No, not really. No. Not.'

'Well . . . ? Are you ill? You haven't got a hangover, have you?'

'Hangover? No no. Well at least I don't *think* so, anyway – really a bit early to tell. Teatime, normally, is when they tend to come over me. Descend, as it were.'

'So you'll come, then.'

'Well . . . *tonight*, you say? Yes . . . it's just that tonight is rather, er . . .'

'Black. We've done all this. What is wrong with tonight? Tell me.'

'Well there's nothing exactly *wrong* with it . . . it's just that it's, well – it's *tonight*, isn't it? Short, um – notice, as it were. Not very good at impromptu, you know. Like things planned in advance.'

'Well this *is* in advance: it's tonight. So you'll come, then.'

'Um. Right-o. Suppose so.'

'And you have been thinking? You will *think*, won't you Black? About my . . . well yes, I suppose it *was* a proposal really, wasn't it?'

'Sounded like it to me.'

'So you'll come. And you'll think.'

'Right-o. Got it. Come. Think. Will do.'

'Seven-thirty all right? You'll get a taxi, I expect?'

'Expect so, yes yes. Seven-thirty. Right-o. Oh and er, Susie – what do you think she'd like? Little present, you know.'

'Who? What on earth are you talking about?'

'Um – Alison. Thought I'd take along a little, you know – gift of some sort.'

'Who in God's name is Alison?'

'Ah. Sorry. Mix-up. Angela, I meant. Yes – Angela, of course.'

'*Angela* . . . ?'

'Mm. Apparently not. Well your little *girl*, for God's sake. Annette, is it? I mean – *you* must know her bloody name.'

'Oh *Amanda* . . .'

'That's the chap.'

'Oh no, Black. Please don't trouble. It's very sweet of you, but honestly, really, no.'

'No? Oh. Quite sure? Oh. I just thought, I don't know . . . maybe – doll, or something.'

'Black. She's nearly fifteen.'

'Oh right. Yes – take your point. Well what do people of nearly fifteen like these days, then? *Weapon* of some sort . . . ?'

'Oh Black – you really are so very lovably silly. Just come. Don't bring anything.'

'Oh. Sure? Really? OK then. Seven-thirty. Come. Think. Don't bring anything. Got it.'

Good, thought Susan as she snapped shut her mobile – it's conversations like that that should maybe make me wonder what it is I'm taking on. Still – means to an end, yes? Never lose sight of the goal, that's the golden rule (though how this many clichés could possibly proliferate in a situation so very singular as this one is something of an intrigue in itself; one to be pondered, if and when I get a moment to myself).

134

Well now, I had better prepare for what I do hope will prove to be a, well, shall we say – momentous evening? I don't want to drag my heels on this one. I feel urgency. I feel it surge. People must cooperate now in doing what I want. The setting for tonight, the aura – it must be quite perfect, though not in the way that someone who knew me might I think imagine I would see it. To begin with, I have decided not to cook. No no. I must not appear as the aproned little wifelet, breathless and eager to delight the men next door – busy amid the steam of a clattered batterie, casting back a flop of hair with the back of my hand, while urging with a wooden spoon a sulking sauce to thicken. Nor, though, do I wish to come across as way on high and in total command (although that is how it will be). More I would like it that the three of us come easily to feel that we are each an equal party, on the verge of a lasting and natural ménage (however unnatural it at first might strike one). So we're having a Chinese takeaway and a great deal of alcohol; this, believe me, will work. I'm sorry if all of this makes me out to be, oh – so cold and unforgiving, so very scientific, unflinching in my approach – because this would be to misunderstand and severely underrate me. You must trust me when I tell you that I have the good of everyone at heart. I feel the warmth of the potential, you see: I am a sensualist, not a machine.

My chink of weakness is maybe betrayed by what I now have done, in the face of my absolute determination through-out to tell no one of my plan, and in particular Maria – a good friend in many ways (we have often fed quite hungrily upon the very meat of one another while feigning a sisterly concern, a profound rapport, as women are wont to; exchanging the one secret for another quite as shocking – condoning any sort of recklessness, indulgence, or even quite blatant insanity, and uniting over the difficulties that men and children will present one with). So yes – in particular Maria, who I knew would pronounce my patient scheming to be thoroughly delicious (one of her words) while really gloating, loving that it doesn't concern her, and then drawing out of me more and more of the purest essence under the twin guises of encouragement and understanding – while even at the moment rehearsing with glee the dripping out of gobbets of the very marrow to unconsidered others. And yet I had phoned her, and suggested we meet. I do not want her to know, I have no compulsion to, oh God – *share* in this . . . I just need to ease myself from under the worst of its weight.

She hates all the coffee shop chains, Maria, and of course so do I. This one is a throwback – comfortably overstuffed and flitting with grim and broken-arched waitresses, seemingly born to it, or else the young and fretful. Trimmed and elegant finger sandwiches are a reassuring feature (I remarked upon them on one occasion to Alan, the finger sandwiches, and he said he'd just as soon have cheese . . . but then, depressingly, that's just so very Alan, isn't it really?) as are the multi-tiered cakestands, pretty with Battenberg, tartlets and Ladurée macaroons. Maria will sometimes enjoy peering through the masking of a steaming mint infusion or else something rare and oriental, while I am true to a succession of espressi, a little jug of just-warm milk alongside. Clustered around our corner table beneath the mirrored panels there is often a slither of rope-handled carriers, the stiff and glossy spoils of her very latest sortie. Today there seems to be even more of them than usual.

'Well I wasn't going to get the navy as *well* as the yellow one, honestly I wasn't. Even I'm not *that* bad. Mm – I say yellow, though it's not one of those ghastly yellows. It's much more . . . it's difficult to . . . I would get it out and show you, Susan, but they do them up so terribly gorgeously – ribbons and everything. But at those prices I just couldn't bear to leave one of them behind. I really saved a fortune. But God, you know – I don't even know where I'm going to *put* the things. Isn't it awful? I had these – did I tell you this, Susan? I had these rather special sort of – *shelves*, really, put up in the dressing room, just solely for all my handbags – but they're already completely full. I'd filled them before the little man had even finished putting them up. So I don't know what I'm going to do. My tea's gone cold. Miss! Oh excuse me – miss! Yes – hallo, thank you. Do you think you could be an absolute angel and bring me another pot of . . . ? Yes. Thank you so much. Very kind. *Now* then, Susan. Do tell. What on earth have you been up to? Haven't seen you in simply ages. Did you want another coffee? I should have asked you when the girl was here. These macaroons, honestly . . . I do wish you'd have one, Susan, or else I'll end up eating the whole bloody lot. They really are too delicious, pink ones especially. Well, Susan? *Talk* to me, heaven's sake. How's work? You make me feel so terribly guilty, you having a job. And how's Alan? Same, I suppose. And Amanda? Is it still term time? I'm so out of touch with all those sorts of things. But it's *you*, Susan, I really want to hear about. Have you got some gorgeous and delicious secret that you're just dying to tell me about?'

Susan sipped coffee, and she just had to smile.

'Well I have as a matter of fact, Maria. I have.'

Maria put down her half macaroon, forced her mouth into a moue and dabbed its edges with a napkin, her eyes inquisitive and alive.

'Well goodness, Susan! Of all the things I might have expected you to say . . . ! Well how utterly delicious – and I didn't even have to coax it out of you. Wonderful. Oh I *am* pleased I came. Well come on, then. Don't keep me in suspense. *Tell* me.'

'Well . . . it's just that I'm getting another husband.'

Maria's eyes were narrow and then so wide as she slapped the tablecloth with the flats of her hands.

'*Ah*! I knew it. I've seen it – I've seen this coming for a long time, you know. I'm amazed quite frankly, my dear – and I can say this now, can't tell you how often I've thought it – but I'm amazed, I really am, that you haven't done it before. I mean – well look at him! Not for you, never was. Never really pulled his weight, has he? I mean I don't *dislike* him, Alan – he's nice enough, course he is – but honestly, Susan. Not what a man is *for* really, is it? I have to say – if my John had carried on like that, well . . . he would've been out of the door just years ago. I mean it. As it is, he earns an absolute fortune doing whatever it is he does – he started to explain it all in detail to me once, the lamb, until I had to just beg him to stop. And his bonus last Christmas . . . well! But *Alan* . . . what has he ever done for you? Nothing that I can see. Well well *done*, Susan, that's what I say. You're well out of it. Now tell me – who's the new man? Is he delicious? When can I meet him? Oh Susan I'm *so* happy for you! It'll be a new lease of life. I've been worried about you, you know. Looked so terribly tired, lately.'

'That's what Alan thought, when I told him. That I was leaving him.'

Maria now was caught in hesitation. She blinked.

'What did you say? I'm sorry, I'm . . . didn't you just say—?'

Susan smiled and wagged her head.

'No. Not leaving him. Couldn't. Wouldn't be right. No – you see, what I'm doing is – and I know it sounds . . . but I'm getting another husband. As well as. Not instead of.'

'You mean you're taking a lover. Well we've all done *that* . . .'

'No. No no. That's not what I mean.'

'Well what else can you mean? You're not about to commit, um – what-is-it, are you? *Bigamy*, for God's sake?'

Susan now was agitated, and she leaned across the table.

'It won't be that, of course – I can't get married again properly, I do know that. I'm not out to get people into trouble. But in all the real senses it'll be proper – a second and parallel marriage. Proper. Sharing one's life. I thought of two separate households, but it's much too complicated. And also, it wouldn't be real. Would it? You can't be with one husband and not with the other. And everyone has to know what's going on. Share it. You think I'm mad, don't you . . . ?'

'Well at the moment I do, yes Susan I do. Frankly. Oh but look you can't be *serious* about all this, can you? I mean how are you going to . . . you know, um—?'

'There's this priest I've got to know. Irish. Quite nice. Name's Johnnie Flynn. Drinks a bit. Lot, actually. Why in the main I think they got rid of him. That and pretty parishioners. Not choirboys, at least. They used not to mind any of that sort of thing, the Catholics, but it's all over the papers now, so they've . . . I don't know – got to be seen to do something about it, I suppose. Anyway – Father Flynn, he says he'll see to it. Service.'

Maria was stirring a slow and thoughtful cup.

'It's gone cold again . . . Can't really be bothered to order any more. But tell me, Susan – this Father Finn . . .'

'Flynn. It's Flynn he's called. I think you'd like him.'

'Flynn, then. But he's – what do they call it – unclothed . . . ?'

'Defrocked. Yes he is. That's why it won't be a legal marriage, but in every other way it will be . . . *right*. In the eyes of God.'

'My dear Susan – I don't think God will even be *looking*. I don't think He could bear it! Well tell me about the new . . . oh Jesus: *husband*. Delicious? Rich, I'm assuming. You haven't *quite* lost all reason, have you?'

'Oh he's got money all right. That's the whole point.'

'Well *good*. So you don't . . . you're not in love with him?'

'Well no. It's a bit like Alan. I love them both, in a way. Hard to explain. But apart from money . . . I'm *doing* it out of love.'

'Mm. And him – what's his name?'

'Black. It's a nickname. Black. Because his surname is Leather. See? It's not very clever.'

'Kinky, though. And *talking* of which . . . ?'

'No. We haven't. It's not like that.'

'No. Like John and me. That's not like that either, more's the pity. He saves all that for his bloody PA . . .'

'Really? John does? I never knew.'

'No. I didn't either until very recently.'

'Oh God Maria, I'm so sorry. How did you—?'

'Usual ways. Snooping, lying, bribery, internet fraud. All the things a good wife does. Anyway – never mind John. That'll blow over. It always does. Tell me – what does *Alan* think of all this? And the new person. Black? What a perfectly silly thing to call him. What does *he* think?'

'Alan thinks I'm crazy – at the moment he's hurt, I think he's hurt – but he won't be soon. When it's all done, he'll be fine. I'm sure of it. Black . . . well Black doesn't actually *know*. Not yet. I mean he knows I want to marry him, because I told him so – just last night, matter of fact. He hasn't said yes yet, but he will, he's got to. But he doesn't know anything about *Alan*, is what I mean. Even that he exists. I've told him about Amanda, though. I thought I should.'

'Uh-huh. But you didn't think to mention that you live with a husband who you've no intention of leaving, and he's going to be imported as Husband Number Two.'

'He won't be husband number *two* . . . well he will in that there'll be two of them, but I'm not putting them in *order*, Christ's sake.'

'Does Alan get points for long service?'

'Oh look, Maria – it's easy to laugh – I know it's a bit—'

'Lunatic?'

'—*different*, but I just know it's going to work. I feel it. Anyway – he's coming round tonight. Black is. Get the ball rolling.'

'Oh my *God*, Susan – can I come too? I'd pay really big money for a ticket to this.'

'Absolutely not. Even Amanda's not going to be there. It's just . . .'

'The husbands and the wife?'

Susan was suddenly coy.

'If you like. If you want to put it like that – yes, that's exactly what it'll be. Shall we go now, Maria? Do you mind? Hundred things to do. Um – you don't *have* to tell everyone about this, you know . . .'

'Susan! I'm shocked. As if I would. It's our little secret. Isn't it? It's just for us. But you will, won't you? You promise you'll keep me *informed* . . . ? Oh my God, but how perfectly *delicious*. Something to *live* for, darling.'

Susan smiled, her eyes uncertain, relieved by her own

articulation. But displeased to have made the disclosure. On her way back home in the back of a taxi, she seriously re-examined these new and altruistic aspects of her growing grand design – benevolence to others, not an element she was even aware of until she had heard herself protesting her own goodness to Maria . . . though she was glad to discover that on balance they were trueish. Because Alan, he very rarely goes out, you know – or at least so far as I am aware. Always just stuck up in that room of his, idling away the day. He's never been . . . what do they say? Clubbable, is it? Not a man's man, so to speak. And hardly, I think we may agree, the other type either. So no sort of a man at all then, if one were to take the more broad and uncharitable view. So he needs someone, really. Doesn't he? A mate, if you like. Someone to talk to. Because I'm no good to him, not in that way, well of course I do see that. All I do is snap and carp, firing a salvo either in earnest warning and barely over his head, or else from close quarters and aiming to wound; thoroughly belittle whatever he does, or else just ignore him completely. And he then breathes in deeply and returns the volley as well as he is able, and so it goes on, around and around. Once, our exchanges – they had been vibrant and gleeful, almost a sporting contest. Now it's just sour, and wholly automatic.

In the hall, by the delftware bowl that I'm really quite fond of, he appears to have left me a note. I wince to remember that when we were newly married, he used to quite regularly litter the house with pretty cream and deckled cards, notes of affection and secret allusion (my oh my, what time can do). But here we have on the mirror a lemon Post-it, annoyingly askew, I assume because he knows that I loathe them (the shade, the tacky backing). 'Out this afternoon, but back in good time for the Fabulous Feast. Wine in kitchen for your approval, ho ho. I assume that jackets will be worn?' Mm. Had he said it to my face, that last little barb, I doubtless would have countered with a withering rejoinder: 'Well *yours* will be, Alan my sweet, in common with all of your rags – practically threadbare, not unlike yourself, my sugar.' Sour, you see? Yes – and wholly automatic.

So he's rather confounded me: having made him out to be practically a hermit, he now informs me he is out for the day. I wish I wondered where and why.

This bloody smoking ban – it's a right bloody pain, and I'm sick up to here with hearing all the positives from all the Green and eco-friendly sodding morons (because I don't give a fuck about my carbon footprint – just like to plant it with force on their collective backside). About the only place left I can light up a Havana is when I'm at peace in my deckchair, tracing the wheeling of a seagull, while my toes get toasty in the sand. And yeh I *know* the bloody air's so very much cleaner and sweeter wherever you go – but in a bar like this (where I am now, one of the seediest I know, and all the better for it) the air's not meant to be clean and sweet – well is it? It's meant to be rank and acrid – eye-stingingly blue and deep-down dirty. They don't serve food here – well, none you'd want to eat, certainly – and it's properly pubby in the worst sort of way – old carpet, old flyers, old bloke with the shakes who lives in the far corner: God, I just love it. No bloody music either. And right this minute, I'm halfway into my second large Scotch (so it might be the third – who's to give a damn?) and there's this fatly seductive Cohiba Robusto burning a hole in my inside pocket. I don't obviously mean literally – well Christ of course

143

not, what do you take me for? I'm not a bloody idiot. But I am aware of its suggestive bulge – my lips are aching for the mellow-scented tang of it. Oh dear me. Why is it I never seem able to do what I want? Why must this be? If it isn't Susan, it's the government. What a way to live, I ask you. And yes, this bar, it's got a couple of cracked paving stones out at the back and a small patch of mud – and the R on the sign, that fell off ages ago, so all of the regulars, among whom I am proud to number, extract a good deal of amusement from calling it the Bee Garden, but still though, you wouldn't want to be out there. It seems always to catch the wind, even if there isn't one – weird, that. And the patio heater, it'd have you broiled, you get too close. There used to be a large umbrella, but Dave behind the bar says some bugger's upped and nicked it. And it's starting to rain now, see? So that's the end of me old cigar.

And she's still looking over, you know – don't think it's just my wishful imagination that's hard at work here. She's been sitting on her own with an orange-coloured drink (could I suppose be orange, now I come to think of it) in the nearest thing this slummy and forgotten oasis could ever get to being a booth – a dark-stained caved-in plywood banquette, curved at its centre, and just clinging on to its sheeny, head-streaked and slashed, once rich crimson plush, burst along the domed and rickety edging of studs where the off-yellow foam is making for the open. On the round-topped table, the rim randomly channelled with scorch-black notches, an abiding memento of a million abandoned fags from the days back when, there is a small and rotting cactus in an old John Courage ashtray, thriftily pressed into fresh service, and also these two long-fingered and slender hands to the sides of the tumbler of orange, the attitude almost prayer-like, poised and tender, as if to keep it from harm. And when I look across, the idle enquiry of my eyebrow is held for the merest moment, and then she quite hastily glances away. And then when I dare to look back, my breath is stopped by the sizzle of the instant as again our eyes are so briefly fused. Those hands of hers are nun-like – white and sepulchral – but the face I can tell is really very worldly. A heavy fringe, as she shyly hangs her head down, is pricking the tips of her lashes. Her air is of someone who is the sole possessor of a sweet and cheeky secret which, with seduction and a gentle insistent goading, she might be lusciously tempted to spill all over me.

'This is . . . quite a surprise, if you'll forgive me . . .'

She blinked up at him quite without expression as he stood over her table, his whisky in his hand. Green eyes, think . . . little hazel speckles . . .

'Just having a drink,' she said, very flatly. But no, he decided – it wasn't quite that, flat, the voice, no it wasn't that. More faraway and wistful as if she had been sleeping, and now was unconvinced by wakefulness, though still barely caring either way.

'Yes yes. It's just that . . . this bar. You know. Not exactly the in place, is it? Not what you'd call, um – "happening". If you know what I mean. Young people, young women – don't come in here much, that's all.'

She shrugged and stared at her drink.

'It's quiet. Don't get hassled. Usually.'

'Ah right – sorry. Well I'll go then. Sorry. I didn't mean to be—'

'No it's all right. I didn't mean that either. I don't mind. You can talk. You can sit if you want to. Won't be here long anyway.'

145

'Oh well that's very, um – nice of you. Thanks. Can I ah – get you a . . . ? Maybe?'

'No thanks. Still got this. I don't drink much. I just like to sit here and think. Quiet, see?'

Alan was nodding over-vigorously as he crushed himself into the flayed and broken hammock of tatters; it was creaking quite angrily before it settled down.

'Thinking, yeah. What *I* do, really. What are you – thinking about? Or don't you want to tell me? I'd quite understand. None of my, um . . .'

The girl laughed lightly. 'Oh God – nothing deep, or anything. Just stuff. I'm Helen, by the way.'

'Ah. The name's Bond. James Bond.'

'Yeh yeh. What's your name really?'

'Well it is *James*, as a matter of fact. Not Bond, though. Christ, you know – I've got this really good cigar in my pocket, and I so damn want to smoke it. Can't get it out of my mind.'

'Oh yeh I know! I got ten Marlboro Lights this morning and I only just had a chance to light one up and then it started peeing down.'

'Bugger, isn't it? Still – there it is, I suppose.'

'I'm just on my way home, actually. Half day. I'll have a fag then. Do you want to . . . ? I mean – you can come if you like. I don't mind. I love the smell of cigars. Makes me think of Christmas.'

Helen had stood up, and was gathering her coat about her. She took her mobile out of her slouchy bag, stared at it hard, and then dropped it back in. Alan was looking perfectly amazed. And then he said something.

'Oh. And you like Christmas, do you?'

'Love it. Doesn't everyone? Well look, James – I'm off now.

146

Live quite near. Don't want the drink. So you coming or not?'

He looked about him at nothing and no one, knocked back the last of the whisky, smacked his lips and nodded.

'Yeh. Yeh I am.'

The rain now was hardly more than a heavy gusty drizzle, though none the less annoying for that. Alan was buttoning up quickly his shabby Harris tweed and he spattered on behind the skitter of her legs, aware that his hair was well along the way to becoming as frizzy as a scourer and that the knees of his trousers were clammy already. She'd said she lived quite near, and yes he supposed it was true – but while he shook off his sleeves as he stood inside the hallway, Alan could easily have wished that it had been a damn sight nearer. The floor was green linoleum and there was a bicycle jammed alongside, the wallpaper's patterning bruised and erased by the routine drag of its handlebars. He stepped across a thick and scattered slick of catalogues, their insistency muted by polythene. She said, 'OK?', and he said, 'Yeh.' Her legs then twinkled away and up into the shadows at the top of the staircase, and Alan's head was booming with only the thunder of his two invading feet banging on the treads as he doggedly followed behind her. Her room was at the top, small and angular, crouching low beneath the eaves, and extraordinarily welcoming with its large divan and a hurling of multicoloured throws, the floor close to seeming upholstered, so gorgeously strewn with outsize cushions. Helen snapped a switch by the doorway and a series of small and globular leaded glass lampshades glowed and were winking in scarlet and amber – purple, lime and golden-yellow. The rain was peppering hard the one tiny window, and Alan felt his limbs uncoiling, so at peace, and terribly relieved.

Helen batted at her fringe with those long white fingers and was screwing up her nose as she shrugged off her coat and stuffed it into a cupboard.

'I saw you were drinking whisky. Was it whisky? Yeh? Well there's a bottle on the table there, if you want some. God I've just *got* to have that fag. Or there's some fizz in the fridge. Shall we have that? Make a party of it – it's such a rotten day.'

'What a lovely idea. And the fridge is . . . ?'

'Oh – just move that screen thing. Yeh – just behind there. Sorry it's all a bit of a mess.'

Helen sucked deep on the Marlboro and whooshed out the smoke in a great big show ('Oh *lovely* . . . ! Thank God'). Alan was stooping low in front of the bijou fridge which was covered in . . . there must be fifty or so of these magnets all over it, each of them bearing a single word in a galaxy of fonts and colours.

'So you like words, do you Helen? Oh – Heidsieck. That's my favourite. How amazing . . .'

'Hey? Oh, the fridge. Yeh – they're all from Shakespeare. You mix them about and try to make a poem. I'm not very good at it, though. I'd love to write. I can't think of anything better.'

'Mm. It is good. I wouldn't be without it. Um – glasses, Helen . . . ?'

'What – you're a writer? Really? I don't believe it!'

'Mm. Novelist, actually. Writing a novel. It's not *Dickens*, you know, but um . . . glasses?'

'Oh yeh – sorry. The door under the . . . yeh. There. Got them? Great. So tell me about it, James – this novel you're writing. God I can't believe it – I actually know a novelist! Amazing. You want to sit here? I'll light the fire.'

Alan was easing the cork out of the champagne – it came away with the merest hiss of resentment (could it be a sigh of impatience at having been disrupted, he wondered quite joyously) and hurtled it foamily into quite the wrong glasses.

'It's popping a bit . . .'

'Popping, Helen . . . ?'

'The fire. Does that. Probably needs a, I don't know . . . clean, or something. I've always wanted a real fire – logs and everything. Pine cones. But gas is the nearest I can get up here. It's quite nice when it's got going, though. Cosy. Bit blue – never used to be blue like that, not when I got it. You see how around the coals it's all a bit blue . . . ? Probably needs a . . .'

'Mm. Clean, or something. You could be right. Not really my, um – thing, you know. Gas fires. Well cheers then, um. Helen.'

'Well I wouldn't expect it. You're an artist. Can't wait to hear all about your novel, and everything.'

Alan now perched himself on the corner of the divan, quite close to Helen and the fireplace. It was softer than he had anticipated and he was very nearly tipped and rolled all the way off the thing, and so he squirmed himself back a bit, his shuffling bottom seeking out a purchase.

'You seem . . . I mean if you don't mind my saying so, your views . . . you seem quite – old-fashioned. For one so young. I mean to say I don't think that's a *bad* thing, or anything. I love it, actually. Well obviously I do. It's just that it's – unusual. In one so young.'

Helen sipped champagne and nodded thoughtfully.

'I think you must be right. My friends say that too. Well – I say friends . . . I haven't got loads of them, or anything. They're all my age, pretty much, but we don't seem to agree on a lot. They're more into clothes and celebs and stuff. I like older people, really. They've got more to say. Know more. Why don't you light your cigar, James? Champagne's lovely. Haven't had it in ages.'

Alan placed his glass on the floor beside him and slid out of his pocket the stubby black-and-yellow tube – tugged it open and tapped out the Cohiba.

'I've already cut the end. I had a feeling . . . I don't know – I just had a feeling there'd be somewhere today I'd be able to smoke it. You're sure you don't mind?'

'Told you. Love it. Are they expensive, those things? Expect they are. Look it, anyway.'

Alan was applying a match, gently revolving the cigar and glancing occasionally at its smouldering tip.

'Well in *this* country they cost an absolute fortune – wouldn't even tell you how much, it's just so embarrassing. But I got a whole load of them in Spain, you know, year or two back. Some ghastly holiday or other. Really cheap in Spain, couldn't tell you why.'

'Oh God . . . that smell . . . ! I really, really love it.'

'Want a puff?'

Helen's eyes were bright in the firelight, wholly caught up in a dazzle of daring.

'*Can* I? I've never smoked a cigar. Oh but look – I don't want to mess it up for you. Make it go all soggy.'

Alan's smile was just a fluttering hint of his enchantment.

'You won't mess it up. Here. Come here – I'll show you what to do.'

Helen shuffled over on her knees Her eyes were blinking in happy anticipation from under the weight of her fringe as she looked up at him expectantly and with a touch of awe

150

(could it be comparable to a pure and credulous child, who after the headiness of all the rumours – night upon night of sleepless excitement – was finally confronted by the vast and smothering benevolence of Santa, in all his warmth and redness . . . ? Conceivably not – but meat on the bone for Alan to gnaw at later on, when he was back at the seaside).

He had drawn on the cigar twice in deliberate succession, and now he blew gently on its smoky end, encouraging the skulking heat to briefly disclose itself in a reluctant glow.

'Now you don't have to suck hard, or anything – you just place the end between your lips, and imagine you are sipping something, a liqueur or something. Close your eyes. Close them, yes. Feel it, Helen. Just feel it. Don't inhale . . . simply fill up your mouth with the total sensation . . . breathe through the scent of it . . . and let it just filter away from you. Just let it disappear.'

Helen did her mighty best to achieve just all of that, seemingly eager for his encouragement and approval. She laughed as she handed it back to him.

'It's like . . .' Her eyes were dancing as she glanced about the room in search of the words she was needing. 'It's like . . . kneeling and receiving a sacrament . . .'

Alan now made out to be studying the cigar as he revolved it slowly between his thumb and fingers. He turned down the offer to just come out with the first four things that had rushed into his head, and instead he stooped down low, and kissed her. The rush of heat and sweetness in the surge of her lips, just tinged with the hint of Havana, and fired by the contagion of her eagerness . . . It was she who eased him back on to the divan – he was carelessly aware of the clunk of his shoe against the tumbler on the floor, the clink and hissing as it toppled and rolled away. When she hoicked up her dress and swung her legs across him, he was not taken unawares by the sight of stockings, their shadowed tops tight against the white of thighs, suspended in the old way by straining straps from a black and lacy cradle. She gasped as he reached up to her and just let the palms of his hands graze and skim, hover and shimmer at the push of her breasts, exactly as he had been imagining since first he had glanced at her glancing at him, ages and an instant ago. She then lay down on her back, her eyes disturbingly childlike and yet so black with hunger and imploring, before the lids fell down and she threw wide her arms. Alan set his heated fingers to the stuttered undoing of each of her dress's fourteen buttons, and laying each wing of it away from her. He bent low over her and closed his eyes as he settled down to snuffling out of her all these scents from the richness and embarrassment of every curve and fold, feeling nearly invasive as he fingered lightly the shocking smoothness, feathery and cool before the rush of warming. He barely had to stir before he came inside her, a shallow communion that at once engulfed him. He fell forward and into the heat of her neck, tasting her dampened hair there, and coughing his exhaustion.

Later, a little later, during his sticky extrication – with care and attempted grace – she lazily smiled at their mutual secret, and seemed then to sleep. Alan picked up his glass from the hearthrug and idled to the table where he poured more warmish champagne. He squatted down on the floor and fiddled with the fire until the blue and yellow flicker licking around the coals at once went dead, and still he was sweating, his glossy forehead prickled and aboil. He drank the champagne and looked across at her, only the rise of a cheek now clear to him beneath the mass and tumble of her hair. He was standing now – eased back on the shabby Harris tweed and bent down over her head, kissed her brow beneath the fall of her fringe. He was pleased when she stirred. Her eyes looked up at him without enquiry as her arms were stretching out wide, the suppression of a yawn tugging and distorting her mouth.

'You off now then, are you . . . ?'

Alan nodded. 'I've left the money on the mantel.'

'Lovely.'

'Bit extra for the champagne.'

'Sweet. Well this was a surprise. Don't often see you on a Saturday, Alan.'

'No. Well. Bit of an odd day all round, really. One thing and another.'

'Next week?'

'Probably. Bye Helen, my dear.'

'Bye, ange. Oh here—!' she said suddenly, holding out to him in two fingers the mashed and split Cohiba. 'Be a love, Alan – take it out with you, will you? You know how I hate the bloody things.'

'Mm.'

'Well don't look so sad. It's nothing personal. It's just the smell they leave behind.'

CHAPTER FIVE

So I came down when I heard like people banging around and I went into the kitchen and I said Hi Mum, the way I'd rehearsed it. Because I've been staring at my face in the mirror – it's quite a cool mirror I've got, actually. A bit like oh yuck sick pink, yeh OK – but it's got all these like light bulbs round it like it's in a dressing room in one of those movies you see when someone like knocks on the door? And says Five Minutes Miss Whatever? And she like goes behind a screen and she's wearing all sorts of corsets and feathers and stuff? It's great, but at least one of the bulbs is never working and all Mum says is yeh well we can't go replacing them all the time because it's extravagant; yeh, like she's so thrifty. If it was in her room, this mirror, she'd have a whole great box of bulbs. And whenever one went, she'd throw something at Dad's head like Tara's Mum does and he'd bloody go and replace it. It's shit, you know, sometimes, the way she treats my Dad – I don't know why he never fights back. I mean, yeh he comes out with all his clever-clever sarcastic-type stuff, but he doesn't ever tell her to just, like – fuck *off*, you know? Yeh well.

So I was looking at my face and I was doing it for two reasons, right? One: to see I wasn't all puffy, because then she'd say what's wrong and I'd say there's nothing wrong and she'd say come on Amanda, I'm your mother, I know when there's something wrong – you've been crying. And then I'd go I haven't been *crying*, OK? And she'd say don't lie to me Amanda – tell me what's wrong. And I'd be like there's nothing *wrong*, OK? Why do you have to keep on and on about it? I *said* there's nothing wrong, didn't I? And then she'd just look at me and then I'd probably start crying again and then the whole thing would go and start up again, right, so that's why I had to check I wasn't looking puffy. And the second reason was I had to make sure I could seem all casual, sort of, and like kind of breezy, or else she'd start trying to dig out of me some big dark secret which I so don't want to tell her. And yeh – I suppose there was a third reason too I was looking at myself – really really looking. It's funny when you use your eyes to look at yourself really closely and all you see back is like your eyes, yeh? Just looking, really closely. But I wanted to know if I'd gone kind of strange. Because although I felt pretty sick about what happened to me, there was something not totally uncool about it as well. I sort of didn't want to tell Tara about it because she'd look at me funny and probably say I was lying? But I had to really because I was different to her now, don't know if I mean different, but anyway she had to know it. But inside, I didn't feel anything, not really, except tired, and that I like really wanted some tea? And I looked the same, so far as I could tell. So I just widened my eyes and concentrated on my reflection and I said Hi Mum. And that was no good because I was nearly shouting and sounding a bit mad. So I went lower and did Hi Mum again, but that was

155

like I was hiding something, which I am. And then I really lightened my voice, like I was really really happy: Hi Mum! Which was OK, but then I thought hang on – do I do that, actually? Do I go into the kitchen and say Hi Mum? Because if I don't, she's going to go What did you say that for? Did you get it from television? You never say Hi Mum. I can't remember if I do or I don't. And if I sound too happy, she'll be like *Someone*'s sounding particularly happy this morning: what's the wonderful secret? God you know, it must be so easy just living on your own and having a car and stuff, just not having to give a shit about anyone. Which is another thing I've been thinking about, actually – going away. Just like, you know: going. I mean, if Mum's really serious about . . . I can't *believe* she means it! What – two dads and one mum and me? All living here, like . . . what is it? *Friends*? No way I'm doing that. And that Harry, I don't want to run into him again. And school, Jesus – they teach nothing you really want to know, stuff you're like really going to need. So why don't I? Just take off? Trouble is, I live in London don't I? And when you read about it, when you see the movies, these young kids, what they do is, they go to like London. Train. Hitch-hike. Whatever. As if that's like the answer. So where do I go? Well I've got a passport – I could maybe go to, I don't know . . . France, and be an artist. Like Bernard Buffet, up where that big white church is in Paris. Or in the desert – like with the Bedouins? Or Australia, where it's hot at Christmas and you just go surfing and eat, like – prawns? Got to be better than this.

'Hi Mum.'

'I'm busy, Amanda. Make something for yourself, if you want it.'

'What are you doing?'

'I'm . . . I'm just sorting out dishes and things.'

'We never use these. Hardly remember them.'

'No well we're using them tonight. Oh yes, Amanda – that's what I meant to say to you. Talk to you about. Now listen, my sweet – Daddy and I are having someone to dinner tonight, yes? And now I don't want you to feel excluded or anything of that sort . . . but I feel it would be better on this occasion if you weren't, um . . . there. All right? Next time will be different.'

Amanda had been idly fingering a blue-and-white serving plate which she just about sort of remembered from when she was a child.

'What are you talking about . . . ?'

Susan slammed her hands down on to the counter and tightly compressed her eyelids; her hair fell over her forehead, and she angrily swept it back.

'Oh God Amanda I don't have *time* . . . Look. It's very simple. Mummy's got a heavy day. I have to plan this dinner, I have a hairdresser's appointment at . . . oh Christ, it's *that* time already . . . ! And I'm meeting Maria later on for coffee – so I really can't . . . ! Look. I'll give you some money. You and Tara can, I don't know – have a pizza somewhere. Something. Cinema. Are there any new films you want to see? I'll leave you out some money.'

Amanda found herself eyeing her closely, while not even wanting to look.

'It's him, isn't it? It's the creep. You're having your new creep over, aren't you?'

'Oh *honestly*, Amanda! How dare you—! He's not a—! And anyway, it's none of your business. Well it *is* – of course it *is* . . . just not *yet*, that's all. Now please, Amanda – do let me get on. I've got a very heavy day. All right?'

'What are you cooking . . . ?'

'Not. Not, no. Chinese. Now please, Amanda. Yes?'

'Yeh Mum. OK. Hairdo. Coffee with Maria. Takeaway. Heavy day. Yeh right.'

So. I needn't have bothered really, need I? All that rehearsing and staring at me in the mirror. She didn't even like look at me once. Didn't think I seemed different – didn't want to know what was wrong, didn't ask me why I'd been crying. I just so don't matter to her, It's just the creep, the sleazeball, the new fucking toyboy – probably like an Italian waiter or something, young and yuck and oily, except he probably owns a whole load of restaurants because it's rich she wants now: rich. If I've got enough Play-Doh left, I'm going to make another model – him I'll skewer in the head. And Dad's just meant to – what? Sit there and just like take it? Oh God. Just so crap. Why doesn't he *fight*? Yeh well – because he's Dad, that's why: stupid question. Well that settles it, really. I'm not going. Running away. Someone's got to be here – someone's got to do something about all this. Someone's got to like just stop it happening. And it's not going to be Dad. Well is it? No. So OK, then: looks like it's going to be me.

'Now, Black – tell me what I can get you. A few more noodles, maybe. God's sake, Alan – *must* you eat your ribs like that? It's just so Neanderthal. Well, Black – noodles? Yes?'

Black touched his mouth with his spread-out napkin, and taking advantage of the temporary camouflage, his fingernails were scrabbling at the wild and livid redness of his jowls. That second bloody shave of the day had of course made the eczema flare, and yes yes yes he knew he wasn't meant to scratch it, he'd been told all that since he was a boy in pain, permanently inflamed, plastered with gunk, swathed in gauze and jeered at by everybody. But *you* try having eczema and not bloody scratching it: yeh matey – you just try it. And this whole situation, of course, this merry little evening – can't really be helping, can it? Breathing's a bit shallow – noticed it earlier on. Not quite chesty, but I know it wants watching: have to keep an eye on it, oh Lord yes, otherwise it's off to the bloody lavatory again with my brace of inhalers. Been there twice already – once to attend to nature (which I wish would cease forever *calling* and just pipe down and leave me bloody alone) and that had involved – well of course it had – the whole palaver of braces and waistcoat and then the bloody corset, we know the routine (my sympathies with the Edwardian matron are practically boundless, do let me assure you), and the second time had been to loosen the laces in my shoes because the swelling down there had been verging on the chronic. Now normally, I am thoroughly aware – if, say, we were dealing with a fully-functioning human being – well then: your shoes are on the snug side, you casually reach down and quickly attend to the little bit of business. Yes well – I attempt bending of any sort whatever and (a) the demeanour of my bowel is going to shift up a notch from its customary irritable to decidedly cantankerous, and from there we will find ourselves but a short hop, skip and a jump away from borderline insane, believe me (chucking around the furniture) – and (b) there would be ruptures, and maybe not solely in the architecture of my dress. And also, where laces are concerned, it's the same scenario as socks, I'm afraid. It's lying flat on your back, you want the terrible details – I wish I were joking – and sort of drawing down your legs, bent like blazes at the knee, and then trying to ball up just that little bit tighter, for all the world as if a

159

dedicated midwife is in the wings and urging you shrilly to expel those overdue triplets from your big and vile and idle gut like so many dum-dum bullets, to spatter the walls and ceiling. And prior to that, all the underpinnings have first to be loosened, hardly needs saying, and then there is the challenge of becoming vertical again – no mean feat at the best of times, but within the measly confines of what I have heard referred to as a 'guest toilet', may the gods preserve me . . . well Christ Almighty. My head was clanging into the bloody brush thing there, and a column of lavatory rolls fell over my face and I was snorting like an engine and spitting out tissue – blowing it away from the corner of my mouth – because both my hands were still messing around with the God-damned shoelaces, I ask you. Jesus, it's all far from easy. My bootmaker has told me that I could have even higher lifts than these (and these are my vertiginous ones – the ones that make me look as if I am poised and terrified on the brink of a diving board) – yes, even higher than these, he tells me, and we could do away altogether with the laces problem, if only I would consider the extra benefits of a gusset-sided and Cuban-heeled boot like the Beatles used to wear because the added sweep of the angle, or the angle of the fucking sweep, whatever the bugger was saying to me, would serve to disguise the extra inserts as well as adding the two-and-a-half inches that would be down to the heel itself. Apart from the fact, as I explained to him, that I should then feel as if I were living my whole life balanced upon the pommel of a flagpole, I am not, by any stretch of the, oh – what is it? – am I, a *Beatle*? And further – I could not contemplate the Cuban heel; I feel, in some unspecified way, that it would somehow diminish me. Imagination. Stretch of the. Mm.

'No thank you, Susie. I seem to be all right on the noodle front, actually.'

And that's another thing: Chinese takeaway. I mean – Jesus. Granted, the wine has been good and plentiful (only reason I'm still just about coping, tell you the truth), but you show me the bod who can match a wine with a limp and tepid prawn and sesame toast, and I shall show you a better man than I am, Gunga Din. Whoever the fuck he was. Being a bookman, I ought to know. And once, no doubt, I did. And I *know* it's a takeaway because Susie, Christ, she hasn't stopped *telling* me, as if, I don't know – it's a *good* thing, or something. First thing she said as I walked through the door – shoved these flowers at her (God, she made a spectacularly big deal of them: it was quite as if she'd never seen any flowers before, maybe didn't know what they even were) and Jesus, I was pleased to be shot of them, tell you the truth. I'd bought them in Liberty's, happened to be round there, remembered that someone had told me that they sold them, flowers you know, and so I went in one of the side doors and, well – you know Liberty's, bloody great maze of a place: go up a staircase or two and you end up on a floor that's lower down than the one you started out on. It's a bit like a magic trick. The shop seems largely to comprise a great big bloody hole, and from wherever you look down into it to check where in Christ's name you've got yourself to this time, all you ever see is an ocean of scarves, and then of course your head starts to swim: mine does, anyway. So I wasn't having all of that so I got into a lift because I could have sworn that the person I'd asked to direct me to the flowers had said Third Floor, sir, which yes, on reflection, and with a handful of hindsight, might and should have struck me as a wee bit odd, but at the time it struck me neither one way nor the other – no, not at all – and so I got into the bloody lift. And I couldn't get it to start. And then it started. And then it stopped on the first floor and some disgusting little lout was sloping in (never used to have them in the old days, louts, not in Liberty's at least) and he of course had this spastic little music toy jammed into his scabby ears, the lout, the bloody *lout* – and all these ludicrous lyrics were fizzing out of the sides of it and I'll remember them for the rest of my days on earth because damn me if the sodding little lift didn't go and stop again and I stabbed at a button and jabbed at another one – and the lout, he didn't seem to have noticed that we had stopped (he seemed unaware, in truth, that he was even alive and on this planet. And just look, will you, at his bloody hair: all the hair in the world this lout's got – and it looks as if someone while he was asleep had covered it in a slick of Evo-Stik and twisted up all these little thickets of it – like a slimy otter or a well-used bog brush, the lout . . .) and of course the lift just wouldn't *move* and so I just had to stand there wincing at these bloody stupid words: Bay Bye Wan Chew, Hernia Knee Jew . . . over and over, well I ask you. Made me yearn to pluck out my hearing thing, but then I knew I'd never get it working again and I couldn't face the prospect of a whole damn evening shouting *What? What?* Into everyone's faces, so I just stood there going mauve and slamming at all the buttons with the flat of my hand. Bay Bye Wan Chew . . . Hernia Knee Jew . . . dear God Almighty, it is a wonder, truly, I am not as we speak under lock and key for having torn the bloody lout's head from his body, the lout, the bloody lout. And then the lift started up again in its juddering way, and as I burst out of the doors on the third bloody floor – and the lout, so serene, had a look on his vacuous and pockmarked face that suggested he might now be strolling through a bluebell glade at twilight – he just stood there, didn't move, and still the same bloody song was boring its way into his cranium, as might an insidious maggot to a forgotten potato. And so I burst out of the doors on the third floor, all right? And I knew I must have filled the space around me like a sturdy and determined one-man commotion (small, I am small yes, but by now I was in unchained bison mode) and some little squirt, when I shouted at him '*Flowers!*', he more or less laughed in my face as if I had said something beyond fantastic, and then he's going 'Flowers? Oh no sir. Ground floor, flowers.' Well why then, I roared at him, did some septic lunatic tell me they were on the bloody *third*?! That, he said, he couldn't say – so I wasn't chancing the lift again, was I? So I settled for the new and fresh hell of charging up and down a succession of Tudor staircases, squinting over the odd could be Jacobean minstrel gallery, wondering whether I was doomed to die here among all this treacly woodwork even older than I – and then, oh mercy! Oh joy! The ground floor was mine. I accosted some woman fooling with a scarf and demanded to know the location of the flowers and she looked at me the way that some women will and she told me that she didn't work there. I shouted back at her that I didn't give a tinker's *thing* where on God's earth she *worked*, and just to tell me, Christ's sake, where the bloody *flowers* are! Well she rushed off, probably to fetch the police, and then some flunkey or other, he oils up to me – maybe attempting to avert a riot – and says that flowers are outside, just outside – through these doors here sir, and outside on the pavement. Well I thought he was having a laugh – turned out it was true: needn't have gone into the shop in the first bloody place. Jesus. And the woman there, amid the flowers, she asked me if I'd like a pre-tied bouquet, and I said to her As Opposed To Tied *When* Exactly? She gave me the look, I gave her the money, I got in a taxi, flowers made me sick and they brought on my hives. So in the hall of Susie's house . . . yes, I more or less threw them at her, fucking things.

'Oh my *God* Black – how divine! How just totally *divine*. Oh they're simply *lovely*, Black – thank you so so *much*. Let me take your coat. We're having a Chinese takeaway – very superior, though. It'll be a hoot. I'll get a vase. Go on in and have a drink. I'll make introductions, yes? And then we'll have a perfectly lovely evening. I'll just get a vase. They're gorgeous, Black: divine.'

Had to go to the lavatory, of course: took some time. And despite what Susie had told me, I had brought a gift, little something for the child, Annette is it. Would have seemed rude not to. Phoned one of the women in the office, Sandra I think: what do girls of nearly fifteen like, Sandra? Christ I don't know, she said: boys, I expect . . . money? Christ I don't know. Mm, I thought: start as they mean to go on, then. So Sandra was no use to me, so I thought I'd ring Samantha, who has always struck me as being of a more thoughtful disposition. Well, she said – what about a really beautiful book? What about one of those limited editions of Grimm we did? With all the lovely illustrations? And this sounded really quite reasonable to me, in the light of the assumption that I wasn't going to bring the child a gift-wrapped boy or a wad of cash. So I put a bit of paper around the thing, bow sort of affair, and that's what I've got with me. Here we go, then. Put on a smile, attempt to cast the thought of a Chinese takeaway far from my mind, and do my level best to not fall off my shoes. Quite nice room: spacious. And there's a forty-five-year-old man at its centre, look. Could be younger or older. Seems a bit wild. Good head of hair on him, bastard. No young girl around. Odd.

Alan came forward clutching a glass, a jammy and slapstick grin draped across his face like a gaudy curtain (rigged up in no time).

'Expect you could do with a drink, couldn't you? I've had several. More than enough. Have another in a minute. Alan, by the way. Ah – you shouldn't have.'

Black glanced down at the ribboned package as he awkwardly fingered it.

'Ah yes. No no. This is for, um – Angela, I think.'

'Mm. You must mean Amanda. Don't worry – I'm appalling with names myself. Perfectly useless. So – drink, then? Scotch? Wine? Got some good wine. Something else? Do sit, won't you. Susan won't be a minute, I shouldn't imagine.'

Black laid Amanda's present to the corner of a console table and sank with relief into an ample sofa and on the whole felt really pretty good about the fact that there wasn't a teenage girl in the room, but a bloke instead – a bloke, moreover, who was offering him drink, and now had placed an ashtray by his side.

'Black, they call me. If you can stand it. Yes – a Scotch would be excellent, not too much trouble.' He hesitantly floated a packet of Rothmans while waggling his eyebrows. 'So you don't mind if I . . . ?'

'Not a bit. Where else can you, these days? Merest touch of water? Not sure about the Black thing, frankly. No doubt I'll get used to it. Fullness of time. Well. This is odd. Wouldn't you say? Here you are: one disgustingly large Scotch whisky – enough water, I hope. Susan said not to say anything of that sort – about it being odd, I mean. But there – I have now. But it is, isn't it? Wouldn't you say Black? Odd. This? Not your fault, of course. But Susan, well – don't have to tell you, do I? You know Susan. I expect. Once she gets a bee in her, um . . . well. No stopping her.'

Black was very uncertain about just every little part of this. He drank deep into the whisky, and that was good; the desperate drag on the Rothman, that was even better. But still, though – what *is* all this? What's all this 'odd' business? Hey? I mean you're all keyed up to blether like a halfwit to some young kid about Jesus knows what, and instead it's all this 'odd' lark with a middle-aged bloke. I've half a mind to voice my confusion . . . do you know, I might easily have done that, asked what's going on, but now Susie is in the room (and oh Jesus, I don't have to *stand*, do I? Can't think I'm up to it. No no – it's quite all right: I did the squirm for form's sake, and she's batted me back with a wave of her hand. Good. Oh bugger – time to take a pill).

'Can I help you, Black? Why are you twisting around like that? Alan – take his glass from him, can you? Take the cigarette out of your mouth, Black – you'll blind yourself. What is it you're trying to . . . ?'

'Sorry. Pills in waistcoat. Bit tight. Big sofa. Be all right . . .'

'Which pocket? Shall I rummage?'

'Left, pretty sure . . .'

'Are these them? Is it these, Black?'

'Are they blue?'

'Blueish, I suppose . . .'

'Let's have a look . . . ah no. These are more azure, you see. Greenish, I call those ones. Maybe the right pocket, then. They're as blue as blue, the ones I'm after.'

'There's nothing in the right-hand pocket, Black. Are you sure you've brought them with you?'

'Ooh God yes – never leave home without them. Maybe my jacket, then. Hang on – let me just . . .'

'Wouldn't it be easier if you stood up, Black?'

'God no – shouldn't have said so. Job in itself. Ah – here we are. These are the boys. Jolly good. Bugger. Bloody cap, now . . . Meant to be childproof. Completely does for *me*, anyway . . .'

'Here, Black – let me. Do you want water? Water, Alan.'

'No no. Scotch is fine. Think they're for my liver anyway, so they'll both be going in the same direction. There. There we are. Splendid. Sorry about all that. Sorry, um . . . Alan, is it? Sorry Susie.'

Alan raised a finger. 'A good liver,' he pronounced, 'is generally possessed of a bad one.'

'*Silly*, Alan,' tutted Susan.

'I thought that was very good,' said Black, in frank admiration.

'A little thing,' Alan smirked, 'and yet mine own. Top you up?'

'I'm sure I've heard that before . . .' Susan was sniffing. 'Read it somewhere. Was that the doorbell?'

'Well it *could* have been the doorbell, Susan,' Alan allowed, with all the unctuous charm and expansiveness he could pile into the thing. 'It emanated from the hall, did it not? And was not the sound distinctly similar to that which the doorbell is prone to habitually make?'

'Yes – all right, Alan.'

'Not to say identical? The very thing, in fact.'

'Well shut up and *answer* it, then. Hungry, Black? That'll be the takeaway.'

'Ah,' said Black. 'Yum yum.'

'We're going to have a perfectly *lovely* evening. Well go *on*, Alan – *answer* it, God's sake. Here, Black – let me help you up. Dining room now, yes? I've ordered plenty of everything. Do you like ribs?'

Mm, thought Black – it's them I'm worried about: strapped up fit to bust, and that whole charade on the sofa hadn't helped in any way at all (sure I heard something go). Oh well – sod it all. Good whisky that, though. Nice chap, Alan, whoever he is. No doubt find out more. Wouldn't have minded the time for another Rothman, if I'm honest. Later. Right, then: let's go forward. Let us embark upon a perfectly *lovely* evening . . .

He noticed nothing about the dining room – low lighting, thick linen, clusters of candles, squat glass cubes jammed with anemones – no no, didn't see any of that; was only aware that the table had been set for three, you see, just three, and that he had been directed to its head – or conceivably its foot, who's to say? A carver at one of the ends of it, anyway, and opposite was sitting this Alan fellow (good of me to have remembered his name) with Susie, then, right between the two of us. At the moment she was fooling around at a sort of trolley affair alongside, busily transferring heaps of steaming whatnot from a seemingly limitless series of cardboard cartons into equally numerous porcelain bowls of strikingly similar shape and form. Whatever else there might be the length of the table, Black did see that it was liberally sprinkled with what looked like more than fairly decent bottles, far as could be made out (going only by the blurred and gauzy impressions of reliably French-looking labels, proper sort of thing, familiar you know – no hope whatever of actually being able to *read* the things, of course, not from this distance) and that already this Alan character was up on his feet and pouring away. This could be a Chablis, if I'm any judge . . . oh I don't know, though – it's unusually lingering, once you get it down you, almost as fat as a red in the mouth . . . might even be Meursault, mm, and if this is the case I can only further lament the acute disappointment that it is to be accompanied by nothing more than a succession of claggy and soy-doused dollopings of monosodium-whatever-they-call-the-fucking-stuff, and not instead maybe a tranche of wild Scottish salmon (a Dover sole, a nice leg of lamb, a fillet of beef, a well-roasted chicken – the sorts of things you actually want to *eat*, God's sake).

'Ah Susie. How lovely. Mm – does smell good. What is it?'

'Well it's the makings, Black, isn't it? Do you not know Chinese? Duck pancake? No? Well you see you spread the sauce on the crepe thing, yes? And then you add the strips of . . . shall I do it for you?'

'That would be nice of you, Susie. Thank you. Good wine.'

'I've noticed,' said Alan, 'that you call her that. Susie. I've never called her that. Have I, Susan?'

'I'll just add the duck now – see Black? And then you just roll it up and hey presto. There's also seaweed, if you want it.'

'Have I, Susan? Never called you Susie, have I?'

'I wouldn't know, Alan. I wouldn't know. Black's glass is empty, my sweet. Do you think you could cope?'

'Oh well – maybe just a drop you know, Susie. Do you, um – object, my dear? To my calling you Susie? I've never thought.'

'Not in the *slightest*, Black. No, not a bit. I like it, actually.'

'Oh well,' said Alan. 'In *that* case, I'll call you Susie too.'

'Don't be ridiculous, Alan, there's a good boy. Are you happy with the white, Black? Plenty of red, if you'd like to switch.'

'It's a fine wine,' murmured Black. 'Perfect with this, um, thing. Red later though, no doubt. You're into wine then, are you Alan?'

'Oh God *yes*,' agreed Alan with eagerness. 'Into wine, all right. Alcohol generally. Fear not, though – I am not an alcoholic. Not a drunkard. I very might well be, though, now I come to think of it – a bit of a *drinkard*. Neither here nor there – but I'm glad you like this one. Cost an absolute fortune, which I wasn't meant to say. In the normal run of things, I'm happy with the more everyday – Oz, particularly the ones with the bloody stupid names, Chile, Argentina. But Susie here, our Susie, she said this was to be special, you see, so the boat has been well and truly pushed. Out. I suppose we ought to have a toast or something, should we?'

'Oh what a perfectly lovely idea,' Susan enthused, taking her place at the centre of the table and flapping her napkin.

'Well . . .' said Alan slowly. 'It's your party, isn't it Susan? Susie? So maybe you should be the proposer . . .'

Susan's eyes were sparkling in the candlelight as she raised up her glass and glanced in turn to Black and Alan.

'To . . . the three of us. And happiness. Cheers.'

Black obligingly bobbed his glass and sipped, but Alan for one could tell that he was puzzled, which I suppose is amusing in a twisted sort of a way, though also rather pitiable. Or is it me I pity? Certainly I am sad. I can hardly see this as a joyous celebration, or as anything at all much really – but still and all, it could hardly be said to be run-of-the-mill. Guest I've never clapped eyes on, best dishes, best cloth, fresh flowers, great wine – and just look at Susan's dress, the earrings, the hair, the make-up: my wife looks so very desirable. I am beginning to think, though – and this has honestly only just this second occurred to me – that Black, poor chap, is not shall we say, au fait. Up with the ins and outs. He seems bewildered, yes, and also rather itchy – and plus, if the way he keeps clutching at his midriff is anything to go by, in the periodic grip of considerable pain. I'll give him more wine, is what I shall do – red, I think: beef him up a bit, poor sod. And the other factor which I can barely avoid, now we are all of us here and I am finally forced to study the man, is that he is really rather old. Well isn't he? Has to be faced. What we used to term – with the shreds of a spurious tact not at all concealing the dismissive contempt beneath – retirement age. Which I am aware ought in some way to make me feel better then, ought it? Well it doesn't. Make me see myself as not, after all, quite so broken and done? Well it doesn't. Encourage me to hope that Susan might some day – maybe even this day – come to her senses, cringe and recoil from the folly of her ways? Well no. It doesn't. Just doesn't, I'm afraid. So all right – red wine now. And then I shall probe – for the sake, I hope, of at least one of us here, though quite which I couldn't honestly at this juncture begin to even hazard. But Black now . . . it appears from the tremor and disturbance about his lips as if he perhaps is about to speak, maybe feeling forced to voice his uncertainties – to if not dispel them, then at least have even partially explained to him this palpable sense of discomfort, his dark and spreading unease. All just a guess, of course: could merely be indigestion – it might be that he is afflicted by some breed of facial tic to supplement the raft of other disabilities he appears to harbour (and maybe others yet not dreamed of).

'So, um . . . Amanda not joining us after all. It is Amanda, isn't it?'

''Tis, yes,' Alan agreed, nodding his head with emphasis, so as to thoroughly dismiss all doubt on the matter. 'What do you think of this red, Black? Second wine of La Lagune. Or at least that's what the man told me, anyway. What would I know? Had to justify the price of it somehow, I suppose. We always liked the name, didn't we Susie? Not La Lagune, I don't mean: Amanda. I have a vague recollection, you know, that we for a short time toyed with the possibility of Georgia . . . ? Am I right about that, Susie?'

'Goodness sake stop calling me *Susie*. Now then, Black – do please help yourself, won't you. Rice. Noodles – Singapore and, um – chicken, I think. Sweet and sour. Sizzling something and black bean something. Ribs.'

'Oh I see yes of *course* . . . !' said Black, rubbing at his side, clawing at his neck, doing his damnedest to defer the need for yet another headlong dash to the nearest lavatory. 'You are Amanda's *father* – oh of course, of course, how very stupid of me. Of course I should have realised.'

'Well *I* think, actually, that you should have been told. By Susie, conceivably. But there – in common with the Great Detective, she has her methods, I dare say.'

'Oh *do* shut up Alan, my sweet. No look, Black – let me just give you a selection, shall I? Assortment. Bit of everything. And then you can pick and choose.'

'And no,' Alan continued, pouring more claret into the glass that Black was waggling expectantly. 'She isn't coming, actually. Amanda. Were you told that she would be here, then? It was never on the cards. In fact I gather from the child's own dear lips that she was expressly barred from the occasion. Packed off for a pizza with a chum. The work of a cruel and unfeeling parent, you might assume – and yes, you might indeed be right. That she might be better *off* with a pizza is hardly here nor there . . .'

'God's sake, Alan . . . !'

'No. No no. I wasn't *actually* told she'd be here, Amanda. No no. The wine is excellent, by the way. Good tannin. Very mellow. Structure. Legs. No – it's just that when Susie said it was to be just the *three* of us—'

'Ah *yes*,' Alan rushed in. 'Point taken. You of course *assumed* . . . Well quite. You would. Completely understood. Woman proposes marriage to you one day, next morning asks you round to a perfectly preposterous little feast – well it's the daughter you'd expect to be introduced to. Isn't it? Only natural. And hence your very kind and doubtless thoughtfully chosen gift for her. But it's a no-show, I'm afraid. And the last thing you'd expect really is the husband instead. I can see how it could come as something of a shock.'

'Sit down now, Alan. Won't you my sweet? You've had your little spell of limelight. Well done. Very good. Clap clap. Now just sit *down*, can't you? Black – just ignore him. You've barely touched any of your food. Alan – stop talking. Black can't concentrate on his food.'

'A sideways blessing, I'd say. A boon. Still, Black – at least the wine's making up for things, hey? Or at least some of them, anyway. I've opened loads. Think we'll need them. But tell me – and this is the real point, isn't it? Why we're all here. No reason shilly-shallying is there, really? Pussyfooting around the thing.'

'Alan – I don't want you to—!'

'No, Susie, I'm sure you don't. But to be honest with you, my angel, I don't really feel I can be *orchestrated* any more. I've just about had it, frankly. And Black – he's quite in the

173

dark, you only have to look at him, poor old sod. No offence, Black.'

'No no – none, um . . .'

'Taken, right. You're a good man. I truly think you are, Black, from what I've seen of you. But here's the big question. Be quiet, Susan: I'm talking. This is the sixty-four-whatsit question, Black. Ready? OK, then: Is You Is, Or Is You Ain't? Or, to put it another way: are you going to – don't laugh – *marry* this woman? To have and to hold. For richer or for richer – oh yes, oh yes, do please make no mistake on *that* score. And is it to be from this day forward? Speak now, or forever hold your thing.'

Black glanced over to Susan, whose face was in all sorts of turmoil, uncertain as to what expression she should even be striving for. The gleam of a collaborator shone from the eye she trained full upon him, while the arch of the brows was an attempt at apology and her own exasperation, while her lips were tugged up into encouragement, the allaying of fears with regard to the very nub of the thing. To Black's eyes, the cumulative impression was that of one who suffered from the colic, if not acute dyspepsia – conditions, alas, that were all too familiar to him.

'I hardly think . . .' he said quite slowly. And then he drank more wine. 'I hardly think, Alan – much as I realise that you were invited here in common with myself, and that your history with Susie is a long one . . . child, and everything . . . I still can hardly think that whether or not I intend to, ah – make Susie my wife is a question for the ex-husband to be posing.'

Alan now raised his arms way above his head and clapped together the palms of his hands. The eyes in his head were dancing, the colours splintered into a dazzle of delight.

'Oh and at last! At last we arrive at the *point*.'

'Alan – I warn you—!'

'No no, Susan. No warnings. It's all out in the open now. How else could it be? What you intended, surely? What you meant to happen tonight . . . ?'

'Not like *this* . . . !'

'No well. This nonetheless is how it is, it would appear. Sorry, Black, sorry to natter on and backbite like an old married couple, which indeed we are – especially over the dinner table, and particularly when the veins are awash with booze, no matter how refined. But the truth of the matter is this: I was not, as you so reasonably assume, *invited* here, no no. To have prevented me would have entailed the packing of me off to have a pizza with Amanda – and I am not saying that had the alternative presented itself, I should not have embraced it with glee as a consummation devoutly to be whatever it is. Because you see, Black – I *live* here. Yes yes. And the reason I live here – wait, Susan, just wait – is because I am *still* the husband. See? Not ex. No no. But still, in name anyway, the real and living thing. Although Susan, our Susie, she might well have something to say on that score, I dare say. Ah yes – here she is now, look. Eager to speak. I know the signs. Shouting through me, for one.'

'Look, Black – just don't listen to him. It's just Alan being bloody *Alan*, which you would know if you knew him. Always like this. Look – have some more wine, yes? Let's eat, shall we? Getting cold. Now, Black – tell me what I can get you. A few more noodles, maybe. God's sake, Alan – *must* you eat your ribs like that? It's just so *Neanderthal*. Well, Black – noodles? Yes?'

'No thank you, Susie. I seem to be all right on the noodle front, actually. But look, um . . . tell me, Susie . . .'

Susan was slightly wild now – on her feet and noisily stacking up bowls and plates, crashing the one into the other.

'Well all right, then – if nobody wants any more food, why don't we take our glasses next door and then we can all—'

'Susie. Listen to me. What Alan was saying—'

Susan's throat was tight, her voice now shrill, and the words spattered out of her, rising in pitch and becoming faster and faster.

'No? You don't want to? Take your glasses next door? Well all right then – you do what you want, the two of you. All right? Sound fair? I'm going to clear away. Wash up. Someone has to. And of course it's going to be me because I'm just the *woman*, aren't I? Yes yes of course. Well look you two – go next door, don't go next door, I really just don't care, all right? I really just don't – *care* . . . !'

And when she simply dropped down into her chair and let her face fall into her hands as she started to sob, and really quite chokingly, Black's immediate reaction was to get up and go to her, but of course for an assortment of the usual awful reasons he could barely even move – and when Alan put a finger to his lips and narrowed his eyes, indicating to Black with the jerk of a thumb that now, believe him, was the time to leave her, he put everything he had into this God-help-me effort to end all bloody efforts – staggered to his feet, clutched his stomach, grabbed at the table, lurched away then, scratching at his face. Because if Alan was leaving, then Black was going too: didn't want to be left alone with her, did he? State she was in. Women, when they start all this . . . well, don't have to tell you. Gets messy, very.

'Sticking with the wine, are you Black? Maybe you'd like to

sit in the easy chair there – not quite so low slung as the sofa. Forgive my asking, but um – are you in pain at all?'

Black sighed as he eased himself down with gratitude and a considerable relief into the buttoned wing armchair by the mantelpiece.

'Usually. Yes – pretty much all the time, I'd say. Well – *pain* is maybe going it a bit, but it's fair to say that discomfort is always with me. My loyal companion. Various reasons. Too dull to pursue, believe me. And the threat, you know – skulking. The possibility of worse to come. The claret was prime, I must say Alan. Although some more of that malt would also be good. Quite hit the spot. Do you know what, though? I just can't be bothered to decide. All right if I smoke?'

'I know exactly what you mean. It starts off, doesn't it, with a sort of a whim, a fancy – and then you feel you maybe ought to urge it on to become a preference, if not an honest to goodness vital necessity. But after a bit, well . . . who cares, quite frankly? Anything will do. Won't it really? Anything will do.'

Black dragged hard on his Rothman and simply nodded; there didn't seem to be anything at all he could profitably add to all that. Alan, in his judgement, had just articulated rather well that quivering butterfly of incipient depression, and then the fathomless trough of apathy into which he these days quite frequently could tumble.

'It's why, you know, I'm giving up my business. You know I've got this little publishing house . . . ? Oh God – what am I saying? Of course you know, of course you do: where Susie works, isn't it? What am I thinking of. Anyway, um . . . what was I saying? Oh damn. This happens to me more and more, you know. I'd worry about it, if I could be bothered. But I start off talking about a thing, you know, and then there's some sort of quite minor digression along the way – and then poof! Gone. Haven't got a clue.'

Alan was strewn across the sofa. He had given Black a very large whisky and had set his own down on the table beside him. Now he was comfortably lighting a Cohiba.

'Know exactly what you mean,' he said, in between a short series of reflective puffs. 'You're not the only one, believe me. Happens to me all the time. Well now let's think back. That sometimes does the trick. Susan works for you, you were saying . . . you can't be bothered to choose things any more – or worry about things, was it . . . ?'

'Oh yes – well done. Got it now. Yes – it's work. When I'm at work. It's quite a well-oiled little place, really. Key people I've got – pretty reliable. But they will keep asking me to make decisions. Well Black, they say – you're the boss, the final say, it rests with you. Well in the early days, of course – can't tell you what sort of a kick it used to give me. But now – oh bugger. Just don't *want* to, you see. Make a decision. Half the time I don't even know what I'm supposed to be deciding about. And small publishers, you know – if you have a decent turnover, steady profit, the big boys, they're forever hovering. We've got a good list. Perennials. Few big names, one or two anyway. And lately I just thought oh sod it – let's put out a few feelers. See how interested they are, or if it's all just talk. Well I've already had a couple of quite remarkable offers, you know. Quite amazed by the money involved. HarperCollins – have you heard of? Murdoch set-up. They're interested. Random House – that's another one. So I'm pretty committed to chucking it all in. But Alan – you must forgive me. I can't imagine why I'm boring you with all of this. When I suppose, um . . . that we really ought to be talking of other things, should we . . . ?'

'Only if you want to. I mean – we've had a great deal to drink, I'm very pleased to say . . . and there's plenty more where that came from. So in a sense, now would be the optimum time for talk. We shan't be quite so careful in what we say. And if something dreadful emerges, well – there's a very good chance that neither of us will remember it in the morning.'

And Black was laughing through his pull of whisky – spluttered a bit, cigarette ash all over his waistcoat.

'Take your point. But tell me, Alan . . . Susie. Susan, if you prefer. What, um – is she up to, as it were? I'm rather confused. Are you getting a divorce . . . ? That it?'

'Apparently not. You would have thought it was on the cards. I mean you can see that she more or less despises me, but still I am not for the scrap heap. All this, you see, it's because I'm so utterly useless and penniless and all the rest of it – no job, you know. It's you Black, really, who's paid for all this booze. Without what you give to Susan, we'd be finished, quite frankly. Anyway – she one day says to me, Susan, that she wants another husband. But not, she said, *instead* of, no no – but as *well* as. See? Well I know. Insane. And yet she doesn't seem to be, I have to say. Another man, well – he just would have walked. This man, however – he didn't. And note the word "husband". She doesn't just want a careless fling with some rich young toyboy . . .'

'Evidently not . . .' Black barely murmured.

'Well quite. No offence, Black, but you're hardly that, I think we can both agree. I find it quite refreshing, actually, that it is you she has alighted upon. Quite restores my faith in her, really. I mean – at least you've got character. And money, of course. Does she know about it? This takeover business?'

'No. Oh no. I've told no one. Just you, rather oddly.'

'Mm. Well – something of a bonus for her, then. Assuming you're even vaguely contemplating any of this nonsense. But do know, Black, that she wants to marry you in the eyes of God. Mad, I know. Not as if she even goes to church . . .'

'In the eyes of who . . . ?'

'God. Old man. Beard. Whose eyes did you imagine?'

'Sorry. It's my ear thing. Might need recharging.'

'Talking of which – let's have another drink, shall we? Sometimes, it's the only thing to do. You're an Aries, of course. That featured strongly in her thinking, apparently.'

'I'm a what . . . ? Oh Jesus, you know – I need to go to the lavatory again. Wish I had a portable potty, sometimes . . .'

'Aries,' said Alan, and smiled. 'The Ram. This is commensurate, is what she said. I'm Pisces, you see. After all that fish, she needed a ram. Is all I can think.'

'You don't believe in all this star stuff, do you Alan?'

'I'd need convincing. In my view, if we woke up one morning and discovered in the papers that the previous day all the people in the world who had been born under the sign of Sagittarius had been hit by a milk truck – that might go a good way in furthering its cause . . .'

'God I've had a lot to drink . . . You really are a highly amusing fellow, Alan. If I may say so.'

'You may, Black. Indeed you may. Certainly I can't remember the last person who did.'

'And that thing you said earlier – about you being a bit of a "drinkard". I did like that. Awfully good, I thought. Remember that. Drinkard. Love it. Um . . . do you think . . . do you think she's all right in there? Susie? Seems awfully quiet . . .'

'Oh she'll be fine. It's probably all a part of her master plan, this. The two of us, alone and half cut, chewing the cud. Believe me, if she wanted to be a part of it, she'd be in here. Conducting.'

'So . . . what do you think we . . . how do you think we ought to, um – go about this? All of this.'

'Well it's largely in your court, you know. Ball, far as I can see. Just let me top you up – there we are. Don't worry – got another bottle. I should've offered you a cigar – didn't think.'

'No no – wasted on me. I just like sucking down all this filthy tar. Don't care for nuance. Like the smell of them, though. Cigars.'

'Really? What – do you mean you *really* do? Like it? Smell?'

'Oh God yes. Absolutely. The odour of, well – not sanctity exactly, although there is that sort of incense overtone to it, isn't there? Civilisation though, certainly. The aroma of civilisation.'

'Mm,' grunted Alan. 'But what I mean to say is, Black – it all, all of this . . . it all rather depends upon your, um – *situation*. Doesn't it really? Your set-up. And, of course, your inclination. I'm rather praying you don't have a *wife*. I mean, Jesus – there is a limit.'

'Ha! No. No I don't have a wife. Did once. Madwoman, basically. I mean – I don't mean mad in the mild and largely acceptable way that all women are mad, no no. I mean out-and-out psychotic. Murderous. Two children, grown up. Tim. He's thirtyish. Loathes me. Quite nice wife, can't remember her name at the moment. Little boy they've got. Adam. I've a daughter too – much older than your Angela, though. Anita.

Amanda, I mean – damn, my mind. Yes – she's twenty-four, pretty sure. Footloose and fancy, um . . . she is. Lucky little bitch. Free. Footloose and fancy, um . . . Yes.'

'Why do you think he loathes you, your son?'

'Mm? Oh I don't *think* it – I know it. And I don't altogether blame him. I was no sort of a father, really. His mother, she used to beat him black and blue – had these mood swings that would leave you reeling. Mocked him in everything he attempted . . . ended up devoted to her. There it is. Blamed me for her condition. Well, I didn't fight it. You can't really, can you? And ultimately, well . . . what's the point, exactly? No point, is there? Not really.'

'Do you ever see them? Your family?'

'Well we have this rather splendid tradition at Christmas, you know. Unfailing. Happens every year. I ask Tim and his wife – can't remember her name at the moment – and the little lad Adam to a smart hotel for Christmas Day. Millie too – that's my daughter. Along with whatever loser and deadbeat she's currently fucking. And then I book it all and pay for every little detail and extra in advance and get my secretary to sort out all the present side of things – and then on Christmas Eve, usually around midday, always make sure I'm in – they all phone up to cancel. Tradition, you see. Unfailing. And then I end up taking along some woman or other instead.'

Alan nodded. 'Like women, do you Black?'

'Don't we all? No I do, I do – one of my failings. Or at least it used to be, anyway. There's a lot about me that used to be. The trouble is . . . I hope I can be frank? I don't on the whole tend to go for the women who appear to go for me.'

'Old, you mean. Oldish, anyway.'

'In a nutshell. I mean I can well understand the attraction of a confident and mature woman, of course I can. They're wise, amusing, know how to dress . . . it's just that they're not, ah – how can I say . . . ?'

'Fuckish.'

Black just looked at him.

'Puckish, did you say . . . ?'

Alan shook his head.

'Fuckish. They're just not fuckish. They're perfectly attractive and groomed – yes yes, I know all that. But it's all too studied. And you know that half of what you're seeing is not what you're going to get. Underneath that veneer of effortless sophistication, we have a very great deal of effort indeed. Opaque slimming pants. Once encountered, never forgotten. Support tights. Dear oh dear. Padded bra. With uplift. Great big scarf artfully knotted to cover up the crepey cleavage. Wig, in some cases.'

'All sounds a bit like me . . .'

'Christ, you say that – if you could be bothered to peel away all of the layers, though, I wouldn't be at all surprised to discover that half of them *are* men. All that "beauty is only skin deep" – it's rubbish. Junk.'

Black shuddered. 'Hate that phrase. Makes me think of all the gore underneath. But I *think* I see . . .'

'You do – you do see. And after dinner, or whatever – you're a bit tired, you're a bit drunk, they invariably live on the other side of London, or worse . . . and there's no – compulsion. That's the point, really. They're just not fuckish. Not like the young ones – the ones that just never even glance at the likes of us, Black. The slim and tousle-haired, long-legged dreams – the sort of girl who has slung on a T-shirt and some jeans and you'd sell your soul and lifeblood just to tear them off her.

That's fuckish. When you'd sell your soul and lifeblood. Yeh. And sell it cheap, as well.'

Black was leaning forward eagerly.

'You know I think you're on to something there. What it is really, you know – is our consistency. When we were young, schoolboys onwards, what we yearned for and swooned over were sexy young girls. Our age, more or less. Right? Right. And over the years, well . . . we see no reason to change our minds. Our tastes remain the same. We are consistent in all of our desires. Sexually speaking, young women are nicer than old ones. Often less nasty too – not the same thing. Isn't difficult to understand, surely. And yet they make you out to be some sort of a, I don't know – pervert, or something. It's just that we like them . . .'

'Fuckish.'

'Yes!' laughed Black. 'That's it! That's it! We are just a pair of old drinkards, who like them fuckish! How perfectly splendid.'

'Well!' called Susan brightly from the doorway. 'And what have you two boys been gassing about? Sorry I was just so . . . And I'm sorry I've been so long. There was quite a lot to see to. Everyone got drinks? God what a *stink* . . . ! Someone's got on one of his perfectly foul cigars.'

Alan was puffing out an ostentatious plume.

'The general consensus of the world is that the very finest handmade cigars emanate from Havana, which is in Cuba, Susan – and that amongst this rare elite, the Cohiba reigns supreme. The undisputed *capo di tutti capi*, as it were. Or, as Susan will have it, "perfectly foul". Take your pick.'

'Another little speech from Alan. Well done Alan. I'm not sure they actually speak Italian in Havana, you know – but there: let it pass, shall we? So, gentlemen – what *were* you talking about?'

Alan softly patted her hand.

'Marrying *you* . . .' he cooed, his smile implying derangement.

'Oh really? Oh good. Is that true, Black? And what have you decided?'

'Well . . .' said Black, shifting in his chair and making to rise. 'Well . . . in the short term, Susie, just that I have to go to the lavatory again. Sorry. Thing of mine.'

'Don't you worry, Blackie old man,' Alan cheerily assured him. 'It's a thing of mine too. Quite common all round, you know, if you care to look into it.'

'Why now,' Susan wanted to know, 'have you taken to calling him *Blackie* . . . ?'

'Don't know, matter of fact. Just came out. You don't mind, do you Blackie?'

'Hardly in a position to, am I?' Black said casually, edging with care across the carpet . . . because I really do need to go now, no bones about it – and Lord, just look at the floor, will you? Pattern on the rug. Zooming in and out at me. Hell of a lot to drink. Still. Case of whatever gets you through the, um . . . 'Do you know, there used to be three girls in the office. At work. These three girls. With names I've never forgotten. Miracle in itself. Luella, Madeleine and Nutella. Used to call them Looney, Maddy and Nuts. Didn't seem to mind . . .'

'Oh Black she *can't* have been . . .' laughed Susan.

'Can't have been? Was, I tell you. Who? What do you mean – can't have been . . . ?'

'The girl. She can't have been called . . . *Nutella.*'

'That was her name, I swear it. Got to, um – go now, Susie.'

'But Black . . . *Nutella*, it's a kind of a . . . *spread*, isn't it?'

'Spread? What's a spread? Not with you. Anyway – got to go now, Susie.'

'It's a chocolate *spread*, Nutella . . .'

'Really? Well I'm damned. Well what did they want to go calling her that for? Some parents, I don't know. Do the oddest thing. Knew a chap once. Oenophile. Great connoisseur. Called his first son Pétrus. I ask you. Back soon. Got to go.'

'Might have been worse,' Alan called after him. 'Could've gone for Second Wine Of La Lagune. Pétrus – not so bad. People will call him Pete, I expect. Or Pet, conceivably. That's not too good . . .'

'Do you have any idea who you are *talking* to, Alan? He's gone, Black. He's left the room. And *I'm* not listening to your pitiful ramblings. *I'm* not listening to you, Alan. Are you *really* pouring yourself another whisky? You don't think you might have had enough?'

'It would surely seem not,' smiled Alan, adding a glug extra and screwing back the cap. 'Else I'd hardly be doing it, would I? So tell me, Susan. Susie. How's it going, would you say? Hm? How's it shaping up? Your little scheme. Or is it a grand scenario? I'm assuming you *do* know what's going on here, do you? That you are aware? Keeping a tight rein on things? Overlooking and tweaking the general shift and drift, are you? Fine-tuning at will? Because nobody else, I do assure you – by which I mean Blackie and myself – has the merest clue. We're just drinking and smoking and chatting, and occasionally the sheer and transparent lunacy of the situation will come to spear or slash at one or other of us. Or possibly we will be struck by the comical element: I hesitate to use the word farce. Bit like the Mormons, isn't it? Except the other way round. Typical. A Mormon, he gets another young and pretty wife.

Me – I'm to be saddled with a pensionable husband. Oh well – if you get what *you* want, I suppose it will all be worth the effort. Do you think you're going to, Susan? Get what you want? Looking good, is it?'

Susan shook her head briefly.

'It's not, Alan, what I *want*. No it isn't. That's where you're wrong. It is how I am prepared to deal with my need. My need, yes – material largely, I freely admit; I am, as you know, a sensualist with certain cravings. And of course to compensate for your truly staggering and boundless inadequacies. I should have thought that was clear.'

'Should you? Yes, I truly do believe that you should. Have thought that. My . . . what was it . . . ? Oh yes: got it. My "truly staggering and boundless inadequacies". Very good. That's a peach. That's a keeper, Susan, that is, even by your appalling standards. I'll use that one next time I'm being cured of all cares by the genial Doctor Atherby. He'll love it. Bring a smile to his little cheeks. Make his day.'

'Are you drunk, Alan? By any chance?'

'Oh God I do hope so. Numb, anyway. Which is nearly as good. Hope old Blackie's all right. Been a while, hasn't he? Maybe he's having a well-earned forty winks. Possibly he's through the window and doing a runner. Break for freedom. Hardly blame him. Don't know, though . . . windows and running . . . not quite his style.'

Susan sighed, and then she smiled.

'You like him, don't you Alan?'

'Oh I expect so. Nice enough chap. Very nice, actually. A whole lot nicer than *you* anyway, Susan – but then let's not be coy: most people are. Got to be faced.'

Susan then actually did scream – jumped up in alarm as the

crumpled boom and then tinkle of a nearby catastrophe was
driven over and into the two of them – just standing there
now, fingers rigid or uselessly limp, their flicked-over eyes
very briefly fusing, lighting up on contact into the frightened
dazzle of fractured suspicion (the dying of hope for the merest
reassurance) before Susan gasped and just ran into the hall,
so completely amazed by the sight of the splintered jamb
and broken glass, the unsettling angle of the hanging front
door – and she whimpered as it grated and was now cranked
open and Amanda spun wildly into the hallway, grog-eyed
and exultant, though seemingly astonished to be finding
herself there. Susan – quite breathless – stumbled towards
her, aware of dishevelment and the hardened blood on
Amanda's neck. As Susan howled for Alan, Amanda dropped
the bottle she had forgotten she was holding – laughed and
half choked, closed her eyes and was fussily beating off from
her the frantic attentions of Susan, her boneless hands quite
suddenly exhausted and now just drunkenly swatting at the
air. Alan said Blu-Dee-*Hell* – was sighing with wonder as he
reached and touched with tentative fingers the dented wing
and stove-in shattered headlamp of, Christ – the fucking *car*,
for Christ's sake – the fucking car's sticking into the fucking
hall . . . !

'Amanda . . . !' Susan tried to scream it, but it came as a
cracked and broken, horrified whisper. Her skittering hands
had hovered and fluttered around and over all of Amanda's
white and soft and tender parts, and now just relented
and attempted an embrace – but were being rudely pushed
and slapped aside by a now quite malignant young woman,
scowling and eyeing her like a targeted animal, on guard,
grudging, and sensing a trap.

'Amanda . . . ! You're – *bleeding* . . . ! Alan – where are you? Come and . . . ! Oh my God, Amanda – what have you—?! You're *bleeding* . . . !'

Amanda chortled and rolled up her eyes, Susan now lurching forward to catch her as her knees just buckled and she stumbled on forward into her arms.

'Not *bleeding* . . . Oh well yeh I *am* bleeding, yeh I am – but I'm not like *injured*. Car crash didn't hurt me.'

She reeled about and nearly fell, Susan's arm now waggling frantically at a seemingly paralysed Alan, still just marvelling at the smashed and ugly juxtaposition of car and front door, a little light drizzle from the black of outside moist and cold on his eyelids. And just staring at it all, he backed away and his arms were vaguely involved in helping Susan to support Amanda whose own arms now were flailing about her head as if in time to an awful tune, her eyes so stark and wide, blazing with the light of triumph, swollen by the surge of victory, all aglow, mad and wicked.

'I took the *car* . . . !' she giggled – thrilled, though hardly daring to clutch at the truth of it.

'Alan,' snapped a now much less agitated Susan, perceiving as usual and quickly her need to take control. 'Alan – help me upstairs with her. She's drunk, I'm pretty sure. I hope she's just drunk, anyway. Oh God. Here – get her, can you? Yes – get her under the arms, and I'll . . . Amanda? Are you hearing me? We're going upstairs now, yes? Get you to bed. Got her, Alan? Yes? Come on then. Now, Amanda – first step, OK? Where are you hurt? Do you know where you're hurt, Amanda? Oh God's sake take some *weight*, can't you Alan? You're just worse than useless. Oh my God it's your *ear* – it's your ear, Amanda! How on earth did you—? Now come along – two, three more steps and we're there. *Lift*, Alan – lift, Christ's sake. *Wrong* with you at all . . . ?'

All of them stumbled up the last few stairs and on to the landing, Amanda now sagging, though still just about slung between the two of them.

'Not *ear* . . . !' she laughed – near-dementedly, it sounded to Susan. '*Ears*! Two ears. Both my. Both ears. *Pierced*, you see? Not hurt, not injured. *Pierced* . . . !'

'What are you . . . ? Oh my God, Alan – she's had her ears—!'

'So? You've got pierced ears,' said Alan, flatly – trying then to shrug away the glare she threw over, with all of its viciousness.

'Are you a *fool*, Alan? Are you? Are you a complete and utter *imbecile*? Look at us, can't you? The position of the three of us. What on earth did you go and say that for? What relevance can it possibly—?'

'Just stating a fact. That's all. Are we going to get her into her room or not? Because I'm pretty tired actually, now.'

Susan just let go of Amanda, which took Alan severely by surprise as he and she were swaying and then lurched over heavily, just about and eventually retaining a sort of balance as Alan reached out and grabbed for the banister rail. Susan continued to stare at him. Her eyes were large and hard in a way he knew well, her lips so very unyielding and drawn back stiffly as she began to slowly and with deliberation spit out the words, and into his face:

'You. Are. *Tired* . . . ? Did I hear you correctly? Is that what you said to me, Alan? That you are – *tired*?'

Alan sighed, and looked away.

'Just stating a fact. That's all. So are we? Going to get her into her room? I wish you'd take her arm. Hell of a weight.

Look at her, Susan – she's, look . . . dribbling a bit. Quite a lot. Seems a bit crazy. Doctor, do you think?'

'She's not crazy, Alan – she's drunk. Just as you are not – *tired*, as you put it. You too, Alan, are drunk. I find myself in a situation where my only child has apparently driven our car into the front door of our house, having drunk a bottle of . . . I didn't see what the bottle was, what she was waving about – not Coca-Cola, I think we can assume. She is bleeding from a rogue piercing and—! Oh my God. Oh no. Look, Alan – *look*!'

Alan was caught by this new and more serious tone – much less oratorical and declamatory, so maybe then worthy of a bit of attention. His eyes did their honest and well-meaning best to follow the quivering thrum of Susan's appalled and rigid finger (because Christ, she was quite right, of course – he was, wasn't he? Drunk, very) and now they more or less focused upon a mess of indigo, a smudge of plum, livid and glowing on Amanda's forearm.

'Christ . . .' he murmured. 'Is that a . . . ?'

'Yes, Alan. Mm. It is, yes. A tattoo. Amanda now is scarred for life. Excellent. Very good. Couldn't be better. On top of all the rest.'

'Tatt-*oooo* . . .' slurred Amanda, sliding into unconsciousness, and out of Alan's wilted grasp.

'Let's just get her into her room, can't we Susan? I can't hold her any more. We'll just have to sort it all in the morning.'

Susan remained silent until – half dragging, half lifting – they finally could let Amanda fall down into her bed, where she bobbed around for a second or so, her arms flopped out over the counterpane, dead at the elbow. And then Susan remained silent no longer.

'That's what will happen, is it Alan? I see. Come the

morning – the fresh and rising dawn – we will sort it all. *We*. That would be you and I then, would it Alan? The two of us – sorting it all.'

Alan exhaled, and turned to go. 'Christ, Susan . . .'

She wheeled around – grabbed him roughly by the shoulder and spun him back to face her. Her cheeks were white, and Alan saw there small and pulsating patches of just that second the deepest rose, shading into crimson, lightening up into the nearest to pastel before shading back down into vivid again.

'Never mind – *Christ*. Christ, Alan, believe me, has nothing whatever to do with this. Or if He does, then He should hang His head in abject shame. What we have here is a case of a child who has, in rather spectacular manner, quite as she intended, run off the rails. And *we* are not going to sort it all, no we are not. Because *we* – *we* don't sort anything, do we Alan? And nor have we – for years and years and years. *I*, Alan – *I* will sort it, along with just everything else, you stupid, dumb, ineffectual little—!'

'Wait!'

Susan was caught by the suddenness, and then by the insistence when he said it again.

'*Wait!*'

Alan's eyes were now dulled by fury. He was amazed to be roused by the thud of anger low in his stomach, an anger that seethed and had rapidly bubbled – up now to boiling. Susan was startled, though she gamely opened her mouth to retort – not enough time though, because Alan now was stabbing at the centre of her face a hateful throbbing finger as his voice started in at a rumble, as low as distant thunder.

'I know you call me stupid, Susan – but you cannot believe it. You truly cannot believe that I or anyone else could honestly be so very very stupid as to meekly accept the blame for this one. No no – not this one, Susan. Because that is what you are trying to do – and in the way you always do it. Beyond belief. You assume control, what you imagine to be control – you do this under the guise of *having* to, because no assistance or even intelligence is ever forthcoming. But you take it, Susan, you take it – you seize control before an issue can even be considered, before any help can even be offered. Because you *have* to have control – it gives you a reason to dismiss me: this time, next time – and historically then, and for ever. And because I am seen to be not dealing with the problem – *quiet*, Susan, don't utter, don't speak, just don't even . . . don't say a damn fucking thing, OK? Right. So – because I am seen to be not *dealing* with the problem, and you of course *are*, you make it appear that therefore I am the *cause* of the . . . problem, the omission, the sin, the slight, the disaster, whatever real or mythical incompetence or crime I am most recently perceived to have committed. Within the narrow of your eyes. And sometimes – maybe even often – I am, of course. The cause. I grant that. On other occasions, I know, I just *know* that this is very far from being the case – but if it is trivial, as, Susan, so many of these frankly hysterical crises of yours so frequently are, then of course I just sit back and let you get on with it. Why not? It's quicker. It's quieter. You can revel in your fat-mouthed smugness. *No*, Susan – not a word: I won't hear a word from you until I'm finished with this, all right? And not even then, because then I'm going to bed – I'm tired, I've had it. Why shouldn't I be tired? Why shouldn't I? Even when I say I'm tired, you round upon me as if I am a brainless villain, an unthinking vandal. But this one, Susan – oh no. Oh no. Tomorrow, you can deal or not deal with it, I just don't frankly care. But *never* . . . *never* try to tell me that Amanda, our child, my little girl, has seemingly taken leave of all her reason because of something *I* have done. This I will not have. You may have forgotten, Susan – I don't know, in your twisted and selfish little mind, you may have found it convenient to let slip from your memory that you have told Amanda that she is soon to have not one but *two* daddies, yes? And that this will be . . . *nice*. Well evidently she doesn't think so, you see? It would appear to me as if she is making some sort of a protest, no? In as touching and sincere and clumsy and heart-rending a way as only an immature child could possibly consider. I can barely stand to look at her, the way she is tonight. This, Susan, make no mistake, is *your* doing. Oh yes. This is so wholly down to *you*, my dear and horrible Susan, that I really think you had best sort it out. And soon. And soon. I leave you now. I'm tired. Goodnight.'

Susan just gazed at him amongst the shadows as he turned to go, her eyes struck wide and mouth fallen open into a box, as if she had been slapped and slapped again, still fearing that this might be far from the end of it. And then she revolved immediately – sat down close to Amanda on the side of her bed. Enough. She could not – would not – squander a single second on even attempting to decipher the rant and ramblings of a madman: men were nothing when set against children, and she had her own child here to attend to. Who now, mercifully, seems to be asleep. All the stubborn fury, the ugliness, gone from her now. Smeared lipstick, which I hadn't before noticed . . . and on her closed and gentle lids a bruising of that awful and ancient kingfisher eyeshadow that I haven't used or thought of in simply centuries: where on earth did she find it? Well. Get some disinfectant. Clean her up. But first I just must ease off this jacket of hers – far too light and flimsy for a night such as this, what could she have been thinking of, might have caught her death . . . and of course I must rifle the pockets: three pounds, a few other coins, a roll of Polo, phone . . . and no I won't let my pain and disappointment remuster and choke me as I pick out and lay aside this battered little packet of ten Silk Cut . . . I shall just note it, and add it to the heap, add it to the heap . . . (And how could he, Alan? How could he say it, that I am twisted and selfish? I am a sensualist, is all I am – one who simply feels things. What I do – I do it out of love.)

Susan started as Amanda's head rolled over and lolled to one side as she began to speak – that soft and enticing tone, distant and dreamlike, that Susan well remembered from so many dank and fevered infant nights, and being in here, cooling and soothing her.

'What is it, Mummy . . . ? What you said? A *rogue* piercing . . . what is that . . . ?'

'Nothing, Amanda. It's nothing. Go to sleep.'

'I think I know . . . *I* am the rogue. I am, Mummy. Because I did it myself, you know. I did. All on my own.'

'You—?'

'Mm. With a drawing pin. And because you're my mummy, I think you ought to know something else as well . . . Oh God, I'm just so *tired* . . .'

'Sleep, Amanda. Just sleep. Know what . . . ? What should I know?'

'Oh . . . nothing. Just that I'm not a virgin any more. Goodnight, Mummy.'

Susan's hand flew up to her mouth and attempted to stem the trembling there. She felt the hot swell of tears expanding her eyes, making them bulbous and sting. She willed herself to be still, to remain so utterly still, until she was sure that Amanda was asleep. Only then she unclenched her shoulders – and as she blinked, the fat warm tear rolled over and away, and then another, and now her face was creased up and sticky with the streaming down of more and more. She felt them, the tears, as they hit her fingers, which were insistently caressing Amanda's arm. And beneath them, her kneading fingertips, the tattoo was pale and blurred and began to run. The pad of Susan's thumb gently rubbed away the remaining inky vestiges of this loathsome little transfer, so very crudely applied. Susan nearly laughed. It was pretend. Only pretend. Maybe like everything else. Just Amanda being silly. And then Susan's throat was caught as she fell with a wail on to the neck of her child, her chest now pumping and racked by convulsions, and quite careless of waking her own sweet baby she held on to her head and kissed at her eyes in desperation as she coped with her rasped-out exhaustion – and even when she was sure she could no longer breathe, she had to continue to sob.

And I had – meant to, I mean. When I said to her, I'm tired, I've had it, I'm just going to bed, that's exactly what I'd intended to do. Why not? Let her wallow in the murk of her own disaster: wash my hands of it. But when I left her – and I didn't storm, I didn't stamp (no door was going to be slammed by me, on that I was determined) – I was almost skipping: had felt so very oddly, um – buoyed up and overjoyed, you might say. High and electric-eyed – like I'd been shot with the whoosh of a full syringe of something toxic and very thrilling that lit me up and made me ripple. Not often I square up to her, just let her have it – can't remember the last time I could even have

196

mustered the energy, let alone the cold raw steel of daring it would have cost me. But this time I was nerveless – just let her have it. The accumulation of just how much resentment had billowed right up in me and taken me over – God, I felt, was on my side; yeah, justice was mine in the eyes of the Lord . . . and I just let her have it.

So still my heels were tripping and lifted by the kick of all that – and only when I was back downstairs could I openly marvel at my very madness, confront the white-out of incredulity in the face of my own and almost magnificent forgetfulness. For there, as if tentatively seeking admission, was the scarred and apologetic snout of my own fucking car sticking its way into my own fucking hallway – splinters of paintwork, a crumble of glass, to say nothing of the house itself so very thoroughly open, not to say breezy, and available to anyone who had simply thought to ease open a little wider the drunken door and have a shufti. And it says absolutely everything about the insular and quite blind exclusivity of the area, you know, the fact that as far as I am aware, no one had. No one, apparently, had heard or seen the collision – no passer-by thought it odd that a car should be seeking entry into a house, the ears of not a soul were assaulted by all of the wretchedness that followed. There is a case for presuming, of course, that there is actually nobody in this street at present (what with it being a weekend, when a good deal of Chelsea invades the Cotswolds), but once one might at least have expected the cold white shaft of a torch-led and flickered investigation by a sole and uncertain probing policeman, in the far-off days of such dim-remembered and fairy tale quaintness. But no – nothing, apparently. I very much hope. And so what, in fact, to do . . . ? And only then I heard it . . . a muffled sort of bump – not my imagination – and coming from somewhere . . . and at once I was alert and frightened close to death: so there *is* an intruder, a thief, a looter, a masked and demonic axeman – on the prowl and bent on blood. If only I had a gun – if only it wasn't illegal to purposefully slay a black-hearted burglar when so joyous an opportunity was spread before you . . . because then I could quickly nip up and get my piece and shoot the scoundrel dead (I think, you know, I'm still a little drunk). The sort of thump, I heard it again . . . and yes I know, it's extraordinary, it's barely believable even from me: just how thick-skulled can one man be? For clutching a table lamp, I had nosily traced it, the crump, the shifting and ferrety noise, to the lavatory door – behind which, yes, oh dear dear me, was still, it would very much seem, my new chum Blackie.

'Blackie, old man. You all right in there?'

Something stirred, Alan could have sworn it.

'Hear me? OK, are you? Coming out at all? What do you think?'

'What . . . ? That you, Alan? Thank God, Can't really hear . . .'

'No well – tell you what: you come out then, Blackie. All right? Then we can talk to one another.'

'What . . . ?'

'Look, Blackie – you see just next to the doorknob thing? The door, yes Blackie? In front of your face. Big white bugger. Got it? Well now right next to the handle thing, OK, there's another sort of thing, sort of snib thing – lock affair. Just turn it to your right . . . no hang on, other way round – left, I think. Yeh, left. Confusing when you're not actually in there . . . anyway Blackie – just turn the thing, all right? And then I'll open the door. OK? Got that? Yes? Hall*ooo* . . . ?'

'What . . . ?'

Alan wagged his head in a sort of careless despair (because enough is enough, quite frankly, and the rush I had earlier, well that's just long gone, and I'm really bloody tired now, tell you the truth). And in the face of really nothing better to do at that precise instant, he waggled the handle – was surprised and pleased when the door swung open.

'Wasn't locked, Blackie . . .'

Blackie was standing – he smoothed the palm of his hand the length of his waistcoat which had taken him, he estimated, all of ten minutes this time (could easily have been more, age I've been stuck in here) to button bloody up – and still one of them, you know, had pinged right off, still around here somewhere, damned if I'm going to crouch down again to look for the little fucker – last time nearly occasioned a hernia.

'Ah yes – wasn't *locked*,' agreed Black. 'Of course, of course. That's what threw me, you see.'

'Mm. Sorry about all the noise and chaos tonight. Not always like this, I assure you. Thought you weren't coming out on purpose. Could hardly have blamed you . . .'

'You'll have to speak a little bit louder, I'm afraid Alan – this ear thing, practically gone. Useless little bloody piece of junk . . .'

'Right-o. Now listen, Black – I truly do think that a nightcap is in order, but first – do you think you could do me the most tremendous favour and help me push the car back out and on to the drive? Then I think we just might be able to jam the door shut and, well – attend to all the rest of it in the morning, hey?'

'Good *Lord* . . .' said Black, frankly amazed by what he was seeing. 'Alan – there's a *car* rammed into your door . . . !'

Alan turned to face it, and his eyes cranked up into enormous.

'Christ Blackie – you're *right*! Well God Almighty – who can have left that there? How very untidy.'

'Want some help? Getting it back on to the drive?'

'Inspired idea, Blackie. I said inspired IDEA, Blackie! Can you HEAR me? Yes?'

Black looked pained, as he narrowed his eyes and touched his lobe.

'Now I can . . .' he said quite quietly.

Alan tried slipping into the driving seat (and Christ it's freezing tonight – I'm going to be in need of that whisky, later on) and releasing the handbrake while signalling to Black to push on the bonnet, but Black – can't think what's wrong with the man – he seemed disinclined to get himself down and bend his back into the thing, so Alan, he signalled with his flattened lips and a flapping hand the abrupt termination of that particular scheme and he got out of the car and indicated to Black that he now should be the one to steer the car while Alan got down to the pain of pushing the bastard. It began to move – but Alan had to call out to Black when the half-detached and twisted bumper was clawing determinedly at the prised-away door frame but soon gave that up when it became quite clear from Black's quite impassive and near beatific expression that he had heard not one bloody single word of it – and so the crumpled up bumper became wholly detached and clanged on to the doorstep and Alan just kicked it away roughly with the absolute contempt that he felt it so very justly warranted. Black jammed on the handbrake and after a couple of failed, though manful and wind-inducing attempts he managed to heave himself out of the car, and was now at Alan's side.

'Bloody cold out there . . .'

Alan nodded abstractedly to that as he eased shut the door. The main lock simply fell off (lay there dead), the other just hanging back in sorrow – but the bolts at top and bottom would surely do the business for the remainder of the night. And then tomorrow we can launch ourselves with a new and palpable vigour into the doomed and forlorn challenge of attempting to prevent the locksmith and the garage from jointly bleeding us white (though no more, really, than token resistance) while squaring up for the usual blank and po-faced stonewalling and commensurate wranglings with the disparate insurance companies which both will make a point of cleaving staunchly to their PR-concocted variations on the promise to not ever conjure a drama out of the merest crisis by the simple tried and tested means of refusing to recognise the merit of the incident, and sweetly declining liability. Excellent: more joys to come.

And now that Black was settled back into his customary chair, malt in hand and drawing heavily on the very last of his cigarettes, Alan just had to admire the man's composure, the very tranquillity of his airy disposition.

'So, *Blackie* . . . !' Yes – he really had to shout: that gizmo he had stuck in his ear, well – it was clearly on the point of expiry. 'You don't feel inclined to ask *questions*—?! Nothing you'd like me to fill you *in* on—?! Car in the *hall*, for instance . . . ?!'

Black was craning forward and was pleased to know that he had fielded at least the guts of all that.

'Didn't think it was any of my business . . . Susie gone to bed then, has she?'

'Mm. Well. After a fashion. But what, then – you didn't hear anything at all? God – you were only a couple of feet away . . .'

'What? Sorry . . .'

'I say you didn't *hear* anything, then—?! *No*? You heard *nothing* . . . ?!'

Black nodded. Mm, yes, more or less. About sums it up. It had, after all, been something of a vintage trip to the lavatory, quite a classic – all the usual sorts of things to think on and cope with. I do believe it's true to say that I was sort of very vaguely aware at some point of a kind of skirmishing, some type of distant shenanigans being enacted somewhere, and not too far distant, but nothing that might have alerted me to the fact that Susie and Alan's hall had become the scene of a traffic accident: this I did not surmise. Did a lot of thinking in there, though . . . well, fell asleep at one juncture, truth be told, but before that, after I'd twisted and wrenched my purple and boiling body from out of the worst of the tyranny of my straps and padding, the bones and braces, I sat there smoking and encouraging the raw backside of me to, Christ – *defecate*, God damn you, now that I've been to all the sweat and trouble of bloody well dragging you in here, you thoroughly useless arse, you . . . yes yes, I sat there puffing away at a good succession of delicious little columns of Rothman, and – with no assistance at all from a stomach still brimful of rebellious whisky – began to think it through, winnow my way through the maze of it all, try to come close to seeing the structure, and what I could make of it. Because it's strange, you know, but when people say to you: you will *think* about it, won't you . . . ? You find yourself just nodding at them absently, rather as if they had told you to be sure to take care, to mind how you went, to put your hand on your heart and swear to them that it is fully your intention to have a nice fucking day. Yes yes, you are mindlessly assuring them – oh all right then, I'll put all my best efforts into ensuring that I do every one of those things, while knowing full well, of course, that your vacuous wellwisher – possibly an Australasian waitress in some or other newly trendy Antipodean hellhole bent on forcing down you a nice little cut of griddled wallaby because it's low on fat and high on protein (whereas I am low on fads and high on Béarnaise . . .) or could be maybe a spellbound Bangladeshi, imprisoned in the cage of a call centre, reading tunelessly from a printed card . . . not someone, is what I'm driving at, who could honestly be portrayed as having one's very best interests at heart: people, in short, who would neither know nor care if you were struck by a truck. But when she said it to me, Susie – when she said to me, you will *think* about it, won't you Black? Well initially I'd just done what I do, nodded away, nodded away . . . but it lingers, you know, the trace and odour of it. The shadow of the instruction, it continues to lurk among shadows of its own. Because Susie, whatever she is, whatever she might be – and I have been awed, thrilled and appalled by the rather more of her I have been privy to witness during the meandering course of this ever wilder evening – I think we can all safely agree upon the fact that she certainly isn't stupid. No no. And so this scheme of hers, her plan, her ploy, the rickety device or artifice . . . surely, I thought, it deserves a glance? Some little consideration? Why I came here this evening, I suppose – although I confess to having been very thrown indeed by the presence of Alan. I was expecting a moody teenage girl, and what I got was Alan. Well well. So is all we have here a simple case of the seven-year itch? I severely doubt it, if only for the fact that they've been married now, Alan and Susie, haven't they, for twice as long as that, at the very least: a thought in itself. Could be that this is the second attack . . .

203

? Well who knows. But the fact remains . . . if all she wants is merely something else, well then why me? You see? Why me? That's what I have to come to terms with. But already I do understand, rather bizarrely, why she wants it to be as well and not instead of. That part isn't a problem at all, very oddly. Because she's rather sweetly old-fashioned in many ways, you know – wouldn't care to be seen to be a bolter – and I can see why she wants him around, old Alan. But what am I? What do I represent? Money? Just money? Well that's a lot of it – but there are younger, richer and better-looking men than me around (and don't think I would hesitate to give the order to have the lot of them exterminated, and preferably lingeringly, the bastards). But then they wouldn't entertain it, would they? All the young and handsome high-flyers, they'd laugh in her face. Because although she's a beauty, Susie, oh Lord she is (and don't think I've forgotten it) – these chaps, the Masters of the Universe (that what they call them?), they never ever have to compromise, do they? And me, maybe I do. Because what, quite frankly, can my future hold? And how much of it is there still to be? Big questions. At my age. Because I've been very conscious lately, you know, of – mortality. My mortality, naturally – don't much care about anyone else's. Which is maybe half the trouble. I am aware of having become something of a rock, amid an increasingly turbulent sea: solid, yes, but so very alone. Why I have made so many large decisions lately – conscious decisions, I'm sure, that will force me to at least appear to begin again. Changes in my fundamental circumstance, as a rather easy and shaming disguise for the same old me, loitering beneath. Because I had this . . . well, *vision* is far too strong a way of putting it: I am not the mystic. But I did sort of see it square on, as it were:

my presiding over my small but rather prestigious publishing house until the dropping off me of yet more bits would force me to retire under yammering and pitiable protest, by which time I no doubt will have tarnished if not riven asunder the reputation of the house as a result of a string of autocratic, outdated, wrong-headed and pipingly peevish decisions (or, much more likely, a yawning apathy and the cancer of neglect) . . . and then what? Hey? What then, I ask you? To do. And where, indeed, to go? So I'm getting out while I'm more or less able – while I can still just about manage to lie down on my back to tie up the laces on my pantomime shoes, while still I can colour my scalp, smoke and drink and eat and bloody do up the straps of my own fucking corset.

And even to the old family house: I am selling that too – complete next Tuesday. Already bought a new one, point of fact – huge, far too big, ridiculous really, early Georgian, Richmond, and a complete and utter wreck, but it does have quite the most amazing garden – a thing I've always coveted, and now, I sense, might need. That is either clear or it isn't: hardly matters. And how much of all this, I have to ask, did Susie simply sense and divine? Or is this just serendipity, at its purest? That undesignable thing, flighty, and far too wily for trapping. It would be lovely to think so – to think so, at least, that alone would be lovely. But I'm at the age now where even the idiot mask of self-delusion need be no bad thing. If it's real, well then excellent; if it's a damn close simulacrum, something that could pass muster when it's dusky and the lights are low, while one's eyes are glassy and one's need is soaring . . . well then that will do very well too. I have seen men, proud, reject with contempt anything that was even remotely sullied or less than complete – but me, I am aware that anything available to me now will and must by definition be partial – gnawed at before by teeth that are sharper than mine, whole layers of contents spilled out or devoured. But I am grateful to even be considered as the suitable and deserving recipient of at least the potential of any good parts that are left me. And this chance, I think – this one, here and now – is more than I might have expected. When you reach a state of resignation, when you have built up as if they are walls the solid boasts of your own self-dependence – not just the lack of desire for another but the supremacy of the solitary state – then the likelihood of encountering a person with whom you could seriously not just contentedly pass away the remaining time, but maybe actually attempt to generate something other, and even vigorous . . . such an idle and withering hope, it diminishes with the passing of each and every moment. And yet here now, at twilight, I have within reach a person I can now truly understand, be easy with, be *me* with – someone who will listen, and from whom I might even learn of the things that have always eluded me. It happens rarely, if it happens at all, and I cannot be the fool who lets it slip away. Soulmate, well – it's an overused expression, a term that is little understood . . . but even the hint of its possibility, the whiff of its aroma, these should always be heeded and inhaled. Because Alan, you know, is that very rare thing.

I am pleased to be rid of the house. Should have done it long ago. All the happier memories of when the children were growing, they have long been overladen by the darkness of all that was to come. And if the establishment of another household is the order of the day . . . well then you do not want to cling on to, to inhabit, to bring along not just a man but a brand-new *wife* to the place where once you recently just found yourself . . . murdering the old one.

PART TWO

CHAPTER SIX

'Well, Alan. It's been a while. My secretary tells me that it's . . .
um, let me see . . . two appointments you've cancelled now.
That right? Two. Alan?'

'Mm – yes, Doctor Atherby. It's true. But I'm here now. Dry
your tears, you sentimental old sausage.'

Yeh – two appointments I've broken. Felt marvellous.
The first time, well – it was just such a lovely sunny day, I
simply can't tell you. Picture-perfect. First of the blossom,
dazzle of pinkness, a zing of freshness all around. Bit of bird-
song – saw them there, flitting about. I felt like something
ugly, a misshapen thing – crude and colourless – fallen like a
meteor down into the middle of a Disney animation. And so I
thought, well while I'm here I'll breathe it in, suck it all down,
before I am rumbled and come to hit the cutting-room floor.
And then it struck me – it was then I laughed, yes out loud (a
mighty good feeling all on its own). I had been smacked by
the reminder of where I was headed: Doctor bloody Atherby.
Even the thud of his name, it depressed me so badly – and
then I mentally projected myself forward – beyond the sour
and curdled receptionist, on into the glumness, the slump of

209

his presence, the still of the room, the smell and shift of the leather on the couch as I fold away the essence of me, resign myself to slipping on the costume of the disturbed, the tick of the clock, the very sight of the man tip-tapping away at his gut-wrenching moustache with the heavy shiny end of his fucking expensive pen . . . and I just didn't, that's all. Went to Hyde Park instead. Delightful. Did me a power. Instead of feeding ourselves into the relentless chomping maw of things like Doctor Atherby, why don't we all just go to the park? Something we have forgotten to do. Bought an ice cream. Yum yum. Closed my eyes against the sun. Felt no longer the brutal invader. It was nearly as good as my own private beach (though I did miss the sand and the seagulls). So yes – that was one appointment blown. The other – quite funny, I suppose. The other time, the next appointment – well, just the opposite, really: pissing down, you know, and I just tweaked aside the curtain, took one look out of the glycerine window and I thought well sod it, actually. Played a game of draughts with Blackie instead; he won, of course, as he usually does, but still – better than traipsing through a monsoon to be confronted by a wall of grey: Doctor Atherby from beneath his shroud, asking me how I feel, urging me to regress, generally wasting a good man's time. I'm here now though, yes I am – on this occasion I have made it, but just you wait to hear what I'm now going to say to the man: let's just watch his face, shall we? When I hit him with this:

'Actually, Doctor Atherby, it's quite odd, you know – that I am here, I mean. Because the reason I am here is to tell you I won't be.'

'Uh-huh . . .'

Had to smile – a smile was twisted from me, I admit. The

tone, the way he had said it, that uh-huh: as if I had uttered not just something logical and coherent, but even a telling profundity. His stock reaction to all I say – and not just what *I* say, I am convinced, but whatever quite pitiable nonsense either falls or is propelled from the mouths of all those other poor and fragile bastards desperate enough to come here. I long ago ceased asking myself whether or not he listened – but it was doubtful now if he even heard. Maybe he had a gizmo like Blackie's stuck deep in his ear – could be he was learning colloquial Cantonese, or maybe just tapping his pen in time to the greatest hits of the Spice Girls. But certainly it wasn't me he was hearing; if it hadn't been clear before, then now it was stark – as plain as the very horrid nose, slammed like dough and roughly in the centre of his big and phoney face.

'Let me make that a little less confused, Doctor Atherby. When I say I will not be here, I mean of course in the future.'

'Uh-huh . . .'

'Indeed yes. Uh-huh. This is to be the last time I shall annoy you with all my goings-on. In this session, Doctor Atherby, during the next however long it is, we have the makings of a swansong.'

'I see. Well, Alan. That is something of a statement. And you think this wise then, do you?'

'Oh God yes. Smartest thing I've done in ages. Professionally speaking, you ought to be pleased. Success of sorts. My dispensing with you utterly. Flushing you away. Flicking you off the lapel of my life like a mote of grit, and into the long goodnight.'

'Why did you say, Alan, that this would be the last time that you would *annoy* me? Do you feel that you do? Are you annoying, Alan?'

211

'No more so than the next quite weak and gullible chap, I shouldn't have said. Your waiting room's full of them. Maybe you should conduct a little poll – see who's the most annoying: you might even win. But did I *really* say that . . . ? I don't recall. That I was annoying you? Well. That could be Freudian, Doctor Atherby. Jungian. Somethingian. Because the reverse is true, of course. As I recently and rather cheekily implied. Yes yes. It's you, you see, Doctor Atherby. It's you who annoy *me*. Practically unto death.'

'I have never seen you, Alan, so openly on the offensive. Always it is there, of course, a latent animosity, but normally your way is to cover it up with attempted humour. To what do you attribute this rather more, um – forthright hostility?'

Alan sat up and just stared at him. He had hung on his face the slap of shock.

'*Attempted* humour? *Attempted*, Doctor Atherby? My, that was harsh. What – you mean you didn't even like my *jokes* . . . ? I am cut. You have wounded me. This could be the very hardest thing to bear. I mean I am aware you would never go so far as to actually *laugh* at anything, Doctor Atherby – not in your nature, probably an unforgivable breach of your hypocritical oath, ho ho – but I did always feel secure in your tacit appreciation of my wilder and more inventive sallies into the balmy realms of the intensely comic. But it seems I was wrong. Sadly deluded. All that reached your ears – aside from maybe colloquial Cantonese or possibly even the greatest hits of the Spice Girls – was no more than the occasional failed quip, feebly lobbed across to you in a touching attempt to conceal the real urge, the truth that what I was really and truly experiencing, deep down in my psyche – and horribly shallowly too – was the need to snatch from your lily-white fingers that fucking expensive pen and ram it up your bloody arse, good and hard, while simultaneously decanting over your head and shoulders a bucket of paint, preferably fluorescent, that so many times I have ached and yearned to have concealed about my person.'

'Uh-huh. I think, Alan, in the light of this, it is time to wind up. For good, as you say.'

'Mm, yes – but be fair, Doctor Atherby: twenty minutes on the clock. Now either this session is gratis, on the house, your little parting gift – again, I fear, just not in your nature – or else you owe me, if not the goodness to hear me out, then at least the paid-for twenty minutes in which to bear it. The grin is optional. I mean – don't you *want* to know why finally I am breaking free of you? Why I haven't taken your stupid pills for, oh – just weeks and weeks. Months, probably. I mean even in you, there must be *some* vestige of curiosity? Yes? No?'

'Very well then, Alan. Tell me. Clearly you need to . . . so if you think it will help . . .'

'Don't need help. Not any more. That's the whole point. Strong now.'

'Uh-huh. I see. And can you put a finger on the turning point . . . ?'

'Yes I can. Absolutely. It was the day my wife got married.'

It was, you know. And I don't have to say that it was extraordinary. I mean – dreadful in many ways, as I suppose we all of us had really to expect, given the singular (if that's the right word?) and tortured circumstances. Now look: you've been to weddings, haven't you? Seen them in films. Everything from the pomp and magnificence of Westminster Abbey to the brisk good sense of the Marylebone Registry Office – yes yes, we know them all by heart, and every variation in between; well strike out all such visions from your mind. Big white dresses, sweet little bridesmaids, emotional mothers, a ridiculous cake and carnations buttonholed by Baco-Foil. No no. None of that. The only traditional element, I believe, were the tears. To say the event was low-key, then, would be to severely over-represent it – though the looming threat of the highest drama was never too far in the offing. The marriage, you see, had been over-hastily arranged (Susan again – 'twere well 'twere done quickly, you know what she's like) and although the intended venue was to have been a marble-floored and sun-filled atrium in a Georgian house in Richmond, surrounded by lawn and trees, it turned out instead to be a building site. Susan's fault. All would have been fine if she hadn't been so bloody impatient – but that's rather like saying, isn't it really, that a picnic might so have been perfect, had it not been for the rain and hornets: we were dealing, simply, with the nature of the beast – it all just had to be now now now.

Blackie, you see, had bought this house. Sold his old one and got this great big pile instead. First I knew of it was when he asked me to drive him out there one morning – Richmond, as I say, just outside, stupendous place really. Pretty much a wreck, though – but with most of the eighteenth-century bits that make you just faint largely present and correct, or at least restorable. It was just everything else: rot, wiring, plumbing – oh God: everything. Well anyway, the architect had briefed the project manager who had instructed the site foreman who had contracted all the subcontractors who had conveyed all relevant specifications to the suppliers and the workforce was in place. Because the plan, you see, had been for the lot of us to live in the Richmond house – God knows it's big enough for an army – but that all the very basic work should be carried out first. Well Christ obviously: you just had to look at the place. Now immediately there were problems – well dozens, actually, but it's people problems I'm talking about now. The sticking points that appeared to be key were roughly as follows: Amanda . . . well, Amanda, she's a story in herself, and one I've got to get on to in the fullness of time (must be faced, can't be ducked, more's the bloody pity) . . . but initially Amanda's main contention was that she didn't even know where bloody Richmond *was*, all her friends and her school were round *here* and why should we all pack up and go and live in this *Richmond* place with some old *man*? Mm, well – problems, as I say, but hardly her fault. Susan weighed in then with all of her tedious and mawkish nonsense about it not being just some old *man*, is it Amanda? Hm? He's going to be Mummy's new *husband*, isn't he? And your Daddy's new *friend* – and we're all jolly lucky that he owns such a big and beautiful house and that he's asked us all to share it . . . on and on. Whereupon Amanda would sullenly reiterate all of her objections, and Susan would more or less repeat to her verbatim the same old screed (as in please see above) . . . and so all of that filled in a fair bit of time. Oh yes – Amanda had also suddenly decided that she loved our house, our lovely old house – had always, she told and told us, always always always loved every brick and tile of the place (that she'd never before even mentioned it, well you have to let that ride). It then emerged that Susan too had evolved a great and enduring passion for the place, and did not want to see it go. For myself, a house is a house; when you've lived over a kebab shop in the iffiest part of Kentish Town, you learn to be grateful for what you can get. There was, however, my secret seaside to consider – that was

215

paining me, the thought of abandoning it, permitting it to be reclaimed by nature. Neither Susan nor Amanda, of course, even knew of its existence (why it remained so pure) – but one evening, Blackie and I were downstairs, quite late, everyone else in bed – he was actually staying in a hotel at this stage, but he used to pop over all the time, and very welcome too. We were building a house of cards, drinking whisky and smoking away (one of the golden evenings, really) and I sort of let it slip into the general drift of the chat, kind of thing. I think we were both of us always aware that what we really ought to have been discussing were the looming nuptials, the practical application – physical arrangements (nuts and bolts of the new machine) – but somehow we always seemed to be talking of other things entirely. And I don't think deliberately or evasively – it's just that there seem to be so many varied mutualities, you see: so many (other) things in common. Anyway: my beach – you could tell he was immediately interested, as I had known he would be (or else why would I mention it?).

'How perfectly extraordinary, Alan – what, sand and every-thing, do you mean?'

'Well naturally, Blackie. Hardly be seaside without the sand, would it old man? You just have to ask yourself. Everything else as well, of course. Up to a point. I tell you what – here's a tester . . . oh here, Blackie: top you up.'

'Shouldn't, really. Go on, then. What do you mean: tester?'

'Well listen. Association. Say anything that comes into your mind when the word "seaside" is mentioned. Go on.'

'Seaside, hey? Anything that, ah . . . ?'

'Yup. Anything. Just say anything to do with the seaside. First thing that pops into your head.'

'Yes, I see. Right, then. Fine. Jolly good.'

'Well then? Go on.'

'Yes well I will. Oh God – you know me, Alan. Complete blank. Absolutely nothing. Hopeless, isn't it? You say anything that pops into my mind and just look at me. Good God. Number of times I've nipped down to Brighton for a bit of a weekend, you know. Some woman or other. Going back a bit. But you'd think, wouldn't you, I could come up with *something*. I like Brighton. You like Brighton? Love it. No sand, though. That's the only problem with Brighton – no sand. Oh yes – there we are: *sand*. How's that?'

'No, Blackie, no. We've got sand. We've done sand.'

'Have we? Have we really? Oh well bugger me.'

'Look – I'll start you off. All right? Seagulls . . .'

'Oh yes – seagulls. Very good. Christ, Alan – you don't mean to say—?'

'No. Just recordings of the noise they make.'

'That's a relief. Nasty brute, your seagull. Knew a sailor once – captain or something. Said they'd have your eye out.'

'And he did, did he? Have his eye out? Captain Hook, was it?'

'Hey? No no. That wasn't his name. Could have been Wilkinson. Needn't have been . . .'

'Knew someone else though, did he? Who'd had his eye out from a seagull?'

'Didn't mention it, no . . .'

'Mm. Think we can take it as gospel, then. Well listen, Blackie – I'll tell you. Be here all night otherwise. Deckchair, blue skies, fishing nets, sea breezes, water to paddle in . . . !'

'Really? *Really*, Alan? I say. That's topping. What about, um . . . I don't know – ice cream?'

'Yes! Little fridge-freezer sort of a thing. Sunlamp. Everything. Do you, um . . . want to see it? Blackie? It's just that . . . no one ever has.'

'Half of me does.'

'What does that mean? Half of you . . . ?'

'Mm. It's just the thought of those bloody stairs. You couldn't bring it down here, could you? No no, Alan – just fooling with you. Of course I'd love to see it. Course I would. What a treat. Honour. Just help me up then, would you? This may well be an easy chair in your book, but for me I can tell you – it's actually bloody *difficult* . . .'

There was a moment of doubt, a shard of fear that went right through me, as I leant into turning the key in the lock – the tumblers had not quite clunked into submission when I quickly glanced over to him with I think it must have been a tremor of anxiety – hesitance, yes, and playing about my ankles the draught, chilly and unmistakable, of rawness and vulnerability. He smiled at me, you know, just as a father would: not my father, obviously, but the sort of father a man really needed, and particularly when poised and nervous upon the very thin rim of not just disclosure, but the hope of true confluence – though still with all the attendant risk of so many carefully placed and pointed blocks toppling over in ruin, and dashing the future of the solid tower that might have been, the air above just waiting. I hung back in the doorway as he tottered on in (he has a strange way of walking – think it could be down to the shoes, which always look to be somehow, I don't know, just not quite right in some way).

'Oh I *say*, Alan. Oh I *say*. This is . . . oh this is just prime. Prime, this is. And how very inventive. The detail – the detail!'

Alan rushed in, and locked the door behind him. He excitedly darted about, flicking switches and minutely

218

repositioning the sunlounger, gently nudging just to one side a cluster of starfish, reconfiguring the fan of scallop shells in the shadow of the suntrap and idly stroking a red-and-white lifebelt.

'You see – you see, when everything's *on*, it's really quite . . . and when it warms up, you know – and this heater, well it really does the business, I can assure you of that. Quite Mediterranean in no time flat. And the dimmer – you can do sunset and dawn as well as the full-on noonday dazzle. Completely adaptable. And the gulls – hear them? I won't put the breeze on because it's actually quite chilly at the moment. And there's old-fashioned organ music, if you want it. Music hall. All the old songs . . .' Alan petered out, and went on nodding with eagerness.

Black just stood there, his heels sunk into the sand, hands on his hips, gazing about him as if at the world's eighth wonder, newly fallen from the sky.

'Superb . . . what can I say? Never seen anything like it. It's perfect.'

'Really? You really think so? Oh . . . I'm . . . pleased. Very pleased you, um – I say, how about this? Would you like an ice cream?'

Black was looking at him roguishly.

'What – cornet, you mean? Proper thing?'

'Oh God yes – absolutely. Vanilla or raspberry thing? Flake, if you want. I've got wafers as well . . .'

'Sit well on top of the Scotch, do you think?'

'Oh no trouble there, Blackie old man. Tried and tested. Many's the time I've been up here, you know – sipping the one, slurping on the other. It's a, well – marriage made in heaven, you might say. Sit down, Blackie, and I'll do all the doings.'

'Sit down? Ah. That, I fear, would be a bridge too far. If I attempted a deckchair, I swear we'd need a crane to winch me back out again. And I shan't even pass comment on the hammock. Tell you what, Alan my lad – at the new house, when we get the Richmond house up and running, yes? We'll have a bench on the promenade. How about that? Little brass plaque on it. Dedicated to Blackie, who always loved to sit here drinking and smoking and wolfing down a cornet – watching the sea and the world go by. Sound all right?'

Alan compressed his lips, the emotion he was feeling was just that great.

'You mean . . . we could do it again? Recreate it, so to speak? You wouldn't mind?'

'Mind? Bloody insist on it. Far better than anything that fool of a bloody architect has come up with. Wants me to have a sunken leisure space with a plunge fucking pool, whatever on God's earth that might be. This is *far* more the thing. We could really push the boat out – literally, if you like. Couple of paddleboats on a pond? Canoe? What do you think? Christ, there's so much garden there – I could build us a *pier* . . . !'

Alan laughed, and touched his eyelid. He placed a hand on Blackie's shoulder.

'A couple of donkeys, I do assure you, would easily be adequate.'

Yes – I said that. And he laughed then. Well I can't tell you what a huge relief this was – what a weight off my mind. It was maybe, selfishly, from that moment on that I became quite absolutely determined to make this whole damn thing *work* – this crazed invention of Susan's (who sometimes, these days, quite slips my mind, there's so much else to attend to). We continued the evening, Blackie and me, on a further slick of

Scotch and an admittedly injudicious gorging of ice cream cones, jammed with crumbly chocolate, and wound it all up soon after we had sifted through a fair deal of my collection of Donald McGill postcards (because they never fail, do they? To raise a smile).

Now of course, if it had been left up to Blackie and myself (and face it – when was there ever a chance of that?) then the show, the sham – the demonstration of a marriage having been piously enacted (in the eyes of You Know Who) – all that would have been indefinitely deferred, and why not actually? Because all of us now, for a growing variety of reasons, were very much committed to the thing, so why the need for so very hasty a formalisation? Well – I say all of us . . . there was always Amanda, of course. To be considered. The main reason, really – and I put it to Blackie and he completely agreed – not to forge ahead into a headlong rush (quite apart from the fact, important in itself, that the planned and proposed venue for the touching ceremony, not to say the selfsame place where we were all eventually to be living, was still just a promise of hopes and dreams – or, more prosaically, walls, and so much rubble). Is there really any point in telling you that Susan would brook no objection? Does it come as a great surprise? The sooner, she said, 'twere done (I know) then the sooner Amanda would come to accept it; when it ceased to be a *notion* (Susan was insistent), an airy cooked-up concept – when it became an actuality, a state, a full-blown ménage, then Amanda would not just buckle down into, Jesus – seeing *sense*, for God's sake, but so too would she come to cooperate, get wise, and extract all the benefits that were dangled before her. Yes well – fair enough theory, I suppose, not beyond the bounds of reason . . . but still, I thought, just to gallop full

221

tilt at it – and Blackie was behind me on this one – it was not only unnecessary, but it threatened revolt and an untimely sabotage of what I think at least the three of us, anyway, now believed (no – in fact I was sure of it) could actually grow, develop – burgeon up into a maybe splendid thing. The only real reason for rushing it that I could see was to make sure of securing the good offices of, oh dear me, ex-Father Johnnie Flynn, before said man of God was thoroughly overtaken or even more ruined by the bends, or else just collapsed and died of rebellion of the liver, whatever came soonest. I tell you, I have never before seen a man so constantly in danger of keeling right over and flat on his face – so incoherent in his demeanour, nor – and let us please face the facts when they very unmistakably confront us – so very *aubergine* in his appearance. Livid is the word – or, at least, from the neck up anyway: the neck, the swell of neck, bulbous over that stained and plastic clerical collar, which seems to cut right into it, his ill-shaved chin, deckled with spittle. His hands, however, are another matter entirely: as white as the dead, and I am sure as cold, though never could I contemplate, oh God no – touching them. Is this, do you think, I gently suggested to Susan, truly the best we can do . . . ? He is, she said, at base, a good and true man. Father Flynn, he has not lost sight of his calling, his vocation, but has simply been denied the I should have said *God*-given right to celebrate the Mass and praise the Lord in the sight of a congregation; it is a gift to us that he yearns to bestow. Mm, yes – so that's Susan's skew-whiff take on it, anyway: our gift (although you should see what he's charging) and the Vatican is doomed to struggling along as best they may without him. One of Susan's many paradoxes – so very fastidious in the normal run of things . . . and yet: this. Well.

In every other way, though, I really must say, she appears to be blooming. New lease of life is barely overstating it – and even more so when Blackie stepped in like the hero he is to resolve the problem of her and Amanda's freshly unearthed and unshakable devotion to the Chelsea house that we're still all living in. He'd talked it over, the scheme, his solution – he'd talked it over with me beforehand.

'You see, Alan – way I see it, it's barely a problem at all. Godsend, in some ways. There's no need, you see. No reason at all for you to sell. Your house. Is there? No financial need. None whatever. Keep it. Rent it out. Fetch a fortune in rent, daresay, place like this. These days. And this solves the other little, um – matter. Delicate this, Alan – so please bear with me if my, ah – exposition is less than perfect. If I offend your sensibilities. But you see – the fact is, you don't have an income. No no, dear boy – not a criticism, believe me. Not a judgement. The merest observation. Now Susie – she won't have one either, of course.'

'No? Oh no. I suppose not.'

'Yes. You see, what with the takeover and everything . . . well I'm sure the set-up concerned would offer her a position. She's really very good, you know . . .'

'Mm. I've no doubt.'

'Mm. And once the trade gets wind of it all . . . still all hush-hush at the moment. Something to do with share prices, they tell me: perceived values. I wouldn't know. But once it's all out in the open, as it were, well – plenty of other houses would be pleased to take her on. She wouldn't be short of offers, is what I'm saying to you.'

'Mm. And so . . . ?'

'Well. Well the truth of the matter, Alan – and I'm telling

223

you frankly now, you see. Won't put it like this to Susie, no, but I'm putting it so to you. The fact is . . . I don't *want* her to, you know – work for another publisher. Just not happy with it. Petty jealousy on my part, it could easily just be. Probably is, actually. But you see – I've got to persuade her, Susie, that she is far too valuable to me – us, to us – for her to be out at work all day. See?'

'I don't think you'll have any problem at all on that score, Blackie. She doesn't want to. Work. Fed up with it. That's the whole point of all this.'

'Ah . . .'

'Well no. Not. Not the whole point – not *now*, it isn't. Obviously. Now she knows you. Loves you. Does she, Blackie? Do you think? Love you . . . ?'

'Couldn't tell you. Shouldn't have thought so. Bit, maybe. Hard to say . . .'

'Mm. I feel the same way. About me, I mean. Me and her. Well. Anyway – at the time, her whole idea – yeah, was to find a way to stop. To cease to be the breadwinner. And give her her due – she perceived at once that there was no way on earth that I was going to come to star in any such a role, and so . . .'

'Aha. Yes I see. Well that's good, then. That's excellent. But still, you see – she'll want an independent income. She will.'

'Oh she will. No argument there.'

'And you – you must have one too. No no – hear me out, Alan. I fear you must misunderstand me. Now you see, at the new house, I shall of course be happy to meet all the day-to-day expenses. Naturally. But I'm not sure that, um – *allowances* would be quite the thing. Clear, is it? What I'm driving at?'

'No, I wouldn't say so, Blackie. But press on, hey?'

'Well you see by renting out your house, this house – well

bingo. Private income for both of you, you see? And all the pain of losing the house – well: vanished. And of course it can only go up in value. And I hate it, you know – the thought of Amanda being dragged away from the house she loves . . . but if you still *own* it, well . . . Better, surely?'

'Indeed. That is . . . this is all very – *generous* of you, Blackie . . .'

'Not a bit of it, my dear boy. You're doing me a great favour, all of you are. Can't you see that? Bought this bloody great white elephant of a house – largely for the garden, really. Well who's going to plan it? The garden. Susie would be prime at that. She'd love it. And who's going to fill all the rooms? Go mad, wouldn't I? Rattling around in a place like that. And once I've sold the company – well, buckets of money all round, not to put too fine a point on it. And what am I expected to do with *that* then, in my declining years? *Count* it? So you see – you've helped me out enormously, you and Susie. Maybe unwittingly, but there you are.'

'What, um – what do your children make of all this? Told them?'

'Oh them. They can fuck off, quite frankly. Never given a damn what I do – why should they start now? Oh I'll give them some money, I expect. Settle something on them, ungrateful little bastards. Tie it up somehow so they can't get their hands on it until they're broken and old. Like me. But talking of children, Alan . . . one of the things I *do* find rather disturbing in this whole, ah – well. Amanda. I mean – I've never even *met* her. Have I? Don't you think that's rather . . . odd? Deliberate, is it? Keeping her away? That the idea?'

'God *no*, Blackie – quite the reverse. Oh no – I hope you don't go thinking that. No – Susan and I, well – it's about the

225

only thing we've always agreed about, really. She's *got* to meet you, Amanda – get to know you, sort of thing. Course she has. Because how else is she ever going to . . . ? But you see . . . well – all rather hard on her, I expect. All this. A lot for her to take in. Not straightforward, you see. Children, they like things cut and dried. Or maybe they do. Truth is, I haven't a clue in blue blazes what children like or don't like. It's just a guess. And I couldn't tell you, Blackie, what it is that's going on in Amanda's mind. I only wish I knew. But I don't. Not at all. Susan – she might be a bit more clued in, but I somehow doubt it. So there we have it, I'm afraid old chap. Time, really. Just give it a bit of time, and see how it all turns out.'

Rare for me, very – allaying the fears in another, seeming sagacious, being a sympathetic party to mutual bemusement, the string of knotted misgivings: understanding, oh but how completely, the fraying nature of a rope's loose ends, the need for neatness and a true conclusion. It is maybe not then children at all, you know, who like it cut and dried. We do, though – it's a virtual requirement.

'So there, if you want it Doctor Atherby, was the beginning of my new-found . . . vigour, if you like. Not power, though. That's for others. But the coming of strength, a rebirth of confidence . . . All that you should have done for me, really. Isn't it, Doctor Atherby? Over the months and years. Instead of just plunging me back into the stale and fetid water, again and again and again . . . and all I could do was wallow and smell it. So yes – as I say, here was the beginning. But the moment when it became absolute – that was at the wedding of my wife. Then it was, well – official, I suppose.'

Doctor Atherby was tapping his pen in a different way altogether – more casually and abandoned, the customary strictness of the drumbeat now hurled aside in favour of something a good deal more wild, impromptu, and involving syncopation: in the new and final circumstance, how could there any longer be a need for rigour?

'Official. Interesting word, Alan. Official, do you mean, in the eyes of . . . ?'

'No. No no. Not His. My eyes. Mine.'

'Uh-huh. Well now, Alan – one minute to go. By my watch. Shall we use it up with a cheery farewell? Hug? Or would you care to squeeze in a tiny bit more? Parting shot? The final rude and derisive outburst?'

Alan now rose up from his bed, delighted to be feeling so very nearly joyous.

'You know, Doctor Atherby – it's funny, really. It's funny. If only you had been like that before. Said things like that before. In all these dumb and wasted sessions. If only to prove to me that you had even been listening.'

'It's hardly professional. But now you see me as just the layman. Tell me, Alan, before you go . . . well – you don't have to, of course. Your business now, after all. But I do remain curious about just a couple of things. Care to indulge me . . . ?'

'We're over time now, Doctor Atherby. By my watch.'

'Think of it as a bonus. An extra. Gift, if you like.'

'Well I certainly don't recall you ever saying *that* before. This is a first. And how very strange that it's also the last. Mm. Well now look – a couple of things, you say. Why not. And I think I can guarantee that I'm damned sure what one of them is going to be, anyway. In your game, prurience, never too far distant. Is it? If not at the forefront, it's always just hanging around. Am I right? Oh I am. I see. How sadly predictable. I did so wish – for your sake really, Doctor Atherby – that you were going to, um – disabuse me of that one. But no. So – you want a little nosy peek, yes? Into the conjugal side of things – that it? The voyeur at the crack of an open door? Or detached and professional interest, allied with the desire for, oh God – *closure*? Hardly matters. Because the honest answer is, Doctor Atherby, that I just don't know. Whether or not I have *wondered* is something else entirely, but I do not know because, well – one, I have not been told, and two, I most certainly have never enquired. I *will* know, of course, when the time is right. Have my suspicions confirmed. It will emerge quite lightly, a raggedy end from the random jumble of one of our talks. He will speak, and I shall listen. But by that time – oh Doctor Atherby, alack and alas – you and I will be strangers to one another. Is that not the case? As if, as if, we were ever even for a moment anything else. So there's your answer: don't know. As to the other little thing that's worrying away at you . . . well, this will come over as fresher, at least, for I honestly haven't an idea. Quite what this one could be . . .'

'Uh-huh. Well it's something you – touched on. Once or twice. Amanda. Yes? How she was coping, what she was thinking. Susan, I am assuming from your virtual exclusion from any single one of your recent experiences, is pleased to have now what she wanted. But Amanda . . . ?'

The hostility, bellicose wrath, that I have constantly harboured for the blighted Doctor Atherby – kept it warm, and close to my heart – has really always been of the subtlest sort, hardly more really than a malignant palpitation. But it welled up now into something so very gaudily lit, that close to brassy – very near to beyond control, and tinged by the fire of violence. My glare was clearly sufficient to make him step back from me – and then I went for the exit whose glamour and fury so very many times I have cruelly denied myself: I strutted, I stamped – I swept with contempt his papers to the floor. And a door was slammed.

There's this coffee place, OK, quite near to where we used to live before we all went like a million miles away to Richmond (believe it?) with the new guy. The like – old guy? Whatever. Not Franco's I don't mean, the coffee place (can't go in there any more) – this one is kind of old-fashioned like your auntie's sitting room, yeh? I don't actually have any aunties, but you like know what I mean. Not designer. I was wearing black tights and my boots and a black sort of like shift-type dress I got at Primark, tunic thing, and this cool like black varnish on my nails? Dad says it looks like I've been digging graves and Mum says it's like in a Hammer film which I didn't know what it was and I googled it and it's all vampires, yeh? And I'm pretty cool with that. And black long beads that I wrap round and round and round and they still hang down. When I'm not in my shit school uniform, everything I've got now is black because pink and stuff for me is just so like over. Except my mouth which I do red. But like – *really* red? Postbox, yeh? And guys, they really look at me differently now. Like him over there, with his paper and his coffee, keeps looking over, and I'm kind of smiling back. Ramming my spoon into the dried-up hunk of brown sugar, chipping away at it, and kind of just like smiling if I see him looking over. It's not my God-you're-*gorgeous*-come-and-get-me smile (which I can *so* do) – it's just, you know – friendly really. See what happens. I followed him in here which is crazy really because I didn't have that much cash and even a cup of tea here, which is the cheapest thing I could find, is like nearly two quid, you know?

Such a rip-off. Maybe Dad should've opened a coffee place instead of trying to sell all like nails and stuff. Except that now he doesn't have to do anything, and Mum neither. He says he's writing a book, and Mum says oh *crap*, he's not writing a book. She's really into design and stuff now – talking to all the builders and the garden people and I think she must be driving them like so just totally nuts because she keeps on changing her mind. It's going to be great, actually, when it's done, the Richmond house. It's just so huge. My room is cool – I got to choose everything and they said no to black walls but the furniture's black and really shiny, Perspex and retro, and it's all wired up for just like everything and I've got my own bathroom which I also wanted to be black but they said no you can have white, right – but I got black tiles, so it's cool. Kitchen's about a hundred feet long – and the big like glass bit at the back? Still all rubble and wires sticking out, but it's going to be, oh wow – just so *amazing*. It's all so much better than where we used to be. Always hated that little house. Hated it. Don't know why. He's still doing it, looking, this guy . . . It's creepy in a way – but you remember all of that ancient stuff, yeh – about Girl Power? You kind of know what they were on about. It's, like – a really great feeling?

It's like I've grown up a lot. When I said that to Tara, she just went oh yeh yeh Amanda – what, because you did it, just because you did it with Harry the Poet and now you're all like – just so *cool*, just so grown-up, just so *different* – so much better than *you* guys. Which was just like so totally *duh* . . . ! But she's been funny lately, Tara – since her mother just so totally lost it, right, and nearly killed her dad with a teapot. And it had, like – *tea* in it? So Tara, you kind of make allowances for – her mum's a psycho and her dad's a conjuror with a fractured skull. But she was wrong like big-time about it being all to do with *Harry*, because it wasn't that at all (wish I hadn't even told her, now). But all that, it was just so nothing. I feel so completely yuck if I think of it, so I don't. And anyway, he wasn't was he? A poet. I've been reading poetry lately – all these thousands of books from the old guy's old place – and some of it, wow, just blows you away. Like Marvell and Donne – and Clare I like (thought at first it was a girl which was a leetle bit embarrassing . . .). Shelley is like to die for. Keats is pretty. Eliot I just don't get – Auden's OK, some of it. Hardy's my favourite, though – by like a million miles. Anyway – the little arsehole Harry, yeh? Yeh well – he's a poet like I'm a, I don't know – brain surgeon or a TV presenter or something. He's just so like *not. Plums* . . . ? Give me a break. So yeh – it's a shame in one way that he had to be such a total like loser, the first one, but it doesn't really matter. Matters to my mum, though – oh God you should've heard her. On and on she was going. It was the day after I did all those really wild and crazy things – God it makes me so go red when I think about it. I'd taken some of Dad's whisky, whole bottle – oh God I can't tell you how disgusting, just the smell of it now, it makes me want to puke – and some fags that were lying around, which I didn't . . . what is it? Swallow. Inhale. Whatever. Tried it, but I like nearly died. So they were just pretty filthy. And I thought what else can I do? Because all this – it's just so *tame*, you know? And I went to this tattoo and piercing place just near the station because I just knew that of all things in the world I could do that would make my mum go just so totally mega-crazy . . . but God, the prices. And also, I hate like needles . . . ? Always have since mumps jabs and stuff. So I pretty stupidly stuck on a fake tattoo that I got on a magazine way back last summer some time and it's been in my bag ever since and I drank some more of the horrible whisky and then I just stuck a bloody drawing pin in my ear! Right through. I just so don't *believe* I did that. And then I stuck it in the other ear! Oh Jesus – blood, everywhere, and I was dabbing on all these little bits of, like – *Andrex*? And then I think what I thought was – I know, I'll take the car, go on a motorway and like kill myself and then they'll have to listen to what I say. Yeh I know – like crazy talk, and I guess it was all the whisky: why Dad just never knows what he's ever doing, I suppose. Must be that. Well I'd never done it before, driving or anything, but the keys were in the blue bowl in the hall and I sort of remembered how Mum and Dad got the thing going and I did that and oh God! It like started to roll away? And I got kind of panicky and just turned the wheel . . . and yeh, that's when it ended up in the hall. Jesus. And I was just so out of it, I remember thinking oh yeh I know – I'll just go through this smashed-up front door and creep up to bed and no one will know. *So* not how it went. I just remember Mum really shaking me and I could see she was shouting and looking psycho and gone all totally weird on me but I didn't know what she was on about or anything. Next thing I was on my bed and the ceiling was all like crazy and going round and in and out and I thought I was going to be sick and then I thought I was just going to die and I really quite wanted to, actually – I remember not minding about it. And I sort of like kind of woke up a bit then, and I thought I can really like wind her up, Mum, get her going, because she thinks I don't know what I'm talking about and so I hit her with the virgin thing and it was great when she cried and stuff, like she was really in pain. I'd wanted to tell her anyway, right from when it happened to me, but I don't know if I ever would of.

Next morning I felt pretty OK, actually – hungry more than anything. Got a shock when I saw the front door and the hall and everything because all that bit seemed to be more like a dream than anything real that I'd been a part of. And I had eggs and ham and Mum said How could you? And then she started on at me: did I remember what I'd said last night? Did I mean it? Was it true? Yeh. And what did I think I was *doing*? I could have been killed. Did I realise I could have been killed? Yeh. And why had I been drinking and hurting myself? Self-harming is what she said. Did I know I could have scarred myself and contracted septy-something and died? Yeh. You seem, Amanda, very unconcerned by all of this. Shrug from me. It's no big: I wasn't killed, was I? Didn't die, no scars, no septy-something: I am sorry about the car and the door, though – I'd pay for it, the damage, only I don't have any money. She was drinking coffee, Mum, but she looked like she more wanted to puke it up than swallow – all gone like white, she was: looked really old. And the – 'other thing', she said: I didn't think you were so stupid. Were you attacked? Were you assaulted? Did you know what you were doing? Yeh. What do you *mean*? What does 'yeh' mean? Why don't you ever talk *properly*? Why don't you make the effort to communicate like a human *being*, Amanda? What I mean is, I said, I knew what was going on, if that's what you're saying: I'm not, like – a *baby*. And then she started kind of snivelling, which was creepy, and she wouldn't like look at me. You did at least, I'm assuming, have the brain to – *use* something. Did you, Amanda? Did you? You did – *use* something, didn't you? Didn't you? *Answer* me! Yeh. I said yeh. What the fuck? And then it was like Who Is He? The boy, the man – who is he (the bastard)? Just someone, I said: doesn't matter. Gone. No big.

And then she was up and shouting: no *big*?! No *big*?! No big *what*, you stupid little girl? No big *deal*? No big *event*? Is that what you're attempting to say? Well I have news for you, my girl: it *is* a big deal. It *is* a big event – because apart from the fact that you are now – oh God, I thought you had more sense . . . well, apart from *that*, I might inform you Amanda, that this – *person*, whoever he is, is in the eyes of the law and in the eyes of God as well – a *rapist*. Oh God. I thought you had more sense. And I will find out who he is, Amanda – whether you tell me or not, you may be assured that I will not rest until I have found this – *criminal*, this dirty little—! Oh God. I really did think you had more *sense* . . . And I will see that he gets what's coming to him. Hear me? Hear me? Do you hear what I'm *saying* to you, Amanda . . . ?! Yeh.

So I just left her to it – Mum and her brand-new game: Hunt The Rapist. Whatever. She won't find him. She can't. No one knows about him, his name, where he is. And anyway, I don't want to get him into trouble. I mean yeah – I'd like to kick him in the face, the fucking arsehole, yeh sure. But I don't want all police and stuff. They'd only start on at me like you see on TV – what did I think I was doing there – *missy* – all alone with him, late at night? Which is a bloody good question, actually: one I've been asking. Anyway. Whatever.

In the living room (and I had to like go real easy through the hall because Dad was over by the door and talking to a, I don't know – carpenter or something, maybe, and hitting this piece of paper, bill I think, and saying You Cannot Be *Serious*, like again and again. And in the living room I was like really so totally surprised because on a table in a heap of about a million empty bottles and dirty glasses (God – and they go on at *me*) was this really cool like parcel? And my name on a label?

It's this book of *Grimm's Fairy Tales*, and I didn't actually go oh fuck me because I'd never seen a book as really great-looking as this one. Heavy and thick – and the pictures! Oh wow! I'm really like loving it. Turns out it's from the creep. The new guy. Who I'd totally decided not ever to meet, but I did of course. Had to, really. Happened later. On my fifteenth birthday, as it turned out. Didn't think at first that it was planned – and then I was like God, what am I *saying*? If Mum's involved, of course it's planned. Like a military thing, knowing her – yeh, and down to the last whatever. We were in this really cool like American diner kind of a place – all retro and really great like in *Grease*, yeh? They asked me where I wanted to go, and I said there. And Mum and Dad, they were like, are you sure? Because we could always go to a *proper* restaurant. And I was like – look, you asked me where I wanted to go, and I said *there*, OK? What's your problem? So we were in this kind of, I don't know – booth thing. Red and shiny with buttons, and on the table there's like a little jukebox? How cool is that? And ketchup and American mustard which is called French like the fries – crazy or what? – and this other cute thing with all like tiny little paper napkins in. I had a Diet Coke, but it was in the proper curvy bottle, with two straws. I thought it was Elvis playing, but Dad, he goes no, it's Little Richard, and I'm like Little *Who* . . . ? Big mistake, because I could see he was going to so – oh God – *tell* me? And that's when this old guy turns up at the table. Hah! And I thought it wasn't *planned*? He was what? Just like passing through? In his three-piece suit and his fucking funny shoes? I so don't think so. God – he was older than the bloody music. I thought it was gaga old Grandad at first, who I'd just been told was coming to the, oh man – *wedding* (and don't get me started on that. Jesus.). But how can he? Huh? How can he come? He's mental, isn't he?

That's what Dad says. That's why we don't ever see him, Dad says.

'Is that true, Alan? Did you say that? Have you said that about Daddy? Have you?'

'Well no. Obviously not.'

'Yes you did, Dad. You did you did you did. You were always saying that.'

'No no. Not at all. I may have suggested that he was less than . . . well look, Susan: face facts. That's why he's *in* that place, isn't it? Wouldn't be there otherwise. Would he? Stands to reason. Which is more than he ever does . . .'

'He is just slightly . . . *distrait*, that's all. Gets easily confused. That's all. And it was cruel and very wrong of you, Alan, to tell Amanda that he was—! Honestly!'

'I never said that.'

'You did, Dad. You did you did you did.'

'God – you certainly get your money's worth here, don't you? This burger's absolutely enormous. No Amanda, I never said that.'

'You *did*! I so can't believe this! You said to me – listen, Amanda, you said, you can more or less write off your old Grandad because he's absolutely mental. That's what you said.'

'Did you, Alan? Did you?'

'And the piccalilli – rather a piquant touch, wouldn't you say? Well yes I *did* say that as a matter of fact, Susan. Yes I did. My very words. Because it's true, isn't it? He's completely bats, your father. Up in the air with the butterflies. No getting away from it.'

'I can't *believe* you can say those things about my wonderful Daddy. He's worth a hundred of you, Alan. Even on a bad day.'

'Mm – well maybe he was once, Susan, possibly one time that was indeed the case – but that was back in the days when he could, oh I don't know – remember his own *name*, wasn't it? When he wouldn't take the carnations out of a vase and drink down all the water.'

'Jesus, Dad! Did he *really* do that, Grandad?'

'Mm. And then he ate the carnations.'

'*Right*, Alan – that's it. I've heard enough. Not another word. I'm going to—! Oh . . . oh look. Oh *look*, Alan – look who's here. Well well. Of all the . . . It's Black! Good heavens! It's Black! Yoo-hoo . . . ! Over here, Black! Yes, that's right. Hello. How lovely to *see* you. Fancy just running into you like this . . . !'

'Mm, yes, as you say. Hello, Alan. All right, are we? What a, um – lovely place. Had the very devil of a job finding it, I have to say. Um – that is I mean—'

'Come and sit with us, Black. Move up Alan, can't you? That's right. Squidge up. Plenty of room. This is Amanda, Black. Our daughter. And you've caught us on a very special day. It's a very special day, isn't it Amanda?'

'Whatever . . .'

'Ha ha. Oh *listen* to her, Black. Honestly – young people! *Whatever* . . . ! Really. It's only her fifteenth *birthday*, isn't it? A *very* special day, I'd say. Say hello, Amanda. This is Black.'

'Hello, Mr Black.'

'No no, dear – just Black. It's a sort of a – nickname, isn't it Black?'

'Tis, yes. Sort of. Well Happy Birthday, I must say. And what a delightful place for a celebration. What's that you're eating, Alan? Looks perfectly gruesome.'

'Not bad at all, as it happens. Want one?'

'Pass, if I may. And that's beer you've got there, is it. Drop of wine, maybe . . . ?'

'Probably got some. Be American though, I should think.'

'Don't think I've ever had it, American. Try it, I suppose . . . So then, young Amanda. Fifteen, hey? Quite a young lady. A very *beautiful* young lady, if I may say so. Oh God. I think I might just have to quickly go to the, um . . . expect it's a little hellhole in there, yes? Ah waitress – could I trouble you for the wine list, when you've a moment . . . ?'

Amanda just sat there and stared at him. She had been going to go through the full routine: Excuse me, don't think I'm being, you know – like *rude* or anything . . . but just who *are* you, exactly? Yeh but look – it's obvious, isn't it? Got to be. Why else would he be here? But no – no way. I mean – look at him. Just look at him. Jesus. He's just like so fucking *ancient*. Like a hundred years old, or something. No. It can't be. But it's got to be. Shit. This is really like creeping me out.

'Anyway, Amanda,' said Susan in what Amanda had once decided she thinks is, what? Her *sweet* voice? And it always comes out so really like lemony? 'As you might have guessed, Black is my . . . well anyway, Black has consented to be my new husband. Isn't it exciting? Now Black – you might care to say something? Few words?'

'Did you catch that, Alan? What the girl said? Don't *have* a wine list. Most extraordinary thing I've ever heard . . .'

'I don't think that connoisseurs make up a good deal of their everyday passing trade you know, Blackie old man. Save your thirst for when you can plunder your own cellar, I would.'

'Funny you should mention that actually – just been looking over the plans for that, the cellar at the new place. They can dig down really deep, apparently, and—'

'Black. Few words? Don't you have something to say to Amanda . . . ?'

'Hm? Oh yes. Course. Happy Birthday, Amanda. No – said that, haven't I? Have I? Truth is, I've just got to slip off to the, um . . . Actually, you know, if you'll all forgive me, I think I'll just get a taxi home. Let's all meet up again when we're . . . you know. When it's not all so . . . well. There it is.'

Amanda registered the placing of an envelope before her, watched him not manage to bend down quite far enough for Susan to be able to plant her kiss, saw his spasm of nearly agony as Alan very playfully cuffed him in the midriff, and then she just simply sat there as he tottered away and out of the door, each of his steps a barely arrested and headlong plummet.

'Well. That was a nice surprise, wasn't it Amanda? Sit up, Alan. There's ketchup on your chin. What's in the envelope?'

'I just don't believe you two guys. Jesus I just don't.'

'We're not "guys", Amanda. We're your parents. What don't you *believe* . . . ? God – I thought we'd done all this. What's in the envelope?'

'He's – *old*. He's got like funny little blobs of black hair. He walks like he's got two wooden legs. He's got a thing in his ear. He's . . . *old*. Dad – what is going down here?'

'Don't be too hasty. He's all right, Blackie is. When you get to know him. No Cary Grant, admittedly, but . . . well, which one of us is?'

'Exactly. Thank you, Alan. He has – many qualities. What's in the envelope, Amanda?'

'Yeh yeh – like he's loaded. Right?'

'He is not without resources. And he is a very kind and sweet man. Should we go now, Alan? This music, it's beginning to get

239

on my nerves. Amanda – why don't you open the envelope, yes?'

'Bobby Vee, this one, pretty sure. Or is it Bobby Darin . . . ?'

'Oh puh-*leese*, Dad. Like we care! I want a pudding. Knickerbocker Glory.'

'Oh *must* you, Amanda darling? Why don't we go home – there's plenty of ice cream in the freezer. And so on. Tell her, Alan.'

'Rubber ball come bouncing back to me-e-e-eee . . . ! Yes. Bobby Vee, I reckon. Might be Frankie Avalon.'

'No because the Knickerbocker Glory, right, it comes in this really cool sundae glass? With like syrup and a cherry? Jesus – it is my *birthday* . . . !'

'Oh – all right then. Alan – get the waitress. Oh look – she's just gone right past you. What's *wrong* with you at all? So ineffectual . . . Amanda – open the envelope, why don't you? Hm?'

'In the jungle, the mighty jungle, the lion sleeps tonight . . . this is by somebody or other as well. Ah – hello. Yes. Could we have please a, um – Knickerbocker Glory . . . that right, Amanda? Yes – Knickerbocker Glory, and . . . anything for you, Susan? No? Sure? Coffee? Nothing? Really? No? Right then – just that, and I'll have the bill. No hang on – I'll have a coffee. Yes. Cappuccino. No – not cappuccino. Espresso. No not, actually – just black, ordinary black. Filter, is it? Yes. And a little milk. Thank you.'

'Well done, Alan. Man of decision. Churchill could have done with you during the war. Black coffee, and a little milk. Right then. Very good. We'll all just sit here a little longer then, shall we, with all this ghastly bloody music and wait for Amanda to consume her own bodyweight in additives and colourants. Oh Christ's sake open the fucking *envelope*, you annoying little child . . . !'

Yeh – and so I did. Wanted to since the second he put it in front of me, the freaky old man, course I did, but with Mum just banging on like that all the time I just thought oh fuck it, let her wait, silly cow. So it was this card, right, with a *pony* on it? And, like – *pink*? So yeh, I was thinking it's good he just happened to have it on him as he just happened to bump into us in the American diner he just happened to wander into (why do they all think I'm just like so *dumb*?). And inside – Jesus. Fifty quid. Fifty-quid note. Oh wow. And then – I go to lift it out, yeh – and what? Only another one underneath. Oh wow. Hundred quid. Never in my life on earth have I ever had a hundred quid, not unless you're talking about like last Christmas when I got it off Mum, but that was towards a new iPod, so it didn't really count.

'There. You see, Amanda? What did I tell you? A kind and sweet man. Very. Now listen to me, Amanda . . . oh God, here's that dreadful pudding you ordered. Can you really, Amanda? Eat all that? It's absolutely enormous. Goodness me. Anyway – give the money to Daddy, he'll look after the money for you – won't you, Alan?'

'*Tssss* . . . ! Jesus. Coffee's hot. Burned my bloody tongue . . .'

'Well yes, Alan. Steam rising, you see. Hot. Well done. If you'd wanted *cold* coffee, you should have been more specific.'

'Hey wait up – no way am I giving this to Dad! It's mine. It's my birthday present from the Ancient Mariner.'

'Don't be so rude, Amanda. How can you be so rude? Black, he gives you an extremely generous birthday present, and all you can do is be rude about him. Tell her, Alan.'

'Yes – what your mother said, Amanda. Should've put some milk in . . . absolutely scalding . . .'

'Yeh well it's my money and I'm keeping it. The raspberry muck in here is just so to die for. Think it's raspberry. Red gunk, anyway.'

'I didn't say you had to give it *away*, your money, did I Amanda? It's just – safe keeping. That's all.'

'Well I know what I'm going to spend it on, so there's no point. Tattoo. Nose ring. Litre of Dewar's . . . joke. Joke. It's a joke Mum, yeh?'

'Not, however, a funny one. Very poor taste, I should have said. Tell her, Alan.'

'Mm. What your mother said, Amanda. Trouble is, whenever I go and burn my tongue, it takes just ages to . . . and I think my palate's caught it too. Wonder if I should ask for some ice . . . ? What do you think? Help, would it? Ice cube? Oh I love *this* one – Jailhouse Rock. Now this *is* Elvis.'

'Yeh, Dad – I think I do know that. This is just so *yum* . . .'

'Stupid, that film. Stupid.'

'Sorry, Susan? What's stupid now?'

'The film. That film. *Jailhouse Rock*. Like all his films. Just stupid. If you're in jail, you're not going to go and start singing, are you? And dance about. So stupid.'

'Oh I don't know, Susan. Over the years, I have found the concept of singing while in jail to be wholly credible – tenable, not to say necessary, if the keeping hold of one's mind is a consideration at all. And dancing about. That too. Don't think I'll trouble with the ice. Bit late now.'

Yeh – so that was my birthday, pretty much. In the evening, Tara came round. Jennifer said she was ill, but I don't know if it was true. I think it's because Tara, she told Jennifer, right, about the arsehole Harry? And Jennifer, I don't know – she maybe found it tacky or something because he like works in a garage? She's like that, Jennifer – sometimes it's like she thinks she's royal, or something. Anyway. I shouldn't have told Tara in the first place really, because I know how she is – that she'd go and tell like everyone? But I did. I knew I would. And she asked me all these piles of questions – it was a bit like my mum. So was it like romantic? No. Was there like all candles and really cool music? No. Is he sexy? Did it feel good? Were there like butterflies? Did he nibble on your earlobe? Were you high? Was there rapture? Did you fall asleep in one another's arms? Yeh well: big *no*. Tara looked like so disappointed, and I did too I guess. Her dad's come out of hospital, she said, but when he got out of the ambulance and they helped him up the steps at home he lost his balance and he like fell over and he broke his leg and so they lifted him into the ambulance and like just carted him back to the hospital. One sad conjuror, Tara's dad.

And all this junk, it's been like going through my head as I'm just sitting in this coffee place – not Franco's I don't mean (can't go in there any more) and I'm wearing black tights and my boots and the black sort of like shift-type dress I got at Primark, tunic thing, and this cool like black varnish on my nails? Got them all with Blackie's hundred (I call him that now) as well as the long black beads, and there's still a bit left, which is good. And yeh, he's still sitting there, the guy, with his paper and his coffee and I'm just ramming my spoon into the dried-up hunk of brown sugar, chipping away at it, and kind of just smiling if I see him looking over. He's old too – that's the point. That's why I'm doing it. Because I thought, no way – no way is a guy of that age going to think he has even like any chance at all with a girl like me. But no. It doesn't seem to work that way. Men, Jesus: go figure. And any moment now, he's going to like come over? So I'll go now, because *ee-yow* – he's just so yuck and old. But I had to know. If it would work. I really really had to know.

And I still do, tell Tara all stuff. I don't know why I do, but I do. And yeh sure – she wanted to know all about the, Jesus – wedding at the new place. But I said no way – there's no way I could even like come *close*, you know? You just had to be there, I so can't describe it. I'm like – nobody could? You know?

CHAPTER SEVEN

I rather think, you know – looking back on what my dear little Susie Q would insist upon always referring to as the 'Day of Days' (dear oh dear oh dear) . . . yes, looking back on it all now from the fairly safe perspective of a good bit of water having flowed under the, um . . . that one is forced to put down the somewhat – singular, shall we say? Yes – singular, I think that ought to do it. Suffice. The rather singular goings-on, then – I think they must simply be seen now as no more than the result of a series of – misunderstandings, want of a better word. Bridge. Water under the, um . . . yes.

On the morning of the day itself, I'd gone over to the Richmond place really very early. Couldn't sleep. Nothing, I hasten to assure you, to do with nerves or anything of that sort, no no no. Just a particularly vigorous and eager coming together of all of the usual – palpitations, stomach of course – head, limbs, you name it really. Itchy as hell – bit short of breath. Had a Bloody Mary and a handful of pills and just got a taxi round there. Can't have been much after eight, but the builders were there, by God were they there – going at it hammer and, um . . . and the dust, oh my Lord – never seen anything like it: thought I could have a seizure. Signalled to the navvies to stop all their drilling but *immediately* – huge great, what are they . . . ? Pneumatic affairs, yes. The floor of the atrium – the very spot where we were all set in just a few hours to be doing the business – well, looked like the recreation of an alien planet, or something . . . thick with craters, pockmarked and powdery. Hammer and tongs is what I wanted to say, although it hardly really matters. So now I start shouting for Clearley – Mr Clearley, he's the site foreman. According to the various reports from the assembled workforce, he hadn't yet arrived, he'd just popped out for a minute, he was 'on the can' – that's what they said to me: 'on the can' – he had to speak to the suppliers and didn't feel well today, so wasn't coming in. Extraordinary, isn't it? I mean to say if you're wholly set on hurling into the face of the gullible old bastard who's actually paying you, you swine, you loathsome ungrateful swine, the most blatant and fanciful fucking fairy story, you would think, wouldn't you, that at least you might run to a little coordination on the matter. Way it is today, you see – sloppy, even in deceit. Anyway, tracked him down eventually, Clearley – stumbling around I was in all this new-found chaos in my perfectly ridiculous shoes (not, though, the even more ridiculous creations that I had had purpose-made for the ceremony to come – black patent they were, upon why-don't-you-guess-who's most explicit instruction, and packed with that much scaffolding they looked like nothing so much as a pair of moon boots, tricked out with treacle. These to go with the dinner suit, you see, I had been told I would be wearing; so not quite so ridiculous as those, no, but perfectly ridiculous all the bloody same). So yes – tracked him down, as I say: sitting in his van, he was, and eating a blameless banana.

'Morning, Mr Leather. Up with the lark. Going to be quite a nice day, look of the sky.'

'Never mind the *sky*, Clearley – what are you doing here? Why are you all here? You're not meant to be here. It's Friday, isn't it? The day we're doing the . . . doing the . . . oh damn – the day we're doing the *thing* . . . !'

'That's next Friday, Mr Leather. Next Friday, that is.'

'What are you *talking* about, *next* Friday! It's not next Friday, it's this Friday. It's today. You think I don't know the day of my own *thing* . . . ? Put down that banana, Clearley.'

'All on my worksheet, Mr Leather. See? States it quite clearly – next Friday. Fourteenth.'

'I don't give a damn what it states clearly, Clearley! It's *today*, I tell you. Seventh. Today.'

'Well that's not what I've got down here. Anyway – no bother, Mr Leather. I'll just tell the lads to pack up. They won't mind. Friday off. Still want paying, though . . .'

'Won't *mind*! Won't *mind*! You think I give a tinker's, um – you think I give a tinker's *thing* whether or not they *mind*? Have you seen the state of the floor in there, Clearley? Have you?'

'Well that's in preparation for the marble tiling. You can't just lay it down willy-nilly, you know. Break up the concrete, compact the hardcore, skim it off with—'

'Yes yes yes – but all that was supposed to happen *after* . . . I wanted the bloody marble floor to be put down *before*, if you remember, but you said it couldn't be put down before and so we all agreed that it would have to be *after*. Yes? You recall? And I've got all these rugs I was going to put down over the concrete and . . . Christ. *Cuss*! Don't give a tinker's *cuss* whether or not they *mind*, God damn you all . . .'

Well there was hardly a point, was there? Going on at the man. Damage done. Nothing for it really but to break the news to Susie. Either we'll have to do it somewhere else or wait a week till the marble's down – which I said we should have done in the first fucking place, and Alan, he backed me up, of course he did. Just like screaming into the wind, needless to say. Strong-willed woman, Susie is. Determined. As, Jesus, I was soon to rediscover.

'Sorry, Black – I can't hear you very well. I'm in a taxi – not great reception.'

'Yes well you'd better get out of the taxi because I'm in a phone box and I've only got another forty bloody *pee*.'

'I just can't understand why you won't get a mobile.'

'Got one somewhere. Hid it. Don't want a sodding mobile. Not a plumber, am I? Always at everybody's beck and thing. And I can't work them. Too fiddly. Now listen, Susie . . . Call. Beck and call. Now listen, Susie—'

'Or at least a phone card. Why don't you get a phone card, then you wouldn't be worried about having only forty pence.'

'Lose them. Always lose the bloody things, phone cards. And I've now only got twenty fucking *pee* because I've just put the other twenty fucking *pee* into the fucking machine because we have been discussing my lack of a mobile and how I'm always losing phone cards! Now God's sake *listen*, Susie—'

'Are you excited? I am. It's finally come. The Day of Days. I'm just on my way to the hairdresser.'

'Yes well – that's what I have to talk to you about—'

'Sorry, Black – you're breaking up . . .'

'I'm breaking up – I'm breaking *down*! Just *listen*, God's sake!'

'Look – wait a minute. I'm just getting out of the cab, all

right? I'll just pay the cab, and then we can talk. Give me the number and I'll ring you back.'

'Number? What number? Why are you going to ring me back if we're talking on the phone . . . ?'

'The number. The number of where you are.'

'What – the number of this phone, do you mean? Well how am I supposed to know the number of the bloody *phone*, in God's name . . . ?'

'It'll be written on it. Just look.'

'Written on it? There's nothing written on it. Jessica Is A Slag is written on the wall, and that's the sum bloody total.'

'Well put in the other twenty pence.'

'I've *put* in the other . . . Susie? Are you there?'

'Can't hear you very well.'

'No well I'm already about to explode I'm shouting now so bloody loudly. Woman outside, I think she's going to call the police. Look just *listen*, can't you? It's about the house. The atrium. I . . . Susie? Hello? You there . . . ? Oh damn. I don't believe it . . . !'

So what did I do next? Run off and get more change? In *these* shoes? I hardly think so. And did I know the whereabouts of Susie's hairdresser? Well did I? Exactly. So I went into a café thing, tea thing sort of a shop because even the bloody pubs weren't open yet and I could have done with another Bloody Mary, I can tell you that – and I said to the woman there, may I please use your telephone? And she said – you want a coffee? You want a cup of tea? Some breakfast? I said oh God all right – all right then, I'll have a pot of tea for one. Toast? Jesus – OK, fine: toast. She nodded, brought me that and I paid and tipped her and I said to her can I please now use your telephone and she looked at me and she said we ain't got no phone. I'm telling you – there are times when I wonder whether this country of ours even deserves a future, I do, I really do. So I went round to see Alan.

'Mm – yes, I see what you mean. But I wouldn't really trouble, Blackie, trying to talk to her, you know. There's no way on God's earth she's going to put it off. No way whatever.'

'Why? Why, Alan? It's only a week. What's wrong with her at all?'

'It's you, Blackie, it must be: it's you. You're clearly irresistible – she just can't wait to take advantage of all your secret folds and creases.'

'God's sake, Alan – this is serious. Christ – we're meant to be on in a couple of hours. Not much more.'

'All right, Blackie. Calm down, hey? Like a virgin, you are, with pre-wedding anxiety. No look listen – she won't call it off because one, she's already in the hairdressers and they've no doubt begun on this most extraordinary creation she has spent quite a time devising. Rollers are the order of the day, I am led to understand. Not to say highlights. Two: caterers are all lined up, such as they are. More to the point is her mad and loony father – one day leave-out from the bin, no doubt with a couple of bouncers in tow – maybe a mask, as in *Silence of the* What-is-it, *Lambs*. Probably thinks he's going fishing. And so that we all match nicely, Susan has rented him a dinner suit because his customary ensemble comprises a motley and varied selection of stains, and someone else's pyjama jacket. Whether the dinner suit she has chosen for him runs to six-foot sleeves that can be buckled at the rear, we have yet to discover. Then there is the matter of the blessed Father Flynn to be taken into consideration. He is being reasonably expensively babysat this morning in order to ensure that not one drop of altar wine should pass those so very florid lips of his. Or surgical spirit, whichever should currently be the tipple of choice. Add to all this, Blackie, the self-evident truth that neither you nor myself could frankly *stand* yet one more week of her wittering on about the glorious advent of the Day of Days . . . No – all in all, as she herself would surely say: 'twere well 'twere done quickly.'

'Mm. Right. See what you mean. Well where, then? Where can we do it? Bloody short notice . . .'

'Ah well now here again, Blackie my friend, you are backed up against a wall. She has it in her mind, you see, that the sacred union must not only be seen in the eyes of God – and hence the defrocked and ludicrous scandal that is Father Johnnie Flynn – but also that it must take place on the very site of all our futures. Symbolic, you see? Touching, in a lumpish and rather predictable way.'

'What – you mean you're telling me that she's going to insist on going through with it – *there*? But Alan – you haven't *seen* the place. It's just – I can't *describe* what it's like there. It's just—!'

'Nonetheless. That's what's going to happen. You know it is. It's Susan we're dealing with here, you know. And if you don't, you'll soon learn I assure you. Me, I'm a postgraduate. If signally lacking in honours.'

So that was that, really. And Alan, give him his due, he tried to get me to, I don't know – buck up, rally round sort of thing, I suppose – kept on telling me that in less than four or so hours it would all be over. Mm, well . . . over for him, very possibly – over for Amanda and the madman father and the dissolute priest, oh yes, assuredly – but Susie, well . . . she has made it very horribly clear to me that tonight, the very first night in

251

our House of Dreams was to be, oh dear God, Our Very Special Journey Into Paradise. I mean I *ask* you . . . ! What does she expect of me at all? Well whatever it is, she won't be getting it, that's for bloody sure. Nervous as hell about the whole damn thing, you want the naked truth of the matter. Tried not to think of it. And especially not the naked part. Even taking my shoes off, that'll be frightening enough. Extraordinary, really – when you consider, Jesus, the only reason I ever paid her any attention, asked her to lunch, asked her to dinner – employed her in the first fucking place . . . was because I really did want to subject her to, well – all manner of rudeness, really. But maybe I just assumed I would never have a cat's chance of getting even close. Because look at her. And now look at me. Quite. The odds were never in my favour. And up till now, it's just been the occasional little bit of kissing, a grateful fondle, the crush of something warm and scented. And an upping of that is truly all I crave: a warming blush of cheeky affection, followed by maybe a blissful release. That would suit me down to a . . . But as to Our Own Very Special Journey Into Paradise . . . ! Oh Jesus. T. It would. Suit me down to a . . . yes well. Oh Jesus.

Alan had explained to me, quite as if I were an idiot, how he had thought that to give all the rubble where the floor used to be, to give it a really good hosing down, were his words to me – he had thought that a *good* idea, you see. And not for the first time with Alan, it quite naturally had proved to be a very bad idea indeed.

'Well Alan now look. I don't really have the *time*, you know, to explain it slowly to you, and in the sort of detail an imbecile would require. I can't really go into it now, how only a very dim and foolish person could imagine that *wet* rubble, rubble that is as we speak deep and running with rivulets and tributaries – how anyone less than altogether sane could have imagined that this would be immeasurably preferable to the *dry* sort. You and Black will be wearing patent shoes, yes? I myself shall be wearing a pale-rose satin high heel – Amanda, white leather pumps. It's not, is it – *conducive*, Alan? It doesn't strike the right note. It verges, Alan, upon calamity. I should have expected nothing else.'

'It was the dust, you see. But there are druggets in the builders' Portakabin.'

'Druggets, Alan? *Druggets*?'

'Sort of canvas things. Heavy numbers. Could drag them out and sort of, I don't know – cover it, maybe?'

'Do it, Alan. Just do it. Do whatever it takes. I am now going upstairs to dress. Where is Black? Where is Amanda?'

'Amanda . . . not too sure. Last time I saw Blackie, he was flat on his back in his bedroom cursing the shortness of his socks, the tops of which he couldn't quite seem to be able to reach. I was happy to oblige.'

'I can't imagine what you're talking about. Now at least reassure me, Alan, that everything else is in order. God Almighty, you know – I really shouldn't have to be doing all this. This is *my* day. Mine. It's a very special moment in the life of a woman, Alan, surely you must see that. It is my wedding day. The least one might expect is a little support from one's bloody *husband*, God's sake.'

'And Best Man. Don't forget that bit. For today at least, I am multi-tasking.'

'Oh yes and talking of that – you have, haven't you Alan?'

'Have? Have what, my peach?'

'Don't play about, Alan. Just don't. I'm nervous enough as it is. You have, haven't you? Got it.'

'It? Got it? Got what exactly, cherub of mine?'

'*Christ* . . . you *know* what I mean. You know *exactly* what I'm asking you. The ring. The ring. The bloody *ring*. You have got it safely?'

'Oh the *ring* . . . ! Hm. Now let me see . . . I know I saw it knocking around here somewhere . . .'

'Alan . . . !'

'But that must have been Tuesday, or so. Don't think I've glimpsed it since, though. Why? Were you needing it?'

'*Alan* . . . !'

'No no. Don't worry. Just a little *jeu d'esprit*, my flower. The ring is safe and sound. All ready for Blackie to slip upon your finger. Have you got one for him?'

'I wanted to. He said he wouldn't. Said rings were for girls and gigolos.'

'Quite right. Well at least you know he's of sound mind, anyway. Solid beginning, that. Who's, um . . . who's that fellow over there? Hanging about. Do we know him . . . ?'

'Where . . . ? Oh him. He's the one who's sitting with Father Flynn until we, you know – get going.'

'Oh I see. And so why, um . . . isn't he?'

Susan's face then clouded, suspicion shading darker into dread and slugging it out with fury to gain the upper hand.

'You! Yes you! Whoever you are. Come over here. Well come on! What are you doing here? Why aren't you sitting with Father Flynn? There's over an hour to go.'

'Well I were. Sitting with him, like. But this girl, she come over, right? Says it's OK. Says I can like shove off. So I been

254

having a bit of a nibble, hope you don't mind or nothing. Sausages is great.'

'Alan. See to it. Now, Alan – before it's too late. Amanda, got to be. What does she think she's doing? Am I that bad a mother? Am I, Alan? Have I truly failed her completely? Why does she – hate me? What is she *doing* . . . ? What does she think she's . . . ?'

'Mm – well I'm sure our friend here doesn't want to listen to all my answers to that, assuming I had the time to give them. Where did you last see them? I'm sorry – I don't know your name. Where were they? Flynn and the girl? Amanda.'

'Amanda . . . ? No – Dave. Dave, my name is.'

'Right, Dave. So where did you leave them?'

'Short for David.'

That's when Susan got him by the throat.

'Look you. Take my husband right this minute to the place where you left them, Is that perfectly *clear* . . . ?'

Alan gently extricated the man from a grasp he knew to be deadly, cooing quite softly the while, and ignoring his amazement, steered him away.

'It's quite all right, Dave-short-for-David. Woman's nerves, you know. It is her wedding day, after all. Which way? Upstairs? Garden? Where?'

'Just by the bar in the wotsit room. But she said you was her husband . . .'

'The bar. Of course. Where else? Dear dear. Yes, but she's getting another one today, you see. Not instead of, but as well as. Now look – I think you might as well pop off now, you know. The cat is out of the bag. Been paid and everything, have you? Good good. Few more sausages, maybe? No? Well bye then, Dave-short-for-David. A brief acquaintance, but none the less memorable for that.'

Yes well. So much for all the flannel – but I've really got to be shot of the oaf now and get to Flynn with all God's speed. Because if his habitual shade of plum has already deepened into anything approaching imperial purple, then we might be requiring all of the good Lord's support just in order to keep him upright. Ah yes – I see them now. I am conscious of a lowering sensation in the pit of my stomach. I have to admit that it's all looking rather far from good.

'Amanda. What are you doing here? You should be dressing. Why did you send that man away? What is in that glass? Are you drinking? And why, Amanda, is Father Flynn lying on the floor with what could easily be a vol-au-vent sticking out of his mouth?'

'He wasn't a couple of minutes ago. We were just chatting about the possibility of me becoming a nun. Like, how cool would that be? Big turn-on for some guys. He made a like really crap joke about dirty habits, and next thing you know – wham. Flat on his back. Crazy. It is a vol-au-vent. They're pretty good, actually.'

'You've done this deliberately, haven't you Amanda? It's unkind. Put that glass down. You're a child. And what do you mean, a big *turn-on* . . . ? Jesus. How much has he had to drink?'

'I'm fifteen. Give me back that glass.'

'A child. Turn-on indeed . . . Here – help me up with him, can't you? Jesus, you're in nearly as bad a state as he is – look at you. Come on Father Flynn – up we get. That's it. That's right. Just get you on to this chair, here. That's the way. How are we feeling? All right? Not too bad? How about a drop of coffee, yes? Amanda – those flasks. Coffee. And you'd better have one yourself. I'm disappointed in you, Amanda. This was not the time.'

'Oh balls, actually, Dad. Of course this was the time. Because like tomorrow, OK? This all isn't happening. So of course it's the time. Isn't it? Oh God. I do feel a bit sick, actually . . .'

'Go upstairs. Shower. Dress. I'll be up in a minute. Come on, Amanda – *help*, for God's sake. You owe it. You owe it to your mother.'

Amanda stood there, swaying like a single and careless sheaf of corn, stirred by a summer breeze.

'I just don't know how you can say that, Dad. After what she's doing to you. Doing to us. I like so don't owe her *anything*.'

'You do. You do. More than you know. That's it, Father Flynn – one more big gulp. That's the fellow. And anyway, Amanda – Black, he's not a bad bloke. Is he? You said so yourself, one time.'

'Not the *point* though, is it? Oh God look, Dad – he's all, like – *dribbling* . . . ?'

'Leave him to me. Do it, Amanda – go upstairs and do what I told you. Save all the issues for later. It's your mother's day. Let's all try to make it, well – a bit less horrible than all of this. Yes? All right?'

'You're funny you are, Dad. I just don't get.'

'No. Well I maybe just don't get either. Go on, Amanda. I'll talk to you later. *Now*, Father Flynn – that's better, isn't it? Course it is. One eye wholly open now, look. Excellent. Let's just see if we can't just prise up the lid of the other one, shall we? Then we'll have a full matching set, up and working. Can you hear me? Do you know what I'm saying?'

'Urrrgh . . . I feel really sick, Dad.'

'Mm, you said. Well add that to your list of things to do then, Amanda. Off you go. Now Father Flynn – I'm going to slap your face for you now. All right? Won't be too hard. Don't take it as a criticism at all – it's a gesture of kindliness, really. Remind your blood to keep on the move. Not to go on hogging the face. Get a little animation into these icy fingers of yours. All right?'

The sudden phlegmy rumble of his voice, when it finally came, caused Alan to his annoyance to bloody slop some of this coffee down and over the man's already disgusting old clerical collar.

'Yous lay a finger on me, my boy, and the wrath of the Lord will show no mercy. Lightning will – eh . . .'

'Smite me down? Mm, yes, thought so. Smite me down. Well OK then, Father Flynn. We'll override the spanking just this once. Want something to eat? No, didn't think so. Well the thing is now, Father Flynn – are you aware of what is supposed to be happening here in – ooh, just under an hour, now? Got it all off pat, have you? Know the words?'

Father Flynn eyed him rheumily.

'Pat . . . is he coming over?'

'No no. There's no Pat. Just us. And the two you're going to marry.'

'Pat. Sure haven't seen him in a long time . . .'

'No no, Father Flynn. Let's get it right. Walk around a bit, will we? That's the way. Now we have met before, Father Flynn, though I would wholly understand if you didn't recall. I am Alan. My name is Alan. The young lady who has gone off to be sick – remember her? Yes? Well her name is Amanda. My daughter. And also the daughter, I might add, of the woman – that's Susan – that you are here today to marry.'

Father Flynn was shocked.

'It is against the laws of the church for a priest to marry!'

Alan sighed. 'Oh dear. We don't seem to be making an awful lot of progress, do we . . .'

'Ah – don't you worry, my lad. I'll be fine. Done this a thousand times. Dry your eyes. His suffering is at an end. Gone to a better place.'

'Oh God in heaven . . .'

'Exactly. Now tell me, boy – when's Pat coming over, the little devil.'

Alan shook his head. What to do with the Irish whisky priest? A comic myth, a thing of fable, stock and stereotypical . . . and yet here he sits before me, just about alive and breathing right into my face really the most unutterable vapour. All I could think of was to lock him into a bedroom with some Alka-Seltzer and a bottle of Malvern and warn him to be a good Father and then hare along the corridor to see to Amanda – seemed more or less all right now, and well into the process of covering her face with all the smacked and brazen allure of a harlot. Blackie next: he was standing stock-still in the centre of his room, dinner suit on, bow tie not too bad – pitched a bit forward on quite the most ridiculous shoes I have ever seen (I don't know what it is about Blackie and his shoes) and so very stiffly as if held rigid in a full plaster body cast. I said to him you could sit down – little while yet. He said Joking. I said, so I'll see you downstairs then, yes? Ten minutes? And he said, those architects, dozy cunts – going to get them to put in a lift. And then he said Jesus, let's just get this bloody thing over and done with, shall we? Yes yes, I said: best of, um – luck then, Blackie: I'll be right beside you. And I went up to him and – well, sort of gave him a bit of a hug, really, not to put too fine a point on it. The look in his eyes, it was nothing but tender. And then of course, there was Susan to attend to: she might, I conjectured, be in need of big assurance.

'Alan. Thank God. When you didn't come, I thought—'

'No no. No need. All is well. False alarm. Amanda and Father Flynn – just flicking through a catechism. Moving sight. He's on top form, I must say. Oh – and she wished you every happiness in the world, by the way, Amanda. Just a bit too shy to tell you herself, you know what she's like. And Blackie, well . . . what can I say? Jigging up and down with excitement, he is – like a kid on Christmas Eve. Says he's the luckiest man alive. I told him he's right. And I know whereof I speak.'

Rather to his surprise, Susan stood up to face him. She was dressed and coiffed and radiant, he only now just realised: her beauty astonished him – again, again. The side of her face was now against his, in a crush and flurry of silk and scent. Alan felt the kick and lurch, a memento of his love. He was sad when she moved away, was no longer against and a part of him.

'Now then, Susan. The other thing. Safe now, do you think? To let him out?'

Susan bit her lip and looked reflective. 'Ah,' she said softly. 'Daddy . . .'

'Nurse said he'd had enough Christ-knows-what to fell a buffalo, but still I think you know – timing is all.'

Mm. Indeed. It was that, if Susan were to be honest with herself – which was always, surely, now the intention (from this day forward)? – that had, among a thousand other and lesser anxieties, been very much a factor to consider: the wisdom of Daddy being here at all. When first she had insisted upon it, she had possibly quite wilfully and childishly refused to have truck with the depth of his condition. It was just that for her first wedding, her marriage to Alan, she had been so terribly eager to see it done – and the eagerness, in retrospect it hardly surprised her because that, well – that was her nature, that was how things had to be . . . but this is *Alan* we are talking about, good God in heaven. Why and how the headlong dash? What sort of urgency could he possibly have inspired in her? Well there. That is the trouble with facts, remembered occurrences – the rigid structures still standing in defiance after the dust and sparkle of all nuance has long since blown away. You cannot, as people say, argue with them (they must be faced) . . . and yet their underlying impetus is lost for ever: they are stripped of reason. Like, I don't know – Stonehenge, say: one can but marvel at this vast and static undeniable presence, while never understanding how it should be there. And Daddy, poor Daddy, I'd given him so little notice he of course just couldn't manage it. He said he would cancel his meeting in Barcelona, reconfigure the AGM (for this is the life he used to lead) and of course I said no – because there would after all be a lifetime full of Daddy, so where was the damage? He was so very handsome in those days – so virile and dynamic. Often browned by the glinting sun from when he fished for barracuda on his sleek and chartered yacht. So very capable and suave as his beautiful hand reached over for the bill in a wonderful restaurant where he was so well known at the close of yet another so very perfect dinner (the slim gold Patek-Philippe just subtly gleaming amid the equally golden hairs on his wrist). I saw him like this so few times afterwards – and then there came the first in a series of disturbing reports: his Bentley was found abandoned in Portsmouth – he was found sitting on a bench in a park not a mile away, determined to see in the millennium from just the spot he had selected at the axis of a floral clock (and this three years before its dawning). He telephoned me so very very late one night to say that he had exchanged the Patek-Philippe with a mounted cavalier upon the moors for a bag of some sort of a savoury snack, though he thought not Twiglets.

And so, in the face of Alan's now wholly comprehensible incredulity, I flatly insisted that upon this next occasion, this brand-new wedding so many years later, that my Daddy should be there – and yes, to give me away. In the glow of the vision I had conjured, I saw myself – younger, even lovelier – and my tall and silver-haired magnificent father, whose tailoring and stature and profile would render all other men there akin to a scattered band of stunted bruisers, clumsy in hand-me-downs – he would offer me his arm and smile his love for me and send me with a kiss sweetly on course for a new and spectacular chapter. Yes well. The home he's in, they thought I was joking, much to Alan's fat satisfaction. And of course, even in the face of, oh dear – sanity, this made me more determined (it is hard, you know, being me all the time). They forced me to endorse every manner of release, the acceptance of all responsibility, the agreement to the considerable costs relating to transportation and accompaniment. And even as I heard the burr of the nib of the pen on the first of the documents – my Daddy's old Montblanc, as a matter of fact, roundly describing the loops of my name and ending with a flourish in the mark of Zorro – I tumbled to the stir and then clamour of warning. And then I signed the others.

'Shall I, Alan . . . talk to him first? I wanted to go to him the minute he arrived, but . . . well. I didn't. Should I? What do you think? See him first? Before the actual, you know – thing?'

'Well . . . there's very little time now. Of course – bride's prerogative to be late . . . but I have a feeling you know, Susan, that if ever your mantra applied . . . well then it surely does now.'

'My . . . ? What do you mean, Alan?'

He stooped and kissed her forehead.

''Twere well 'twere done quickly . . .'

Susan smiled in fondness and maybe resignation. She briefly touched his hand, and Alan was shocked to discover that this had so very stupidly thrilled him.

'I'll get the nurse to decant him downstairs, Susan, and then I'll haul down old Blackie. Give Amanda a knock. See to the clergy side of things. One good side to us all just being here, though – we don't have to drive round and round in circles in Rolls-Royces and things, waiting for someone to turn up. Yes. Right, then? OK. Ready? Good. Oh yes and I forgot to mention – the flowers, they arrived, look marvellous. Bit late, but they're all here now. And, um . . . this, Susan . . .' and Alan was reaching into the wardrobe as he stuttered out this oddly difficult little bit – 'this . . . this is for you.'

Susan gazed at the ball of palest pink old roses, flecked with gypsophila and trailing a ribbon of, oh – just exactly the identical shade. Her eyes dipped down and her shoulders were relaxed into maybe ease or a voluntary defeat.

'Oh. Alan. I hate you . . .'

'Right. No change there, then. Um – why, particularly . . . ?'

'Because my maquillage is perfect and if it all just runs and smears I shall look like a . . . well. I'll just look a mess. Thank you, Alan. Thank you.'

She kissed him soft and full on the lips, a sensation he barely remembered. He gripped her shoulders and tried not to sob and so much wanted now just to rape her, here and at this very moment, to rip, tear into and spoil, ravish and repair this once holy union of husband and wife.

Stood there like a bloody statue until I thought I'd bloody become one. Alan, he'd popped his head in at some point earlier and suggested I might like a sit-down – bloody laugh that was. Done a really thorough job I had, with all the straps and buttons, but Jesus, when it came to the cummerbund – always an ally when a paunch is on the menu – I could barely get it to do up. And the jacket itself – could hardly believe it: not just the body of it, not just the fastening, but the sleeves, even the bloody sleeves! Thought they were going to burst as I was boiling like a pig and trying to stuff my big porker arms into and down the fucking things. Can't have been that long, can it? Since I wore a bloody dinner suit? I mean, am I expanding then conceivably daily? It's extraordinary, really. I mean to say, I look in the mirror, a fat man doesn't gaze back at me. Granted, the reflection is anything but gratifying – the real hair, the natural stuff, what there is of it – that's growing in like it had been paid to (white, but of course) and the punched-in darker little wiry knobs of it just sit there with resentment, not so much ever getting longer as fizzing out sideways like spat-out furballs. No – more the air of a pubic bush, really, randomly dispersed by a salvo of buckshot, then quickly flash-fried as crispy seaweed in the merest smidgen of corn oil. Hands are horrible – hanks of albino bananas, foxed like the pages of my second edition of Sam Johnson's *Dictionary*, and no doubt altogether as musty. Face, well – handsome once, it pains and amazes me to recall, now more akin to a gourd that a spade's just clanged into. So a relative mess, it's fair to say – but not, strangely enough, a fat man. So is some malevolent goblin (and can there be another kind . . . ? Doubt it, doubt it) sneaking into my wardrobe under cover of darkness and substituting all of my clothes for sets that have been similarly well-tailored, though with comparative dwarfs in mind? People, that is to say, even smaller than I? Or maybe they have been just deftly inserting the odd tuck here, taking in a dart or an inseam there – just sufficient to render me foolish and so damned uncomfortable that all I can do is just stand in the middle of the room like a bloody statue until I thought I'd bloody become one? And my arches, they were now strained in pain, my head just clinging on in fear to the guardrail of borderline giddiness. My bootmaker, idle sod – he says if I get easily used to these little beauties, then the next pair he might even be able to jack up that all-important extra inch, bloody deluded fool that he is. Can't he see that if he goes on at this rate I'm in danger of becoming not so much a pillar of a man but some sort of a Barnum's fairground attraction with my head rammed up into any passing chandelier and half my stature made up wholly of *shoe*. I tell you, if I can lift it without the aid of two strong men, next time I see him, this clown of a bootmaker, I'm going to get one of these patent numbers and clout the cunt round the skull with it: dead before he hit the floor. I'd send no flowers.

Couldn't tell you how relieved I was when Alan finally came to get me. I'd made sure I'd taken my puffers, scratched my neck into a lurid and pustulating smorgasbord (slathered all over it a cortisone cream) and swallowed all relevant pills along with a small handful more just to be on the safe side. I was as ready as ever I can be, and God I was grateful to him, Alan, for getting me down the stairs. I am, you know, going to get those bloody architects of mine – one of them's a homosexualist, you only have to look at him, the other's barely more than a simpleton who still seems to worship Le Corbusier. Wanted to build me a conservatory along the lines of a cigar box, and jacked up on concrete stilts. Jesus, the only thing that should be that is me. You might wonder why I engaged them: I know I do. No, I said – I want one with a pitched roof and trefoil crenellations and bloody great finials, not to say glazing bars and pilasters. Close to tears he was, stupid bloody bastard. Just as well his nancy partner was there at his elbow with a lacy hanky. Anyway I am – don't think it's too late: going to get them to put in a lift. Escalator, maybe: there's an idea. And in the mornings, for coming down to breakfast, possibly a fireman's pole.

Jesus, though. When finally we were down on the ground floor and out the back and into the atrium, I barely could believe the sight that met me. An undulating battlefield – well yes, that was expected, but it was all loosely draped with thick and green sort of tarpaulins, stained and holed, can't describe them. Sort of thing you might in desperation sling over a house in a storm when the roof was blown to kingdom come. But Alan, I whispered to him with urgency (whispered, yes, because Amanda, she was there, swaying and goggling at me quite glassily, seemingly holding up or maybe leaning on a parboiled party with a pink-and-sepia clerical collar. Another man in white had a drooling old man in an unrelenting clinch, encouraging him to suck upon what appeared to be a dildo; all these people, do you see? So I had to be discreet). Alan – where are the rugs? What rugs, he said: don't know what you're talking about. The rugs, the rugs – I've got this collection of Persian rugs, some Turkoman, three Chinese, a

266

couple of dhurries, one or two runners: I *told* you about them. You never told me, he said – maybe it was Susan that you told. No no, I said – I wouldn't have troubled Susie with it, no no, I wouldn't have told Susie. And so I was left with the creeping and not unfamiliar suspicion that I had in fact told nobody at all about my collection of rugs, not a living soul, except of course for myself – out loud, yes, and no doubt repeatedly. Oh dear Lord. And it's not as if it's going to get any better, you see: that's the worry.

And that's when I felt it go. A sort of greasy slippage from deep within the ear, and then just the kiss of a draught. The plop it made as it then leapt away from me was the last thing I was destined to hear for quite some considerable time. Even though I caught the slightest glimpse of it from the corner of my eye as it hit the nearest hillock, bounced, rolled and recoiled like a stir-crazed Mexican fucking jumping bean, maddened with delight at its gutsy bid for freedom. I'm frantically signalling to Alan, but damn and blast him, he just won't look over – staring at the doorway – and me, well I couldn't move, well how could I? Jammed in the spot he'd dumped me. Things were grim enough already, but if my clothes were now suddenly to explode and I were to break a limb falling off my shoes in shock, then I think we might have on our hands a debacle too far. There are a couple of violinists over there, look – astounding, really, I hadn't seen them before . . . three actually, now I come to focus, seem nice women, and another one, a man, with one of those – what are they? Big violins. Those big buggers they pluck and carve away at with a thing. And going by the arm movement – Jesus, these women . . . seem intent on sawing the fiddles in half, and he, the bloke, he's no slouch either when it comes down to the old

267

in and out . . . yes, so there's probably music then, filling the air. And Susie's father – got to be him, I presume: there was no plan I was aware of to have more than just the one gaga and slavering derelict to attend this communion . . . he seems to be enjoying the tune: waving his arms about and singing along, conceivably, although it could be no more than a protracted yawn. His dinner suit seems huge on him, and there's yellow all down the front of it. Cello, is it . . . ? Think so. Bass, could be. Priest person. He's come over to me now – patting my hand and beaming like a child (and the fumes, I can't tell you – something on a par with an industrial patio cleaner, strong and surgical, with a top note of maybe ammonia: Christ, he'd go up like a torch). So I have another half-hearted attempt to wave over to Alan – I can almost sense the stitching in the seams straining at their utmost to keep this impossibility together and intact – but he's rapt, you know, thoroughly entranced is how he's seeming . . . and I crank round my neck a bit, and then I see why.

And Susan, now that she was quite sure that everyone had looked, that everyone had seen, abandoned with reluctance her pose in the doorway and picked her way with determination and gingerly up and down the potholes, across the treacherous swathes, the green and undulating mounds that carpeted her bridal path, aware that it was her own quite implacable insistence that had ensured that this was the spot where all of her dearly beloved were to be gathered here today. She smiled at Alan, who simpered back – a dart of worry stabbing her face as she caught sight of Amanda – and signalled imperceptibly with just the one brief closure of her eyes that the burly nurse clasping firmly her once so fabulous father should now and this moment begin to shuffle him forwards . . . and then on

Black she lavished her very most liquid and enveloping smile, a tangible blandishment that made him sigh. And his eyes, she saw, were just about molten. Father Flynn was moaning softly. Susan's father jerked away suddenly as if shocked by a current and shouted out and wildly '*Jacaranda* . . . !' before he saddened, and subsided.

'Daddy – don't make noise. Just hold my arm. There. That's it. You are now to give me away. Oh Alan – there you are. Ask the musicians to stop now, would you? I think we can begin. Ready, Father Flynn?'

Father Flynn grinned quite worryingly.

'You look . . . lovely.'

'Thank you, Father Flynn. You're very kind. Shall we proceed?'

'Quite . . . lovely.'

'Yes. Thank you. Shall we, then? Alan – try to get Daddy to understand that now he must give me away.'

'I've tried to. He says we ought to haggle.'

Amanda said, 'I think I'm going to be sick.'

Susan whispered something reassuring to Black, who gazed at her wonderingly, and then she turned back to face Father Flynn.

'Begin, yes? Let's start now, shall we?'

'We will. We will. Oh God yes, we will. And may I just say to you, Susan, how very very lovely you are looking today.'

'Alan . . . why does he keep saying that . . . ?'

'Jealous of your husbands, I think. So come along then, Father Flynn – let's kick off the proceedings, shall we? All right, Blackie? Yes? All right, are you? Hello? No – Blackie's gone mute. Fair enough. Amanda – do try to remain vertical, won't you? Off you go then, Father Flynn.'

'Oh yes, oh yes. Oh yes. Oh God, yes. Now then I have to tell you all, that this wedding, this holy, em . . . wedding, yes, oh God yes, it's going to be conducted, em – informal. Not, that is to say, the usual, em – formal wording, and so on. Do you see? More personal, it'll be.'

Amanda guffawed. 'You can't remember it, can you? How it goes. Oh man, this so blows! Earlier on he was going to me how he couldn't, like – remember? Thought he was joking.'

'It will all be there in *spirit*,' insisted Father Flynn. 'Now then – who is, em – come here to give away this woman in holy matrimony . . . ?'

'*Panorama* . . . !' shouted out Susan's father, and his nurse smacked him firmly on the wrist, which nearly made him weep.

'I think,' adjudged Alan, 'we can sort of take that bit as read. Now come on now, Blackie. Edge up. You're on. This is it. Why do you keep staring at me like that . . . ?'

'Oh God,' groaned Amanda. 'I so think I'm going to be sick . . .'

'Ignore her, Father Flynn. Let's get going.'

'Yes – oh yes. Oh God, yes. Now then – do you, Susan, take this man . . . oh but by God you're looking so lovely – do you know that? I'm sure you do. Lovely. Just lovely. Well now – do you, Susan, take this man, em . . . oh do you know, his name now, it's just slipped my, em . . .'

'Black. It's Black.'

'What's black, now?'

'The name. His name. It's Black.'

'His name is black?'

'Yes. Get on with it.'

'Ah but sure you can tell me. I'll never give it away to a

living soul. And sure it can't be as black as that . . . I once met a man in Drogheda, name of Lucifer . . .'

'Just . . . oh Jesus. Say Black. Do you, Susan, take this man Black . . . ? Yes? It's his *name*. Just say it.'

'Oh well now – if that's the way you want it. Susan . . . oh God, Susan, I do have to say how lovely it is that you're looking this day . . .'

'Alan . . . I don't think I can bear it . . .'

'Come on, Father Flynn. Mind on the job, yes? Do you, Susan . . . ?'

'Yes. Right enough. Yes yes. Oh God yes. Do you, Susan, take this man, em – Black? Is that right? Black? Thought you were having me on. Do you take this man Black to be your lawful wedded husband? You know – before you answer that, I'm just thinking it's the feller I ought to be asking the first. I doubt it matters, though. Will we go on the way we are? We will? OK, then. Do you, Susan, take this man, em . . . oh God, do you know – his name, it's gone clean out of my head again. Oh no – tell a lie. Got it now – it's Black, is it not? 'Tis, yes. Is it really that? Black? Well God in heaven. Thought you were having me on. Well. Do you, Susan . . .'

'Yes. I do. I do. Yes.'

'You do? Well that's very nice. And now – Black, is it? Do you, Black, take this woman Susan to be your lawful wedded husband?'

'Wife. Oh God, Alan . . . !'

'Wife. I said wife. Did I not say wife? I'm sure to God I said wife. Well there now. Well of course, wife. Do you – Black, is it? Do you, Black, take this woman Susan to be your lawful wedded wife?'

Amid the silence, everyone's eyes were shifted on to Black.

All was hushed until Susan's father was suddenly screaming out '*Macadamia* . . . !'

'Come on, Blackie,' Alan was urging him. 'Answer the man . . .'

Black just looked concerned.

'What . . . ?'

'Do you, Black – you heard him. Come on. Oh . . . ah. Oh dear. He's pointing at his ear, Susan. I think he's lost his thing. Yes – he's nodding. He's lost his thing. Right – have to find it. Help me Amanda, will you?'

'Urrgh. Can't. So like sick . . .'

'No, Alan,' said Black. 'Get up off the floor. Don't bother. You won't find it. It's quite undetectable. That's the whole point of the thing.'

'Oh Jesus. All right, Blackie. Well just say "I do" – OK? Watch my lips. I DO. Yes? Got it? Hear me?'

Black was nodding. 'I do.'

'Yup. But not quite yet. When the padre says so. Jesus – I don't know why I'm talking to him. Man can't hear a bloody thing . . .'

The nurse was ramming a pill in between Susan's father's tightened lips and keeping his hand flat across the mouth as if in an attempt to smother his next exclamation. And Black had a couple as well.

'Will we try again, my brethren? We will. Do you – Black, is it? Do you, Black, take this woman Susan . . .'

'Don't say I look lovely or I'll kill you, all right?'

'Susan, my child! This is the House of God!'

'It isn't.'

'Well no, it isn't. Fair enough. And how can I help it if it's lovely you're looking? Well now, Black is it? Do you, Black,

take this woman Susan as your lawful wedded husband?
Wife. I said wife.'

The pain from Alan's pinch to Black's arm was severe, he
couldn't deny, but nothing compared with the acid in his
stomach and the bite and breaking aching from each of his
arches.

'I do. That right? Right moment? Good. I do.'

'Well then. If any person here knows of any, em – lawful
impediment to this man and this woman being joined in holy
wedlock in front of the congregation and before the eyes of,
em . . .'

'God.'

'God, yes – I knew that. Of course I knew that. Em – let him
speak now or forever hold his, em . . .'

'Yeh – I do. I *so* have a reason.'

'Oh God's *sake*, Amanda . . . !'

'And what, em, young lady, would that reason be?'

'Oh don't listen to her, Father Flynn.'

'I'll tell you the reason. The reason is, she's already married.
Like *so* married. To my Dad who is standing right there. *Jesus*
. . . !'

'Oh yes, my child – I know all about *that*. I mean any *other*
reason.'

'Any *other* . . . ?! You're mad, you lot are. How can there be
another reason? You talk about like lawful wedded wife – well
it isn't, is it? Lawful.'

'Shut up, Amanda. Tell her, Alan.'

'But it *can't* be, can it? Lawful. You know that, Black – tell
them.'

'What . . . ?'

'No good talking to him, Amanda. For ever holding his

273

peace. I'm the Best Man, so talk to me. Or rather, don't. Here, Father Flynn – I've got the ring.'

'Oh that's very kind . . . oh I see – for Susan, yes of course. Yes. Oh God yes. Well then I now pronounce you man and, em. Wife.'

And Black slid the ring on to Susan's finger so that it just touched the simple platinum band that Alan had placed there, how many years in the past? When she looked at him, the way that she looked at him, Black felt his more prominent features warm and dissolving into a mash of placidness and knew for certain that if his stomach had been not quite so punishingly restricted, it would surely have suffered a major lurch, even maybe so much as a convulsion. He glanced up at Alan, whose lips were compressed and there were tears in his eyes. Sometimes, he thought, it was good to hear nothing. Just sometimes, silence is all.

After, the string quartet threw themselves with gusto into exhausting their repertoire, and struck up again from the top. Black went to the lavatory for seemingly an age, and Alan just stumbled across the hearing aid a little to the side of Susan's father's mad and energetic foot – and the poor old sod, he roared out '*Taramasalata* . . . !' as he was more or less kindly bundled away. The last Alan heard of him was his urgent and insistent questioning of the totally impassive nurse before the ambulance door was clanged shut and locked up noisily: 'Why am I here? Why am I here? What *is* this place? Tell me, please – what is its *nature* . . . ?' Father Flynn had been persuaded to go out into what some day would evolve into a remarkable garden; he had a bottle of Jameson in his left hand, and in his right he clutched another. And just by the caviar that everyone had agreed they didn't really care for, and that Susan had insisted upon (being, as she said, a sensualist by nature) – just by the crystal bowl of ice in which it was glisteningly suspended in a frosty silver sling – Amanda was sick: said she felt fine, cool as, and then she was sick. And Alan sat with Susan, sipping champagne. And he was right, the whisky priest – a ruined idiot, well yes of course, but he saw it, didn't he? As how could anyone fail to? That she was lovely, quite lovely. How very lovely she looked this day.

CHAPTER EIGHT

Yeh so that, it was all like a zillion years ago? My first really proper hangover? Dying, that would have been totally good. And vodka, though – it doesn't smell like all the others do, and if you have some you feel like really a whole lot better, which is something I've learned. The house now, oh God – it's just so really cool, it's just so really fantastic. All the rubble in the atrium, that's all white marble, if you can believe, like a hotel in a movie or something. The stairs, they kind of wind round and you can see right through them and the rail thing, that's all chrome like in a bathroom? And this you *won't* believe: there's like a *lift*? No really. And Blackie, he's in there all the time – says it's made a new man of him, but he still looks like a bloody old one to me. He's OK, though – pretty cool, in an old man way. Tons of money, which has got to be good. I don't have to invent all stuff about needing something for school – I just go, hey Blackie, can I have some money? And he's like, sure. And he gives you, I don't know – whatever, yeh? Say twenty. And if you just like stand there, he gives you more. So cool. Oh but my room! That's the best bit. In the old house, in the crappy house, I had like nothing. Laptop, CD thing and that was about it, if you don't count all the Barbie pink shit, which I can't believe I really used to go for. In my room now – oh wow. I've just got *everything* – and Tara, Jesus, you just should've seen her, her face, when she came over the first time. She said oh wow, Amanda, this is *so* the room I'd like just *die* for, and I can't tell you how good that was. You know – made me feel. She went through all the cable channels and looked at all my DVDs, loads of them 18s, and the Bose iPod dock I've got, she really went for that like big-time. And I've got all like mirrors and fitted window seats and my very own bathroom all shiny and I've got these huge like framed photos in there of Marilyn and Humphrey Bogart, just so cool. It's funny how old people are totally OK when they're dead and in black-and-white. And then she started going on about her mum and dad, who are going to split up, yeh, because her mum says she's worried that if they like stay together for much longer she might end up killing him, Tara's dad – and Tara's dad, yeh? He's pretty worried about it too. She went on and on – like I give a shit. But it got me thinking, though – my set-up, it's really OK. Not too bad. Pretty fucking cool, actually. Mum, she maybe isn't so crazy, just lately, I don't know. Still don't like her, though. She's weird. Spends all her time with this like landscape gardener and they talk about vistas and pleaching and pergolas and box bloody balls: Jesus. But the other two – Dad and Blackie? They're OK. Like kind of two old fogies. Like Statler and Waldorf, if you know them. Like from *The Muppets*? Anyway. And then Tara, she starts going on about school and how she can't keep up with the coursework because at home there's always like teacups flying around and blood and stuff and all over the floor there's like crunchy bits of dishes, and sometimes her dad. And I was like – there's *coursework* . . . ? Oh yeh – and talking of school, we've got this really sick person there, real saddo called Miss Levin, so totally creepy, and she's something like . . . I don't know what they call her, pastoral something, which I thought was all fields in the country and *Shropshire Lad* and ploughman's lunch and crap old music but it can't be. Anyway, it's Miss Levin you go to if there's something you want to talk about that isn't to do with lessons and shit. She's got glasses which are red a bit and she probably thinks they're really cool and make her look, I don't know, intelligent or human or something, but they don't – they just make her look old and sick and totally creepy, and she kind of looks over them at you, and her voice when she talks is just like stupid?

'Have you been attending the sex education classes, Amanda?'

'Yeh. No. Some.'

'Mm. Not maybe enough. You do realise that what you did was wholly irresponsible?'

'Yeh. Suppose.'

'You suppose correctly. Well the good news is you're not pregnant, at least. You don't seem very pleased.'

Well no I wasn't, if you want the truth. That's what I came to find out. Because yeh, I've been seeing Harry again. OK, right – I know he's a shit and everything, but I just like bumped into him in the newsagent, right, and he goes hi and I go hi and he says, so what – you want to like, do something? And I'm like what, and he goes I don't know – just stuff. Hang out. And I'm like cool, OK then. Yeh. But it's not like I want a *baby* or anything – God, I'm not stupid. Messy little shitbag puking and screaming? I so don't think so. But I'd been kind of rehearsing going up to Mum all like sorrowful and pious, you know? Slow low voice like I'm doing a sermon in church. 'Mum . . . I'm late. I think I might be . . .' – and then she just so totally losing it? So great. Anyway: not.

'But luck, Amanda, we simply cannot rely on. Can we? Now I do not recommend any sexual activity whatsoever for girls of your age. Let me be clear. You are fortunate that it is the school's custom not to immediately inform your parents. But if you do find yourself in a . . . situation, then you really must be prepared. You cannot depend upon the boy. And quite apart from the risk of pregnancy . . . are you actually listening to me, Amanda?'

'Yeh.'

'Quite apart from the risk of pregnancy, there are some very nasty diseases out there if you fail to protect yourself. Some of them fatal. Let me be clear. There are videos, Amanda . . . I'm sorry, Amanda: am I taking up too much of your time? Am I keeping you from an urgent appointment? Will you kindly do me the goodness of hearing me out?'

'Yeh.'

'So obliged to you. Videos, Amanda, that would make your hair stand on end. Believe me. So – take care, my girl. Care – that is the watchword. Let me be clear. So – off you go then. And if anything else should arise, anything at all you'd like to discuss, you know where my office is, don't you?'

'Yeh.'

'And that the door is always open.'

'Yeh.'

'Well goodbye, Amanda. And you will remember, won't you? Care – that is the watchword. Let me be clear.'

'Yeh.'

Yeh. And *shit*: that is the watchword – let me be fucking

clear. So-called adults, you know – they're more like kids than we are. They just never grow up. And as for sexual bloody activity – puh-*leese*! What the fuck does Miss *Levin* know about it? I doubt she's ever had a shag in her life. Like – who would want to? Who, oh yuck – *could*? And look how she's ended up – a Miss in a school telling girls to always pack a rubber. Gross, right? And like really really sad, and just so totally creepy.

I cut the last class of the day and went home. Went to the fridge soon as I got in because I was like really starving, and then I was going to go up to my room and have a slug of vodka because I've got a bottle in there now and it really, like – cheers me up? But Mum was in the garden as per bloody usual, yacking away to bloody Herb the gardener, yeh – and don't get me on to like how she went on and on when she discovered his name was Herb: what a simply *wonderful* name for a gardener, yeh yeh, on and on, like I could give a fuck. And then she was like calling and calling to me so I had to kind of go, but I crammed into my face all this like really tasty Polish sausage? So I could talk through it, which so really gets to her.

'Oh Amanda – it is you.'

Amanda's wide eyes looked down at herself in wonder and then they stared at each of her open palms in turn.

'Yeh . . . ? Yeh – it really is . . .'

'Yes well I couldn't quite see through the glass. Please finish whatever is in your mouth before you speak. Say hello to Herb.'

'Pa-lurrgh, Burb.'

'Amanda!'

'Jesus. You said talk and don't talk. What am I supposed to do?'

'I apologise for my daughter's behaviour, Herb.'

Herb put on his cheesy grin – big on cheesy grins, is Herb. I think he thinks it makes him look kind of, I don't know, boyish or something – but Jesus, he's got to be like thirty.

'No problem, Susan. No problem at all. OK are you, Amanda?'

'Yeh.'

'Black and your father are doing the dinner tonight, so it might be a weeny bit late. Have you got prep?'

'Yeh.'

'Well it'll give you a chance to get it all done then, won't it?'

'Yeh.'

'How long does it take, Herb? This hedge. To grow.'

'Oh it's a real fast worker, this one Susan. Next summer, you won't recognise it. Basic shape will be there. Then we can clip it.'

'Mum – can I talk to you?'

'What is it, Amanda?'

'Well like – in private?'

'Can't it wait? I'm right in the middle of . . .'

'Not really.'

'Oh . . . all right. Sorry about this, Herb. I won't be a couple of minutes.'

'No problem, Susan. No problem at all. OK are you, Amanda?'

'Yeh. So – you coming, Mum?'

Susan followed Amanda through the double doors and into the kitchen.

'Well what is it, Amanda? I was right in the middle of . . .'

Amanda looked sorrowful and pious, and in a slow low voice she murmured:

281

'Mum . . . I'm late. I think I might be . . .'

Susan clutched at the counter top and was gaping hard-eyed at Amanda.

'Oh my God. You *think* you . . . have you—?'

'Yeh.'

'And is it . . . ?'

'Yeh.'

'You're *sure* . . . ?'

'Yeh.'

'Oh my God. Oh my God. Oh Jesus, Amanda. Jesus. Right: that's *it*!'

Susan wheeled away in a rush, grabbing up her car keys and barging her way through Alan and Black who had just ambled into the kitchen, in their matching butcher's aprons.

'Hey hey! Steady on! What's all the rush?'

'Oh get out of my *way* Alan, God curse you. Just get out of my—! I'm going out. I don't know when I'll be back. Your darling daughter will fill you in on all the whys and bloody wherefores, stupid little tramp.'

Alan and Black just stared at the blur of her as she hurtled out of the room.

'Perfectly extraordinary . . .' Black was muttering. 'Amazing display. What was all that about, Amanda?'

Amanda shrugged. 'Couldn't tell you. Just Mum being Mum, I guess.'

'But Amanda,' said Alan. 'She must have had a *reason*. I mean – even Susan, she doesn't just become the lunatic without a simple *reason*, even if it's often a very small one indeed.'

'I don't know. I just said hi, I'm back from school – got heaps of prep. And she said you two were doing dinner, yeh – and then she like just lost it. Go figure.'

Amanda smiled her sweetest smile, and wandered out of the room. Hee hee hee hee hee bloody *hee*. Well shit: how could I resist it?

'Do you think,' Alan was wondering idly, 'that if you couldn't eat fruit . . . I mean if all fruits were inedible, just sort of, you know – looked nice . . . do you think people would still go on growing it? And buying it? Just because it, you know – looked nice?'

'Mm . . .' thought Black, as he deftly diced a pepper. 'Working on the principle of flowers, I assume to be your train of thought. Same goes for some vegetables, of course – such as this rather beautiful red and rubbery pepper I have here, for instance. Not potatoes, though. If you couldn't eat potatoes, that would be the end of them, obviously. Ugly bugger, your potato.'

Alan was tilting a pan over a flame, this way and that, coating the base with butter, and adding just a gloop of extra virgin.

'It's the rotting, I think, that might upset folk, you know. Fruit I'm talking about now. I mean to say – yes, flowers die, course they do. In a vase. There is though, with some, isn't there – that final blown-out glory? As if they know their time is due and they sort of generally rally round and put on all of their whorish greasepaint and tattered crinolines for a last and vast, final gaudy hurrah. Anemones come to mind. Ranunculi. Roses, most obviously. But a bowl of fruit . . . a bowl of fruit, if you couldn't eat it . . . have you done the onions, old fellow?'

'Spring onions. Less vicious. In the little bowl there, look.'

'Ah yes, got them. Now then, what was I . . . ?'

'Full-blown blooms. Fag-end of glory.'

'Christ. Well remembered.'

'Sometimes I amaze myself.'

'But I'd gone on from that, hadn't I? Moved on to something else?'

'Well I'm the last person to ask, aren't I Alan? Really. I mean if you remember your thread I'm sure I'll be right there behind you, but until that moment, well . . .'

'Oh yes – I know. Fruit. The fruit in a bowl. Well you see it's the rotting factor, isn't it? Unlike flowers, you'd have to ditch them the second they were less than perfect. Too much like flesh. Memento mori. Specially peaches.'

'I think peas with this, you know. Usually we do beans, don't we? But peas, I think. Agree? Yes? Jolly good – peas it is. Yes I take your point, but the Bard – didn't he use flowers in a lot of his analogies? A rose must bloom, it then must fade: so does a youth, so does the fairest maid? That's him, isn't it? Fairly sure it is. Or else some other poet. Take the point though, don't you? Women, you know – never understood how they could *stand* a vase of flowers, never mind love it so bloody much. Just watching, within a week – the fading, the sag, all the colour going out of them, the sheer bloody stink . . . and then bits – bits drop off. Jesus. I can't go on.'

'Chicken in strips, pork in chunks. Think that's best. Yes well – all in all, I think we're pretty fortunate that you can eat fruit, really. Gets no chance to rot. Very alluring, fresh fruit.'

'Mm. Like girls. Not original, but there you are.'

'When they're fuckish, you mean.'

'Quite. You know it occurred to me, Alan – what would a woman say, what would she think if ever she heard us saying all of this? Might call the police. Certainly there would be odium, if not outright hostility. Amis, he came in for a good

284

deal of that. Fine writer, Old Amis, I mean, not the young shit.'

'The thing about this meal is, when you've done all the preparation, the actual cooking takes no time at all. The tomato, the sauce, that's been ready for ages. Just have to heat it up. Don't quite know what to do now. You've read a lot of books, haven't you Blackie? Christ knows when Susan will be back. What did she have to go storming off for, when she knew we were just about to get going on the dinner?'

'It was my life, you have to remember, Alan. Always loved books. Wanted to write them once, but had to face the facts. Actually . . . thinking about it, I'm not at all sure I *did*, really Want to write them. I wanted to have written them, that's the key. That's what I wanted. Like so much bloody else. Just to have it done without all the endless palaver of actually *doing*. Publishing, though – it suited me better. More in control. Or used to be, anyway. Not recently, obviously. And writers, you know – well, when you meet them on a daily basis, when you get to know one or two of them, well . . . nuts, for the most part. Pathetically insecure. And, unless you've heard of them, broke of course. Not, now I come to think of it . . . that he is young any more, the young shit. Not broke either. Mm. But all in all, I think it turned out all right for me. You should probably turn off the heat, you know. We'd better wait for her.'

Alan nodded, and did that.

'I've, you know – started one. A novel. I expect that's true of everyone you've ever met.'

'Pretty nearly. Depressing, sometimes, I can't deny it. And all these adverts you see – they don't help. You've seen them, haven't you? "Why Not Become A Writer?" Christ. They never run adverts saying "Why Not Become A Plumber?", do they? No – because with plumbing, you see, they assume you require a modicum of skill. Ignorant bastards, the lot of them. But you're a bit of a dark horse, aren't you Alan? Never mentioned this before. Had no idea.'

'No well . . . I got out of the way of mentioning it. I also got out of the way of writing it. Susan, of course. She used to say that if I was a writer, then she was a trapeze artist. Or a mountaineer. Lion-tamer. Deep-sea diver. Varied in detail, but the thrust and intent were always made plain. She's not that savage, these days. Not since you came along. She continues to sneer and ignore – that's just her stock reaction with me, of course. But the blades, they come out less frequently.'

'Shall we have a drink? Might as well. While we're waiting. What's it about, Alan? This novel of yours. Actually, writers always hate that. When you ask them what it's about. But what else are you actually supposed to say? And nine times out of ten, it's not as if one actually *cares*, or anything. It's only politesse. Not in your case, obviously, Alan old man. Of course I want to know. Scotch, do you think? Or finish off this wine and open a good deal more?'

'I refuse to bore an eminent ex-publisher with any of the non-news about what Amanda would doubtless refer to as my *so* non-novel. A Scotch would be good, actually. Or maybe wine . . . Oh hell – let's have a Scotch, and then we can have some wine. Touch of a mild hangover. Only known cure.'

'*Mild* hangover . . . ? How fond. How very blissfully nostalgic. I do just distantly remember those. Mine's been an absolute sledgehammer all day long. Cheers, dear boy. As to your novel, well . . . if you really don't want to talk about it . . .'

'It's about a man who wants to take on a challenge. A challenge, yes. And not just something that would challenge him personally, no, but something that would astonish the world. Something that had never been attempted before, let alone accomplished. And I thought: swimming.'

'I might just have put a touch too much water in this . . . it might have been a splash too far. Have a taste, and top it up if you think so. Did I miss something there, Alan? Lord knows it would hardly surprise me. Did you say – swimming . . . ?'

'I did, yes. Don't know what put it into my head. I'm no sort of swimmer at all – flounder around like a turtle. Maybe what put it into my head. Or it could have been – you know, listening to the sea, cosying up to the sand. On my own private beach. Which now, thanks to you, my dear Blackie, would I think put even Bournemouth to shame.'

'My great pleasure, Alan. If nothing else is remembered of me, then at least let it be said that I was the instigator of the best and largest private indoor beach in the whole wide world. Well – at least in Richmond, anyway. Oh yes and by the way – that seat I told you about, old boy – coming next week. Tuesday, I think.'

'Oh really? Oh God how marvellous. I can't tell you how grateful . . . it was really a kind thought. Really thoughtful.'

'I think the chappie was pleased to have someone take it off his hands, quite frankly. Not much of a market for a lifeguard's seat up a flight of steps, shouldn't have thought. Said it came from Miami. Probably balls. And there's the loudhailer thing there as well. You know – thing they shout through.'

'I can't wait. What a finishing touch. And I'm pleased that you come in there now, you know. Wouldn't let anyone else even near the place, goes without saying. Because that was the only thing wrong, really: got a bit lonely. You want to, don't you, discuss the fading light, the receding horizon. Share a pot of whelks. So I think – yeah, it must have been all of that, put it into my mind. The swimming. God Blackie though – you must think I'm an absolute *child* with all this seaside stuff . . .'

'Oh I *do*, Alan – I *do*. And I mean that in the best and kindest way. We're all of us boys and girls, whatever our ages. Or the best people are, anyway. And us in particular, the male of the species – we never grow up, I'm delighted to say. And women, you know – they say that of us in pity, amused contempt. But they are just the same. They just don't laugh so much. But all of us, don't we? We surround ourselves with toys. Either the toys we remember, in a more sophisticated version, or else the toys we never had but always yearned for. With you, it's the seaside. Me? A lift. A huge garden. Thousands of books. All toys, aren't they? Playthings that bring us delight. And what of women, with all their coloured handbags and pretty little bottles of scent and so on. The bloody shoes. Naughty chocolates. Saucy clothes, if you're lucky. Toys: fripperies. And nothing wrong with that. And you know what else I think? I think that sometimes, just occasionally, we catch a glimpse of someone that we truly believe to be a *real* adult, a proper grown-up person. The genuine, as it were, um – article. People used to think that of *me*, for God's sake, and I don't have to tell you how very wrongheaded that was. Grief. And we subtly ape him, this paragon of maturity, in the hope that no one will twig that we're really just kids, dressing up and mouthing the words of manhood. But in truth, everyone – everyone is just looking over their shoulder, checking that they at least *appear* as adult as the fellow behind. But no. It's just a front that some become more used to than others, and hence can render the more convincing. But at base, we never change. Boys and girls, that's all we are. Boys and Girls. And what could be better? You see? Anyway. Seem to have got off the . . . got off the . . . what is it we were on actually, Alan? Talking about.'

'Um, let me see. Touch more Scotch? Good man. Um, let me see. Fruit, flowers, turn off the gas . . . oh yes: swimming. My non-book. Swimming. I got to thinking of those people who do the Channel, don't know why. You know – cover themselves in something unspeakable and thrash off to France. Pointless, I agree – particularly now there's the Eurostar. But they do it, don't they, because it's a challenge. Well I looked it all up on the thing. You know – internet. Amazed. I was totally amazed. I was looking for some method, some angle – some sort of twist that had never been tried. Well I tell you, Blackie – there isn't one. People have done it both ways, without a break. Three ways, one fool. Backstroke. Married couple holding hands. Kids have done it, with the deranged and driven parents in a boat alongside. Even ancient old bloody wrecks have done it, I couldn't believe it: ninety, one of them was. In fact it's so damn common that the ferry lanes, they must be choked with them, all these deluded morons, gangs of them, dog-paddling to France and back, for no bloody reason on earth. So – no good to me. No sort of challenge at all. But I was keen to stick with the swimming idea, can't really tell you why, and so I got to thinking well right then, OK then, what has never been done before? And then I got it.'

'You did? You got it? What's the time . . . ?'

'I did, I did. Why? Expecting someone?'

'Well just Susie, you know. Getting a bit hungry. What, though? What did you get, Alan?'

'Get? What are you talking about? It's early, actually . . .'

'Oh Jesus Christ – you're getting to be as bad as me. You said you got it. What did you get?'

'I did? Oh yes I *did* – of course I did. Yes yes – the great challenge, the mountain to conquer. Not a great image in context, but there. Yes, Blackie – I got it: the *Atlantic* . . .'

Black sipped whisky before he spoke. Lit a cigarette.

'Atlantic. I see. Yes. That would be the ocean, would it, that the *QE2* and so on take, um – what is it? Six days and nights to, er . . . That the Atlantic you mean?'

Alan sighed and drank a bit.

'Well yeah. You see the point. Why it didn't – progress, really. The idea. The book. Oh well. Ah . . . ! Was that the . . . ? That was the door, wasn't it? Think she's back. Right, then – let's get on with things, shall we? Yeh – I'm pretty hungry too, now I come to think of it. Pasta'll take no time. Heat on under the sauce, I think. Bung in the pork and so on. Gone quiet. That *was* the door, wasn't it . . . ?'

'You're asking me?'

'Sure it was . . . She's not coming in though, is she? Oh Christ – you don't suppose she's stamped upstairs, do you, this fine and cherished wife of ours, for not so much a wash and brush-up as to indulge in one of her serious sulks? Hell for us if she has. Broods for ever about whatever atom of nonsense she has this time magnified into a meteor of life-threatening proportion – and then it is us, my friend, who will be called upon to withstand the barrage of unremitting missiles which in a just world – that airy-fairy mythical planet – would be directed elsewhere. Why don't you go and have a shufti, Blackie? See how the land lies.'

'Well without wishing to too much rely upon the repartee of the playground, Alan – why don't *you*?'

'Couldn't possibly. Were I to present myself before her, naked and unashamed, as it were, then I and I alone would be bearing the whole brunt of her latest antagonism. And – as I see you are beginning to assimilate, dear Blackie, by your deft, nay, very adroit evasion – no one else's antagonisms have brunts so whole as hers. We could send in Amanda. White flag – rifle cocked. Where is Amanda?'

'I'll just refresh your glass, shall I Alan? Going to have to get in another case of this, I think. She was mumbling about prep, or some such.'

'Prep. Oh yes – prep. We spend the whole of our lives engaged in that, don't we really? Prep. Preparation for something or other, which never seems quite to arrive. Like an eternal advent calendar, where you never ever get to open the twenty-fourth door. Better not tell Amanda any of that, though. It would only depress her.'

And then Alan and Black locked glances as the unmistakable pitch of shrill and female altercation recoiled from the walls above and filtered down the staircase. The unspoken consensus was to now lie low, then – clink glasses and wait for the bullets to cease their flying, the dust to settle, the air to clear (Black turned the gas off under the sauce). And overlaying this muted caterwaul – rising and falling, but always embittered – Alan, at least, heard reasonably clearly the smashing of something glass into splintered and resounding spangles, and he had no wish to know that this had come about as a result of Susan's very wildest gesticulation, an outflung arm, the cuboid amethyst on her ring finger catching the large and pearlescent globe light just by the plasma TV screen in the draped and candlelit, chill-out and deeply private area of Amanda's room.

'I can't believe you just *did* that!' Amanda was screaming, clutching her hair at the roots in both of her bunched-up hands, as if to keep it in or rip it out. 'That was so my favourite *lamp* . . . !'

'Oh Christ and Jesus keep to the *point*, Amanda!' Susan was raving – pacing around in tight and seething circles, revolving swiftly, retracing again her hot and angry circuit. 'It's a *lamp*. It's a *lamp*. It's just a bloody *lamp*! We can always get a new *lamp*, can't we? But what about *you*? You have destroyed yourself – and all for the most ridiculous and impudent little *shit* it has ever been my displeasure to encounter!'

Amanda – caught at the start of a putative howl – just stopped right there and gaped at her.

'Now just sit down, Amanda, and be calm. We have to *arrange* things.'

'*What*—? Now look – just like wait a minute, you! What do you mean – *encounter*? What are you talking about – *encounter*? You don't mean you—!'

'Sit down, Amanda. Be calm.'

'Fuck off! I don't want to sit down. *You* be calm. Don't tell *me* to be bloody calm. *You* be calm. Look at you – you've so like just smashed up the place.'

'That was an accident.'

'Yeh? Well so was what I did. You know? And just never mind that. What I want to know is—!'

'My accident was a *lamp*. A *lamp*, Amanda. It's just a bloody *lamp* We can always get a—!'

'Yeh yeh bloody *yeh*. You've done all this, haven't you? Said all that. Just tell me what you mean by whatever you fucking said about *encounter*, or whatever you said. You—!'

'Enough swearing now, Amanda. Just sit down.'

'Listen, you! I just so can't, like – *believe* this . . . ! I don't *want* to sit down. Just *tell* me, can't you? What you're saying. What you mean. Are you telling me you've gone and *talked* to him? You can't of. Not possible. You're lying. You don't even know his—!'

'Yes – oh yes Amanda, I do. I do know his name. I know the ghastly house he lives in, and I know the equally ghastly and dirty little garage where the shitty little shit has a so-called job. I know everything, Amanda – of course I do. I *always* do. You, I thought, were aware of that. I told you I would not rest.'

'*God . . . !*'

'Yes well. He may or may not help you now. But I will. I am determined. I am your mother. I wasn't going to . . . confront him, do anything. I was going to keep quiet. But when you told me you were – oh God, I can't bear to even *think* it . . .'

'But I'm not! I'm not!'

'When you told me you were . . . *pregnant*, well that just—!'

'I'm not! You listening to me, or what? I'm not. I'm not I'm not I'm not!'

'Bit too late for lies now, isn't it Amanda?'

'Oh God . . . I'm *not*, I tell you. I just . . . and anyway – I don't believe you. I don't believe you, what you said. You just said all that to, I don't know – frighten me or something. Well it doesn't work. Or to stop me like seeing him, or something. Well that won't work either. You don't know the first thing about him. You're just a liar.'

'Oh yes? Then how did I know he worked in a garage?'

And Amanda was struck by the question. As well, Susan was reflecting bitterly – as well she bloody might be. Because it wasn't that the seeking out and tracking down of this young little bastard had been that much of an effort . . . the intimidation of children, after all – when was that ever a challenge? But there was disgust along the way, and many were the times she had been touched by the shiver of humiliation (for she had later determined that the finger of shame, it was icy at first, then soon scalding, and the same for evermore). Why had she been reduced to hunting out this gormless little friend of hers, Tara – a monosyllabic mutant, is how she had come across to Susan, and who, as little girls always do, initially protested her puzzlement at the questions, her ignorance of the answers. Cajoling and money had failed to work, much to Susan's surprise, and so she was forced to resort to inventing (and on the spur of the moment, too) a series of articles she had just been commissioned to write for the local paper – truthful and amusing profiles of residents in the area such as, ooh – I don't know . . . your father the conjuror, say. The entertainer, yes? And his wife and child. Mm . . . poor little thing, I almost felt sorry for her. Anyway – that got me the name, at least, as well as the whereabouts of a newsagent and a coffee shop, and also the fact that the shit, he worked in a garage – and what had I expected? A member of the Cabinet? Captain of Industry? The Secretary General of the United Nations? That he worked at all was something of a surprise; I had fully been prepared for a long-limbed, smug and stupid idler on the dole – though having seen the state of the garage (there aren't that many left any more – it didn't take too long) and not just the garage, but the grease on the boy's hands as he wiped them with a rag, the caked-on grime of his oversized overalls . . . idleness might almost have been preferable; he might then at least have been clean. He wasn't really smug – just vain and hopeful, as young men will be, and not so much stupid as careless, really, and apparently disconnected. His limbs, though – they were long and lean. That one could see, even with the overalls.

'Harry, isn't it? Is there somewhere we could talk? I am Amanda's mother.'

Harry looked happy, and then rather wary.

'Is she – all right?'

'Well that rather depends, you see, upon exactly what you mean. Doesn't it really? Is there? Anywhere? We can talk? Yes?'

Harry looked about him helplessly. There was an ancient 3.4 Jaguar jacked up on to a tilted ramp, and practically eviscerated. Black and sticky parts were laid out on a workbench. All around was hard and rusted apparatus that Susan was eager to be far away from.

'Not really . . . this is where I work.'

'Yes – I see that. Not an office? Shed? Something?'

'Not really . . . I'm due for a break, though. We could go and have a coffee, if you . . . but she's OK though, is she? Amanda?'

'That is what I am here to discuss. Will it take you long to – clean yourself? A year, by the look of you. No – let's just do it here then, shall we? I shall be brief. You know of her state. You know she is underage. What are you intending to do about it? And before you answer, you may care to consider what it is *I* intend to do about it.'

Harry's eyebrows were low in concentration. He sat down upon what could have been an anvil.

'I'm sorry, I . . . *underage*? I don't know what you mean. She's the same age as I am.'

'I think not. You are, what? Eighteen? Nineteen? Twenty?'

'Seventeen. I'm seventeen. Yes.'

'Oh really? You look more . . . mature. Well I have to tell you that Amanda is just fifteen. Yes. And, when you first . . . met

295

her, rather younger. I don't for one minute believe you didn't know that.'

Harry was standing now, and Susan could have sworn that what she saw, alive and fidgety all over his face, was a genuine consternation.

'Oh my God – no, you've *got* to believe me. I had no – idea. I'm shocked. I'm, I'm – just amazed. She looks so—! Please – honestly, if I'd known, I never would have . . . I mean, that's just disgusting, frankly. I'm not like that. I never knew. I'm really, really sorry. Listen, look – I'll never see her again, if that's why you're here. I mean – I don't want to, frankly. Man – I'm not into . . . *children*. Jesus. And if there's anything I can do to, you know . . . I don't know. If there's anything I can do, or anything . . .'

And Susan, she had to admit, was rather thrown by all of this. She had been intending to convey to him her fathomless repulsion – to forbid him to even so much as lay eyes upon Amanda again – and so now the ground beneath her, it had all gone soft and marshy.

'Well . . . that is as may be. But still you should have taken the most basic, God – *precautions*, shouldn't you? Harry. Now of course she will have to undergo an abortion, that's understood, but still—!'

'What? Wait a minute. *What*? You mean she's—!'

'You mean to tell me you didn't know?'

'But she can't be. Jesus. We've only done it a couple of times, few times, and – oh Jesus, sorry sorry sorry, I forgot you're her Mum, I didn't mean it to come out like that. Sorry. Sorry. But what I . . . well I *do*, you see. I do use stuff. Didn't the first time, but that was ages ago.'

Susan felt giddy, and just a little nauseous.

'Well. Something or someone evidently failed. And you mean she didn't tell you?'

'Tell me? God no. No. First I've heard of it. Jesus. I just can't believe it. Oh God. Oh *God* . . .'

Susan watched the flicker of his dark thick eyelashes as he stared at the ground. His worried face was active with energy and his lean long limbs were twitching. Her voice, when she heard it, was steady and a good deal calmer.

'There is also the question, Harry, of whom I involve. Your parents? The police? You are, Harry, guilty of – *rape* . . .'

His eyes were searching and frantic now as they darted with nerves all over her face. Twice, he nearly spoke.

'Maybe,' said Susan, 'we ought to. Go and have that coffee. Shall we?'

And yes – we did that, it astounds me to remember. Not at all the scenario I had envisioned during my endless and spitting, furious journey over to the garage, agitated fingers banging on the steering wheel, determined upon blood and at the very least the cruellest sort of vengeance. And in that awful coffee place, I became convinced of his sincerity. And his pitiable uselessness, cluelessness, his general and inept confusion, I found so very familiar. Are such people – men – really up to it, one has sometimes to ask oneself. The shouldering of blame. Assuming responsibility. They're not, are they? They are boys, you see – that's all. It is beyond their capabilities.

Yes, well – that was then. But by the time I had driven home – swung the car into the drive, left it just anywhere – anger and sickness were back within me: he was a shit, just a shit, nothing but the most ridiculous and impudent little shit – of course he was a shit. No more than a careless invader, no matter how charming his smile or demeanour – and now

Amanda was spoiled, and it is I, of course it is I, who must now press forward for a resolution.

'And so, Amanda. No please – don't argue: just listen. There is no *debate*. I shall tomorrow make an appointment, This – situation of yours will have to be terminated. No discussion.'

'But listen! Listen! There *isn't* a situation. There isn't – there isn't. I'm *not*, I tell you . . . !'

'Enough. You are becoming hysterical. We will both now go downstairs and attempt to have a civilised dinner – over which poor Black and Alan have been slaving, little dears. Not a word to either of them, please. I shall take care of this alone. Oh yes – one more thing, Amanda.'

'*God* . . . !'

'Harry. Name ring a bell? Yes. He asked me to tell you that he never wants to see you again. Never. I said I would. All right? Plain enough for you?'

Amanda's eyes were immediately blazing, and glassy then as she blinked at the pain. She wanted to rush her, attack her mother, tear at her eyes, or else just be welcomed into her arms, to be stroked and cooed at throughout the coming hours of sobbing. Instead she just stood there, her face quite taut and jerking in the terrible effort to look, at least, cool.

'I don't *believe* you . . . !'

'No. Well. I think you do. Now come along. Dinner.'

Amanda nearly spat and nearly wept and then just clumsily scooped up her jacket and bag and rushed out of the room. Susan smiled in a lemony way and quietly followed her down the stairs. She had not yet reached the hall when the thunder of the front door slamming caused the house to tremble in the aftershock.

'Bloody hell,' said Alan, walking quite quickly and wiping his hands on a cloth. 'Thought it was World War Three.'

'One less for dinner, I think,' said Susan calmly. 'Smells divine.'

Alan fell into a low and courtly bow, flapping the tea towel as if it were a coloured silk.

'A humble thing, but our own. What's wrong with her? Isn't she hungry? Where's she gone?'

Susan touched his cheek.

'Don't know, don't know and don't know. Is it nearly ready? I'm hungry anyway. Have you both been working so terribly hard, you poor little drones?'

'When you are naturals, as Blackie and I have surely become, the art of cooking is surely just that: an art. It is not work – just the instinctive and inspirational fusion of variables, sprinkled by the dust of creative genius.'

'Fool. And I am not so sure one can *become* a natural, but never mind. So what is the result of the labours? No, not labours: *inspirations* of two such Renaissance gentlemen? Food, surely, fit for the gods?'

'Mm, well – fit for us, anyway. It's only pasta and meat – few vegetables. Sauce should be good, though. Been licking the spoon for ages.'

'More than one wished to know. I'm glad it's you who does the sauce, else it'd be covered in all of Black's fag ash. Well let's eat, God's sake. Starving. So you don't use recipes any more? Just wing it?'

'Oh Christ no. Follow them religiously. Swill, otherwise. But seriously, Susan – about Amanda. What's going on? What were you two screaming about? Is she OK?'

'She is what she is, Alan. Leave it at that. Now – enough. Why don't you just say to me those three little words? The words that every woman longs to hear . . .'

'Uh-huh. And they might be . . . ? Not, I am presuming, the obvious?'

Susan giggled, and kissed the very tip of his nose.

'Dinner. Is. Served.'

Alan smirked, offered her the crook of his elbow, and arm-in-arm they swaggered away, and really quite chummily.

'One thing that pleases me about you, Alan . . .'

'Mm, well – there had to be *one*, I suppose . . .'

'. . . is that you don't pretend to be mad any more.'

'No. Well I ceased to consult the doctor who professes to help the mad ones – has to be a cure in itself, really.'

'But it's not that, is it?'

'No. Not really. I suppose, Susan – and I shouldn't really be saying it, should I? Tempting, what is it . . . ? That thing? Providence. But at the moment – currently, the way we are now . . . I just don't find anything maddening.'

Susan tugged at him and looked quite earnest.

'And nor the need to put up defences? Whitewash? Smoke-screens?'

'Could be. Could be. And you no longer seem compelled to call me your sugar or your sweet. Always was your very *sourest* thing . . .'

Susan nodded her satisfaction.

'I know. But you though, Alan – it's a bit like Black, but in a different way. I mean – well *you* know: how he doesn't do all those ludicrous things to himself any more. All the – hair and shoes and, well .. I don't suppose you ever saw his underwear, did you?'

'No, Susan. We're just good friends.'

'And he takes far fewer pills, you know. Mostly he just forgets, it's true – but it doesn't appear to be doing him harm.

300

He's . . . well, it's like you said just a minute ago, I suppose. He's a natural now.'

Alan could only smile. It was true, of course, all that Susan was saying. Blackie, he did – he looked and behaved quite differently. What Susan maybe wasn't aware of, though, was all the sweat and horror, the fear and irresolution, the long and rocky road that had led him, poor bugger, to this new-found nirvana. Because yes, dear Susan – I may not be a first-hand party to all of the mysteries of dear Blackie's underpinnings, but I do *know* about them, oh yes I do, and plenty else besides. Because who do you think he talks to? Not you, my dear – no, not you. We both of us, Blackie and I, exchange with you every manner of pleasantry, tidbits and all the day-to-day nonsenses, of course we do, we do – but when it comes to actually *talking*, well . . . that we do with one another. In private. As consenting adults. It started – properly started, I mean, because we've always had an understanding, rapport, a good deal of substance in common – but I suppose the epiphany, the defining moment when we became to one another true and trusting confidants was the very day following your romantic betrothal. That time of sweet memory. Because I had ages before divined that that evening, at truly the end of the day, his first and blissful night of marital warmth and harmony . . . well, the very thought of it had him practically deranged – though not I fear, dear Susan, in the way of a lusty young buck driven so close to the edge by the fevered agonies of anticipation, a just barely reined-in and salty libido. Well no, be realistic – this is Blackie now who is under discussion, let us not forget. His tensions were all of a different kind, that much at least I was aware of, and the very next day, well – he told me all about it. How it had

301

gone. All the, as it were, ins and outs. Would this shock you? I wonder if it would. When you conjured it up, this ménage, this extended union – when I not so much agreed to it (for I wasn't, was I, asked?) as, well . . . succumbed to its apparent inevitability – did you know how things would turn? Or have you been as frankly amazed as the rest of us? How far down the route into the future did your scheme and imagination lead you? Were we all from the start to be co-dependent? I suppose so – or else why not a coming and going between two quite separate households? But to what degree, though? Equals? Not possible, is it? In any family, really, and certainly not in this one. You, of course, were to be the common (sorry) denominator – a phrase with which you would surely have a bone to pick – but were Blackie and I intended to exist within our own and quite distinct vacuums, intercommunicating only during the moments when the common (sorry) wife was shared and sharing? Is, in short, what has come about no more or less than a happy accident? An agreeable fluke? Or are you really so terribly brilliant, Susan – your insight into nature and personality as keen as a twinkling scythe – as to have not just foreseen the development and outcome, but to have selected the ingredients for so rich and surprising a confection with flair and the surest touch, the hand of an impresario? I will never know the answers to this welter of questions, and not just solely for the reason that they will never be posed. The only idea I could ever have is by watching, judging your unguarded reaction, if ever I let you know (and I won't, not ever) that the morning after the night before, Blackie had told me all about it. Would it shock you? I wonder if it would. Or, if not by the fact of his telling me, then maybe in the face of the detail and selectiveness of his frank recollection, the very depth of that initial and unadorned dread. You might wonder too whether I minded – his telling me, my hearing it: how I was feeling about the whole thing. And as he spoke, I wondered it too – quite what shape I was going to be in, once he was over and done with it. And nor was I alone: he, I could tell, was wondering also – how now maybe the two of us might stand, following this . . . by turns, you know, really impassioned and pathetic outpouring, this literal confession clearly quite vital to him. It was only later, much later, that we both could honestly reflect upon the incipient humour, shy at first, and then coursing through the narrative like a wheezy and more or less preposterous rheum.

'The bull by the horns, Alan. The bull by the horns.'

I blinked, I think. Waited. All I could do.

'By which I mean, dear boy – tackling right now the subject with you. Thought about not. You know – pretending that last night was, well – just another night. And you – you're a good fellow, Alan. You would not make any allusion, not even jocular, let alone crude. Prurience, I am sure, is by no means a hallmark of your make-up. Mixed, um – thing, that. Pretty sure. Never mind. And then, you see, there would forever be between us a, Lord – what's it called? Big bugger. In the room, you see. Something impossible for either of us to ever ignore. Metaphor, mixed metaphor – that's not the big bugger, I don't mean – that's the thing before.'

'Elephant. In the room.'

'That's the chap, quite so. Yes. And so look, Alan – for right or wrong, I'm going to charge ahead with it, you see. Rather like an elephant, I suppose. Bull by the horns. Mixed thing. Never mind. And then we'll be clear. All right with you? Uncharted territory, isn't it? Can't go on precedent. Husband telling husband. Queer one. Anyway – got to be got through, far as I can see. All right with you? Well – got to be really, I'm afraid. Have to do it. Bull by the horns. And then we'll be clear. Going to light a fag now.'

'Drink?'

'Bit early, isn't it? Had a load last night. Partly to blame. Well – not really. But you've got to, haven't you? Have something to blame. If only partly. Make it a large one, would you? But what about you, Alan? Sort of lost track of you, as the evening wore on. Missed you, you want the truth. Sounds ridiculous. What did you get up to?'

'Watched a bit of television. Read. Did a crossword.'

'Really?'

'No, not really. None of those. Drank. Went to bed. Got up. Drank. Went to bed. Stayed there.'

'Yes. I see. Well quite. Only course open to you. Do see that. Ah – lovely, Alan: the golden nectar. And just that drop of water. Perfect. Most people – well, everyone but you, in my experience – you say a touch of water, just the merest touch, and they make as if they're mixing you up a batch of Ribena, or something. Mm. It's good. Hitting the spot. Looks like being quite a nice day . . .'

'Bull by the horns . . . ?'

'Mm. Yes yes. Quite right. Well you see the first thing that threw me was all the bloody candles. In the bathroom. Must have been hundreds of the buggers. Big ones, tiny ones – all over the place, even on the floor. Telling you, if you'd been wearing a nightshirt you would've gone up like the fifth of November. Stench was perfectly overpowering. Me, I was in a headlong dash to get to the lavatory, as per bloody usual – put out two of the bastards without even trying. Bit of a sizzle.

But women, they've got a thing, haven't they? About candles. Seem to. I mean to say, I've nothing against the candle per se. Useful if the fuses have blown. Perfectly fine on the dinner table – not the stinky ones, obviously. But I ask you: covering a bathroom with the fuckers to the degree that it looks like a shrine to, I don't know – St Francis of Assisi and smells like an inflammable brothel, well really. They worried me, quite frankly. A relic of my timid past. Parents, largely – very cautious, you see. But they didn't have to tell me not to play with matches, Lord no. Wouldn't even touch the box for fear it might explode in my face. I was no hero. Always remembered that a plastic bag is not a toy. Never had anything that could be construed as even approaching a choking hazard – and nor a single thing unsuitable for a child of less than thirty-six months, not until I was at least about, ooh – fourteen or so, anyway. And so as for leaving all these candles unattended, well . . . heart was in my mouth. Because Susan, you see, she wasn't, um – actually in the bathroom itself. No no. Bath full of bubbles, so obviously it was a part of the eventual plan, but for now she seemed content to be next door, sprawling on the bed. And well – you know that bed, don't you Alan? You remember the nightmare when we had it delivered. Had to take the window out in the end. Remember? Yes. Course you do. Nightmare. Size of the very first digs I had when I came down from Oxford, that bed is. Well I had a glass in my hand, goes without saying – fag on the go. And at the sight of her, all in pearly silk, hair sort of fanned out and away from her, framing her face, sort of style . . . and I don't have to tell you of all people, do I Alan? About that face. Stop anyone in their tracks. And what I felt was . . . peckish. Yes – decidedly in need of a snack of some sort. Nothing fancy, you understand.

305

A Ryvita and Philadelphia would have done for me perfectly – maybe a few of those leftover sausages. What did you say . . . ?'

'Nothing. I didn't say anything. Just sitting here and listening to you, Blackie.'

'Oh. Thought you . . . oh. Could've sworn. Well anyway. It all sort of became rather like a film from that moment on. A film I was watching, yes, but also had a part in – if not, very signally, the starring role. Dreamlike, I suppose you'd call it. In a nightmarish sort of a way.'

Damn right, Black thought then: exactly how it was – I can see and hear the spools clicking and streamingly unfurling through a rackety projector, dancing dust caught in its beam, the images just so clear and very rowdy.

'Black – be near to me, darling. Sit by my side.'

'Right-o, Susie. Coming right over.'

'And bring the champagne.'

'Champagne. Check. Got you. Jolly good. Gosh – big bugger. Magnum. Pink as well. Clicquot – excellent. The widow at the wedding. Get it? Bit of a joke.'

'Not a funny one, though.'

'No no, granted. Not funny, not at all. Here you are then, Susie: glass of bubbles. Did you know – the pressure in a bottle of champagne is equal to six atmospheres?'

'No Black, I didn't. What does that mean, in fact?'

'Not the least idea. And in a magnum, who knows? Could be *twelve* atmospheres. Quite a thought. Anyway – cheers, yes?'

Susan sat up and leant upon an arm. She held out her flute to him.

'What do you propose, Black, my new husband . . . ?'

'Mm? Well – hell of a day, hasn't it been really? Good night's sleep is what I propose.'

'I meant . . . toast.'

'Oh God yes – toast would be lovely. I could really do with a nice bit of – oh: right. Take your – well quite. Well now, Susie – here's to my beautiful bride. I am humbled. I do not deserve you. But I'm glad I've got you. Lord yes. And so here's a toast to, well – *us*, and all the happy years that await us in both of our golden futures.'

'That was beautiful, Black . . .'

'Mm. Read it in a book, pretty sure.'

'Come to bed, my darling man. Don't you want to . . . touch me?'

Well I do, I do, of course I bloody do. Those accursed breasts of yours, ripe and pulsating like so many apples – been yearning to get to grips with them since the moment I thought of Ryvita, which I grant you is odd. Not that apples are known to pulsate – but Jesus, who cares about a thing like that at a time like this? And the narrow waist, you know – and then such a swell. The mouth, painted and shiny. Yes – the hips and the lips, oh dear me. But you see . . . what I *don't* want to do is anything more. Can't, very probably. But also don't want to be – involved. To such a depth, as it were. Just really want to pick and choose, squeeze and maybe lick a bit, have a fag, throw together some sort of a sandwich and get a bit of kip. But mostly what I don't want to do – can't even think of it – is to even hint at the beginning of my numbing deconstruction. To let her see, by way of her probing and my increasingly horrific disclosure, how I quite literally just come apart – to let her see the inexorable diminishing of the man I was, to let her see – cast aside and about the floor –

307

the vile and sterile lumps of apparatus that go into keeping me vertical and if not standing tall, then at least preventing me from altogether vanishing. But if I approach, God curse it, if I touch her – then she will, won't she? Touch me back. It's the nature of the thing. And while my fingers are thrilling to the abandonment of the plump and creviced warmness of her, she can but rummage through hardware and a torpid sort of swaddling, the impersonal buttresses of my outer being – which, when unbuckled, unbuttoned, unstrapped and unzipped, leave bare and foolish and so ashamed an alternately stringy and distended, white and lifeless, stripped and cringing clammy little thing, criminally old and yet just puerile, so very truly hideous in its every single aspect that even I myself can frequently recoil in disgust from just the inkling, and not even sight of it.

'Come on, Black. Come on. *Touch* me . . .'

Well there you are – caught, wasn't I? No way out. And most of me, of course, wasn't at all wanting it – way out, I mean. Way in, that's what a good deal of me was tangibly yearning for, Lord yes. But well look – I've said it all, haven't I? The fear was there, plain as day. And then (Jesus, I amazed myself) I just *did* it – tried to black out the light of thought, every sort of vision, even any sensibility. Got about a pint of Clicquot down me, and threw off my jacket. Hauled away the tie. As I prised out each of the waistcoat buttons from their safe little crannies, the thread throughout could almost be heard to sigh and then shriek at their blessed release from such arduous duty, and the stays beneath began to stir with a maybe quite giddy anticipation of their own. And while I did this, I stood there deliberately, four-square and before her. I did not approach, and nor did I cower. I wanted this to be a quite thorough admission of all of my guilt. An appalling show. The devil's own striptease. When I shrugged off the shirt, I awaited her gasp – could not dream of looking at her, naturally enough: my ears were my sole source of detection, the gauge to her reaction, the extent of her revulsion (and the battery, I could tell, was on its very last legs). It was quiet, though, as I began upon the corset, the very core of this terrible installation. Could be she was struck mute by the blossoming horror before her wide and disbelieving eyes. My stomach began to surge forward as its cruel constraints were one by one and purposefully released – I could feel the progressive collapse of rolls and pouches of defeated flesh where once had been muscle and tone and the tingle of pride. As the whole of the buckled contraption clattered down on to the floor, the avalanche soon was complete: my belly fell over into one quite vast and molten fold, hanging right down to where once I was sure were a grown man's genitals, strong and sensate. And still there was no choke of puking that came to my ear, no hit and then splatter of spew. So now it was time for the grand finale to this most repulsive burlesque: I leant, with difficulty – stooped right down and undid first one of my clumped and lunatic shoes, and then unfastened the other. When I rose, I could take shelter only in the belief that I would barely now be visible above the satin counterpane (across which Susan was still maybe sprawling? Or was her face now clutched and distorted, protected by a rampart of pillows?). It was only now I dared to look. She gazed at me. I bowed my head – in honour and penitence, yes, but also in order to make quite plain to her the nonsensical battlefield that my scalp had become – a stained and riven landscape, with only tufts and desolation. I watched her closely, then – was astonished, after the first hot tear, that I still remembered how to cry.

'And well . . . do you know, Alan? She was smiling. Not, no no, in any sort of a jeering way. Not even in embarrassment, far as I could tell. Just . . . smiling. You know? Fond, I think is the word. Think it'll do.'

'Mm . . .' murmured Alan. 'I know that smile, Used to.'

'And so I . . . went to her. Yes I did. Touched. Lovely. Was a boy. Excitedly feeling. And the figure . . . hourglass, really. Would you say? Reminded me of the very first girl I had ever cupped and handled. She had a name, fairly sure. Damned if I know it. We were both in our teens. Little thing, she was. Tiny, really – but so well developed a figure, and she can't have been five feet tall, you know. Not so much an hourglass, then – more of an egg-timer, really. She looked up to me. Half the point. And we touched one another. Fumbled around in a scramble of cloth. Loved it. Susie – she came over as just a girl too. All she is. Underneath. She just goes to the dressing-up box, time to time – that's all it is. As, I suppose, we all of us do. And you have to remember, Alan – yes, you might want to know this, hard to tell. But I still had my trousers on. *All* I had on, granted, but a fairly key garment, I think you'll agree. Susie . . . I think she understood the game we were playing. The hurried thrill and the blurring of fingers. The delighted surprise of a squirming satisfaction. Boys and girls, you see? Boys and girls. There's no more really, and nor can it ever be better. Alan . . . you're quiet, suddenly. You've receded. I do so hope I haven't . . . I mean to say, the last thing in the world, old man . . .'

'No no, Blackie. Rest easy. I'm all right. I didn't know how I'd be. But I seem to feel . . . all right. I admit, yes – when you started in on the thing, I thought that maybe for form's sake I should stop you. Halt you in your tracks. Seemliness, and all that sort of thing . . .'

'Why I very nearly didn't go ahead with it . . .'

'But then I began to appreciate the honesty. Would "coming clean" be quite the term here?'

'It was the need for honesty that made me plough on. Could have been a world-class error. Had to risk it. You see, in one sense there is something between us. Well of course there is: Susie, obviously. But I didn't want there to be anything . . . malignant. As silence sometimes can be. I didn't want to plant the germ, incubate the fever of a taxed imagination. Nor can I abide the dreaded shilly-shally. Out in the open, that's the best way. Because we've always been, haven't we Alan? Open with one another? I hope so. Straight down the line, and no bloody nonsense. That's why there's a, that's why we have a, well – bond, if you like.'

Alan smiled, and poured more whisky.

'I'm going to light a cigar. Traditional at nuptials, I believe.'

'Oh good. I'll join you in a fag. Killing ourselves, I suppose. Still – can't be helped.'

'Blackie . . . ask you something?'

'Oh Lord . . .'

'Don't worry. I am not in quest of lurid detail. Nothing of that sort. It's just, well . . . I wonder why you, um – well your hair, for instance . . . ?'

'Ah yes. The coiffeur. The grand pompadour that never quite was. Sad, isn't it? I know it is. How many people must have wagged their heads in wonder? You and Susie, how did you stop up your laughter? Amanda's reaction I can only shrink away from. And I can't now even remember . . . isn't it funny? Isn't it strange? I honestly cannot remember what made me even contemplate it. I mean I ask you . . . having divots of vile and scrubby fuzz from the back of your neck plugged into your bloody scalp! And then painting in the pink bits, as if by numbers. I even tried a toupee, you know. Oh yes I did. On the grounds that at least it wouldn't fucking *hurt* – because it does, you know, all that plugging. They say it doesn't, but they lie. It's not their head they're digging the holes into. But a toupee, well – don't have to tell you, do I really? What a complete and utter arse I looked. Just sat there like a rissole – and always the fear of it blowing away. And yet I never thought of myself as a vain man. But I must have been, I suppose, because then came the corsets. You will observe, Alan, that today I am sporting something of the, um – fuller figure? Why I'm still in a dressing gown, matter of fact. None of my clothes will fit without the armour underneath. Going to get a whole new wardrobe – can't be jailed by all that any more. My scalp, that can do as it damn well pleases. I'm leaving it to its own devices. You will notice too that when I rise you will be seen to tower. You were always a good deal taller than me anyway, Alan, but from this day forth, dear chap, believe me, you will tower. I couldn't give a damn. Not any more. Just to feel again the earth beneath my feet – to not be dizzy and aching, to walk across the room and not feel *precarious* . . . ! Joys to come. I am, Alan, undone. Undone, yes – though willingly. And, oddly, quite made up. Well there it is. There you are.'

'Top you up, will I?'

'Oh Jesus, Alan – I can't drink any more. Right-o, then.'

'Well cheers, Blackie. The worst is now behind you.'

They clinked.

'Cheers, Alan. Cheers. And, um – well thank you, really. For everything. I mean it. I think now I'll just pop off to the lavatory.'

And so that, dear Susan, is how I came to know. About it. All those months ago, when we were still, maybe, the three of us, raw, and yet untried. Would it shock you? To know I know this? I wonder if it would. Now, though, we are different. And somehow, just lately – no more than just the wisp of an unformed intuition, no more than that – but just lately I have been sensing that before very long, we are to be different again.

When she rang the doorbell, Amanda had heard the grating of a sash window from somewhere above her, and then its immediate closing. When she rang the bell again, there was nothing but silence. When she rang the fucking bell a-bloody-gain – leaving her finger there and jabbing repeatedly, her other hand beating at the knocker with a frenzied and staccato energy (and she was more than ready to holler obscenities through the letter box) – a light was distantly glimmering through the dappled glass panels of the door, and then the shadow of somebody looming.

'Jesus, Amanda – what the hell are you doing here?'

'What the fuck do you think, Harry?'

'My *parents* are here . . .'

'Like I give a shit.'

'Look – go away, can't you?'

'As *if* . . . ! You letting me in, or am I going to start screaming?'

'*Jeez* . . .'

Harry stood aside and very quietly closed the door after Amanda had barged her way into the hall.

'Well – come up to my room, then.'

'Don't want to go up to your poxy little room. We'll do it here. In your ghastly so-called, oh yuck – *lounge.*'

'Jesus, Amanda – my parents, they're right next *door* . . . !'

'Well you'd better not make a noise, then. God – you are just so like *pathetic*. My parents! My parents! Jesus . . .'

'Well go in, then – but for God's sake lower your voice.'

'Why? What will they do? Will they, like – stop your pocket money? What is it, Harry? Don't they know that you're screwing a schoolgirl?'

'*Jesus* . . . ! Just get in. Get in the room, OK?'

Harry bundled her into the room and firmly shut the door behind them. He could not begin to analyse the emotion that was jumping and jerky all over her face – where hurt maybe ended or collided with the anger – but he was aware of big hostility there, that was for bloody sure. And she looked a bit, I don't know – high, or something. Could be drunk.

'I didn't know you were a – *kid*, fuck's sake. I feel – awful. Why didn't you tell me?'

'Did tell you. Told you the very first time. *Before* the very first time. In this shitty smelly room of yours. You laughed. You didn't believe me.'

'Yeh but then you said—!'

'Yeh yeh. So I said. So fucking what? And how do you think I feel, Harry? How do you think *I* feel? Having my mother telling me you don't like fucking want to *see* me again? How do you think that makes me feel?'

'Well . . . she told me you were . . . and that she'd fix it. Deal with it. I don't know. And I just said fine. It's best. Isn't it?'

'You're a creep. You know that? You're just a low-life fucking *creep*.'

'Fuck's sake keep your voice down! My—!'

'Yeh, Harry – yeh I know. Your manky *parents* are just next door. Well maybe I ought to go in and talk to *them*. Seeing as we all seem to be having meetings with each other's bloody *mummies* . . . !'

'She just came. Your mom. I didn't ask her. She thought we weren't, you know – using things. And I told her we were. I just can't understand how you can be—!'

'Oh *Jesus*, Harry! I'm not. I'm not. I'm not I'm not I'm not! I just said that to her.'

'You . . . ! You're *not*? Well why the fuck did you—?'

'Don't know. I don't know. I just said it. I do that sometimes. Just, like – come out with stuff.'

'You're nuts.'

'Yeh right. And you are so a creep.'

'Look, Amanda . . . why don't you just go? Hm? Just go.'

Amanda was stung. Her face, when she glared at him, was as if it had been slapped.

'Why? Why? I don't want to.'

'Please, Amanda. Just go. I think you're drunk.'

'*Why*?! Why do you want me to—?! Not *drunk* – fuck off!'

'*Quiet* – Jesus! Keep your voice down, God's sake. Your mom was right about you – you can get kinda crazy.'

'What is this with you calling her my "*mom*"? What's "*mom*"? And "kinda *crazy*"? Oh man. What are you – like some sort of a Yank now, or something?'

'Amanda. Look. There's nothing else to say. Is there? Just go. Yes? Why don't you?'

'You're a shit, Harry. You know? That's what my mother called you. My "*mom*". A shit. And she's right. Because that's exactly what you are. A Grade A, like – *shit*.'

Harry was grinning. Stroking his chin.

'I don't believe you. I don't actually believe your mom said

315

that to you. Our conversation, the way she came on, it just wasn't like that.'

'The way she – came *on* . . . ?'

'Yeh. Your mom – I think she's kinda cute.'

Amanda just stared at him.

'Ex-*cuse* me . . . ?! That is just *disgusting*. I *so* feel sick . . . !'

'Amanda – piss off, can't you? Just *go*.'

She nodded, turned, and slammed her way back into the hall. Before Harry could even get near to her, she was pounding on the door panels of the room alongside.

'Hey! *Parents*? You in there? Yeh? This is the fifteen-year-old girl your son's been screwing, and he's just told me to – get *off* me Harry, you fuck, just like get your bloody hands *off* me, OK . . . ! Yeh – hey *parents*! He's beating me up now, so I'm going to go. He's a shit, your son. A real, like – *shit*!'

Harry was close to weeping in his quite frantic effort to drag her away and out of the house. Just before the front door was slammed in her face, she glimpsed the agitated bustle of two stupid fucking like *spastics*, OK, red-faced and all over the hallway. Harry's face was blazing at her wildly, so she punched it square and right in the fat shit middle of it, and then she turned and ran away up the length of the street, the heart within her hammering, rictus face a plaster of tears, wailing and nearly demented.

CHAPTER NINE

I am hardly the first to discover solace in the bliss of a garden. I was amazed to realise that I had never really had one before, not really – not, anyway, the sort of thing to which I could devote myself, become quite lost in. And Black, he's been really so terribly good – better than I'd dreamed of. Left me to hire a firm of professional landscapers, gave me complete carte blanche, the little sweetie – told me he had total confidence in the magnificence of the outcome. I've had great input too in the house itself, well of course I have – Alan and Black deciding on colours and the positioning of plug points? Not really there, is it? There was an interiors person, obviously, whom I didn't take to at all – dictatorial, basically, like the worst sort of hairdresser. So what I did was, I extracted from him all of his technical know-how – because it is astonishing really, when you're starting with a large and beautifully proportioned virtual shell, how much business there is in it all, how much nitty-gritty and undreamed-of arcana – and then quite joyously sacked him, the ghastly little man, and worked out all the rest of it with the help of the contractor, Mr Clearley, and a load of books and just piles and piles of all these monthly house magazines. There are dozens, all of them seemingly touting just a couple of recipes – doing it with chic on the cheap, or splurging a fucking fortune, which they cleverly term as investment in the future. Yes well – I need hardly tell you that I went down the fucking fortune route, that fortune, I am ashamed to admit, closely followed by at least another one. He doesn't seem to mind, Black – he encourages it, in fact: so sweet. And he needs so very little in return, and I do find that endearing. He likes it when I wear a skirt, which sometimes I do, so he can slide his hand up – and he just adores to suck a bit on each of my breasts, can't get enough of them, just like a baby boy. I simply close my eyes, and it's quite all right then. I rub him against his trousers – you should see his little face. It's more than Alan gets, anyway. Poor Alan. He gets nothing – not from me, anyway. Hasn't for just ages. Not ever a conscious decision on my part, I don't think. Just how it all turned out. I sometimes wonder whether he minds. Still, however, I can't quite care enough about it. Which is more than a pity, it is actually rather a shame, because I know he loves me – more, lately, even more, and maybe far too much.

But it is in the garden, I think, that I really do feel I have come into my own. I would be foolish to say that now it is finished because some of the frustration and most of the joy will always come from the truth that a garden can never be that. The rolling seasons, the vagaries of the soil, the force or punitive absence of sun and then rain . . . one is truly prostrate at the feet of the gods, playing to one's best advantage the hand one is dealt, no more really than an earnest titivator, ever looking forward and simperingly delighted by whatever new and blossoming treats are thrillingly bestowed upon one. When I was a child, our garden was big enough, I suppose

318

– scope for skipping and running, a Wendy house, an alpine rockery that was said to be mine – but all it came down to really was an overgrown and sprawling lawn, a crab-apple tree and another one that every so often would grudgingly yield just a few damsons, sour and pappy – and a lovely old bent-over pear tree, Conference, the long ones, and I used to love the pears when they were still so hard I could snap them in half. Gardening, I suppose, in those days, it wasn't really seen in terms of design, as an art form or anything of that sort. Bedding, bulbs, a run-out with the mower from time to time – spot of weeding if you really had to. My father, he never lifted a single finger – just stretched out in the summer on a steamer sort of chaise-type affair looking quite mighty and even majestic, in my eyes. Poor Daddy. And Mummy though, I don't remember her doing anything either – there must have been a man, or something, but I honestly can't recall. There was evil at its perimeter in the form of stinging nettles – dock leaves, though, for the antidote – and viral-looking ferns sprouting from the very mortar in the bulging retaining walls. And I had a vision of him, Daddy I mean, in that garden, when just the other day I got a call from the people at the place he's in. They had just brought him down from the roof, they told me – wearing only one of the lady carers' pinnies and a paper hat from a Christmas cracker – where he had been chipping at a chimney stack with a small pair of nail scissors telling everyone and no one that the topiary had been very cruelly neglected, and further that his uncle was the Duchess of Argyll. None of the terrified staff who had been forced to clamber up there was allowed to descend until they had joined him rousingly in two choruses of 'Yellow Submarine', and promised to give up cheese for the remainder of Lent. Oh

Jesus, I thought, he didn't really do all of that, did he? Oh God he can't have: not *again*.

So no, the garden is not and never will be *finished*, per se, but dear me, I am so very pleased with all that now I have here. And I am well aware, don't worry, that gardeners, particularly recent and ardent converts, can easily become the most dreadful bores on earth, so I am not about to deliver a lecture, nor to conduct the grand and endless tour, replete with commentary and a bewilderment of Latin terminology. Let it simply be said that the garden is on four quite separate levels: the terrace, that's the first thing, proper York stone – that opens out from the atrium doors – quite heaven on a summer's evening with a glass of champagne, I so can't tell you – and then there is this very attractive baluster, also stone, and a few steps down to the lawn, practically perfect now that one of Herb's workers has finally got rid of the clumps of moss and even a *molehill*, if you can believe. I practically lost my mind when I saw the mound of earth almost tauntingly bang at the lawn's very centre and immediately wanted to lay waste to the creature or creatures responsible – gas, guns, bombs, whatever it took. Herb, he said I was making a mountain out of it, and we laughed about that. Made sure he got rid of it, though. So this lawn, it's bordered, will be, by a low, thick and cubic hedge – Herb says it'll grow really quickly and I believe him about that because already the shape and breadth are quite plain to see. There's a ha-ha beyond, so you can't from the house see the seemingly natural meadow beyond – you have to just come upon it, strolling. It's so very beautiful – willow, honeysuckle, the splatter of poppies, all sorts of wild grasses and those tight and wiry little clusters of yellow, the name's just gone from me at the moment, but you know what

320

they are when you see them. Months of work and unspeakable sums of money to get something seeming as natural as that. The vegetable garden, the country garden, the swimming pool . . . There's a pergola with the sweetest little roof that just tips up at the corners like a Japanese pagoda. Conservatory, of course – divine for breakfast – and a little rustic summerhouse just before the trees that you can revolve to get the best of the sun, and then the shade. It's all very marvellous, and I love every inch of it. It makes me laugh when I think back to the Chelsea house – the obligatory pair of bay trees in Versailles boxes standing sentinel outside the front door, and at the back just a stunted mutation of a Lutyens bench, box balls in tall zinc cylinders and the most dreadful sheet of aluminium all down the rear wall, and over which water coursed, highly annoyingly, although more often that not it just didn't work, leaving as the focal point of the garden what looked like a piece of an aeroplane's fuselage. Just didn't think about it at the time. Black, he was asking me only recently – yesterday morning, coffee on the lawn – whether the agents had yet found a tenant for it, the Chelsea house, which had always been the idea, and I told him no.

It's the meadow I'm in now. There's a small wooden hut, heavily distressed in order to make it look not so much rustic and ancient, but more as if it had actually grown up from deep down in the ground, and in it we have all these traditional deckchairs – green canvas slings, though: nothing stripey. I am slumped in one of them now, seeing red through my eyelids, closed against the sun. My fingers and thumb are sliding over the silky cool of a petal as I trail down my hand into the long rush of grasses – I am trying by touch to assimilate its colour. Only a sensualist such as I could even dream of such a thing.

And so why, into such an Eden, must hellish thoughts intrude? Amanda. God curse the stupid little child. I have already spoken to Charles, my doctor, about the position she now finds herself in, and he assures me that this is easy, no problem at all – fixed up with a single phone call, private suite, nicest people, out the same day or else she can stay for as long as she pleases. Well yes – but it still has to be *gone* through, hasn't it? The whole thing. And I suppose her mother, she ought to be by her side? And Charles, he said to me – but Amanda, she's a minor, isn't she? Is this a situation that is involving the law? And I thought back to the boy's utter helplessness, Harry, the boy, and his credible surprise. I thought of his wide and open vulnerable face and troubled eyes, and then of his golden future (because at his age, all futures are that). And so no, I said: no. Not a situation that is involving the law.

I am, you know, going to go out again this evening. I'm rather looking forward to it. I got this most divine and silky floaty dress from Valentino – made for a warm summer's evening, so such a wonderful chance to wear it. It is a muted floral and one of the colours is a nearly fuchsia which but precisely echoes the shade of shoes I had bought just the very week before in Harvey Nichols, and neither was ever intended to match – it's just a happy coincidence. Serendipity. The falling of things, as if from the sky, and perfectly into place. And before, I shall light a dozen candles in my bathroom – Diptique, and this new one I've found in Penhaligon's – and give myself up to the deepest and hottest bath I can bear, with Nina Ricci bubbles, the kindest and the sweetest of all that I've tried. And imagine myself being borne away by the lapping waters to somewhere else and quite enchanted, where the light is brighter, and the warmth of love is all around. Because still, there is a hole in me. I have all this, everything I planned, and still there is a hole in me. The practical side of my nature, that has been so utterly satisfied . . . and yet I have to face it: still there is a hole in me, and it must, just has to be filled, you see. Only a sensualist such as I could even dream of such a thing.

'Out are you, Alan old man?'

'Am, yes Blackie. Thought I would. Pleasant evening, and all the rest of it. Stroll. Stretch the legs a bit. You're very welcome to . . .'

'No no. Perfectly content here with my book, you know, and the glass that warms. Rereading Hardy. Never tire. Spent a devil of an age tracking down my glasses. Can't tell you how good it is not to have to poke those bloody lenses into my eyes any more. Think I ought to have a pair in every single room . . . glasses, you know. Susie, she went off about, ooh – half an hour ago, I expect. Said she wouldn't be horrendously late. Looked lovely, I must say.'

Mm, thought Alan, I imagine she did. Hadn't actually seen her, this time. Didn't, in fact, know she was out. But lately, quite recently, she had taken to going out in the evenings – not every evening, no, but more than once or twice – and on the occasions when I was caught and assailed by the shock of her perfume, the glint of a necklace, the fall of her hair, the confident stride high up upon such daring heels and then the mouth, that mouth of hers, and just as the poet put it – roses filled with snow . . . at the times when I had been aware of the sumptuous fleetingness of her quite astounding presence amid the air that she scented, and then just the trail of it when she was gone, I had indeed noticed that yes, she did look lovely, quite as Blackie had put it. More and more, to my mind, and flushed with a vigour I had long believed to be forever extinguished, a full and burgeoning, yet all the time secret glow that murmured of a second coming.

And then I was on a bar stool in the shabby old boozer that soon, I suppose, will be wrecked by making it splendid – patting a tubed Havana in my pocket and wishing to Christ I could smoke it. God it's so utterly *collapsed*, this place, not unlike a lot of the men here. No gastropub, this one – not at all family-friendly, no siree, not this one. Just men drinking, and wishing they could smoke. Weren't all men, of course – there was a knot of penniless students, looked like, over by the door, all dressed to be more or less identical, and very horribly indeed – ex-army fatigues intended for Titans, shoes that had been used for target practice, chewed-up hair, the odd bit of metal punched into their flesh, a smattering of tattoo – and the boys, Jesus, they were just as bad. But now look over there . . . on the stove-in and greasy banquette. Girl on her own, maybe a cider. Still looking over, you know – don't think it's just my wistful imagination that's hard at work here. Studying the classified in the *Evening Standard* – possibly for a job, could be for somewhere to live. Just wander over, have a friendly word . . .

'This is . . . quite a surprise, if you'll forgive me.'

She blinked up at him quite without expression as he stood over her table, his whisky in his hand.

'You say something . . . ?'

'No no. It's just that . . . this bar. You know. Not exactly – the in place, is it? Not what you'd call, um – "happening". If you know what I mean. Young people, young women – don't come in here much, that's all.'

324

'Yeh. I'm beginning to see why. Look – I'm not interested, OK? So if you don't mind . . .'

'Yes yes. No no. Quite. Sorry to, um . . . It's just that—'

'Look – just piss off, all right? Jesus . . .'

'Sorry, sorry. No offence. It's just that—'

'Look you – I been nice. Now do you want me to call the manager?'

'No – no need. I'm leaving. I'm off. Sorry to have, er. Yes. It's just that—'

'Oh just fuck off, can't you? What's wrong with you? Just fuck *off*.'

So yes – did that: fucked off. Flew out of there, frankly – ears were purple with the burn of shame. And so there – one more lesson in life, and not one I should need to be taught: you don't buy and pay for it, it's not going to happen. Dashed into another pub – though not, alas, nearly so nasty – and wormed my way up to the bar for a whisky. Shaken, quite candidly. Hadn't had time to phone her, Helen, and now I'd got reality completely confused with all the other side of it. First signs of something, though nothing good. Or did I really think I'd be able to get away with it? Fool if I did: fool. Found myself confiding in a complete and total stranger all the details of my newest humiliation.

'Mistake you made,' he growled back darkly – large man, red in the face, though blueish too: wore a fat gold signet ring whose dimpled inscription was all but eroded. 'Mistake you made, son, was going for a young one. Pick and choose, they can – and face it, you ain't no kid. No oil painting neither, no offence. You want to go for the older ones, they're the ones what's grateful. Reminds me of a joke I heard one time.'

'I have to go now,' said Alan quite hastily, wondering why

in God's name he was in fact standing here in the first bloody place.

'Man – in a pub, right? Could be this very hostelry in what we're wossname. And there's this woman, OK? Sixty if she's a day – nearer seventy, might easily have been. And she turns round, right, and she says to him—'

'Really have to, you know. Be off.'

'No no listen – sit down, sit down. Have another drink. It's not long, it's not a long joke – it ain't one of them shaggy fuckers. So yeh – old woman, right? And she says to him, says to this bloke – Well how about it then, darling? Fancy it, do you? And the bloke, right, he's going Oh Gawd – do us a favour! I ain't that desperate, am I? And she's like—'

'Look—!'

'Listen! Christ. So she's like, don't be so bleeding hasty, sunshine: I bet you never done it with a mother and daughter before, has you? And the bloke, he gets to thinking mmmm – could be interesting, could be interesting. So he go off with her, right? Her place. And she gets in the door, OK, and she shouts up the stairs, "Oy Mum! You awake?!"'

And the man went redder and bluer and chortled very throatily, his eyes quite lost in pink and puffy folds.

'Dear oh dear oh dear! "Oy Mum! You awake?!" Christ Almighty. Get it? Up the stairs, she's shouting, "Oy Mum! You awake?!" Killer, that is. Classic. Here – where you going . . . ?'

Out of here, mate, that's for bloody sure. This whole evening, it's not really working. Cut my losses, I reckon: head back home. Best thing. Much earlier than I imagined it would be, but there you are. So what – I really did believe then, did I, that I could just saunter up to a girl in a bar, and the next thing I knew I'd be . . . oh God: imbecility. Doesn't bear thinking

326

about. Too too shaming. And particularly in the light of just everything, now. Well. Right. That's that. At least there weren't witnesses. Put it right out of my mind, that's what I have to do now. I'll just . . . what shall I do? I know – I'll go and disturb Blackie. Keep on chatting until he casts aside his Thomas Hardy with a gentle sigh of indulgence. Then we can have a drink. Yes, that's the plan – so I'm surprised, I suppose, when I go into the drawing room and there's Blackie, not in his usual chair and knee-deep in Wessex, but standing up and way over by the curtains, patting his considerable stomach and seeming rather agitated, looks like to me – although it could be, I suppose, just a touch of the recurrent dyspepsia (to which, he will tell you, he is a consummate martyr).

'All right are you, Blackie?'

Black's eyes were flickering as he looked around and nearly at Alan.

'Perfectly, perfectly. You're back, ah – soon.'

'Yes well. Limit to how far one's legs are going to stretch, isn't there really? Fed up with reading? Book's on the floor.'

'Yes. Dropped it. Can't bend down. Can't be bothered. And, um – you, you all right then, are you Alan?'

Alan exhaled, and fell back into an armchair.

'Oh I *suppose* so – yes, I am really. I suppose I am. It's just that . . . oh, I don't know. Yes yes – I'm fine. Fancy a nightcap?'

Black looked about him, as if there might be lurking a furtive surveyor.

'Well, um . . .'

'Yes – course we'll have a nightcap. Have a bit of a chat. There's something, actually, I'd quite like to, um . . .'

'Like to what? Something on your mind, is there Alan? Maybe wait till morning. Little bit tired, you know . . .'

'Nonsense, Blackie – barely nine o'clock. Early even by your standards. Here – I'll pour us a Scotch.'

'Still, though – think I might just turn in. Call it a, you know – day.'

'What – not just a quick one? Poured it now.'

'Oh well – right-o then, Alan. Right-o.'

Black now eased himself with care and resignation down and into his chair by the mantel, making the deep and throaty harrumphing sound habitual to his sitting (more final and an octave lower than the guttural grunt he would always come out with whenever he had to bloody well get up again). Alan pulled a side chair right up close to him.

'I think, Blackie – well, now's as good a time as ever, I suppose. I mean – I don't want to, um . . . alarm you or anything, but . . .'

'What? But what? Alarm me . . . ? What on earth are you talking about, Alan?'

Alan compressed his lips and narrowed his eyes. He touched Black's hand, and then he swallowed. This is it, then:

'Well . . . it's just that . . . our wife: I think she might be having an affair.'

Black just gaped at him, it was all he could do, and Alan – until the doorbell suddenly rang and made him jerk and then stand up – he could only goggle right back at the man in sheer and utter amazement at hearing in the air his very own words.

'Who in Jesus name can that be? Back in a minute, Blackie.'

Black was gazing at the back of him as Alan quite hurriedly left the room. He put down the glass, and his rigid fingers went up to his eyes. He did not hear Amanda as she reappeared from behind the sofa – but he heard her cackled remark as she darted away and out into the atrium:

'Well fuck me, Grandad: that was a close one, wasn't it?'

Amanda flitted through the hall and up the spiral of stairs, just as Susan was distractedly bustling her way through the front door and batting away all of Alan's anxiety and ministrations.

'Just left my *key* behind, that's all . . . it's nothing to . . . yes I'm perfectly all right, of course I'm all right – don't I look all right? I'm quite all right, I tell you. I decided to come back early, that's all – not a *crime*, is it? Look, Alan – I'm sorry, I just want to go to sleep now, all right? Pounding headache. Oh Christ's sake don't ask me any more *questions* – what's wrong with you at all? I just want to go to bed, that's all. It's not hard to understand. No – I'm fine, I'm fine, I'm perfectly fine – I *told* you I'm fine. Oh Christ just fuck *off*, can't you? Leave me alone. I'm going to bloody *bed*.'

Susan rushed up the stairs just as Alan turned and quickly glimpsed the wink of the ascending lift, no doubt with an equally somnolent Blackie inside it. Well. Right. I'll just do that, then: fuck off. Getting quite good at it.

So I spent the night on the beach. Thanks to all the technology that I don't understand (it's only a matter of time before it all goes wrong on me) I was able to watch the sun go down, and many hours later than it had actually done so in that other and awful place, the real world – a place where again I find myself wounded – and hence, I suppose, my headlong escape from it. Dazzlingly orange, and then the very most intense sort of crimson, my kind and warm and vibrant sun, as it sizzlingly touched and then dipped down with a majesty and grace into the deep and vivid sea, when all was swallowed by indigo – just the merest turquoise and hazy halo to guide my hand to the glass of Scotch.

I hated myself for thinking it – had tried so hard to smother the idea before it had breathed its life into me. But no: the seed was sown. And nor was it tender – it got no nurture from me, nor a sympathetic bed . . . but still the roots were shooting, and they seemed quite sturdy (grimly anchored and snaking with venom). And yet – I should not maybe have confided my suspicion. Not to an innocent. But here, of course, is no suspicion – this is something I know. Not an iota of evidence – and nor, Christ, have I sought any. I know it, though – just know it, that our Susan, she has strayed from us. I did not have to ask myself: But how could this *be*? Because I knew that too. I had no detail, and it hurt me. But detail, oh dear God – I run from even the thought of its heat: that could come near to closing me down.

Just before dawn – whether mine or the true one I can hardly care – I bullyingly was buoying myself up with a sadly hopeful and wilfully contorted construction on the matter: that Susan had been in so dully impassioned a state because she had at last been flooded by a bright and inner realisation . . . the smack of how foolish she had nearly been, a tremor on the rim, but now she was safely come home to us. And then I spent minutes straining with pain to become so stupid as to swallow the half of it. I couldn't. So what if . . . before even the thing took hold, a jagged and ugly break-up? Possible, surely? Well yes, but only in the way that miracles are constantly said to be. In truth, the state of her had given me not an atom of encouragement. Only depth moves us to the core – and Susan, believe me, was moved to the brink of turmoil . . . whereas fancies, on the other hand – well, these are famous only for passing.

Susan, though: her room is locked. Whether or not she is inside it, I simply couldn't say. Blackie, then. Couldn't, could

I? Just abandon him to thinking whatever he's thinking. Gone
ten, now: strange that he hasn't sought me out. His caring will
be of a different order from mine, but already he must surely
be sour and unsettled, if only from the looming of something
new. It is a beautiful morning – perhaps he is in the garden,
the pergola, maybe. Because he rarely if ever goes away from
the house now: says that all he wants is here.

No one in the pergola, nor on the terrace or the lawn. He
wouldn't be in the meadow because he says it's just one hell
of a trek and when he gets there there's something growing
wild, couldn't tell me what, that makes his nose so itchy, and
then it goes down to his knee. I like to think I know of all
his irritants and foibles, though fresh ones are arising daily.
One of the younger gardeners, trainee maybe (there seems
to be a never-ending roster of them), is planting densely a
long low row of geraniums – the total length of the lawn,
as far as I can see. Red ones – the only colour in the world
so very akin to new-dripped blood. But Blackie, though . . .
no sign. The vegetable garden was a strong possibility – he
had some fine vine tomatoes under glass and was always
quite fascinated by the dexterity and athleticism of the
runner beans, whipping their way up and around the canes.
He wasn't there. I only caught up with him, Blackie, much
later on in the drawing room, where very stupidly I hadn't
even thought of looking. Told him where I'd been searching,
and who I had found there instead: Amanda – stretched out
on a lounger alongside the pool, a forearm flung over her
eyes. Quite the young woman . . . and wearing only what
appeared to be bunting – a few triangular strips of white,
and loosely knotted simple string. Her hair was frizzy and

nearly dry. Just a short distance, but still I had thought I'd better call over – didn't want to startle her by my soft and sudden approach. I told Blackie this, and then I told him how the rest of it had gone: went into all the detail that I could remember. Wanted it to be as shocking for him as it had been for me.

'Hello, Amanda. Morning. Not at school today?'

Amanda raised her arm from across her face and peered in the direction, waving him on as she squintingly focused.

'It's Saturday, Dad.'

'Is it? Is it really? Yes, I suppose it would be, by now. So. Had a swim, have you? Warm, is it? Water?'

'Dad – sit down, can you? Wanna talk.'

Alan lowered himself warily on to the lounger beside her which was far too low and pitched a bit, till he was settled. Which was worse? Silence? Or people who wanted to talk?

'What about? Had breakfast, have you? Thought I might make some coffee . . .'

Amanda looked hard at him, and seriously.

'Mum, Dad. What do you think? We never like talk, OK? But now I think we should.'

The sun was beating hard on the back of Alan's skull. He put a hand there and his hair, it felt so warm. And another heat – the very smoulder he had failed in his earnest and repeated efforts in damping down, snuffing out, now took light and licked up before him. His eyes flicked over to check on Amanda; still she looked at him hard, and seriously.

'Your mother? What do I think? In what, um, sense do you . . . ?'

'Oh come on, Dad. You know exactly what I mean. Blackie told me.'

'Blackie? *Told* you . . . ? Really? Told you what? I'm amazed. He *told* you . . . ?'

'Yeh. Sort of. Anyway – doesn't matter. Now just listen, OK Dad? Because knowing you, you're just so like going to do nothing, like you always do. But you've just got to this time – because this time, OK, it's just like so *disgusting*. I mean yeh OK – I thought at the time that with Black it was like *gross* – but this, oh man, this is just . . . !'

'What are you saying? How can you know what—?'

'I'll tell you. I'll tell you how I know. I know exactly what she's doing, and it makes me like just so *sick*, OK? Because I know him. The guy, yeh? That she's doing it with.'

Alan shut his eyes, as his mind tore away in a frenzy. So wished he hadn't, now – come to talk to Amanda. And his heart . . . a fist inside him was gamely fumbling, but it was just too late to catch it as it fell down hard and into somewhere black where at first it lay there dead and heavily, before there came the slicing. Because merely an inner and solitary certainty, that still can be just about tolerable, blinking in the dimmest shadow of a glint of battered hope; corroboration, though – that just brings despair. And Amanda – despite his pleading at first with her not to, and then insisting she did so immediately – Amanda, she told him, yes she did, and with a fierce directness, who it was her mum was doing it with.

'Amanda . . . that *can't* be right . . . ! It just . . . who is this man? How do you . . . ?'

'Not a man, Dad. Boy. Not yet, like – eighteen? Harry, he used to be my kind of boyfriend. Mum, shit – she went to see him.'

'Why did she—?'

'Because I guess I told her I was knocked up. Pregnant.'

'Jesus, Amanda! You're—?!'

'No. Not. I'm not. It's just what I told her.'

'Jesus, Amanda! Why did you—? Are you or aren't you, Christ's sake?'

'Not. I'm not. Why did everyone believe me when I said I was, and now like I'm saying I'm just so *not*, everyone's just going to me oh yeh, *right* . . .'

'Well I just can't understand why you'd—!'

'No well I don't either. It just like came out. She was giving me a hard time, you know? Anyway – not the point. She told Harry not to see me again, OK? And man, did he go for that big-time. No argument at all. Chucked me out, more or less. And now I know why. Mum, when she was talking about him, she'd gone all kind of creepy on me? Weirded me out. And then Harry – do you want to know what he said about her? Do you know what he called her? Eee-*yow* – just *so* sick.'

'Jesus . . . !'

'He said she was "cute". "Kinda cute" is what he said. Shit. How sick is that?'

'He's . . . how old did you say? *Eighteen* . . . ?'

'Nearly. Yeh. I know. Sick, right?'

'But are you *sure*, Amanda? How can you—?'

'Sure. I'm sure. You know when you just, like – *feel* something? You just look at people and you *know*?'

And Alan nodded, because mm, he did, he did. He did, yes. And all this later, as he just blankly stood there, was what he woodenly repeated to Black.

'I have been into all the detail I can remember. I wanted it to be as shocking for you as it has been for me.'

Black nodded, and sipped his whisky. Lit another cigarette.

'You have succeeded. I am . . . shocked. No – more than

334

shocked, actually. I'm in – pain. Physical pain. How perfectly extraordinary. So . . . your suspicions, Alan, would appear to be sound. When you said that to me last night, I thought you might be drunk. Delusional. But Amanda . . . it's all a bit . . . is she absolutely positive? I mean to say – one must be sure. Mustn't we? Thing like this. We don't want any slip-ups here.'

'Slip-ups? What on earth are you talking about?'

'Well I mean to say, Alan old man – we've got to do something about it, haven't we? Can't just – let it happen, can we? Got to do something.'

'Do something? Like what, Christ's sake?'

'Well I haven't the slightest idea. I'm still in a state of . . . but we can't just stand idly by. What do other married couples do in a situation like this?'

'But we're not, are we? A married couple. We're a married triple. That's the problem. I doubt if there are people who get into a situation like this.'

'See what you mean. God though, Alan – I just feel so . . . !'

'I know. So do I. Didn't, when you came along. Not for a minute. Funny. But now I do. Very. This is different.'

'But what can have *possessed* the woman at all? I mean – hasn't she got everything she wants? Wasn't that the point of all this? Haven't we been good husbands to her? Why are women always so—?'

'Because they're always chasing more and more. That's why there's never a good answer to "What do women want?" Because the only answer is always *more*. For us, I think, it's the other way round: we want less and less – and certainly, Christ, nothing *new*. But good, yes – we've been good up to a point. And this is the bit that kills me, frankly. I mean, you – you pay the bills. Gave us this wonderful house. You were the means whereby Susan could stop working and I could stop pretending to look for a job. Me? Well – old time's sake, really. That, I imagine, is why I'm still around. Is all I can think. Never could really fathom why she wanted you as well as, and not instead of. Amanda's father, of course – might have something to do with it. But ask yourself, Blackie – and this is painful, I warn you. You – me. What's missing? What else could she be craving?'

Blackie was nodding slowly as he lowered his glass.

'I know. I'm ahead of you. I've just been trying not to . . .'

'Mm. Yes. Hurts.'

'Furiously. Strange. How I've come to . . . love her, really. Only woman I ever have, except for Letitia. And that was decades ago. Long before I lost my mind and married fucking Mylene.'

'Why not Letitia?'

'Oh. Well. Long story. But would you want to marry some- one who was out every evening, serially unfaithful, slobbed around the house all day, smoking and drinking?'

'Mm. No, I suppose not . . .'

'No well – nor did she. Dumped me. That was that. But look we've just got to, you know Alan – do something about it, I mean. *Eighteen* . . . ! Jesus Christ Almighty . . .'

'Cruel. Too cruel. But that's the ghastly thing – that's why it makes a terrible sort of sense. Not going to be mooning around another old fart, is she? No offence, Blackie old man.'

'No no – none, ah . . . I assure you. Taken, dear man. Christ, though . . . But yes I do see. Beautiful woman. Still quite young . . .'

Alan pulled his chair right up close to Black's – topped up their glasses and looked at him frankly.

336

'Blackie . . . there's something I don't understand. Why did you go and tell Amanda what I'd said to you? And *when*, Christ's sake. I only said it to you just before you went up to bed.'

'Yes. Well I'm glad – I think I'm glad – that you, ah – asked me that, Alan. Because I would've had to tell you at some point. And this, this might as well be it. The point, I mean. Seeing as it appears to be a day of discovery . . .'

'Sorry, Blackie. Lost me.'

'Well you see, Alan . . . I didn't in fact *tell* Amanda, no. She heard you say it. To me. She was here, you see. At the time. Yes. Behind those curtains over there, in point of fact. Or was she behind the sofa . . . ? Makes no odds, really. All sounds very cloak and dagger, but there it is. Point is, she was here. With me. In this room. Yes. Couldn't understand what on earth she was up to, but now, maybe, I more or less do. I mean to say – no psychologist, but in the light of what Susie has done to her . . .'

'Look I'm sorry, Blackie, but I haven't the slightest bloody idea what in God's name you're talking about. She was here in this room, you say? I never saw her. Be plain, can't you?'

'I can be, yes, and I shall be. Last evening – you were out. Susie was, Christ help us, out as well. I was reading. *Mayor of Casterbridge*. Know it? No? Do recommend it. Riveting. One of his finest. About a man who sells his wife. Oh Lord. Anyway – here I was, in this very chair, and Amanda, she walks in and sits down. Just about where you are now. Starts talking to me.'

'Amanda? Sat down and started *talking* to you? Good Lord. Never done it before, has she?'

'Not ever. Not once. I should have remembered that. So yes, I do recall thinking to myself, mm – this is all rather odd.'

337

An understatement. Well look – this is Amanda's father, after all, who I'm talking to now. So I think it is as well to be circumspect. I tried not to notice her at first, made a pretty poor fist of it. Well Jesus – you should have seen her, you really should have been there. Let's face facts: what I was doing was my damnedest not to *ogle* the poor child. Never seen her in that light before – never so much as even crossed my mind; not so much an admission of my ever-encroaching age as the facing up to the daily need for a candid confrontation with reality. Because my years of self-delusion were now, I hoped, finally behind me. And by the time she eventually shifted from her chair, I'd read nearly three whole pages of Hardy and had failed to absorb a single bloody word.

'Amanda . . . what do you imagine you're doing . . . ?'

'Just touching your hair . . . why? Don't you like it?'

'Why are you doing that? It's rather . . . thin.'

'Silky, though. You like Mum, do you?'

Her skirt, well of course I'd observed it was short, but now as she moved up her arms – sifting around still on the top of my head, she was, as if for treasure, or maybe for the lurking of lice – it rode up on her thighs, bit by bit, higher and higher. The scent all over her was maybe Susie's, but I have to admit that she wore it well. Her eyes were glassy: she might have been drinking.

'Not silky, is it Amanda? More like a scouring pad.'

'Yeh . . . it is a bit. So do you, Blackie? Like her?'

'Well of course I . . . Wouldn't be here otherwise, would I? Would we all? Amanda . . . what in God's name do you think you're—!'

'Just *touching*, Blackie. What's the matter? Are you, like – what are you? Freaking? Don't you like to be touched? I think you do. But she's old, isn't she? Mum. I thought men liked younger girls. I mean – you're old, yeh, like mega . . . but still.'

Black so yearned to be firm. To be amused and adult over this. To take up her fingers from close to his groin and bid her quietly to resume her seat or else – better – leave the room entirely. On the other hand there was not the slightest possibility of his doing any such thing; so far, he was still clutching on hard to the covers of his book, but it was touch and go how much longer that was going to last. Her hair was teasing his forehead, and her little breasts, plumply cheeky little plums, were beginning to dance before his eyes. So Black just closed them, willed himself to become a young boy again – just a boy and a girl is what they'd be then, and where's the harm in that? The innocent thrill of exploratory contact . . . And at that moment, for good or bad, there was a shuffle and slam in the hall, and Amanda had made a dive for it. Black was on his feet in the blur of an instant – fastest he'd ever done it, and he didn't even grunt. *The Mayor of Casterbridge* fell to the floor, and suddenly the room was filled with Alan. Black had tried to put him off, but he'd insisted on a drink and a chat. He was barely aware of what he was talking about – just saw Alan moving his mouth – until he said what he said about Susie. And then the doorbell was clanging – Alan shot away, thank God, and there was that little minx Amanda again.

'Well fuck me, Grandad: that was a close one, wasn't it?'

Black was reddened – shocked by the implication of collusion, and stung by this new and cruel note of jeering. At least, Jesus, he hadn't . . . touched her. But still, but still – he should not have been playing the boy: he should at least, shouldn't he, have striven to be the boy who was imitating the man? But the thing is, Jesus oh God . . . when she was there

339

and then all over him . . . she just had looked so very terribly *fuckish* . . .

'So you see, Alan . . . she sat down and started talking to me – and then you came in, and that was that, really.'

'Mm. But why did she—?'

'Yes well. Hide, you mean? Yes well. Been asking myself the very same question. Children, you know. Bit of a prank, I expect.'

Alan was watching him closely.

'But earlier you said . . . that you weren't now too surprised that she had done what she did. What is it, Blackie, that she did . . . ?'

'Nothing. God. Well nearly nothing. Tell you the truth, Alan, I think she was just making fun of me. Wouldn't be the first time a young woman has. I think . . . well, if she perceives Susie to have gone and messed up her, I don't know – relationship with this boy . . . Jesus Christ: can it really be *true*? Too too incredible. What's his name, by the way? The boy. Not that it matters.'

'Harry, the sod's name is. And she gave me his address.'

But what I was saying, Alan, is . . . um . . . oh fucking hell. What was it, Alan? What I was saying?'

'Er . . . what, before about Harry, you mean? Oh yes – what Amanda was up to.'

'That's it. Good man. Yes – I think it was maybe just a child's attempt – touching, really – to spoil, um, something of her mother's. Think so? Could be. Needn't be. Might be total balls.'

Alan nodded briefly.

'I'm sorry, Blackie, that you were put through . . . taunting, shall we say. Having seen her in the garden just now, I would fully understand it if – even fleetingly – you saw her as looking, well . . .'

'Mm. Well she did look a bit . . . now you come to mention it. But there we are. Water under the, um . . . The thing we've got to put our minds to now is Susie, and this blasted Billy problem. Bridge, Water under the, um . . .'

'Harry, his name is. The bastard. Well what do you suggest we do? I mean, Christ – you know Susan. If she wants something, she's bloody well going to have it, isn't she?'

'Yes, oh yes. There's no point whatsoever in our confronting Susie. Only add coals to the, er – damn, *fire*. No no – it's this Harry we've got to approach. That right? Harry? Teach him the folly of his ways.'

'How do we do that?'

'Well there are two methods, tried and tested. Bribery or intimidation. Reason is out – you cannot reason with a boy in lust. Envy the bastard – well of course I do. To be so very young that one day you have nothing, not even leeway, and then God goes and bestows upon you, oh – such a gift. Then you know that everything in the world is suddenly possible. Except, of course, ageing and death, which will never ever strike you down. Bliss. Shame, really, that we have to stamp on it – if it were any other woman on earth, I'd wish him the best of British. But we do have to, stamp on it – and soon. And firmly. If he's broke, as I imagine he is – all people of his age are, aren't they? – I daresay a grand or two might do the trick. Otherwise . . .'

'Otherwise what? You come out with a knuckleduster?'

'Ha ha. Very droll. Obviously not. But I have, you know, had dealings in the past with a certain party who is no stranger to certain, um – tactics. Met him through the friend of a friend of God knows who. Huge man, he was – black as coal and covered in jewellery. Extraordinary. Went by the name of Beef Jerky.'

'You're joking . . .'

'No no – I assure you. He gave me at the time all sorts of pointers and tidbits of information when I realised I could no longer allow my wife to go on living. It was her or me, fundamentally.'

Alan sat back in his chair and widened his eyes to the utmost.

'Yes – it is rather shocking, I suppose. Hearing it for the first time. But me, I'm thoroughly used to it by now. I'd offered her everything, you see – divorce, house, money, anything a woman could ask for. But no. She seemed to exact the greatest satisfaction in life from staying where she was, and tormenting me beyond endurance. When she became openly psychotic, Mylene, I tried every avenue open to me to get her locked away, but there was always some damn reason why she couldn't be. Then she started to come at me – with a meat axe once, as I recall. Regularly hit me with things. Can't have it, can you? One day, I have no doubt, she would deliberately or else as a result of yet one more quite insane and instantly forgotten assault, have killed me. Simple as that. So I thought I had to get in first. You see. And I got all sorts of information – poison, gun with silencer, certain knots – very interesting, those were – and the guarantee too to supply all the equipment. I am obliged to you, Mr Jerky, I said to him, but I think I need something altogether simpler, more natural and explicable – less *criminal*, if you know what I'm driving at. And that's when he told me: cases like this, he said – Lord, had he seen life, that man . . . death too, of course – cases like this, he said, falling down stairs is always favourite. Explained about rucked-up rugs and maybe faulty stair rods. Mine of knowledge. I paid him – said to him oh *thank* you, Mr Jerky, I am indeed indebted to you. He smiled so broadly, I remember – took a pride in his work, you could tell. He patted my shoulder, grinned his grin. And then he said "Call me *Beef* . . . !" Nice chap.'

'And . . . you . . . ?'

'Yes yes. Best way, really – because she was always prone to a bit of a tumble, Mylene. Gin, you see. So yes – got it done, you know. Wasn't smooth. Made sure she'd drunk a bit on top of all of her pills – it was her, in those days, took all the pills . . . mm, the pill has yet to be invented that could have turned that one around . . . and yes, anyway, got her to the top of the stairs, you know – and the seam in the carpet, seen to it that it was frayed a bit, had marginally, ah, come undone, as it were . . . and then, well – *whoosh*, basically. Clatter clatter. Bit of a thump.'

'And . . . she . . . ?'

'Well no: wasn't. That was the problem. I mean to say, she didn't look too merry, just sprawling down there – all in a twisted heap, sort of style. Unconscious. But dead she wasn't, no.'

'So what did you . . . ?'

'Well only one thing I could think of. Had to, so to say, stay within the system, didn't I? The master plan? So I – and Jesus, don't ask me how I managed it, because she'd grown big, Mylene, over the years, big woman she'd become – but somehow I dragged her all the way up again, and then sort of encouraged another little tumble. Clatter clatter. Bit of a thump. It was all becoming somewhat familiar, and even a little bit fond.'

343

'Christ. So what happened then?'

'Well then, of course, I had to canter down after her and assess the situation. I hadn't quite decided whether to phone her doctor or else plump for 999.'

'So what did you go for? Christ, Blackie – this is all so amazing.'

'Mm – 'tis, I suppose. Well neither yet, as it happened. Bitch wasn't dead, was she? Could barely believe it. Stubborn, you see – always was. Thought I might after all have to summon up a weapon from my friend Beef. But then you've lost the element of domestic accident, haven't you? You see. So there was only one thing for it.'

'Up again . . . ?'

'Oh yes. Hauled the bloody woman all the way up again. Weighed a fucking ton, I can tell you. Kicked her down, this time. A good deal less clatter, a lot more of a thump. It struck the right sort of a timbre. Trotted down again, and bingo! Third time lucky.'

'She was . . . ?'

'As the doornail, yes. From then on, it was pure formality. Had to do a bit of acting, of course. Went very well, I think: I was weeping, weeping – joy and relief and not a little exhaustion is what it all expressed, but they weren't to know. Everyone bought the story, yes. Except for Tim, of course That's my son – remember I've mentioned him? Yes. Well he – you should have seen the look in his eye. Was convinced I'd murdered his mother. Can you credit it? Your own son, believing you to be capable of such a thing. Why he hates me, you see. Always will. Can't really blame him. Never told anyone any of all this, goes without saying. So anyway, my dear Alan – just to scroll forward to our present predicament,

I think in the first instance we must, the two of us, pay a visit to young Billy . . .'

'Harry.'

'Harry, and flash a little cash. Don't think there'll be any call to put on what I believe are termed the frighteners.'

Alan now was agitated.

'But what if he won't? What if he spurns us? Spits on the money. Says he, I don't know – *loves* her, or something? What if he just laughs in our faces, the fucking little upstart shit. What if he tells us to go to *hell* . . . ?'

'Mm. Well in that case, of course, we'll just have to.'

'Have to . . . ?'

'Mm. Kill him.'

'Joking . . .'

'Well in a sense I am. In that nothing I think or say can these days be taken to be anything close to one hundred per cent, um – in earnest. Or even totally sensible. Though equally, I am never given over to flippancy, the glib remark, pure and simple. I think you may take it, Alan, that while the idea of just killing the bastard is by no means a psychotic determination, still though it need not necessarily be out of the question. Circumstances, I daresay, will eventually dictate. There is also the truth, of course, that my knowledge and skills with regard to the despatch of another of our fellow creatures, my first-hand experience, are considerably limited. Specialised, you might say. Basically it comes down to this: if the cunt lives in a bungalow, we're buggered.'

Susan was sucking into her the strong black coffee as if it were a vital elixir, the only thing now that could claw her back from the maw of eternal damnation. As she asked the waitress for another plate of croissants, Maria could barely fail to notice the light of energy, an unnatural awareness, aglow and fidgety in both of her eyes.

'It was good of you, Maria, to just drop everything and come. I know you're very busy.'

'You are a complete and utter liar, Susan. You know perfectly well that from one day's end to the other there is not a single little thing in the world that I have to attend to. When you rang, I simply told Lolita that she would have to attend to the flowers herself this morning – although she never does them very well, always makes them appear really quite funereal, or else so very, I don't know . . . *plebeian*. There's a word you don't much hear any more. And then I simply put forward my hair appointment. A life of ease, dear Susan – and one that you are finally enjoying for yourself. Best thing you've ever done, the importing of wealth – you look positively radiant, so very young and vibrant. New lease of life, my dear. I shouldn't have a croissant, but I shall.'

'Is she really called that, your woman? Lolita?'

'Mm. But cast from your mind any vision of pre-pubescent loveliness. Husbands, they really don't need that kind of distraction. Something you learn along the way. No, my Lolita is large and strong – flat at the front and rather broad of beam. Like a Routemaster, really – though lacking the colouring.'

'Oh Maria! You really are so awful.'

'I know – but you love me anyway. Now listen to me, Susan – I have been most dreadfully patient with you, but there is a limit. You did not ask me here to watch me grow obscenely fat on croissants and nor to discuss my dear Latino treasure. I do hope there is something delicious you have to tell me. If it's less than spectacular, I shall be sorely disappointed.'

Susan needed no encouragement: she had been carrying within her this, oh – damn great *thing* for so bloody long that if she didn't very soon and rushingly unload a good deal of it she felt she must then just atomise into a zillion dazzling stars and pinpoints (for in such girlish terms she found herself more and more compelled to couch her sensations). She replaced her cup, hunkered down her shoulders and extended her neck and hands across the table, Maria unthinkingly mirroring her actions. Exclusive intimacy was therefore established, the bright and buzzy hubbub of the rest of the coffee shop blurred and muted, pushed out far to the periphery.

'I think, Maria . . . the reason I look as I do, if what you just said is . . . if I do look like that, radiant, alive, all the rest of the stuff you – well it's not to do with the money. I mean, don't get me wrong about the money – it's been a total godsend, I just can't tell you. And the house, the garden, it's all so heavenly. Particularly the garden. Just heavenly. And this is why I feel so, oh God – guilty, I suppose. Because the atmosphere at home, it's all been rather wonderful. Everyone's been getting on so terribly well – mm, that is if you discount Miss Amanda, of course. She, oh – I can't go into it. Another story altogether.'

'She's a teenager, Susan. The constant column inches in the press concerning teenagers? Can't have passed you by, surely. Everything disgusting they're really quite famous for. Sloth, rudeness, drugs, promiscuity, grunted-out monosyllables – no sense whatever of personal hygiene. Boys, that is – they're the worst by far, apparently.'

'You wouldn't say that if you had a daughter, believe me. But listen, Maria – never mind that. Forget Amanda. It's not Amanda I want to talk about. It's . . . someone else.'

Maria's eyes narrowed, and then they were dawningly glowing as the slyest smile crept on to her face.

'Oh my *God*, Susan – you've got another one! My goodness – this is becoming quite a collection. It's really just you and Elizabeth Taylor, isn't it? Do you label them all so you don't forget their names? Oh but how perfectly *delicious* . . . !'

'God's sake, Maria – it's not like that. And it wasn't intended, or anything. It just, well – it just sort of came out of the blue, really.'

'Mm. As such things will. Well go on – don't stop now, God's sake. *Tell* me, Susan. Tell me all about it. Does Alan know? Does the other one know? Can't remember his . . .'

'Black. It's Black. No, he doesn't know. Neither of them does. Got to tell them. Haven't yet. Got to, though – got to tell them soon. Last night, God – I made such a bloody fool of myself. Had this terrible sort of, I don't know – insight. Realisation. Had to rush away from him. God knows what he thought. And Alan, when I got in – I must have looked a bit mad, I think. Sorry, Maria – rambling. But all this, it's why I wanted to talk to you . . . you see – it's really quite serious.'

'Oh dear. Serious. Serious isn't too good. Serious can rather take the fun out of it, you know Susan. And isn't fun the whole idea? Isn't that, after all, why we do these things?'

'I didn't start it as fun. I didn't start it as serious. I wasn't really aware of . . . starting anything at all, really. It just . . .'

'Happened, yes. Sort of out of the blue. You said. Well who is he? Don't tell me – Alan's best friend! The classic story. Who is Alan's best friend actually, Susan? Does he have them? Friends? I've never known.'

'No – he's never really had one, a best friend as such. Not to my knowledge. Or even a *friend*, really . . . But men, they're different. Not like us. They don't seem to need them as much as we do. But now . . . Black is. His best friend, yes. Sometimes I feel rather . . . and actually, this is maybe a part of it. I've got these two husbands, and I don't really . . . I haven't actually thought of this before, but what I feel is, a bit, um – well, excluded. Really. They're together, the two of them, and yet they're apart from me. Which I didn't intend. Why I maybe, I don't know – let this new thing happen to me.'

'Right then – can't be Alan's best friend, I see that now. Because you've already got him, haven't you? In your portfolio. So who is it, then? Where did you meet him?'

'I didn't really – meet him in the normal way. He just sort of . . . fell into my life.'

'I see. And I'm guessing now, Susan – but he's young, yes? Good-looking brute, is he? This man who fell to earth. Oh do say yes.'

'He is young. Yes. Very. That's the point, I suppose. Attract-ive, I'd say. Quite strong physically. "Fit" is the expression, isn't it? But certainly not a brute. Didn't like him at all at first. By no means an instant thing. But his hands . . . and his hair. His eyes . . .'

'And no doubt other parts as well. So let's get this straight then, shall we Susan? Alan is there because . . . well I suppose because Alan always *has* been there really, hasn't he? Since time began. And this Black person you got because of the money . . .'

'Not wholly. Not just for the money . . .'

'This Black person you got for the *money* – don't interrupt me, Susan, and don't, please, attempt to be naïve. Not at this stage of the game. And now, to complete the triumvirate, as it were, you have a handsome young buck – no doubt more than

349

competent in the area in which your other two, um – *beaux*, are sadly lacking?'

'That's crude, Maria.'

'Mm, though broadly accurate I would guess. Well once more I feel congratulations are in order. I salute you. I'm also beginning to hate you just a bit. My own little life now is suddenly seeming so terribly *dull*.'

'I used to envy you, Maria. Your life, rich husband, lovely home . . .'

'*Three* lovely homes, if we're counting, Susan. Don't forget Spain and Aspen. And what on earth do you mean you *used* to envy me? You mean you don't any more? I'm not sure I can actually live with that. I make it a golden rule to only know people who envy me to *death*. How else is one expected to survive? To maintain that all-important *edge* . . . ?'

'Oh Maria. I never know if you're joking or not.'

'Well you can probably tell by my face. What's it doing now, my face?'

'Beaming malevolently, I'd say.'

'Mm. Well I'm probably joking, in that case. Botox, you see – I am seldom in charge of it. But otherwise I think I'd look like thunder. Are you having more coffee? I might just have another tea and get the girl to remove from my sight these perfectly scrumptious croissants. But listen, Susan – why, please enlighten me, why in God's name are you going to *tell* them? Your two old fogies. Do you imagine they'll be *pleased*? What if this Black person takes it into his head to withdraw all funding? Chuck you out into the cold? Why don't you just go on hugging it to you? Your thrilling naughty sexy little secret.'

'I don't know. I just feel . . . I should, that's all. It's a household, after all. Ménage, if you want. My idea, getting us all together. And the thing is, we're all meant to *share* . . . No – I don't want any more coffee. It's not actually that I feel I should. It's because I have to. I just must. It's . . . complicated.'

'Mm. Well this is one part I think they'll both want no piece of. And the new boy. Is he rich too? Or just one of life's quite gorgeous and penniless playthings?'

'Oh God no – not rich. In fact if it weren't for Chelsea, we'd have nowhere to, you know – go. I was meant to let it out, the old house. Rather pleased I didn't, now . . .'

'Goodness me, Susan – you're a strategist as well. How the need for furtiveness does so bring out the best in you. Susan – this has all been most perfectly *delicious*, but I really must now fly to André and get him to attend to my roots. He's already indulged me today, and if I'm late for this new appointment I could become, oh God – horror of horrors – persona non grata to the finest colourist in London. And without my highlights, I might begin to resemble someone rather too close to my own age, a thing a woman can never dream of. We'll do all this again when you acquire number four, shall we? And you, Susan – what are you up to now? Is this enough for the tip, do you think . . . ? I never quite know. I wish they'd just add it in and be done with it. Maybe they do: I never look.'

It's not, Susan was thinking, that I have to talk to her, Maria. It's not that she has anything for me; I just need to hear what it is I am thinking.

'Me?' she smiled. 'Oh – I've got an appointment too. I'm going now to see my lover.'

So adored that, saying it to Maria, adored the flavour of the word in my mouth. And later, it was him I was tasting, the youth, who touches me like a girl and then is so excitingly boyish and eager in his efforts to be manly. We made love on

351

the floor of what used to be my bedroom in the old house in Chelsea, the very room in which I had so often wondered if ever again I would have such a thing – countlessly, for it seemed like years. The carpet is quite new and fluffy there, where the bed used to stand, and still there are the flattened indentations from its feet (my elbows scorch, there is such friction). After, he caressed me with a feather: where on earth did you get that from, I asked him. Do you know what he said to me? From a Bird of Paradise. Believe it? So poetic. Once I tried to write a poem for him, but I couldn't. Alan, had he ever done such a thing (inconceivable, really) he would have told me that the feather was one of many, the result of a burst-open duvet – and as for Black, well.

I must, though, talk to them – it's important that they know, now. I said to my boy: I really have to go. The tang of his sweat was sour, and so sweet to me. He told me I was beautiful; I know it to be true – I see it in the eyes of every one of the men I encounter, but no one ever tells me. I have to go . . . I have to go . . . I kept on sighing it, feeling no compulsion. I could have stayed in his arms for just ever.

I left, I had to – already yearning for the moment I could return to him. And back at Richmond, it was all so strange: I barely had the door shut behind me and they were there, the two of them, peering at me with eagerness and maybe (or was I imagining it?) a dread anticipation, as if they could have sensed that all was not well. This was more than just my guilt: I felt they knew, and I was thrown. I had not expected instinct.

'So, Susan,' said Alan too loudly. 'You're back.'

And then he glanced over to Black for assistance – who, quite suddenly, was as lost as Alan. This was not how it was meant to be: they had worked it all out, how it had to be handled, and here they were like a couple of wide-eyed, hungry and useless spaniels, superfluous around her feet.

'When she comes in,' Alan had said, and not half an hour earlier, 'I think we must be stern.'

'Stern yes, I see. Sort of brooking no malarkey, type of thing. I've got you.'

'Tell her we know everything, and that we're just not standing for it. While making it clear that when she stops all this nonsense and comes to her senses, we are prepared to display both compassion and forgiveness. Confront her with the letter, if she tries to wriggle out of it.'

Yes, the letter . . . well, not much more than a bit of a notelet really, but that's hardly the point. Because just a short while ago, I had been into Susan's room. Had to. Not for any solid reason – was not my intent to rummage, couldn't even think there would be anything to find. It was just the bare fact of the door being locked, that's what I simply couldn't stand. It served as a symbol of the exclusion I was feeling. I think I might just have smashed it in, you know, so powerful was my impulse (do I have a jemmy . . . ? I remember wondering) – but Mr Clearley, he was busy with some or other bit of finishing off in the attic region, I rather thought, and so I raced up there and I said to him Oh there you are, Mr Clearley, afternoon, afternoon – wonder if you can help me out at all: stupidest thing, lost a key, don't want to cause any unnecessary damage . . . well, the man had the door open in an instant flat with the twisting of some little gizmo or other – and that, I don't know . . . it certainly makes you think. So I got rid of Clearley, and then I was in. And the scent, just the scent of the room, it had me nearly reeling – so utterly redolent of Susan, and all that I had loved and remembered. There were high-heeled

shoes, pink, one on its side – the bruise on the inside where
her toes once had been clustered, it made me gasp, it stroked
my very heart. In the sheer of a discarded nightdress, still
there was the whisper of her. The unmade bed, that spoke of
recent turbulence – buckled-up sheets . . . fresh, but somehow
meaty. And on the dressing table, a gorgeous woman's litter –
unclasped pearls and perfumed pots, a lemon tissue smudged
by mascara. And a sheet of lilac paper, folded. I had been
dreading the glimpse of a diary, for I knew I would have been
driven to impale myself upon each and every spearpoint that
it doubtless would contain . . . but the sheet of lilac paper,
folded – this was bad enough. I flapped it open – held it away
from me in case it might burn.

H. I tried to write a poem for you, but I couldn't. So am
writing this instead. I love you. S.

It did not burn, it froze me. My eyes were tight in a squint,
shying away. I came downstairs and, wordlessly, held it out
to Blackie; he read, but did not touch it. Said nothing at all.
We both sat down and had a drink, then. Blackie smoked a
cigarette. I toyed with the idea of a cigar, but couldn't face all
the fooling with the thing. And then Blackie, he suddenly said:
'Bad.'
And Alan nodded to that, whatever its meaning. He decided
then that they had to be stern (the other more yielding things
too). He thought . . . Susan, she is in the midst of just loving the
very best game that boys and girls can ever play, while Blackie
and I, well – we seem to be jointly cast in the role of no more
than a caring and disappointed father . . . Alan thought all that,
yes, but he uttered not a word of it. It was also decided that

they would not now rush to ring her on her mobile (which, Alan judged through the cut of pain, would anyway be left to its futile warble while a could-be abandoned Susan was taken and taken over by maybe even rapture) . . . no, they would not rush to do that, but instead just patiently and with a degree of dignity, they would await her return. She would then go upstairs to change, as was her custom, and soon come down again to possibly make some tea. Then and gradually, the big bold subject would be gently broached. Yes. But as they heard the key in the lock, they each of them and quite independently near bounded into the hall and were gazing at her with hurt and a sort of longing, seemingly eager for the smallest of treats, while at the same time cowering away, cringing in fear of an undeserved slap.

'Alan. Black. There's something I need to tell you. I think that maybe you already know. Is Amanda here?'

Alan and Black glanced across at one another so terribly briefly, the spark of fright and then the wince of dread being altogether too much to hold for any longer. So – no going upstairs to change, then; no coming down again to possibly make some tea. And the big bold subject, it has thundered down and is already among us, so massive, jagged and looming, and feebly we quake in its shadow.

'No, she's . . . no. She's out, Amanda.'

'Good. It isn't for her ears, this. Shall we go into the room?'

'Oh no,' said Alan, in as throwaway a manner as he could possibly muster. 'Don't think that's really necessary. Let's do it here, will we? Shouldn't take long. You just tell us what you need to, and then we'll say what we have to say, and then that I hope will be the end of it all.'

Susan blinked at him.

355

'I think . . . maybe not. You see, the thing is . . . now I'm aware that you're both going to think me quite horribly awful, you probably do already – and we'll talk, of course we'll talk . . . about all this. In detail. But later. For now, I think – just the very bare facts. Alan, Black, there's no other way to put this . . . I want another husband.'

Alan and Black now just openly goggled at one another – Alan very nearly laughing out loud, but no not quite.

'Well . . .' he said hesitantly. 'I think I can speak on behalf of old Blackie here when I say that we are both, um – collectively shocked. Fair to say, Blackie? Mm. Thought so. Now listen, Susan – oh no, oh no, you can't hope now to just barge in and interrupt me at this stage, Susan, no no no. I've got to say *something* before you drive your damn bloody steamroller all over us, haven't I? And what I say is this: it's a big house, yes granted. And it's Blackie's house, of course, and it is he, therefore, who will have the final say . . . but speaking for myself, at least – well I should have said that two husbands, you know, a pair, it's really quite sufficient. Ample. Is my view. And to add a third, well – it might, I suggest, be somewhat over-egging the pudding. Wouldn't you say?'

'Hear hear,' said Black quite gruffly. 'Second that. Jesus, Susie.'

Susan smiled quite sadly. She approached them both – lightly laid a consoling hand on each of their shoulders.

'I think you maybe don't quite understand . . . oh dear. You see – I don't mean as well as, no. I mean instead of. Yes.'

Black was silent in the car, while Alan drove the two of them home from that shabby and, to Black's mind, really rather lowering tenement building where they had boldly bearded and confronted the little bastard. And then he simply could resist no longer expressing his high jubilation.

'Saw him off, hey Alan? That sort, boys – never too much of a problem. Feelings, not deep-seated. Take what they can get and when they can get it, fundamentally. Knew it wouldn't be too much of a problem.'

Alan could only nod, while the car was idling at a zebra crossing, a stream of uniformed schoolgirls filing in front of their eyes.

'It did seem to go exceptionally smoothly . . . Glad, on the whole, we didn't have to throw him down the stairs several times. He was a wiry thing, yes, but he seemed quite strong, I thought. Physically, I mean, Christ curse him. But now, well – it's just a question of whether Susan accepts it. You know Susan.'

'Got to though, hasn't she really? Got to buckle down. Now she has. Nothing else she can do. I say, Alan – did you see that last one? Blue eyes, plaits? Little gingham thing on her?'

'Did. Course I did.'

'Fuckish, hey?'

'Exceptionally. But listen to me, Blackie – how do you think she's going to react? Just pretend that it all never happened? Carry on as usual? Not in her nature, is it?'

'Oh I don't know. Time we get back, he will have told her. She might go round there, have it out with him. Tantrum, shouldn't wonder. She'll be difficult with us for a while – but Jesus, when isn't she? The entire idea was always quite perfectly preposterous anyway. Wasn't it? She couldn't have been thinking straight. Fit of, I don't know – passion? It can do that. But getting rid of her home and family – the very ones who love her! Marrying an infant. A penniless child. How long

357

before that particular novelty would have faded? Susie, well – expensive woman. Expensive tastes. We can only assume that briefly, well – she simply lost her mind. Consumed by . . . let us just call it the *moment*, shall we? Can't dwell. No no. But now, well . . . over, isn't it?'

It certainly, thought Alan, would appear that way; the boy's enthusiasm for the offer on the table had been both palpable and nearly immediate, callow little sod. And young! My God, how young. I mean, Amanda had told me exactly how young he was, so it wasn't as if I hadn't been primed – but Jesus, when he opened the door I could barely believe it: that this long-limbed child with the eyelashes of a fawn could really be a rival in love for these two pent-up husbands with a collective age of over a bloody century. Standing there on the doorstep, the lad in jeans and a T-shirt with one arm draped over the door, so very languorously, like a careless and sedated ape . . . it was all so very shaming. This . . . thing, this insignificant little shit: he'd fucked her. Repeatedly.

'Help you?'

'Harry, is it?' ventured Alan (Alan, it had been agreed on the way over, Alan was to do all the talking). 'Mind if we have a word? We have someone in common, you see. Susan . . . ?'

'Susan . . . ? Who's Susan. Oh yeh right – *Susan*, got you. Well what about her?'

'Well . . . maybe we could come inside? This might be to your advantage.'

Harry shrugged and stood away from the door.

'My parents are away at the moment, so the place is a bit of a tip. Who actually are you guys?'

There were odours in the hall that Black for one did not care to identify. And the dark and dampish room where now he found himself had somehow, how could he say . . . ? The air of having altogether surrendered.

'Would you mind,' he said, 'if I smoke?'

And as Harry briefly closed his eyes in complete indifference to that, Black was thinking, hm – and would you mind also not being so damn well fucking insolent by just standing in front of us like a casual clown, you unutterable little dirtbag? And would you mind too making this all as pain-free as so pain-fraught an expedition can possibly be? And would you mind as well making it on the quick side, yes? Because already I need quite badly to go to the lavatory, though maybe not quite badly enough to contemplate using yours.

'The thing is, Harry . . . my name is Alan, by the way. I'll make it brief. Best way. I, you see, am Susan's husband. Susan's husband, yes – and this, this is . . . my very great friend who also has, um – shall we say a vested interest. And so I think—'

'Hang on. What – you're Amanda's dad. That it? Blimey.'

'Yes, I – yes. But it is not Amanda we are here to discuss.'

'Isn't it? Oh.'

'No. Now, I look at you, Harry, and I don't see a stupid person.'

'Thanks.'

'Not stupid at all. And you're – young. Whole life before you. Don't want to mess it up, do you? Get bogged down?'

'No I bloody don't.'

Alan glanced at Black, quite excitedly.

'Well exactly. So that's why it's got to end. Here and now.'

'What the fuck you on about?'

'Oh God that's *it*,' Black was now fuming impatiently. 'Sorry, Alan – sorry to, um . . . but I simply can tolerate his attitude for not a moment longer. Now listen to me, young man – I'll be plain. In return for never seeing Susie again, I am prepared to give you one thousand pounds.'

Harry just looked at him.

'What? Never *see* her again . . . ?'

Black exhaled, and was glaring.

'Very well: two thousand pounds. Here and now. Take it or leave it. Speak up.'

Harry now sat down heavily into a lopsided armchair.

'Two thousand pounds . . .' he whispered, as if to himself.

'It's a good offer,' put in Alan.

Harry's eyes were blinking with energy.

'What's with you two guys? You are, what—? You are offering – in exchange for, Jesus – never like seeing Susan again . . . you say you're going to give me two grand. Two grand.'

'Oh *damn it*, Alan – what's wrong with the fucking little idiot? On drugs, do you suppose? In common with all the rest of them. Right then – *Harry*, or whatever your damn bloody name is: I'll double it.'

'Jesus, Blackie . . . !'

'No no, Alan. Got to be done. Got to be out of here. Got to get rid of him. Well, boy? More money than you've ever seen. Speak. Last chance.'

Harry looked up at him.

'Cash . . . ?'

'Got it right here in my pocket. Fifty-pound notes. Four thousand. Well?'

Harry stood up, and was smiling.

'I'll take it.'

Black nodded briefly and hauled out of his inside pocket a thickish manila envelope. As he was counting out the money,

360

he beamed over broadly to Alan, who was appearing relieved. Harry was agitated, and biting his lip.

'You'll sign this,' barked Black, very curtly. 'It's no more than a receipt. And it must be understood that this is immediate. This happens right now. From this moment onwards you will have nothing further to do with Susie. Understood?'

Harry held the money and nodded dumbly.

'Right,' he said. 'Got you.'

There was a brief bit of nonsense at the front door – Black just stamping away, Alan having instinctively half-extended his hand and then withdrawing it sharply when he saw that both of the boy's were filled up with cash. Harry watched the two of them walk to the car, his mouth now jerked by a spasm of glee. He slammed shut the door and ambled the length of the hall, eyes alight, though seemingly in a dream. He went into the back room this time, the used-to-be dining room, and dropped the packets of notes on to the table.

'Bloody Jesus. You won't believe what just happened . . .' he said quite quietly.

'Fucking *hell* . . . !' screamed Amanda, jumping up at the sight of it. 'Jesus, Harry – what the—?'

'It's just so like incredible. I don't believe it . . .'

'What, Harry – *what*? Where did you—?'

'It was your Dad. I can't believe it . . .'

'My—?! What the fuck are you—?!'

'Your Dad. It was him at the door. And some other old fucker. Jesus, man! I so can't *believe* it . . . !'

Amanda was shaking him now because he'd gone and had this like really fat spliff, right, just before the doorbell had rung, and now with all of this – shit, all of this fucking *money* – he just seemed like so out of it. God – if I couldn't see it and like feel it for myself, OK? All this cash. I'd think I was tripping too – and I only had like what? Couple vodkas. Because man – this day, OK? Started weird and just got weirder. Yeh see – what I decided to do is like make a couple of new Play-Doh dolls? Because my Harry one, I'd torn that to bits just the other night, OK, and now I needed one of my Mum as well to stick like fucking great skewers in? And then I thought no – fuck that. What's the point of messing about with kid's stuff when I can do the real thing? I had to get them, OK? Really like hurt them for what they'd done to me. Because it's so a bummer getting dumped – but when like the guy is dumping you for your *mother* . . . ! Oh please. So at first I'd just gone – OK, fine: you fuck up my life, I can fuck up yours. And I did try – I did all that yuck stuff with Black and I might have gone on with it if Dad hadn't come in . . . but later, ee-*yow*! So sick. I mean he's just like so *old*, you know? Stinking of fags and whisky. And then I thought of Harry, and how I could kill him. I really wanted to, and thought of all the ways. Knife in the bath is what I liked best – to see his long and wavy hair in all that like *red*? And then I guess I'd go to prison or whatever, but I'd be bound to get out soon because like everybody does. And Mum, she couldn't have him then, could she? If he was all red and dead and everything. So I thought OK then – that's what I'll do: kill Harry. And I had a little drink or two and I went right over. When he opened the door, I crashed right in because I didn't want him like shutting it in my face like the last time I was there, the fucking shit.

'Right, Harry – I am *so* coming in, OK? Just don't give me a hard time, right?'

'Oh hi, Amanda. My parents are away. Come in.'

Amanda looked at him. 'Yeh . . . ?'

'Yeh.'

So Amanda sauntered into the hall and then remembered
that she'd brought this flat half-bottle of Smirnoff especially so
that she could smash it against the wall and cram the jagged
edge into his jugular, and so she attempted to do that but it
just wouldn't break, and now she actually felt a bit drunk.

'What the fuck you doing, Amanda?'

'Don't you – don't you fucking talk to *me*! I'm going to kill
you, Harry, for what you've done.'

'Jeez, Amanda – I only chucked you out because of my
parents. They could hear everything. Had to tell them you
were nuts.'

'I'm not talking about that! You so *know* what I'm talking
about! What do you mean – *nuts* . . . ?'

'Let's go in the back room, yeh? You wanna drink?'

'No I don't fucking want a—! Got any vodka . . . ?'

'Yeh, pretty sure. So what you been up to, Amanda?'

'Listen, Harry – you're so not getting this. I'm here to *kill*
you!'

'Why? Here – here's some vodka. Want anything in it?'

'*Why*?! *Why*?! Because you're bloody screwing my, oh shit –
mother, that's fucking *why*, Harry!'

Harry put down the bottle and just looked at her.

'Man. You *are* nuts.'

'Oh *Jesus*, Harry! No – nothing in it, just as it is . . . *Jesus*,
Harry! You're not, like – *denying* it?'

'I don't know what you're talking about. I've only ever seen
your mother once – Susan, isn't it? Yeh. And that's when she
came to tell me not to see *you*. And that you were pregnant.
Which you're not. Weird, yeh?'

'Oh yeh *right*! I *so* don't believe you. Nearly every bloody
evening I've like watched her getting all like tarted up and

coming over to see you. To – *fuck* you. You think I don't *know* . . . ?'

'Coming where? Here? With my parents? Joking. They only went away this morning. Whole house is empty. Cool, hey? Listen, Amanda – it wasn't *my* idea to stop seeing you. It was hers. I like you. You're real foxy.'

'Yeh – but not like my mum. She's kinda *cute*. Remember?'

'She is? I don't remember, actually.'

'That's what you called her, Harry. Don't like tell me you forgotten.'

'Well I have. Told you. Only saw her once. I maybe just said that to wind you up. Here – have another drink.'

'Don't *want* a—! Yeh, OK. Look, Harry . . . you telling me the truth? You better be telling me the truth, because if you aren't I will so like kill you. Are you listening to me, Harry? Because I was really *sure* about this. I tell you, if you're, you know – like just messing with my mind, you are *so* dead. No . . . No . . . just take your hands off me, Harry. OK? No . . . You hear?'

'But you like that, don't you Amanda? When I touch you there. You like that. Don't you? Don't you . . . ?'

'Just . . . oh God – *don't*, OK. Oh God, Harry . . . Oh *God* . . . !'

'Come on, Amanda. Come on. Whole house is empty, yeh? Come on. Come on. Why don't we . . . ?'

Yeh because God – that Harry . . . well, it's just like the very first time when I saw him in the newsagents, he just like makes me just go so melty, you know? And his hands, his fingers – shit, he so starts me up. So we were there on the floor of the room and he was like ramming me really hard and stuff and I hadn't like had it for really ages and yeh, it was good, OK? And after, he lights up all this really gigantic weed and I don't do weed, right, so I had another drink. And the doorbell, yeh . . . I kind of remember that . . . and then maybe, I don't know, slept a bit or something . . . and next I know he's back in the room with like a trillion quid all over the table. So yeh – this day, right? Started weird and just got weirder.

'So what are you telling me now then, Harry? That my, God – *dad* just rolls up and gives you . . . Jesus, how much money *is* there here? Looks like . . .'

'Four grand. Four fucking grand! Can you *believe* it . . . ?'

'Jesus. But . . . I just don't . . . !'

'Well it was the same thing you were on about. I can't understand it. This money, I got it so I wouldn't see your mum again. No *listen*, Amanda – *listen*! Put that bottle down and just listen to me, OK? Watch my lips. I. Haven't. Been. With. Your. *Mother*. OK? I don't know why everyone thinks I have, but I haven't. What can I say? And who was that other guy? Little old guy?'

'Hm? Oh – that's Black. He here too? He's Mum's other husband. It's complicated.'

'Her *other* husband . . . ? Oh man.'

'Yeah. I know.'

'But listen, Amanda – why does your dad think I've been—?'

'Oh man. Because I told him. Oh shit.'

'You told him? But why did you—?'

'Oh shit oh shit oh *shit*! Because I thought it was *true*, you stupid bastard! Why else would I tell him?'

'How the fuck should I know? Same reason you told your mum you were up the duff. Nuts. But listen – you now know it isn't. True. Don't you? You know it isn't true, don't you . . . ?'

'I . . . guess.'

'OK then. Good. Well look – have another drink, OK? And then we'll decide what to do.'

'How do you mean, decide what to . . . ?'

'With the money, Amanda. The money. Look at it all. We're rich!'

Amanda looked, and her eyes were glittering.

'Yeh . . . we are, aren't we?'

'And I'll be keeping my side of the bargain. I promised your dad that I'll never see his wife again, your mum – and I won't. I won't. The fact that I wouldn't have anyway, well . . . Course, I'll be breaking my word to your mum, because I said to her that it's *you* I wouldn't see again. Intense.'

And Amanda, on impulse, just hugged him.

'This is kinda cool,' she was laughing. 'Let's – go!'

'Go where?'

'Doesn't matter. Just – go, you know? Anywhere. Just away from here. Let's do it now. Let's just go.'

'Well I don't know, Amanda. What about . . . well, your school? Your parents . . .'

'Oh fuck my *school*! That's the *last* bloody thing. And as for my, God – bloody *parents* . . . ! I used to, you know – worry about them. Like a million years ago. But not now. Not now I don't. No way. Come on, Harry. Yeh? Will we? Just go, yeh? Just take *off* . . . !'

Harry was smiling as he stooped down to kiss her.

'OK then, Amanda. Yeh. Let's just do it.'

PART THREE

CHAPTER TEN

Hard to believe sometimes, you know – the way time passes. Just been glancing through my, er, oh Christ – you know, date thing, date book, can't remember the name of the bloody thing, and it's been weeks now, weeks, since they both of them have gone, Susie and Amanda. Tip of my bloody tongue . . .

Not saying it wasn't odd at the beginning – and for Alan in particular, I rather think . . . but the passing of time, you know, it brings a sort of salvation all of its own. *Diary*, that's the chap. Yes. One does find oneself adapting remarkably well, rather extraordinarily. But God, though – that first night, the very bloody day we'd both of us been horsing around in that bloody little twister's bloody awful house . . . I really do believe that when we'd each of us in our bewildered turn read through Susie's letter (and then read the fucking thing again) we thought, we really did think it, Alan and I, that we might have, I don't know – completely lost our minds. Had we not had one another's sanity to cling to, for frantic reference and gabbled verification, we – well Alan, anyway – could very well have fragmented on the very spot he tottered. Because still we were bold and jovial, you see – I remember our mood of mighty triumph, the conquering heroes returned from a determined campaign and deserving if not gilded laurels and palm fronds strewn before us (rose petals fluttering in the sunlit air) then at the very least a damn big Scotch. Because we'd canned the little worm, well hadn't we? Observed from on high the lowly erk scrabbling for the money, betraying his true and ludicrous being. And although we neither of us said it – it was, rather nobly, not once even alluded to – I think the coming prospect too of Susie's eventual returning, this added considerably to the general rather carnival feel – hangdog, bruised, she might be (though I think we can rule out penitent) . . . maybe even simpering rather, and making her eyes go wide and liquid in the way she was of course aware was always so thoroughly irresistible. Champagne, really, was the order of the day – and none of the usual stuff either: this called for Krug. We had done for the kid, and now we could get on with things the way they used to be. Mm. The letter, I don't know . . . must just have been pushed through the box at some point, while still we were clinking glasses. Alan was still talking about Amanda, and I had been distantly and maybe even vacantly agreeing with him, what he was saying – because it *was* odd, it *was* of a sudden, it *did* seem out of the blue – but truly my mind was cleaving still to the shivery thrill of all the tremor that remained, the gleeful ripples of aftershock relating to our masterstroke. So Alan, he was still, as I say, in rather full flow as I ambled easily out of the room, and was then just passing through the hall on my way to the pantry in quest of another decent bottle.

'I mean to say, Blackie . . . if it's a school trip, why didn't I know about it? You see? I mean – Amanda, she said I'd had a letter. Said I had it ages ago. I don't remember getting any letter. Maybe Susan did – maybe she got the letter, but I certainly didn't, that's for bloody sure. She didn't mention it – if Susan did get a letter, well she never mentioned it to me. Anyway – I suppose it's all right. Switzerland. Decent people in Switzerland, aren't they? Just as well you had some cash left, Blackie. Christ – what would we all do without you? Tara's going too, Amanda said. Think it's Tara. Could be Tamara. Doesn't really matter. She didn't take much, pack much, Amanda. Anyway . . . I suppose it's all right. Have to square it with Susan when she gets back. Don't want the blame. But it's odd though, isn't it Blackie? School trip all of a sudden – completely out of the blue. Oh well. There it is. But you'd think it would've come up, wouldn't you? In conversation. If you're going to Switzerland . . . Have to ask Susan about it, when she gets back. See if she remembers any damn letter. When do you think she will be, Blackie? Susan, I mean. Coming back. Shouldn't be long. Do you think she'll phone us first? Or just come back? Poor little thing – I do, you know, I do feel quite sorry for her. She'll be hurt, no doubt about it. But it was a cruel-to-be-kind sort of a situation, wasn't it really? We acted properly. In the long run we did, oh yes. We did the right thing.'

'Um . . . talking of letters, old man – seems to be another one here. No stamp, or anything. Just stuck through the, ah . . . you know: hole thing.'

'Ah! That'll be from Susan. Poor little thing. Paving the way, I expect. Here – let me see it, Blackie. Yes – her writing, look. On the envelope. "A & B". That's us. Husbands A and B. Sweet. Right – see what she's got to say then, shall we? Poor little thing.'

Yes well. You just had to take one look at his face to

know that something was up, to see that something was off. Eyebrows – at first just hoicked up in anticipation, I supposed . . . then they contract, and soon they're dark and knitted. Next thing, though, they're just all over the place, the eyes beneath hurried and flickering, as if quite stunned by confusion. And then he wasn't looking at the letter at all any more – just gaping blankly ahead of him – so I prised it gently and then quite forcibly from the white tight grasp of his fingers. Read it. Looked up sharply to find Alan's gaze, alight with the need for assurances (we're *not* mad, are we? We *haven't* lost our senses . . . ?). And then I read the bloody thing again:

Dearest Alan, Dearest Black. You must both think me the most heartless woman, if not insane. But the awful truth is – I now have <u>found</u> my heart, you see. We have gone away, I will not say where. It's no good trying to contact me – I've got a new mobile. My wardrobes and so on are cleared – anything I've left, I don't really want. We will talk again, but I can't say when. I hope you both won't think too badly of me, and I also hope that in the future we can all remain friends. The dry cleaning dockets are in the red and gold box on my dressing table. Take care of yourselves. Love, S.

We looked at one another, Alan and myself. No real words yet, though our eyes were splintered by half-put questions, and smothered in bafflement. I could hardly bear his pain and silence . . . I was on the verge of saying something, then – not sure what, can't have been much – and that's when Alan, he finally spoke to me:

'Blackie . . . what the *fuck* . . . ?!'

372

'Mm, yes. Well quite. Our elation was clearly premature. We appear to have been diddled, Alan. Made fools of. I can't say I like it. Not only has she left us, gone off with the bloody little shit, but I have just funded their expenses . . .'

Alan was wagging his head, his flat eyes pleading for reason.

'Can't believe it. I just can't—! He didn't seem to have it in him – deception on that sort of a scale. Just a kid. Little kid. What does she want with a fucking little *kid* . . . ? Christ, Blackie . . . did they – *plan* it, do you suppose? Did Susan *know* we were going to go round there? Attempt to buy him off? She's capable – Jesus is she capable! Christ – they must both be laughing their fucking heads off. Right now. At our expense. We walked right into it. Four fucking grand! I can't believe it, I just can't believe it . . . ! Christ, I feel so . . .'

'Can't have been. A plan. Susie – she's got lots of money. I see to it, I'm afraid. She doesn't need four thousand.'

'Oh Jesus. Well – can't you get it back? Freeze the account, or whatever they do? *Christ* if I ever see that little bugger again . . . !'

'No. Money's cleared. Clears every month. Hers now. Nothing to be done.'

'Well . . . at least she won't be getting any more. Have to bloody work for a living, same as . . . well, most of us. Because him, the little shit, what can he earn? Yes. Well . . . at least she won't be getting any more. Will she? Blackie . . . ? You're not saying anything, Blackie. Why aren't you saying anything to me?'

'Well, Alan – we can't, can we? Let her – starve. She'll come to her senses, of course she will eventually. But until then, well – can't just cut her off, can we? She is our wife, after all . . .'

'Great. That's just great. You've given them four grand for their honeymoon, and now you propose to maintain them both in the manner to which you have accustomed her! Excellent. And what sort of a wife is it anyway? That would hook up with a, Jesus – *toyboy*, and walk out on her husbands! "Take care of yourselves", she says. Huh! No fucking *choice*, is there . . . ?'

Bitter, bitter, oh Lord how bitter he was. We drank a lot that night, I mean more than usual. Alan, he came up with all sorts of, well – schemes, he called them, but each one was really only a recipe for vengeance: Let's go back round to his house, the shit. Why, Alan? He won't be there, will he? Remember? He's gone away with Susie. I know, I know . . . but at least then we can tell his stupid parents what a *shit* he is. Or OK then – let's hire a detective to find them! Why, Alan? She won't come back if she doesn't want to, will she? I know, I know . . . but at least then we can shame them in public – tell everyone what *shits* they are. Or what about this then? We take out a full-page advert in all of the papers . . . ! On and on. Poor Alan. Bitter, oh yes – Lord, how very bitter he was. And I suppose at the time, we neither of us could see, project, not beyond the black and hurt of the night – could not imagine how anything other could one day be. But time, as I say – and of course one has noted it before, but still you know, it always rather delights and amazes me . . . how, just by its passing, it can not only mollify, dab at one's tears and smooth the jagged edges, but somehow it will heal, like a tacky mastic shot from a gun, the way it fills up all of those voids and cavities, bestows a welcome evenness and polish to a new and somehow more durable surface. Changes in the procedure, adaptation to the new-found road, ways of going about things that never one would have thought to even float, or tentatively fly . . . and though unsought, they become so surprisingly quickly not just grudgingly acceptable, but a mighty step beyond. Maybe even . . . the very consummation that had always been desired: true companionship, without somewhere at the back of your mind being constantly frightened to death.

At first, though, there was a very strong sense of . . . what might you call it? Displacement. Yes, I think so. Odd, in one way, because Susie, she had never been the personification of the hausfrau, and nor, to be fair to her, had so humdrum a role been ever her remotest ambition. Her absence, however, was everywhere. Not just in the vastness of the silent vacuum, but in the little things as well. Alan would say, Where are the Corn Flakes? Aren't they usually here? Isn't this the shelf they're normally kept on? Well I couldn't help him, of course. Didn't know we bought Corn Flakes – never eat them, stick in my teeth, as do most things: might, you know, need dentures soon (yet more delight in the offing). And then he'd say. You know Blackie – while never understanding why it was she ever stuck around, still you know – I never thought she'd leave me. Poor Alan. He'd worked out, you see, that by importing me on to the scene, Susie had put into train the only solution to her loathing of the situation as then was standing. Joyous, he said he had been, when it all seemed to be going so smoothly. And – he said this repeatedly – and now all *this*. Then he would marvel at the fact that she hadn't phoned, not once, to check that the two of us were still alive, if not very kicking (young people, you know – they say that: I've heard it on the television. They say that this or that is 'kicking'. Extraordinary, isn't it really? No idea what it means). Now then . . . what was I . . . ? Oh good Lord, it's happened again, you know. More and more this is happening to me now. Start off talking about a thing, some other damn bit of nonsense suddenly strikes me and *poof*! Gone. Thin air. Awful, isn't it? Bound to get worse. Everything does, in the long run. Might be the first stages of . . . can't remember the fucking name of it. Went to my doctor the other day – nothing to do with that, this was something else. Said it's my knee. Aches like blazes. And then sometimes when I walk, it sort of gives out a twingeing kind of a thing and buckles in on itself, best way I can describe it: one of these days, it'll have me over. So he checks me over, gave me a check-up, the doc, and he says to me it's my hip. Jesus, I don't know – how can my knee be my hip? You wonder sometimes whether it's you or just everybody else who's losing their minds. *Alzheimer's*, that's the chap. And much to my surprise, I've just remembered my thread, so I'm not completely gaga yet, at any rate – but don't hold your, um . . . Alan, yes. And then he says, Well you'd think at least she'd phone to see that Amanda's all right, even if she doesn't give two fucking hoots about either of her husbands. Breath – don't hold your breath, God curse it. And I remind him that in the first place Amanda isn't here (bloody long school trip, is all I can say – don't say it to Alan, though: it would only worry him) and in the second place, they both have mobiles, don't they? Could be chattering away thirteen to the dozen twenty times a day. Alan says: I doubt it. I doubt it too, but you've got to say something, haven't you?

Yes, so in the early days I was heartily engaged in bucking him up to the best of my ability on a more or less wall-to-wall basis. I didn't mind. What friends are for. And for his part, well – he's just been marvellous, you know, with all of the running about. If I've left something upstairs or in the garden, say, he'll hare away and fetch it. Do it a lot, goes without saying. Constantly leaving things all over the bloody place, and more often than not, of course, I'm damned if I can remember where. But Alan, he always seems to track them down. I call him The Bloodhound. Actually, that's an arrant lie – never called him The Bloodhound in my life. Maybe I ought to start. Doesn't matter. And he does all the shopping, you know, because I don't even drive now. Truth is, in Alan's car I can't reach the pedals, and I don't want to be fooling around with adjustments all the time; did toy with buying a car of my own, but even as I was toying, I knew that I'd never get round to it. And never mind a car – it's a hip, apparently, I'm going to be needing now, according to the doc. That's the latest. Maybe two, he says. Well why not? More the merrier. The things they can pull off though, these days – remarkable, isn't it? What did people with useless pelvises do in the old days? Lie down, I suppose.

But time, you see – that's what I was saying: the passing of time, and how it affects things. Now, Alan buys the – well, Corn Flakes, say, and puts them on whatever shelf he damn well pleases, knowing they'll be there for him the next time – not moved, and not eaten. We dine, you know, not so much at mealtimes, but just whenever the fancy takes us – and nearly always simultaneously, as chance would happily have it. He cleans – and very well too, I must say. New pin. And I do the accounts. We both of us continue to cook, and we're becoming rather good at it. The gardeners go on gardening, and everything there is lovesome (God wot). We formulate ideas, that's another thing we do. Well, I say ideas – more viewpoints, really: conclusions reached in the face of the evidence. And because, I suppose, we each well know our respective audience, we're not at all afraid to express them, Lord no: eager for it, really. We store them up. Other evening, I postulated the theory that the reason this country has now been quite thoroughly overrun by yobboes and foreigners is that the decent English people, the proper ones, were too polite to lock the doors (certainly true of the BB bloody C). And when it became plain to all that this upsurge of moujiks could barely express themselves, they somehow contrived to make inarticulacy a lovably fashionable idiom, if you can fucking believe it. Why now with even highly educated and literate people you have to machete your way through a throttling overgrowth of sortas, kindas and likes (know what I mean?). Alan was right behind me on that one – no huge surprise, I confess – and in return suggested to me that as one gets older and is seeking to improve one's lot, it is no longer a question of ambition nor frantic acquisition, but first a process of shedding, and then one of simple barricade: ruthlessly excluding all that one very certainly does *not* bloody want. Much the principle with first-class travel and accommodation, really: it's not really about what you get for your money, so much as all of the horror that can be loftily avoided. Yes. I sometimes think we ought to be on *Question Time*.

One other evening recently, we were in the drawing room watching a delightfully titillating DVD directed by somebody called Tinto Brass (odd name, I agree – Italian, Alan was telling me, although if that's true you'd rather more expect him to be called Brasso, wouldn't you really? Anyway). Yes – watching this film (he has a thing, old Brasso, about young ladies' bottoms, and who can mind?) – and we had a bottle of Scotch between us, new discovery, Glenmorangie Port Wood Finish, indescribably mellow, and Alan was pulling on a fine

Havana and marvelling at the wonderful truth that no one was about to barge into the room and complain about the stink, condemn the film for objectifying women, and nor to suggest that we had both had quite enough whisky for one evening, thank you.

'You see – what it is, Blackie, is that we don't really need them. Women. Not, you know – all the bloody time. They make you *think* you need them . . . maybe they have to think it themselves. But because they make sure they're always *around*, they lead you to believe that their presence is vital. When clearly it isn't. I mean – look at us. Fine, aren't we? Perfectly happy. Got our own little ways, and no damn harpy to mess them all up. But do you know what they'd accuse us of? Do you? Tell you: misogyny. Yes, oh yes – that's what they'd say. Whereas I would call it self-sufficiency. Well . . . self as in . . . I mean I don't think that on our own, Blackie, either of us would be that – self-sufficient, no. But as a *couple* we are – oh yes, by Christ. But that doesn't make us co-*dependent*. Does it? Don't know. Maybe it does. But it's *women*, in my view, who despise men, not the other way around. And there isn't even a word for it, so far as I'm aware – not misanthropy, no, that refers to the whole of mankind. But a woman's hatred of men – there isn't even a word for it, so therefore, they would have you believe, such a thing can't possibly exist. Wrong. Look at TV: man puts up a shelf, what happens? Bloody shelf falls down. Woman sighs, wags her head, rolls up her eyes. Look at all the endless bloody articles in the papers and magazines: a woman, a mother – she has a cold and stoically gets on with her ten thousand cares and responsibilities: breast-feeding, slaving over and servicing horrible men, running the government, whatever.

But a *man* . . . ! Oh – he's convinced he's got *flu*, poor little hypochondriac diddums, and takes a week off work; woman, of course, becomes a long-suffering night nurse. And they'll illustrate it, this piece of blatant hokum, with a library picture of a red-nosed great fat oaf with a towel draped over his head and his feet in a fucking galvanised basin of steaming hot water. Just not *true*, is it? And at Christmas, Christ – the woman, she multi-tasks twenty-four fucking *seven*, as they will keep on saying, fucking journalists, so that everything is prepared and beautiful for the slobbo man who lies on the sofa watching football and drinking lager and buys her a crappy little present late on Christmas Eve in a bloody service station. Or, if she's lucky, Chanel No. 5. Again. Just not *true*, is it? Now women – I don't say they're useless. They're not. Obviously. But do you ever see an article *saying* they are? No you do not. Why not? Think I'll write one, just for the hell of it.'

Amusing, Alan's diatribe – diverting, yes – but irksome nonetheless because all through this latest little polemic of his I had been gamely trying to discern whether or not there was even a suggestion of plot somewhere lurking in this Italian film about young ladies' bottoms. Didn't matter, as it turned out – we didn't get close to the end of it, because just at that moment the doorbell rang.

'Late, isn't it? Not expecting anyone are we, Alan?'

'Course not, Blackie. We're never expecting anyone, are we? I'll just see who it is.'

Alan still held his cigar, and tugged on it briefly as he swung open the door. Delight, he later decided, was his overriding reaction when confronted by these two young girls there, lolling against the columns of the porch.

'Hi,' said one of them – Nordic blonde her hair was, with almost creamy stripes. 'Sorry to bother you but we're doing a charity walk, yeh? British coastline. And we were wondering if you'd like to sponsor us. Got a certificate here, and badges and everything.'

'Sponsor you . . . ?'

'Yeh,' said the other one – smaller, darker, with bright-green eyes, which you don't often see. They both wore the same school blazers – maroon, with a pinkish piping. 'Like, you agree to give us so much per mile we cover, see? All the money, it goes to this, like – charity? It's all written down here. It's official, and everything.'

'I see. It's rather nippy, isn't it? Why don't you come inside so we can discuss it?'

'OK then,' agreed the blondie brightly.

And they must have felt it, you know, Alan was reflecting – nippy, he meant – because look at them, won't you? Just these little pleated skirts, and nothing on their legs.

'Come into the, um – room, yes? And then you can tell us all about it. Yes, that's right – just in there. First door. Good good.'

'Nice house . . .' murmured the smaller, darker one, with bright-green eyes (which you don't often see).

'Oh I'm glad you, um . . . we like it, yes. Look Blackie – two young ladies here in quest of our sponsorship. That's right, isn't it? Sorry – I didn't catch your names . . .'

'I'm Lucy,' said the blondie, 'and this is my friend, Crystal.'

'Crystal . . . and what bright-green eyes you have, Crystal. Don't often see it.'

'Yeh,' she agreed. 'People are always saying that.'

'Come over here,' offered Black, sitting up and craning his head around (very pleased indeed that he'd managed to snap

381

off the television just before everyone had walked into the room). 'Maybe you two girls would like a, um, I don't know – drink of some sort? There's chocolates there, if you . . .'

'Yes, girls,' enthused Alan. 'Do sit. And then you can bring us up to, what is it? Speed. Yes.'

'Really nice house . . .' said Crystal again. 'You got any Coke?'

'Um – think so,' said Alan. 'Diet, probably – suit you? And you, Lucy? Coke? Tell us about your charity walk. They're going to do a walk for charity, apparently Blackie. Coastline – that right? British coastline. Not all of it, presumably.'

'No,' said Lucy. 'South. Hastings. Bognor, round there. It's the school's idea, but we're quite into it now. And you, you sort of sign up for so much per mile, see? Any amount you want.'

'Hm. And how many miles do you think you'll cover?' asked Alan idly (and he was thinking that the both of them, you know – they really did fill out nicely those little white shirts of theirs, ties just slightly awry).

'Well – don't know, really. Depends on the weather and stuff. We're doing two overnight stopovers so, could be . . . don't know. Fifty miles? What you think, Crystal?'

'Jesus – fifty miles!' Crystal hooted. 'That sounds like endless.'

'Yeh . . . ?' doubted Lucy. 'Might not be fifty. Forty, maybe. Don't know.'

'I see,' said Alan, smiling and nodding and really quite gleeful. 'Well I reckon we could stretch to . . . hm, what do you think, Blackie? Oh – this is Black, forgot to mention. And I'm Alan, by the way. Sorry – should've . . . Yes. Well let's see now . . . say, what? Pound a mile? How's that sound?'

'Tell you what would sound better,' Black was chuckling. '*Two* pounds a mile. How about that?'

Lucy was clapping her hands in delight.

'Oh yeh – oh wow! That would be great. Oh wow thanks a lot. Most people, they go oh OK then – ten pee. And it is for charity, after all.'

'Indeed,' agreed Alan. 'Now then – two Cokes, is it?'

Lucy paused, and looked up cheekily.

'Um – look, I know it's a bit, um . . . but you don't have any ice cream, do you? I could really just go some ice cream. What about you, Crystal? Like some ice cream?'

Crystal nodded eagerly. 'That would be great . . . but it doesn't, you know, matter if you haven't, or anything.'

Alan glanced over at Black, and briefly their eyes gleamed in fusion.

'Well it just so happens,' he said, 'that you two young ladies are in luck. What's more, you might even learn a little bit about the coastline in the process. We can have our ice creams on the beach . . . !'

Lucy and Crystal eyed each other, slightly uneasily.

'Sorry . . . ?' Lucy ventured. 'Don't quite . . .'

'Well follow me and all will be revealed. Blackie – you'll pop up in the lift, will you? Meet us up there?'

'Oh wow!' cooed Crystal. 'You got a *lift* . . . ?'

Black was already on his feet.

'All mod, er . . .' And then he tailed away. 'You know – what is it? Cons, yes.'

'Shall we go? I promise you, you'll be amazed. But in a pleasant way, rest assured. And don't, um – worry, will you? You're perfectly safe. Coming?'

Lucy and Crystal had a swift and whispered conversation

– a thing of eyebrows, squints and elastic lips. They both stood up and were smiling, indicating to Alan and Black their willingness to go for it with a puppylike eagerness overlaying a more modest undertone of sisterly courage and mutual support.

Their reaction upon stepping into the room was more than Alan could have wished for. He had briefly left them just outside (could hear their muffled giggles, bless them, through the panels of the door) while he rapidly set up a gorgeous sunset, the sounds of the gulls and then the lapping of waves at the shoreline. The sand was warm to the touch.

'Oh – *wow* . . . !!' they yelled in unison. And they repeated it several times more and increasingly softly as they wandered in wonder at the seaside – fingertips outstretched, though reluctant to touch, and eyes as wide as wide.

'Well girls!' Black regaled them, coming into the room and closing the door behind him. 'Never seen anything like *this* before, I'll warrant.'

Lucy seemed reluctant to disengage the sweep of her eyes from over all of this magic around her.

'It's just . . . oh my God, it's just so . . . ! Isn't it, Crystal? It's so *real* . . . the look and the noises and . . . even the *smell*, Jesus . . . !'

'Mm,' nodded Alan, quite as pleased as ever he could recall. 'Salt and ozone and just the merest hint of Sarson's vinegar. Took a while to get it right . . .'

Black was in a deckchair, holding the blade of his hand across his eyes to shield them from the livid orange glow of the slowly sinking sun.

'Well come on then, Alan! Ice creams all round, I think.'

'On my way, Blackie. On my way.'

384

Yes I am – oh God yes: I am. On my way, yes yes yes, and very much so. Because this bit is nearly new, and I love it so much. Blackie, he arranged it all for my birthday. I nearly wept with joy. He'd somehow tracked down a derelict nineteen-fifties ice-cream van – I know, I know: just so thoughtful. And he'd had it sawn down the middle, longways, and completely and beautifully restored, the half of it, inside and out, and now it stands so perfectly against the whole of the far wall. It had to be assembled on site – and still he managed to keep it all a secret. It's powder-blue and a deepish cream and covered in hand-painted pink lettering and original tinplate signs showing all the varieties of cornets and lollies of the period, each of them sixpence. And does the whippy ice cream nozzle actually work? Why of course it does, and splendidly. I have become quite good at this – and the girls, very gratifyingly, are watching me now as I do it – twirling the cone around in my fingers as the ice cream squeezes out, just to create the ideal whirl. Flakes – we get them wholesale – I now slide into the finished works of art. A grunt of satisfaction from Blackie, squeals of nearly rapture from these two lovely girls – and then Alan plonked himself down in the remaining deckchair. And even the following day, he wholly failed to put into words the extraordinary stab of sensation that jolted him when Lucy, smiling impishly, sat down across him and put an arm about his shoulder. But it was as nothing compared with the very next instant when she blobbed her ice cream onto his nose, laughed quite gurgily, and then licked it off cleanly, with a darting little tongue. Black had beckoned to Crystal, and she sauntered over to his side. He closed his eyes and swallowed quite hard – on the very teetering brink of a now-or-never moment. And then his fingers just barely grazed her calf – lay there frozen, poised to take flight . . . and then in the peace that ensued, he slid it up softly the length of Crystal's leg. Crystal looked over to Lucy, who now was kissing Alan, and deeply, and came quite close to a chortle as she crouched down low and laid her head in Blackie's lap. He just longingly exhaled, more than content to just let her get on with it. Alan now stood and guided Lucy to a private section of the beach, and laid her down on to the sand. Only sighs and a gentle moaning, as the burning ball of sun was now extinguished; the scene was then one of indigo night, overlaid by whiffs, and then the stench of pleasure. Tomorrow is not a concern tonight.

It came, though – as next days will, no matter how tenaciously you cling in desperation to the one before, striving to keep a hold on it for just one moment longer. Not though, when it came to it, how Alan felt at all: he bounded out of his bed, wholly refreshed, noting only that it was a little bit past his time, and eager for coffee and Corn Flakes. When Tarzan was awoken by his chimp of a green and sunlit morning with a nice big cup of freshly macerated jungle juice, and uppermost in his mind was just the coming joy of swinging through the trees on ropes of vine, this swiftly to be followed by an energetic bout of chest-thumping and the lowing undulations and then irrepressible echo of his very own siren call . . . well Alan for one knew exactly how he felt. It was the freedom, that's what did it – the absolute and uncompromised freedom to do precisely as one pleases with the added pleasure of knowing that one's sole cohabitee either shares with enthusiasm your tastes and urges, or else is quite careless and wholly indulgent to all of your other impulses, your every passing whim: those that are peculiar to you. A basic human right, freedom is –

that's what people say: but in truth it's a rare thing, very. We become inured to kowtowing at a horribly early age – civility, it's called, manners, selflessness, concern for the happiness of others . . . but all it comes down to, if, in the process, it messes you up, is a grinding pain in the bloody arse and a build-up over decades of yearning and resentment that one day when you realise that here is the pattern for, oh my Christ – just *ever*, the dam can burst with irreparable consequence. But the thundering stew of my turbulent waters, it has receded – the boiling of the mountainous waves subdued now, and tranquil, merely a pond with a shallow and silky surface. We live a very regular but not rigid existence, and this suits both of us. Clean and tidy – everything in its place. Order, within and without. Pleasing, and very calming. I am – very calm. And we don't discuss it, you know, but you can see quite plainly the selfsame thing in Blackie – he doesn't erupt at the slightest thing: life no longer appears to him as an eternal inconvenience, a jinxed and worrisome obstacle course, plotted by fiends and goblins. Doesn't even seem to need to dash off to the lavatory quite so frequently. He reads a lot – he's forever reading; just become a member of the Folio Society – he does so much love just the touch and heft of a beautiful book. (I got him a little present recently: Picasso's very late erotic – some would say pornographic – drawings and etchings, rather lovely edition; Blackie immediately dubbed it his Pubist period.) He goes out and encounters people less and less, that's certainly true, not through dread or evasion but simply because he has seen to it – and I, I hope, have abetted him in this – that all he desires is here, with me. And sometimes, in order to spike and enrich the warm and creamy everyday flowing and lapping of our lives together, treats and surprises are in order.

'Morning, Blackie – morning morning. Your Earl Grey is all set out, look – you just have to boil up the water. Sleep well, I trust?'

'Like a lamb, dear boy, like a lamb. Eventually. By golly though, hey? Those two little firecrackers . . . !'

'I know. Are you having toast? I thought we might have an early lunch, if that suits you. Sort of picnic affair, maybe. Gorgeous day – I could set it all out in the pergola.'

'Capital idea. What time is it, Alan? Not that it really matters . . .'

'Not sure. Tennish, I think. Which one did you prefer?'

'Tennish, hm. That's a very interesting question, Alan. A very interesting question. Anything in the papers?'

'Not really. Murders, war, higher taxes. The lies of dullard politicians. I only really look at the weather and the crossword. Obituaries, of course.'

'Don't think I shall – bother with the toast. Not if it's tennish. I think on balance it has to be Lucy, really, if only because I've always had a particular thing about blondes. Well we all have, I suppose. Especially in that dinky little uniform. But Crystal's curves . . . dear me. Dear me. And the kiss . . . so much more than a meeting of mouths. It was as if she was supplying a taste of her lips as the sweetest sample of all that was next to come. How old do you reckon, Alan? Crystal, I mean.'

'Hm – she's the younger one. Twenty-two or so, I'd say. Not her real name, of course. Lucy, well – I don't have to tell you about Lucy, do I? Just knows every trick there is to know. She could be twenty-five easy, maybe more. Who knows? But she's in beautiful condition. Not cheap, of course, but you'd hardly expect it, would you? Not if you want a decent sort of a show.'

'It was just so good of you, Alan, to set it all up. So terribly thoughtful. What a treat! And you divined it exactly correctly, you know – well of course you know. What I – like, and everything. Thought I'd take my tea out on to the terrace. Coming?'

'Mm. Why not? Have a glance at the crossword. What are you up to today? Anything? I've got to see to the beach. Took a bit of a pounding. What was that . . . ? You hear that? Was that in the hall . . . ?'

'What? Didn't hear anything. Not too surprising. Can hardly hear *you*. Got to take this thing in . . .'

'Mm. Could have sworn I heard a . . .'

'Could be the post. Could it have been the post?'

'Could have been, I suppose. Oh . . . better take a look . . .'

Alan wandered into the hall, expecting only the usual slew and clutter of plastic-wrapped catalogues to be littering the doormat (don't get much in the way of regular post these days, and that just suits me fine). But what he saw there instead was a large and grimy canvas bag, recently rifled and spewing rumpled denim and magazines. Also on the floor – quite recently polished by Alan in the old-fashioned way, hands and knees and beeswax – were kicked-off and streaky wellingtons, the track of the soles thick with dried-on grassy divots. A dented can of Diet Coke was on its side and askew on the hall table, harming the arrangement, and it had dribbled its dregs on to the surface, brownish globules shivering. Alan heard Black now padding out behind him and he whirled round to gaze at him, aghast and open-mouthed. The returned expression on Blackie's face was one of at first uncertainty, and then a cold and looming horror. Not only would it appear, then, that Amanda had returned to the

389

bosom of her family, but going by the yelps, initially, from the floor above, and then the more outright screaming . . . it would further appear that she has just encountered, mm – Lucy, yes. And also Crystal. Asleep and sprawled out Christ knows where, almost certainly naked (more bosoms to her family than Amanda could frankly shake a stick at) . . . or – and Alan now winced as he acknowledged a rather stronger likelihood: in rucked-up pleated skirts, and strewn about them with the abandon of the hot now so cold moment, cobalt knickers and pink-piped blazers. Mm.

What, thought Alan, next . . . ? Well next, Amanda had hurtled back down the staircase, her hands clasped over her ears and was shrieking out the word 'dis-*gusting*!' over and over and over again. And then the word '*sick*!', repeatedly. She streamed through the hall, knocking aside Black and colliding into Alan – and lest there be the slightest doubt as to just who in this house formed the butt of her repulsion, she drew back the lips from her teeth and in a shrill now cracked voice she was screeching that *both* of you, oh God yuck yuck *yuck*! You are both so totally sick and fucking dis-*gusting* . . . ! Her face seemed caught in a panic of revolt. She ran out of the house, crashing shut the door behind her.

In the shimmering silence, Black was idly massaging the shoulder that had borne the full brunt of a rioting Amanda. He glanced across to Alan, his eyebrows raised. And then he looked up at the sound of a voice from the landing above.

'What was all that then, boys?' Crystal was calling. 'The *day* shift . . . ?'

Her jumpy breasts were dangled down over the banister rail, their rosy nipples singling him out. And Black could only sigh. Alan held a hand across his eyes. My waters, he thought, are turbulent . . . they are rapidly becoming a thunderous stew: the walls of the dam are being hammered by the boiling of the mountainous waves.

Amanda, for once, had sounded genuinely distraught, and so I rather rashly told her to come straight over. Already regretting it. I could just slip out, I suppose – be gone by the time she gets here . . . but that would seem a little cruel. I said to her on the phone: Amanda, my darling – five days now and you haven't called. I am your *mother*. Remember that? You said you'd call me every day. Didn't you? Didn't you, darling? Don't ask me if she heard or not – wailing and babbling, she was. Distraught, as I say – and not, I thought, her usual teenage 'freaking', as she terms it, and general overreaction to even the very slightest thing. Something clearly was amiss – and I felt quite fond, I suppose, that it was me she sought to talk to. But then she'd hardly ring her father, would she? What use has he ever been in a crisis? Or at any other time, really.

But I didn't want her here. Because we hadn't spoken, not properly, about my moving away. And oddly, she hadn't bombarded me with an eternity of questions and all of the customary recrimination. Seemed wholly engulfed by some-thing of her own, which at the time I must admit was something of a relief. Because whatever questions she might have asked me, I doubted whether I had the answers. I had been quite flighty – hadn't thought things through, and perhaps deliberately. One of the curses of growing older is that you are forever doing that, thinking things through, pursuing the course to its logical end, investigating the possibility of alternative avenues – yes, and judging how the mood will take you. And then either ducking the whole thing, ditching it completely, or else trudging on through it with a lowering sense of premonition and the expectancy of doom. And so yes, it is entirely possible that I willed myself into my current irresponsibility, and I must say it did feel so good. Just to leave all the old behind – hurry away with my brand-new lover. Yes. It seemed, as they say, a good idea at the time. But now, whatever had so selfishly consumed Amanda had clearly withered away, or else exploded, and so now of course, when I have done with consoling her, there will be nothing between us to protect me. She will be 'on my case', as she so horribly says. Well . . . it has to be faced some time. Maybe just talking about what I have done might help me to understand it. She will, quite naturally, be furious. And possibly even revolted. Which I would expect, in the circumstances. I don't, of course, have to tell her. And that is the doorbell.

'God,' was the first thing Amanda said, dropping her jacket on to the floor. 'This is so like *creepy* . . .'

'I can't see why you think that,' sniffed Susan, while seeing it exactly, for she felt it herself. 'You lived here for years. It's not as if it's strange to you.'

'I know. That's what's so creepy. What are you doing here? Why have you . . . ? I thought this place was let or like sold or something.'

'Do you want tea? You look perfectly ghastly. What have you been doing to yourself? It was to be let out, yes. Or sold. But I didn't get round to it. Quite a good thing, as it turns out. I mean, quite apart from anything else it has already considerably risen in value. Tea? Yes or no.'

'Don't want tea. I just want to *die* . . . !'

'I don't recall a single year passing when you didn't, at one point or another. What is it this time?'

'You don't care. So long as you're all right, you just like so don't care about me.'

'That hurts, Amanda. And it's quite untrue. You're here, aren't you? And I've asked you what's wrong. How much caring do you want?'

Amanda just threw herself on to the sofa and held a cushion across her face.

'I can't hear you, Amanda. If you want to talk to me I suggest you don't hold a cushion across your face.'

' I *said* . . . !' bawled Amanda, hurling the cushion aside, 'that just everything everything *everything*'s wrong, just like *all* of it, OK? And I so just want to *die* . . . ! And you! And you! Why are you back in our old bloody house? What are you *doing* here? I just don't *understand* . . . And listen, right? Before you say like anything, you've just got to tell me this because I've got to *know*, OK? And you've got to tell me the *truth*. Yeh? Right? Right, then: have you ever . . . oh God *yuck*, I can't even *say* it, it's so . . . !'

'What on earth are you talking about, Amanda? Have I ever what?'

'Oh God. Have you . . . ever been with Harry? Oh *God* . . . !'

'Harry? That odious little shit, you mean, who took advantage of you? Well yes.'

'*Yes* . . . ? *Yes*?!'

'What are you so upset about? I told you I went to see him. I told you that.'

'I don't mean – *that*, I don't mean then. I mean again. Have you? Like – you and Harry . . . did you ever . . . ?'

Susan just stared at her.

'Am I picking this up correctly? Are you seriously asking me – me, your mother . . . may I yet again remind you,

Amanda, that it is your *mother* now you are talking to? Are you completely *mad* . . . ?'

'Well *did* you? Just like *tell* me, OK?'

'I find the very suggestion quite utterly repellent and deeply, deeply insulting. Christ – I can't even understand how you could have borne him to be even near you. His skin is appalling. What put this perfectly slimy little idea into your head? Did *he* say so? Did the lying little *shit* say so? I'll have him arrested if he did.'

Amanda sighed – a mixture of fractured and tainted relief, creeping weariness and a tumult of confusion.

'No . . . he said you didn't. It was me who thought . . . I don't know. Maybe I am mad. I don't know . . . I just don't know *anything* . . . !'

But it is like a thought – could be, couldn't I? Like, crazy or something? Because I really did believe he, like – cared for me? A bit, anyway. And at first it was just so great because what we did, Harry and me, is we like got on the Eurostar? To like Paris? Which I'd never been to, and it was just so cool. And he got us this most amazing hotel and we went up the Eiffel Tower, like just so scary. He bought me this so cool scarf from a really expensive shop called Hermès and it had like red and yellow flowers on it and it felt like heaven. Food was great and we got so like smashed, you know? It was great. And then one evening in this like brasserie – famous one, can't remember – he just starts chatting up this *girl*, if you can believe it. In like *French*? Me just sitting there. Touched her hair and stuff and they were both like *laughing*? And I was just so angry I copped off with this boy at the very next table and I walked right out of the place with him and I was thinking yeh well screw *you* Harry, you bastard. And it was awful because the boy, right? He was called Pascal which is a pretty geeky name, I think, and we went to a bar and we were on, like – Pernod? Which tastes like sweets and medicine and oh man, I was just so out of it. And he got me up to this room and I was so like woozy and he shoved me up against the wall and like pulled down all my things and just fucked me then and I couldn't stop him and it was only for like less than a minute but it really hurt me and I was crying. He got me a taxi – oh yeh *great* Pascal, you fuck – and I went back to the hotel and Harry wasn't there. And when he came in just like hours and hours later, I told him what I'd done except I made it sound all like kind of romantic? I did it so he'd be jealous, but he wasn't. He just said – Cool, babe. Grinning, eyes all wild and crazy, like high on some shit. So next morning I just like hated him and I hated me and he gave me some of Black's money – there was so little left – and I got the train back to London. And before I left, I went to him Yeh and I bet you *did* – you did, didn't you Harry? You did go with my mother – you were lying. And he said Haven't, I swear I haven't . . . yeh, and I so like didn't believe him. And why did you go with that *girl*? Why did you do that to me, Harry? And he just went, she was 'kinda cute'. Yeh – like my mum. I chucked the scarf right in his face just before I ran right out of there, and I so like wish I hadn't, you know? It was just so beautiful, and it felt like heaven.

'Why don't you,' suggested Susan, 'go back to the beginning?'

Amanda blinked at her, suddenly bereft of anger and scorn. I'd love to do that, is what she was thinking: go back to the very beginning. Before all the shit started happening. Whenever like that was. But yeh – I know what Mum means: tell her what's been going on. And I will, actually, because I think I need some help.

'See, Mum . . . I've been away, OK?'

'Away? What do you mean away? Away from me, do you mean?'

'No. Well yeh – but no, I don't mean just away from you. I've been, like, on a sort of a . . . holiday?'

' Don't know what you – but you're at school. How could you . . . ? Are you telling me you haven't been at school? Is that what you're telling me? But what was your useless *father* thinking of? Where have you been? How long have you—?'

'Look, Mum – if I'm going to talk, right, you've just got to stop being *Mum* all the time. I'm going to tell you what's been happening, OK – and then maybe we'll all be just like less crazy.'

'I'm not crazy. You may be crazy – I'm not crazy.'

'You going to listen or what?'

'Oh . . . I'm listening. And the truth, mind. Otherwise there's no point to it, is there?'

'Yeh – I'm going to tell you the truth. That's what I'm going to do. So – I've been away, OK? Like – to Paris?'

'To—!'

'Oh Jesus just *listen*, can't you? Just shut up and listen, Christ's sake. I went to Paris. I told Dad it was a school trip to Switzerland, don't know why I said Switzerland, but I did. And, well – you know it wasn't.'

'And he *believed* you? My God, what a man. But the school, though – haven't they been in touch? They must have noticed you weren't *there*, for God's sake . . . !'

'Don't know. Maybe. Don't know.'

'And were you on your own on this . . . holiday of yours?'

'Yeh. No – I was with Tara. No – I wasn't with Tara, I was with . . . Harry, OK?'

'Oh – *Amanda* . . . ! And that little bastard – he *promised* me—!'

'Yeh well. You said the truth, so I'm giving you the truth. Anyway, it didn't work out, and I came back. Just today. And I just got so like confused, because if you and Harry weren't . . . well why have you moved out? And to *here* – why are you *here*? It's just so weird. But then – well then the *really* bad thing happened. I just can't . . .'

'What? What bad thing? Tell me.'

'Well actually – another bad thing happened first. I'm like – pregnant?'

'But . . . you're not any *more*, Amanda . . . The clinic . . .'

'Yeh. Didn't go to the clinic.'

'You didn't keep the appointment? Well why on earth *not*?'

'Because I wasn't pregnant.'

'You weren't . . . ? But you *said* to me—!'

'Yeh. But I wasn't.'

'And, what – now you *are* . . . ?'

'Yeh. I am now. Bummer. But we can see about that, can't we? Just like make a new appointment?'

'Oh God, Amanda – you make it sound like going to the *dentist* . . .'

'Well it is a bit. Get something rotten taken out.'

'*Jesus*, Amanda . . . Maybe you really *are* crazy . . .'

'Anyway. That's not the big bad thing. The big bad thing is, I get home, right? And I really feel like tired and stuff so I just drop everything and I go upstairs for a shower, OK? And just kind of chill. And oh *God* . . . ! It was just so . . . dis-*gusting*, I can't tell you.'

'You'd better tell me, Amanda. What is it, Christ's sake? Are they all right? Alan and Black? Is one of them—?'

397

'Oh I'd say they're *very* all right. Oh yeh. Oh yeh. What a filthy pair they are. There were – *women*, Mum. Like – *girls*? One on the floor, the other on top of Dad's *bed* . . . !'

Susan was just so amazed.

'*Women* . . . ? You mean—?'

'Yeh. Young. Slags. No clothes. Christ, I'm so like *sick* . . . Why did you go? Why did you leave them? They never would've done it if you'd . . . well Black would, probably. Ee-*yow*! Tried it on with me once. Sick.'

Susan sat forward.

'I don't believe you. Black did? I don't believe you.'

'Yeh well – believe what you like. He did, though. All over me. If Dad hadn't come home I would have had to brain him.'

'I can't believe it . . . when did this happen?'

'On one of the nights you were out, like all tarted up. I thought with Harry. I, um – told Dad that's like what you were doing. He and Black, they went round. Gave him money, Harry, so he'd stop seeing you. Loads. How we went to Paris . . .'

Susan was staring.

'Did they *really* do that? Alan and Black? That is just so . . . and *girls* – I just can't . . . I mean, Alan of all people. Oh dear. Oh dear me. Well this . . . this just changes everything.'

'Like – what's left to *change* . . . ?'

Well yes – but the ground is altered, and it is largely my doing. All that's left that now must change are more, yet more of my plans. In which, I have to confess, I am increasingly losing faith. I no longer, in truth, actually had one, a plan – more it was a hastily devised possibility of escape, a bandage over the seeping wound, a hopeful attempt at salvation (and my own, of course my own) . . . but now, in the light of things, even that – it just seems to be beyond, beyond. I believed that I had been flooded by an unstoppable force for good (and my own, of course my own) and suddenly, girlishly, all the old, the clinging on to all of the old, it seemed not just ridiculous but such an encumbrance – accumulated ballast that was holding me down. I had forgotten – or certainly I chose not to recall it – that it was I who with such great care had made sure that such an anchor was firmly keyed, and then, for certainty, I added to its weight. This much was wise. But since I cut away, that total freedom that we all of us, I suppose, so stupidly dream of . . . it appears to have resulted in aimlessness and shame (and not just my own, of course not just my own, although I know I am alone in feeling ugly and foolish). I doubt whether others, the two old boys, will be thinking this way. They must at first have hugged to themselves with a hot and mutual hurt and fury the righteous outrage of the wronged and badly done-by – and then, very touchingly, they had attempted repair. They still cared for me that much, at least. I had never wondered quite how much – and yet when I was gone, I thought of them not at all. I was in love. And Amanda too – that appointment at the clinic? And how I was going to accompany her? I thought of her not at all. I was in love. Who can there be left who is still in the heaven of ignorance as to just what love will do? You feast so greedily on all its sap and sugar – and, in your eagerness to suck up more, are blissfully careless of how much you have torn. And so it was love, not calculation, that made me know I had to go. It could not be 'as well as', no not this time, for here would be a heinous infidelity: for you must be true to love. I imagine I was not the first person to be so dazed, so knocked, so struck and damned and dazzled as to have hardly thought at all. One's being, it comes into its full-blooded own – headily, with the anticipation of yet another coming together with the adulated other, and then so very wildly on impact. Other people, other lives – they were quite as wholly irrelevant as anything but he whom I held in my arms. Is it my fault I am a sensualist?

At first, I had hardly known he was even alive. Because in the early days of trying to get the house and garden together, there were men just all over the place. It consumed me. I was running around from this project to that, consulting with Mr Clearley – constantly on the Net, tracking down not just all these specific and typically elusive materials, but also such details as doorknobs and tie-backs. A hundred decisions a day. It was fraught, but I must say I adored it. I am a manager by nature. There was also, well . . . I did derive a very large satisfaction in seeing the household I had envisaged, the confluences I had engineered, surely and steadily pulling together. Black's blind faith and seemingly fathomless resources, Alan just being there as just always he had been – Amanda, by degrees, accepting with reluctance at first this new situation, and then with the thrill of her very own suite, embracing it madly. I felt, in truth, more of an architect than the architects, whose services eventually I quietly dispensed with. Once the marble floor in the atrium was finally and beautifully done (it turned out we were lacking just three square metres to finish, and Mr Clearley, he had to order it specially from the original quarry somewhere in the south of Italy, though still the problem of actually matching it was quite a thorough nightmare) . . . but yes, that was the key to it – once that floor was down, it acted as a sort of a bridge, is the way I saw it, to all the other rooms and floors. It joined things up – the disparate sites were becoming a whole. And that's when I felt freer to concentrate on what was for me the most exciting part of all – my fabulous schemes for the garden.

The first lot of gardeners we got, they turned out to be utterly useless – and Mr Clearley, to give him his due, he spotted it fairly early on and got shot of them. The new team we got in I had read about in one of the endless stream of monthlies I was buying. They'd done quite a lot of work for the Chelsea Flower Show, medals and everything, though I nearly didn't bother even ringing them because I thought it highly unlikely that they could take on so big a job as this would be at such very short notice. But they didn't seem even remotely fazed by the scale of the thing; sent over in the first instance a gang of navvies to clear the ground – I lost all count of the number of skips of useless clay and tree stumps we got rid of – and then the landscapers there, they went over my plans with me, pointed out all manner of practical considerations that of course would not have occurred to me, but generally were very encouraging. All of it was possible, they assured me – 'quite do-able' was their phrase – though the final cost, they said, would be . . . well, 'considerable' I think they plumped for – that was their word of choice. 'Massive' comes closer – and all the time it was being revised, upwards and upwards, very often because of me, it must be admitted – all my glorious afterthoughts and so swish refinements – but sometimes too because of unseen complications: the rerouting of the drainage, for one – and then the discovery of what seemed to be a subterranean boulder, quite vast, that no one could explain and in the end it had to be blasted out. When finally the layout was more or less apparent, I could start in on all the earnest discussions with the plantsman, the man in control of the project on the ground. Herb. Though at first I had hardly known he was even alive. Saw him around – didn't know his name. And then I did, and I just thought . . . well I *said* it to him, actually: I know people must have remarked on it before, but it is a perfectly wonderful name you've got, isn't it really? For a gardener, I mean. He grinned and said he was grateful his parents had resisted calling him Daisy.

And, like the garden . . . it just grew. I tried to remember, I have tried to decide . . . was it his eyes, warm and peeping from under the long mop of hair? The first thing to tweak me with a strange delight? Or was it his big and bony capable hands, crescents of earth beneath the nails, so very tenderly peeling away the layers of a tiny little pod, so that he could show me the seeds within . . . ? At first, I doubted my senses – I could not possibly be attracted to so unsophisticated a person, let alone one so very almost laughably young. He had a rather odd voice – a bit sort of strangulated, his accent, quite weird noises, sometimes. Never in my life have I felt myself drawn to such a thing – maybe, I don't know, why the allure was daily proving stronger and stronger. He flirted in a rather clumsy sort of a way – but what man have I ever met who didn't? I laughed, I parried – I glanced over my shoulder at him and smiled, whenever I walked away. The day, though, he just roughly took hold of me, I could not call up even a show of resistance – I sighed out loud with so huge a relief that all the waiting now was over. The sex at first was brief, gratifying and very literally dirty, often on a bed of mud: I was surprised to remember how much I liked it. And soon I lost all caution. God – I remember one day when Amanda had come home early from school and I rushed to call out to her, so bathed in gratitude that she had not arrived just five minutes sooner when she might just have spotted us emerging from behind

402

the pergola, my back so wet from having been just mashed down into a bed of petunias. I was no more than babbling, really – the scent and essence of him still sticky on my fingers. That was the day she told me, Amanda, that she was pregnant. But, it turns out, she wasn't. But now, however, she is, or so she says. Christ. But anyway – all the risk and discomfort, it could not go on. And that's when we started to meet in Chelsea – in the old house, yes. I went there every evening I could, daytime too. The thrill of the journey nearly choked me. When I was not with him, I dangled at the mercy of the give and pull of a long elastic yearning. And one night, gazing at the mere and slightest shimmer of blue on the twitch of his sleeping eyelid, I simply fell in love. And so everything then just had to be changed – for this, you see, was it: the bare and true and longed-for thing. Not the outcome of a calculation, nor a canny move. From the blue (if just the slightest shimmer) – here was now the bolt, thudded into me. And this, no – it could not be as well as, no no – this just had to be instead of. And yes I know it was contrary to, oh – everything, all of it, which before I had seen quite plainly to be right – yes, and proper; I knew that, of course I did – but somehow there was now a new and more valid propriety, all the contracts of old quite suddenly null: I saw them just as dust. This great man whom I loved . . . I must marry and be with him, and him alone: it must be good in the eyes of God.

And I remember that night, remember it utterly – will remember it for ever, as well as all that came after. So impatient was I for him to awake, my mouth formed into an 'O' and I blew with care on to that slightest shimmer of blue on the twitch of his sleeping eyelid, so that at first I could be gently anointing his stirring consciousness with the merest whiff and then a smudge of unction – a tiny brilliant speck of love – and then when he embraced me, we both would be engulfed by the full great weight of it: it would fill us up and we could laugh at our own amazement.

He awoke, and I kissed him. His eyes were lit with a lazy ease. I breathed the words . . . I love you. He smiled and touched my hair. I breathed the words . . . I love you. He sat up then and stroked my arm. My glance was urgent and I whispered the words . . . I love you. He swung his legs away from the bed, picked his shirt from a tangle on the floor and said to me, 'Susan.' I pulled off the shirt he now had half on and I said to his face that I loved him. He tugged the shirt back over his shoulder and stood, detaching my hand from whatever escaping part of him I could quickly catch a hold of. Doing up trousers, he walked to the bathroom. I called out the words – I *love* you . . . ! He closed the door behind him and I was left alone, and in a different amazement, one not of our own, but only mine. And when he came out and jangled his keys – I rushed to him, rushed, and in a voice now cracking I just failed to scream at him all of my passion . . . and his eyes were lit with a lazy ease, he touched my hair and stroked my arm: Have to go. Why? Why, I said – why do you have to? It's late, he said, and looked at the floor. It's been late before – it's been later than this, so why? Why? Why do you have to? I *love* you . . . ! Before he slipped away and out of the door and into the dark he said quite simply, Because I do.

Disappointed, so let down – but no more than hurt: here was not a devastation . . . I had maybe, simply, been too premature. Men are like boys – they will shy away. And yet . . . I have endured a lifetime of gangs, dozens and scores – bustling throngs of hopeful hopeless men, all of them battering with crudeness and determination against my strong defences, the towering limit of me, just for the sight of a glimmer of light. Here the gates were flung their widest – the flooding beams were dazzling. But, he said, he had to go. I tried to write him a poem, and couldn't. So on my special lilac paper, I wrote him a note instead, saying simply, 'I love you'. But because of what came after, I never did give it to him. Forgotten it till now. Don't know what became of it, where it might be, and nor do I really mind.

He came again the next day, with not good champagne. He knew I liked champagne, but did he know I would not care for this one? He is ignorant of champagne. He brought as well some truly tawdry flowers. He knew I liked them, flowers, and well he knew I would not care for these: he is an expert on flowers. He said, Mellors is come, my Lady – a joke, I suppose it is a joke, that he had made before, and not just the once, and each time I had asked him not to again. We made love soon and quickly, and I remember with wonder that I barely even was aware: my mind was elsewhere and onward. After, he drank the not-good champagne – I held my glass, and didn't. And then I told him – my voice was steady – that it was not just, did he see, that I *loved* him (was that a wince? Did he slightly turn away?) but that I needed to give myself to him quite utterly: the bestowal of my body (which always made him grunt and gasp and fill up his hands) . . . my red and eager heart, only tinged with bruising . . . and then my very soul – still close, at least, to the core of me. I need, I said, to be his wife. He drank a good bit more of the not-good champagne. And then he said Susan, you've got a husband: at least. He, I said – they – must go: I need to be your wife – and yes, exclusively. Well . . . he said. Well? Well what? (I think I quelled most of it,

405

my rising anger, my lowering shame, the quiver of impending terror.) Answer me, please: well what? Well you see, he said – scratching, now, at the back of his head, his eyes alive and darting, seeking out snipers on every rooftop – well you see, Susan . . . I have one of those, a wife. You see. And one, he said, is quite enough. Very quickly I had to wall up the vastness of all that would soon crash down and crush me – because for now the vital point had rapidly to be pursued. *One* wife, yes – I agree, I agree: and that one wife . . . will be *me*! His eyes were lit by an active unease – his hand came up to my hair, and then towards my arm. He looked away and shook his head.

He did not come the next day (following my tears, and then the shrieking – after I hit him with a chair, I was not too surprised) and so I set myself hard to plotting his recapture . . . which for me was a new game, very. His, oh God – *wife* . . . what could she be? Nothing. Nothing much at all. Or else why would he . . . do what he does? Well no – that didn't quite follow. Didn't, did it? Because with me, what man wouldn't? You see? This is not an average situation. But whatever she was – his, oh God, *wife* – she could be just snuffed out. Guttered. Like the old flame she was destined to become. And suddenly, I hated her, this woman, whoever and wherever she was – hated her with violence. And then, later . . . it was he whom I hated, for betraying her: for reneging on his contract. And then, I suppose inevitably, I came to hate me, myself, for just understanding everything so horribly clearly . . . and even for being around. So, I thought – that is that then, really. There will be no plot after all, no scheme – and no recapture either. Let the fugitive flee. And me? I must smother the flaming of shame, damp it down to a smoulder, and then embrace regret. Reparation, now, is all I can think of. But through all

406

of this – it was long, yes long, and so terribly lonely – I would keep coming back to this one and stark marvel: the love that had filled me, that had impelled me to be drastic, that had opened my eyes and set my sensuality ablaze – the love that was to have fuelled me for the whole of the rest of my life . . . was gone. Done with. My eyes were deadened, and I felt only lassitude . . . just so terribly empty: outrage, then, and a barely simmering fury. And so this, I thought – well it does, it changes everything. And had Amanda asked me then: what's left to change? I should have answered, well – just one more thing: to get back, to get back – I have to change it back. But in the light now of what she tells me . . . Black with Amanda . . . his and Alan's belief that I had simply had something so casual as a fling with a *boy* . . . and now even the glimmer of the thought of their – *girls* . . . oh, can it ever be possible? Well yes – because they want me, you see. They must do. Well of course they do – they always did: they paid out money to get me back. And so – get back, get back . . . we all just have to get back. It's what I want.

And Amanda – was she in love, as I was? Did she feel all that I did? I doubt. She is no sensualist – so never ablaze. Although whatever she was feeling, it had impelled her to be drastic – it had certainly opened her eyes. And now, poor girl, she is done with. Her eyes are deadened, and she feels only lassitude . . . just so terribly empty: outrage, then? And a barely simmering fury? Well. So we must all, now – just get back. I have, after all, always done everything for them – Alan, Black, Amanda. Haven't I? And who is to say I cannot again? But the boys, the taste they have had . . . the flavour of the two young girls. Because it is always true – even if ultimately you do just everything for a man, he can and will find another –

one who is willing to do anything at all, the distinction being clear.

'All I have, Amanda, for us both . . . is a hastily devised possibility of escape. A bandage over a seeping wound. A hopeful attempt at salvation.'

Amanda just gazed at her mother and shook her head so slowly.

'Jesus. Jesus . . . OK – look. I'm like – out of here, yeh? And you, Mum: listen to me – you just so have to get *over* yourself. You know?'

Susan nodded sadly. I know. I know. But it's hard. And it's going to be harder. Because I'm lying. Getting back? I don't want it at all. It's just . . . necessary. And my love? It is not done with – it has simply done with me. I cannot think of it as only a loss along the way. It's just . . . necessary. And yet, she's right. I do – I just so have to get over myself. I know. I know. But it's hard. And it's going to be harder. Because me, you see – I'm so very steep as to be practically unconquerable.

CHAPTER ELEVEN

Black was enjoying a cigarette – enjoying too the deftness displayed by Alan as he trussed up a bulging plastic rubbish sack.

'I must say, dear boy – you really are so very adept. So good at all these little jobs around the house. I could watch you for hours. Often do.'

'Never used to be. Susan – she did all this sort of thing. And very much more efficiently. The rubbish, she used to separate everything. Very diligent. Damned if I can be bothered. You know – recycling.'

'Ah yes – heard of it. Saving the planet. Lord, you know – it's all one can do to save oneself, never mind the bloody planet. Why are you doing all of this now though, Alan? It's late.'

'Well they come in the morning, you see. Bin people. Best not to have it all hanging around. So the planet can just look after itself – that the way you see it?'

'Got to be, hasn't it really? Go mad otherwise. I can only think it's all, well – faddism, really. Like the latest food scare, or what have you. Soon, you know, people will be dying of vitamins. Or else malnutrition, because they just don't dare eat *anything* any more. And as to fucking units of *alcohol* – well Jesus. You either drink or you don't, and there's an end on't. Johnson.'

'Who's he? I'll just drag this out, and then maybe a nightcap, hey?'

'You really are rather illiterate, Alan. I think we're going to have to see to that. Johnson. Sam. Dictionary man, yes? Good God.'

'Oh him – oh yes I know him. He wouldn't have had a lot of time for it all, would he? Food scares and units.'

'No well – a man was *meant* to be a man, in those days. Now, you hardly dare. Well – *I* do, *we* do . . . but people, I mean. Oh bloody *hell*, Alan – this is my very last cigarette. I don't believe it. Thought I'd just started the packet. Oh Christ – this is going to be a difficult evening, I must say.'

'Don't worry, old chap. I'll nip down to the place on the corner. Open all night.'

'Oh *no*, Alan – no no. Wouldn't hear of it. I'll be fine. I'll just drink myself into a stupor and take a slug of Night Nurse. I'll be fine.'

'No honestly – won't take a jiffy. I'll be back before you're into your second jigger.'

'You really are too kind. What would I do without you?'

'Same as before. Like me. Muddle along. Right then – I'll dump the rubbish, and then I'll be off. Two minutes. Suck a stub while I'm gone.'

Watched him toddle away. Warm night it was, yet still he was pulling on that wretched Harris tweed of his. Habit, I suppose. I always feel, I don't know – somewhat *fond*, really, whenever he wears it. So much a part of *Alan*, if you know what I mean. We had it invisibly mended not too long ago, semi-successfully, and leather on the cuffs. Looks perfectly ghastly, of course, but in some ways I'm quite as attached to it as Alan is.

Yes . . . all this, I remember it perfectly clearly. And then I went into the drawing room – I'm quite sure about this stage of the events – poured a Scotch, another one, grunted down into the chair and yearned for a cigarette. And then I . . . I don't know . . . almost certainly had another whisky or so, because why would I not, and then . . . Christ, don't ask me . . . some time thereafter, the nightmare began. How will I ever begin to forgive myself? Next thing I knew – well I was being pushed about, roughly handled, and someone was shouting at me, hoarsely. I opened an eye in fear and astonishment – my mind was still in fractures. Amazed – couldn't speak – when I registered lamplight and the appallingly distorted features of *Susie*, dear God – and she was bearing down on me, spitting and shrieking at me all sorts of clamour, wild and incoherent things – and then she started hitting me, hitting me yes . . . palm of her hand, and then she punched me and there was blood in my mouth, yes I could taste it, and I slithered off the chair and I must have been roaring at her now, my hands getting slammed as I tried quite vainly to deflect this quite maddened flurry of all her kicks and lunges.

'Wake up! Get up, you pig and villain! How *could* you? How *dare* you? Get *up*, Black! Get up because I'm going to *kill* you . . . !'

'Jesus, Susie! Christ's sake! Stop it! Stop! Stop kicking me, Christ's sake! Let me up! I'll get up, I'll get up! Stop, Christ – *kicking* me . . . !'

His hands now were over his eyes, the whole of his battered body in the utmost turmoil. No extra pain now seemed to be coming just yet, and he dared to peer through the lattice of his juddering fingers – her two defiant legs astride . . . and then on up to the snorting flare of her reddened nostrils – those blazing and lunatic eyes. He stretched up and towards her a pleading arm and she hauled on it, but then he screamed and fell back down to the floor: the agony at the centre of him was biting down and he could not move. Susan knelt down to him.

'What's wrong? What's wrong with you, Black?'

Black's eyes were both tight closed.

'What's . . . *wrong* with me? *Jesus*, Susie . . . ! What's *wrong* with me . . . ?!'

'Why did you *do* it, Black? At what point did you – you of all people in the world – become just such an . . . *animal*?!'

'*I* . . . ? I don't know what you . . . Christ, Susie – oh God I'm in such pain. I don't know what you're . . . Alan. Where's Alan? Get him to help me. Oh Jesus *Christ* . . . !'

'Ha! That's a good one that is, Black you bastard. Why should he? Why should he help you after what you've done to him? What makes you think he *can* help you, the state's he's in. How could you have *done* it? Did you use a *hammer*, or what?'

Black was desperate now to clamp down on all of his tortured core and just will himself to simply . . . *understand* . . . !

'Is Alan . . . all right? What's wrong? Oh God. Is he all *right* . . . ?!'

'Of course he's not all *right*! How could he be, after what you've done? You're a bad bad person, Black. I was so very wrong about you. You attempt to rape my daughter, and now you viciously assault my husband!'

'I—! I didn't! I've never—! I've never laid a finger on either

412

of them! How could I? *Alan* . . . ? I – *love* him . . . ! Why do you think I—?!'

'Because he *told* me, Black. All right? Yes he did. Just lying there in the hall, bloody and just half-conscious. He *told* me . . . !'

Yes he did – and I shall never forget it. I had hardly known what to expect as I determined to drive straight round here, as soon as dawn had broken. I had tried not to rehearse, to compose no speech. I knew it was too early for just all sorts of reasons: they both would still be asleep – and Alan for one takes just so bloody long to rouse himself, even with a pint of the strongest coffee. Also, the place might be littered with, oh God . . . girls. But as soon as day could be said to have struck, I could simply wait no longer. Whether or not I wanted to get back – I had to, you see, I had to: I just simply had to. The first thing I noticed was that the door, the front door, it was not quite to. My mind – spun back wildly to the time when a drunken Amanda had driven the bloody car into the old house, yes, that first night, yes, when Black was there. I gently pushed it open – I thought I might pluck out an umbrella from the stand as a sort of weapon in case of marauders. But all I did was gasp – I gasped and was hurt and sickened by what I saw there . . . Alan, poor Alan, askew on the floor, his jacket all torn – blood on his hands and clotted into hard encrustations in the wrenched-around and sweat-matted tousle of his hair. I rushed to him, and he stirred.

'Alan! Oh my *God*, Alan . . . ! What has . . . ? Are you . . . ? What happened? Who *did* this to you . . . ?!'

Alan twisted around his head, and opened an eye. His voice was no more than a groan.

'. . . Black . . .' he said. 'Bloody *bastard* . . . !'

Susan's breath was caught, her heart a welter of pain and shock. She ran upstairs to her bathroom, her mind now useless in the spin it was in, and hurtled back down again with armfuls of everything she had randomly gathered. She stung him with disinfectant, she cooled his forehead with a dampened towel, she dabbed at his contusions and she wrapped his hands in gauze (the tube of fake suntan, the tampon dispenser and two packets of dental floss she hurled away with impatience). She could see he was aware of comfort – his eyes were smiling the faintest thank-you, and she knew he would not die. And after the fleeting peace of that, there then came the blinding wall of fury. She flew back upstairs and crashed into Black's bedroom – plain and calm and quite untouched – and then she was running all over the house, banging doors and yelling out his name. When finally she found him, quite sweetly asleep in his armchair, a whisky at his side, her eyes were mauve with uncut rage and the need for attack. And here now – after all of that – before her on the floor was yet another bruised and damaged bastard of a man who of course, like all men, denies all knowledge, any culpability – he protests his innocence, and begs me for mercy. Well he won't get it. And yet . . . since I told him to his face just what Alan had said to me, Black . . . he was crying. I would have punched him hard for that, and yet . . . there was a pain of a different sort alive in him, now – he seemed at least remorseful. I might have relented, then – an attempt at human compassion – but then there was this vision that cut me: his fingers on Amanda, crawling – and now the splice of Alan's blue-and-red and bulbous face . . . and I drew back my fist and – *God*, I would have hit him, and just so hard, but my arm now, it was being constrained, but oh so very weakly. I glanced around and was shocked to see Alan, bent double and swaying above me, my wrist in his tentative grasp, his other hand holding his side.

'Susan . . . ! Christ's sake. *Leave* him . . . what are you – *doing* . . . ?'

The effort, then, was just too much: Alan fell back into a sofa and just lay there, breathing hard.

'But Alan – he—!'

'He's my – *friend*. He's done nothing. He's my – *friend* . . . !'

And Alan now was crying too. He eased himself forward and down on to his knees. Susan just watched him as he shuffled his way over to Black, his hand still clamped down on to his side, and he was wincing. One of his tears fell down on to Black's face – and Black, he did his damnedest to prise open his eyes and try to see above him. He smiled, then, at the sight of Alan, and Alan tried it too. Susan could only stare as Alan's stiff and bandaged hands clasped a gentle hold of one of Blackie's, and then more tightly. Alan stroked his brow and said shhh, shhh . . . and told him, softly, not to worry, not to worry, because everything now was going to be all right. Black had flattened his lips, and he nodded calmly, his eyes so very tender. He managed by degrees to lift up Alan's gauzy paw so that the tips of the fingers were just now touching his lips, which then so very slightly stirred. And in the silence, it was Susan, then, who was weeping.

Mum, she's like – out? I don't know where she goes, and I so used not to care, you know? But she's kind of been having a hard time lately, like everything's really done her head in and she never lightens up. Sometimes when she goes out it's got to do with getting stuff for my – omigod, *flat*, can you believe? I mean it's not like a new flat or anything, it's just the basement

415

really, right here in the old house. But when I said to her, Mum – listen, OK? There is no *way* I am going back to Richmond, not after all what I saw. And it kind of broke me up in one way though because my room there, oh wow. And my black-and-white bathroom and everything. And Mum, I thought she was going to go Oh don't be so *silly*, Amanda – of course we're going back, it's our *home*, isn't it? And your *father's* there, isn't he? But she never. She just said she was like hearing me, and what she'd do is she'd get Mr Clearley's people to come round here and like break in a side entrance? And that would be just for me? And there's going to be a proper bathroom, yeh, and a chill-out space and even like a microwave and other gear. I just said cool: what's not to like? And she's been really amazing about other stuff too – like when I told her that to cover for this so-called Switzerland jag I'd written this like note to the school? Doing her signature and saying I was ill? And then I said to her, Mum: I so don't want to go back there either. Yeh – and I was just like ready for all of her usual stuff: what are you *talking* about, Amanda? Of *course* you have to go back to school – you're not yet *sixteen*, and there's the sixth form and then there's university and—! But she never. So I've got this, like – tutor? She comes every day – Eileen, her name is, and she's really pretty cool. I'm even like learning stuff because she doesn't make it all just so boring like they did at school, you know? So yeh – Mum, she's just so like not being Mum any more, and so when she said she was going to come with to this new appointment at the clinic, I told her what I'd been thinking. I half wanted her to tell me I was nuts and like drag me there, but if she did that I was so going to go crazy at her. But she never.

'Oh, *Amanda* . . . I don't really think you understand what it is you'd be taking on. You're so terribly *young* . . .'

'Yeh but a lot of girls do it now, don't they Mum? And you'll be here and help me and stuff, won't you? I just feel it's . . . right. You know?'

And Susan could only sigh, not really sadly, and nod at the inevitability. Because despite all of the more practical considerations, well – it *is* right, of course it is. In the eyes of God. But Amanda, she's never had to cope with even a minor responsibility, let alone something such as this. Though she's quite correct when she says that I'll be here and, yes – that I'll help. For where else now could I possibly go? And what have I left to do? It is a relief in many ways that I'm not getting back – it was never, at base, what I wanted, and yet I did believe that it had to be done . . . though I can't now even remember why. But the morning following that most hideous night . . . when Black was in the hospital with Alan close by him in constant attendance . . . well, I did not consider even broaching all that I had determined – bestowing upon them the gladdening news that I was repentant of my actions, that my passing insanity was cured, that I was prepared to be large and overlook too their recent . . . misdemeanours. No. No no, I said not a word. Even simply standing there, I had felt as an intruder: it was they who were together, Alan and Black, bonded not just by their raw and crusted injuries. And some days later I received from Black just the sweetest little note: no recrimination, not an atom of bile – just the insistence that I continue to forward onto him all incurred expenses and to in no way consider myself a stranger. Alan had added his name, and a kiss. More hot tears from me – my eyes were always then so thoroughly reddened and sore – though if someone had asked me quite why this time I was crying, I could not possibly have answered them. And of course, had Black not continued with his infinite generosity, all the new plans could just never be. As it is, the house, the old house, is well on the way to being split into two quite separate but intercommunicating entities; Amanda, for once, seems actually to be applying herself to her coursework and curriculum, and the Harley Street gynaecologist is nothing but encouraging.

'But what about . . . the father, Amanda? Why should he be able to get away with it? The bloody shit.'

'It wouldn't be like that. I just so don't care about him. I mean, yeh – we could get him banged up, I suppose – but what's the point? You know? And he's got no money or anything. And it's not like I, oh God – *love* him, or something. I just so don't care about him. I can deal. Anyway – it's *my* baby. Mine. Got nothing to do with him, the bloody shit.'

So it's easy then, is it, Susan wondered idly. If you have help and you don't love someone – it's easy then, is it? I suppose it is. I suppose it must be. I wouldn't know, because I do love still: I continue to dangle at the mercy of the give and pull of a long elastic yearning. He rang me, Herb: he said – What's wrong? Susan? What's wrong? Why can't we, you know . . . go on the way we were? Susan? You listening? Why can't we? I just put the phone down. And then I said Because we *can't*. That's all. It wouldn't be right: you're married.

'Well, Amanda . . . if you're really really *sure*, my darling . . . But know it won't be easy. Like the way you were so terribly sick this morning, yes? Well . . . that will happen again.'

'You *think* . . . ?'

'Yes well. So long as you know. And I suppose you have not given the slightest thought to what you'll be doing to *me* . . . ?'

'To you? Don't get . . .'

'What you'll be *making* me. A grandmother! At my age!'

418

'Oh. Oh that. But you're beautiful, Mum. You're beautiful.'
Susan was so surprised.

'You've never said that to me before, Amanda.'

'No well. I guess everyone else in the world has. I never said it before because I always wanted to be as beautiful as you.'

'Oh but, Amanda – you are, you *are* a beauty! What are you saying? And you're *young* – so very very young. The very essence of beauty, youth.'

'I'm not *really* young – don't feel it. I'd like to be sometimes – just rocking up to whatever and just being like fifteen, you know? But I don't feel it. I'd like to, like – *believe* in stuff. Like I was reading that book again – *Grimm's Fairy Tales*? I read it just over and over and I want to believe it's true, but I can't. I mean – I know they're *fairy* tales and they're not meant to be true, but you still kind of have to *believe* them, you know? I maybe didn't put that right. Anyway – I know what I mean. Susan felt again the heat and sting of impending tears.

'I have to go out, Amanda. Mr Clearley and another of them are working downstairs. Offer them – you know: coffee and things.'

Amanda watched her as she got up to go.

'You cool, though – aren't you, Mum? About, you know: stuff?'

Susan harnessed a smile as she gathered up hurriedly her handbag and a jacket.

'Oh *thoroughly*, Amanda, I do assure you. I am perfectly "cool" about "stuff".'

'Yeh, OK . . .' smiled Amanda. 'But you know what I mean. Where you going?'

'Oh, I won't be long. Maria. Coffee. Back soon.'

Amanda nodded and looked at her as she waved a good-bye. Even now, when she's in a bit of a state (because quite a lot, I guess, is kind of freaking her), she's still got such a way of . . . I don't know: just like – *being*, really. That walk that women can do and I can't no matter what. Not like, you know, those weird and skinny models whose hips are sort of pushing out at you and they're in your face as if their whole like middle wants to be sick . . . but just – together, you know? Comes with age, maybe. Which I guess I've been kind of like thinking about quite a lot lately. Sometimes, when I go to myself: 'You're going to have a . . . *baby*,' I get all excited and feel so like really mature and I'm really up for it, you know? Like going and getting all the stuff, and things – and what was always the dining room that we never used, that's going to be the nursery, yeh? And I'm going to have it in pink even if it's a boy because I still like really go for that colour, actually – with a really fluffy carpet: how cool is that? I could find out – you know, if it's a boy or a girl. They're both good, one way, and they're both pretty bad. Girls are nice because you can, like – dress them up? And you've got, like – dolls and stuff? But I wouldn't really want her to be like me. And boys are OK too at first, but then get violent or just dumb. I wouldn't mind if he looks like Harry with the eyes and stuff, I just don't want him to be a shit or anything. And I'm already thinking of names. I think it would be really cool to call this kid like just a *word*, you know? Not like a name that everyone else has got, but just something that's really different. I thought of Zam, which is good for a boy or a girl, if you think about it, and I really really liked that for a while, and then I got thinking it maybe sounded like a, I don't know . . . sink cleaner? Issal is

420

another one – to, like – rhyme with missal? And then I thought of the Bex Bissel carpet thing we got in the cupboard and I just went Jesus, why are my names all sounding like . . . *housework*? Sta is what I like at the moment, pronounced like star . . . but then I went and read somewhere that S.T. stands for 'sexually transmitted' . . . which he is, of course, the kid. Isn't he? Like every single boy and girl in the whole wide world.

Yeh. Anyway – I like go through all of this when I'm high on it . . . but the other times I go to myself 'You're going to have a . . . *baby*,' and I just get so weirded out, you know? And totally stressed because I don't want it to hurt or anything. But I'm really glad my Mum's here. Because she is, now – it's different. I think she's really really *here*, you know? Not just in the same house, but sort of . . . with me? Don't really like it when she's not here.

I would go down and offer Mr Clearley something, like Mum said, but the reason I don't like to is that the less coffee and tea and stuff they have, the quicker they're going to finish my flat. (My flat! So cool.) Might even have a coffee myself, actually, because I so don't do all the vodka anymore. And also, the other guy down there, the younger one, black dude, Phil he is, he like – looks at me? Like they do. Man – he'd be so wiped out if he knew my . . . condition. God . . . I suddenly feel sick again, Christ, it's the worst, this . . . you just feel so . . . oh. How weird is that? It hits you – like in waves? And then it's gone. Totally over. Weird. I feel fine now. So weird. So yeh maybe I will – I'll go downstairs and ask if they want tea or coffee or whatever. Actually, that Phil, if I'm honest, he's like well fit: kinda cute. Except boys . . . I don't know . . . just so not into them at the moment. Just happy to be here, on my own. With my Mum.

*

Well – what a time it's been. But we're both of us on the mend now, I'm delighted to say. Blackie – he's out of hospital tomorrow, yes, picking him up first thing. Don't really like it when he's not here. He'll be back in there though in a couple of weeks, of course, because they're going to do his hips. A latent problem for quite some time, but Susan's onslaught, well – it rather brought matters to a head, shall we say: fell rather awkwardly. He's in a very charming suite in the hospital, terribly swanky, and he could, of course, have had the operation straight away – the specialist was there, ready and willing – but . . . and quite rightly, in my opinion, he said he'd really like to come home, rest a while, get a bit back to normal. Yes well – I'm all for that, goes without saying: *normal* – oh God yes, that's for me. And also, it's his birthday, you know, in just under a week – don't want to spend your birthday in a hospital, do you? No matter how swish it is. I asked him if there was anything in particular he wanted for a present and he said that now I came to mention it there was, yes, but he was damned if he could remember what it might be. Anyway, I have something in mind. And then I asked him how old he was – he managed a smile: a hundred, Alan . . . but I do feel so very much *older*. Dear fellow.

That night though, when finally the ambulance came – and it was I who had to ring and ring for it, you know: Susan, she was just in pieces. Rather a laugh, in retrospect, seeing as she was the only one of us who hadn't been reduced to a twisted and bloodied pile. Anyway – ambulance came; they took one look at me and started trying to get me on to a stretcher. No no, I was protesting – it's not me, it's not me – it's *him*, it's him inside. So they go into the drawing room, these para-whatever-they-are, and they're tending to Blackie (poor old man – every

422

time they budged him he was wincing so bravely) and then they're looking up at me again. Eyeing me, you might say.

'Bit old for this sort of thing, aren't you? Fighting.'

And before this, of course, it hadn't so much as occurred to me: how it would look.

'No no, I assure you. The states we are both in, they are wholly unrelated. Coincidence, really. I was attacked in the street – and I fully intend to file a police report, or whatever one does – whereas my friend here, well . . . that was more of a, um . . . domestic accident. You see. But is he all right? How bad is he?'

One of the ambulancemen had Black now safely and reasonably comfortably, it seemed to Alan, strapped on to the stretcher. The other turned his attention to Susan.

'That right is it, madam? Domestic?'

Susan looked up from her handkerchief, into which she had been sniffling quite ceaselessly.

'Oh . . . yes, yes. That must be right. It is I . . . who is partly responsible. To blame. I became a little bit annoyed.'

The ambulanceman nodded. 'Yes right, I see. A little bit annoyed. Heaven help him then if you'd been out-and-out pissed off. And you, sir,' he said to Alan as the two of them wheeled out the stretcher, 'it looks like you'd better come along as well. Get you properly seen to. And if you wouldn't mind, sir – for our report – telling me a bit more about this, um – attack of yours.'

Yes well. As usual, I suppose, with these bloody things, there's not much to tell. Happens in seconds, with you for the rest of your life, but there's not much to tell. Got to the shop in no time, bought Blackie's Rothmans – and it was late, of course, dark . . . next thing I knew there were these young

423

thugs all clustered around me, couldn't tell you where they came from. Two of them were almost luminously white in the pale cold drizzle of light from the one remote street lamp – bald, bony, eyes were spinning. Other two, black as hell and bloody big. I remember, through the weightlessness and the soaring nausea of my clammy-handed terror thinking well well well – half and half, that's not something you see every day. And hands, then, they were rifling my pockets and one of them had me by the throat. And I so wished I'd *had* something, but no – I'd come out with just a tenner for the fags: no wallet, no phone, I wasn't even wearing my watch. You could see the malevolent fury in their eyes. One of the white and shaven morons, he spat in my face and turned away. A black one hit me in the stomach, almost by way of a parting gesture – he swore quite a bit – and then the four of them set to trudging away, no doubt in search of some other careless innocent to traumatise and injure. And then I heard myself muttering – but it must, I suppose, have been quite loudly – 'Bastards . . . !' Oh dear. And one of the black ones, he came back – ran back, don't know if it was the same one who had winded me, and oh Lord, he was so very severe, so totally hard and vicious: my cheekbone, nose – the whole of my head was just coming apart and I felt like I was dead – and then oh Jesus, the kicking and kicking . . . I felt numb and in agony and my consciousness was slipping. I must have been roaring, though – because the others, they were suddenly urgent and dragging him off me. I lay there, smelling and tasting the hard and cold of the pavement, aware of rips in my clothes and person. No one came. And I could not move. And then I could. Although I don't remember the journey, I must of course have got myself back home. I *do* remember closing the door with care behind me (didn't want to disturb) . . . and then I was so lightheaded and booming with pain, I can only assume that I must just have passed out. It didn't feel strange or even remotely odd to see Susan hovering above me when I eventually came to. I was aware that she was asking me who *did* this . . . and I twisted around my head, and opened an eye. My voice was no more than a groan:

'. . . Black,' I said. 'Bloody *bastard* . . . !'

Yes. And it was only, oh – just hours and hours later that I understood her consequent actions (but if she'd only stopped to think, you know: I never call him Black – I always call him Blackie). Anyway, by this time they'd attended to me very well in the hospital, I must say: bound up my ribs – none broken, rather miraculously, but fucking painful for all that. Nostril felt a little gummed up, ear a bit roary. I hadn't noticed my bleeding hands and torn-up fingernails: I must have, I don't know – crawled my way home. No recollection. Black was asleep by this time – they'd given him something for the pain in his pelvis – and apart from a fat nose and a split lip, he looked at peace, and really so angelic. Before they'd given him the jab, though – he needed it, you could see it behind his eyes, the hurt he was feeling – he was anxiously regarding Susan as she just distractedly was fluttering alongside. And then he looked at me. I swear, you know, that in our eyes were flashing the very same lightning zigzags of alarm as that shocking moment in the hall when we had registered the return of Amanda – uncertainty at first, and then the cold and looming horror. Could it be now that Susan too was back in the bosom of her family? That thing for which we had once, Blackie and myself, so thoroughly abased ourselves in order to secure? She said nothing though, Susan, much to my surprise; and we said nothing too.

And as for this evening, well . . . I'm just pottering about the house now, really, and making sure that everything is perfect for the morning, when Blackie comes home. The lift will be a mercy I must say, because he'll be in a wheelchair up until the operation. Not after it, though – he's quite on course for a full recovery, the doctor seemed convinced. They said we could rent a state-of-the-art model – wheelchair, I mean – one that he could drive himself and turn on a sixpence. But I said no – we'll just take the regular kind: I don't mind pushing. So – that's the end of that chapter. And on the whole, you know, we haven't been bad boys, Blackie and me. I mean . . . Amanda coming in when Lucy and Crystal were here, well that was bad – but was it bad for us to have had them? Susan, she got it into her head that Blackie had assaulted Amanda in some way or another – and that of course would have been bad, but the plain truth is he *didn't* (which is good). Susan and Amanda, however – they have been bad girls, no getting away from it, and yet they neither of them, I am sure, set out to be bad. Things that at the time seemed to them to be good . . . just turned out badly, that's all: they're both good people at heart.

My jacket, you know – the old Harris tweed? It might just about have had it, this time: terrible state it's in. And oh look – in the right-hand pocket . . . a mashed packet of twenty Rothmans. Maybe just chuck it out. Forget the whole thing. We'll see. But for now, I'll just draw the curtains and then I'll pour myself a drink. Getting dark. Flower beds are in a bit of a mess. Haven't seen the gardener for ages.

And just lying here like this, somewhat preposterously, I do, of course I do – I wonder why I came. Everyone must, I imagine. Alan, he surely must have done so, week in week out. Amazing he kept it up. I can only conclude that it is a need to commune with your very own self that drives you into the arms of others, to chatter away to them, professional or otherwise. Maria, however – on this occasion, she just would not have done. She feeds on me, and she whoops like an American audience. I am, to her, a spectator sport. What I needed now, I had decided, was education in its strictest sense; just that – an elicitation. Or possibly, I was just rather lonely.

'Did you hear me, Susan? Did you hear the question?'

'I did, Doctor Atherby, yes I did. I'm thinking about the answer. And I don't really know, quite how I see them. In terms of their relating to me, I mean. I can see them perfectly clearly as they *are*, as they are in themselves. Or what they have become, anyway. I suppose there were elements there before . . . well of course there were, of course. But sometimes now it's as if they're . . . I don't know . . . Higgins and Pickering, almost. You could say. Though there never was an Eliza. Not that I know.'

'They have a lot in common?'

'They always did. I didn't know how much . . . but now I would say – everything. I saw it most clearly just after I had injured one of them, you know, and they bled together. In the hospital . . . Alan, he leant over. While Black was still asleep. Kissed him. Just once. On the brow. So . . . tender, it seemed. What they were meant to have in common, of course, was me. Me, yes. That was the, oh God – *idea*. What they now have in common – one of the many things – is still me, in a way . . . in that now I am no longer there. Funny. To some that might seem funny, I suppose. Maybe my presence was the sole reason, once, that there was always so much, um – sympathy . . .

empathy, is it? Between them. I was the thing that had to be mutually borne. And then I no longer felt a part.'

'When did you begin to feel that?'

'When I ceased to have . . . control, I think. When they went their own way. Their own *joint* way, I might say. They spent a lot of time in Alan's room. Secret room. I've never been allowed into it. Never really wanted to – never been interested in any of Alan's little escapades. Can't imagine what goes on in there. I suppose . . . nothing. What goes on in any room? Once, Alan was struggling in with a big box marked 'cornets'. Cornets, yes. Which struck me as strange. Well I don't know – maybe they have an entire brass band, or something. Wouldn't know. I've never been allowed into it. Never really wanted to. Though I must say I doubt the band idea. Not remotely musical, those two. No coordination, you see. And then there were the jokes . . .'

'The . . . sorry? The jokes?'

'Mm. All the time. Not there was an Irishman and an Englishman in a bar sort of jokes, not that. But suddenly, one of them would say something that I thought frankly rather silly, rather – childish, yes. Just like little schoolboys. But the other would always be hugely amused. And then reciprocate.'

'I see. Do you recall an example? A particular instance?'

'Oh . . . so many of them, really. Well one I remember . . . Alan, yes it was Alan. He said that as all the members' clubs in London were only open from Monday to Saturday, why didn't they start one up that would be in business solely on the Sabbath? And call it the Sunday Joint. Yes. Well that seemed to tickle Black terribly. Laughing away. And I just found myself going Oh good *Lord*, Black – what's wrong with you? It's not *that* funny – in fact it's not funny at *all*. It's not, is it, Doctor Atherby? Not funny, is it?'

'Black, he evidently thought so.'

'Well yes I know. That's what I mean. And then another time I remember Alan asking him, um – what did he say . . . ? Oh yes – he said: Blackie – he always calls him Blackie, Alan. I don't, but he does. Blackie, he said, what are you doing to save the planet? And Black, he says: I'm not saving the planet, Alan – I don't collect *anything*. Well. That was just *riotous*, seemingly. Laughing away into their whiskies . . .'

'Susan. Are you . . . sad?'

'I think I must be, don't you? Of course you won't answer that. You people never do. But I suppose I am. Although I don't yet feel it. Maybe it won't come over me. In one way I'm quite – light. Less, well – luggage now.'

'But you did feel . . . excluded.'

'I did, yes. I suppose so, mm. But that's not why I . . . I mean I didn't go actually *looking*, you know. I didn't seek out another man in order to upset them. Not even for the company. It just . . . happened. Everyone says that, I expect.'

'What was your . . . husband's opinion of that?'

'I don't know what their opinion was. I've never asked. I've never even properly talked to them about it. I think they still believe it's the boy I went with – you know, Amanda's little shit, the little shit who . . . And I'm not sure that any longer they even *care*. Well actually, that isn't true.'

'No?'

'No. I *am* sure – perfectly sure. They don't care a bit. I don't mean they don't care *about* me – or even *for* me, because I think they do. They're both of them very . . . kind. Black is more than generous. And, thinking about it . . . even that isn't right.

429

Because I was saying, wasn't I, that they don't now care if I'm there or I'm not. But no, not true. The awful thing is . . . they care very much that I . . . *mustn't* be. And I just don't think I *deserve* that . . .'

'Do you . . . do you need a tissue? Susan?'

'No. No thank you. I'm fine. I'm perfectly fine. There are now, after all, other things. Well – I told you, didn't I, about Amanda and everything. It's quite a challenge she has set us. Already though, if I'm not dreaming it . . . all this, it has, oh – that dread phrase: brought us *together*. It has, though. We two girls. Three soon, I hope: don't want a boy. Then there's the house to see to – redecoration. I enjoy that. Used to, anyway. And the garden. The garden I shall do all on my own, I've decided. So it's not all awful. Not by any means. Unfortunate, though, that the sensualist within me has been so very thoroughly . . . roused. What to do? Without, I suppose: just do without. Managed it before. Years and years. Strange, though – I ought to have been so utterly sated with it, the sex . . . but I never really was. Is the oddness here. Feasting daily, and always I was left with a hunger. Why, I suppose – it's the only reason I can think of . . . well maybe it isn't – why I did go back to him, that one rainy day. Harry, I mean. The long-limbed shit with the eyelashes of a fawn. In that dirty and hateful little garage he worked in, we briefly impacted – I remember only his sheen, and the tang of diesel. Is that awful? Maybe it is. Paid him to keep his mouth shut – and he has done apparently, which I hardly expected. I also repeatedly made him swear to me that he would never again see Amanda and, well . . . the little lying shit. Didn't know or care what he *thought* of me. Is that awful? Who cares, actually? On the way home, I rehearsed my gentle surprise, a gesture of the hand, when Alan or Black

430

would remark upon the smear of engine oil along my forearm. Neither of them did. I think I had already entered the realm of the invisible. Never mind that. That was just nothing. But with Herb, you know . . . it's not even his love that I miss, because in truth he, well – he never gave me any. Had none. What I miss is . . . having him to love. I love him still, but I don't, you see, any more . . . have him. As to the future . . . I can only hope that my heart has chambers yet uncharted. A vain hope, very probably. Yes. And so . . . after all this . . . I now have to get a divorce. Two, in a way.'

'Why do you feel that?'

'Oh because it's *right*, you see. It's the right thing to do. In the eyes of God. You have to be seen to be together properly, I believe, or else, well – just not at all. I tried to shore it up, my first marriage – didn't I? To enhance it, to make it into something, oh God . . . *noble* . . . and this is where it has led me. I just can't do it again. I am exhausted. I am also excised. You see. And of course I shall have to work again. Eventually. Can't go on just *taking*, can I? Have to get a, you know – job of some sort. The very thing I . . . well. And that, Doctor Atherby, is where I now stand. I just must confront the truth.'

'Which is . . . ?'

'Oh. Simple. It's terribly simple. I was ignorant of everything, really. And now . . . it's over. All of it. I've just run out. It's terribly simple. They are gone from me. I don't have a single husband to my name. Nor even, now, a married one.'

'Time's up, Susan . . .'

'Yes, Doctor Atherby. I know.'

I'm sweating like a pig, but still I toss another log on to a fire so thoroughly blazing as to be giving off enough heat I'm sure to

431

effect a smelt. But Blackie, he just loves it – and I have to admit it's a dazzler to look at. Huge and very handsome mantel in the drawing room, don't know if I ever mentioned – original to the house, shouldn't wonder: fluted Corinthian, egg-and-dart, you get the picture. It's been quite a day – I think we're both a bit tired; I said to him – Blackie, you're close to overdoing it, you know. Nonsense, dear boy! Life, it's for the living – yes yes? Well, can't argue with that – but it's me, of course, who's doing all the pushing. He just sits there like some sort of imperial pasha, while I have to negotiate all the ramps and kerbs and things – things you don't even notice if you're not out and about and humping a wheelchair: I don't mind. Rather like it. Blackie, he says I visibly *thrive* on it: there you are, he says – Alan Peacock, and you're actually *strutting*. He once said he thought of us forming a limited company (Lord knows with what intention) – Peacock & Leather, or Leather & Peacock – but he abandoned the idea almost immediately because it sounded, he said, like a purveyor of sexual aids to a bunch of shirtlifters.

Since he's been out of hospital, he insists that every day we go out, if only for a short time – and the weather's just lovely at the moment, so it's really no hardship. Today we went to lunch in a splendid old restaurant – very cosy and panelled, little brass sconces, speckled glass shades . . . it's a famous restaurant – heard of it, never been there, damned if I can remember the name. Anyway, the food was prime and we were terribly well looked after. He ordered the most wonderful claret – no, don't know what it's called; he's much more into that side of things than I am – he's actually a bit of a connoisseur, on the quiet (and he made me laugh: what sort of water do we want, Alan? Still or troubled? Or shall we not bother with it? Boring muck anyway). Seems that Blackie used to go there all the time in his publishing days and the head waiter, he made an awful fuss of him. Name of Smales, apparently – amazing I remember that, but Blackie, Christ, he said it often enough: Good man, Smales, he kept on saying, and I could only agree. We talked of this and that: how the police, predictably were absolutely nowhere in terms of apprehending and nailing to the wall and preferably with a rusted riveting gun the band of fucking hoodlums who hurt me so badly and left me in pieces. We are aware, the Inspector I spoke to had said – in that unblinking, atonal and perfectly maddening drone that they're maybe taught at Hendon – of a teenage gang answering to your description who are known to operate in the area. To which, of course, I said the obvious: so pick them up – nail them to the wall, and preferably with a rusted riveting gun. And he said it was not so straightforward as that (although you would, wouldn't you honestly? Think it bloody was) and that the situation was being monitored. Which meant what? They were keeping a tally of all their daily and nightly victims? I would, he said, be kept informed. Which – and here's a surprise – I haven't been. I think they work on the principle that eventually you become bored, fed up with pursuing it all, and then just forget it. And they're right in a way: I am bored, I am fed up with pursuing it all: but Jesus, I'll never forget it.

And we talked of Susan, of course, and Amanda. Turns out she's pregnant – Amanda I mean, thank Christ. Amazing – don't know what to feel; seems only yesterday she was playing with her dollies and Play-Doh and so on. And here's the extraordinary thing – she's quite determined to have it, which completely bloody amazes me: she can barely look after herself – as I think we have seen – let alone a baby boy (which yes, would be quite nice, I suppose). But *Susan*, I said to her: she's only a little *girl*. Oh yes, Susan explained to me, but she's really changed – her situation, the new tutor: she's come on leaps and bounds. Maybe, maybe – but what about me? I'll become a bloody *Grandad* . . . !

'Yes well,' chortled Black, dabbing his lips with a napkin. 'Join the, ah . . . Do you know, Alan – talking of one's children and all the rest of it . . . club, yes, join the, ah . . . I had the most extraordinary phone call.'

'You did? When? I must say these profiteroles are quite sinfully good. How's your crème brûlée? All right? Excellent. What phone call, Blackie?'

'Yesterday afternoon – forgot to mention it. While you were out, that time. Accidentally bumping into your Jezebel – Helen, is it? In that perfectly frightful old pub you seem to love so very much. Can't understand it. Anyway, yes – didn't even recognise him at first – you know, the voice. Can't remember the last time I spoke to him. And he had the nerve to say to me—'

'Who, Blackie? Who? I haven't the slightest idea who you—'

'Oh. Didn't I say? Thought I did. Tim. My son, you know.'

'Good Lord.'

'Well quite. And even the phone, you know – I thought it was odd when it rang. You know – my ghastly little mobile thing. Hasn't rung in months. Only had it for work. Bought it under duress – around the time in history when the perfectly unassuming oblique stroke became a forward fucking slash, I ask you. They even wanted me to get one of these, what are they? Pod things, is it, that everyone seems to have stuffed into their ears. Christ – I want music drilled into my skull, I ring up a bank. Good though, was she . . . ? Your little Helen?'

'As ever, Blackie – as ever. Fell for my charms, and the author in me. So what did he want?'

'Who . . . ?'

'Your . . . Tim . . . Your . . .'

'Oh yes, course. Tim, yes yes. Well they were my very first words: Oh, I said – Tim. Well what do *you* want?'

'And . . . ?'

'Well – most extraordinary thing. He'd got wind, don't ask me how, of our, um – situation. Amazing, really. Of course he'd got it all wrong – thought I was cohabiting with a married woman . . . which of course I was, in a way, short while. But it's so very strange, isn't it? How he would have heard anything at all. The phone call of course had nothing to do with his concern for my welfare, no matter how he tried to couch it. It's *you* I'm thinking of, Dad – kept on saying that. Balls, of course. He was just worried that I'd fritter my fortune on some gold-digging fancy woman and there'd be bugger all for him when eventually I pop off. I didn't actually tell him that it had long been my resolution that there'd be bugger all for him when eventually I pop off. He probably would have wept, or maybe had me assassinated, who knows? And as to frittering my fortune . . . well it's rather fun, isn't it really? I like a good fritter. They do them here, you know – apple and banana. Very tasty indeed. Bit late though, I thought, for him to be suddenly taking an interest in anything I might be doing. Barely exchanged a word since the day I killed his mother. Suspicions, you see, they're still very much there, but of course he can't prove it. If he could, he'd have the police on to me like a shot, no question about it. I did him a favour, if only he knew it. She only would've knifed us all in our beds. You having coffee, Alan? Armagnac, conceivably . . . ?'

435

'Is it an illusion, do you think? The bond one feels when one's children are . . . well, still only children, really. Still, you know – just fooling with their dollies and their Play-Doh and so forth. Or is it just the pull of their dependence? You know – they cleave to you because they need to. And then when they don't . . .'

'Couldn't tell you, old boy. Far too deep for me. Expect it's different for, you know – women and suchlike. Good Lord, you know – that fellow sitting over there – know who that is? Can you see him, Alan? Couple of tables down. Beaky nose, white hair. Yes, that's . . . what was his name? Published the most excruciatingly dull book by that man once. Years back. He didn't write it, of course. We got in a professional hack, ghost sort of thing, and still by page five you were yearning to put a gun to your head. Biggest remainder in the history of the house. He was the, um – the RAF equivalent of the First Sea Lord. Top man. I always used to call him the Air Head, which never seemed to endear me to him.'

'Oh Blackie! That is highly amusing. We might go an Armagnac, mightn't we . . . ? Drinkards that we are. Sterling notion. Shame I can't have a cigar . . .'

'You can have one when we get home. Yes . . . sure that's him. Said to me once his wife had become a voluntary mute. Never spoke to him from one week's end to the next. He was divorcing her at the time.'

'Silly man. Such women as that are damned hard to find.'

'Ha ha! Very good, Alan – very good. Ah – Smales! Excellent. Yes – two large Armagnacs, if you'd be so good. So much. Now listen, Alan – I'm just off to the little boys' room, yes? Won't be a jiff. Christ, you know – when I used to truss myself up like Sir Lancelot, it used to take me so bloody long that by the time I'd done the business and bolted myself back into everything, I needed to go to the fucking lavatory again. You know . . . now I look at him again, I don't think it is him. You know: the Air Head. No. Doesn't actually look like him in the slightest . . .'

Yes: jolly good lunch, that was – but it's nice now to be back home, even if the temperature is that of a kiln. We had virtually nothing for supper, we were both that full still: couple of oatcakes, few ripe figs and two good bottles of Alsace. And then I lit up a Cohiba.

'So we're agreed then, are we Blackie? Have them over, Susan and Amanda?'

'Oh yes I think so. Only for an evening, after all. They're all right, aren't they? The girls. Small doses. Give us a chance to try out that new osso buco recipe – Barolo, I think, with that. But I don't want a great big fuss made, you know, just because it's my birthday. My age, well – farce. Don't want, you know – presents or anything. Nor candles. Christ, there isn't a cake in England big enough to take them.'

'You'll want my present though, Blackie. I promise you that.'

'Oh no *really*, Alan – honestly. There's nothing I want. Nothing I need. Just your company alone, dear boy: present enough.'

'Oh but my dear man – you must have something to unwrap. It's traditional. Pulling at bows, tearing off the paper . . . especially if inside you can discover, oh, I don't know . . . Lucy and Crystal, maybe? What say you? Girl Guides, I rather thought – reinventing the bob-a-job. Singlehandedly, you might say.'

'Ah! Now that's *different*. Dear Alan – you think of

everything. Those two, they're just so very, um . . . And I know you say they're expensive, Alan, but actually, they're really such a bloody bargain. You know – when compared with running a woman full-time, so to say. Like a taxi, isn't it really? Any sight in the world more welcoming than that little orange light aglow, when all you are is alone and desperate? Yes. Takes you precisely where you want to get to, and then it fucks off and out of your life until the next time. And who buys a taxi? See what I'm, ah . . . ? And so delicious little things like Lucy and Crystal, well, of course it's very lovely when they arrive – because those two, my God, they're just so very, um . . . but it's almost even better, isn't it? When they go. Very heaven. So yes indeed, Alan: what a gift. And maybe later . . . a picnic on the beach . . . ?'

'All laid on. The gift that keeps on coming. Hardly a *selfless* present though, is it? Good Lord – this Cohiba, you know: prime, quite prime.'

'Glad you're enjoying it. "A woman is only a woman, but a good cigar is a *Smoke*". Kipling, you know. Amazing that poem hasn't been banned – promotion of poisons, the doing down of the eternal goddess . . . Fuckish, fuckish, that's the word I was, um . . . How's the book coming along, old man?'

'I didn't think professionals were supposed to ask that sort of thing. Not a question that an author can decently answer. But . . . well, I've done a bit, you know. Bit more. Little bit. Don't know if it's any good, or anything . . . but yes: done a bit.'

'Good man. Stick at it. Still got contacts in the trade, you know. No guarantees, of course, but at least I can promise you that it'll be *read*, at least. By somebody good.'

'Mm. Just got to write it, then . . .'

'Well there is that . . . Women's market. That's what you've got to aim at if you've any hope of selling. Title's important too. I'd call it something along the lines of *Mr Darcy's Chocolate Manolos*. Can't miss, shouldn't have said.'

'Blackie, oh Blackie . . . Do you know – I'm feeling rather weary. Could be all the wine. Early night, do you reckon? Tate we're going to tomorrow, isn't it? Looking forward. Old Tate, of course. Heard it's marvellous since they weeded out all of the rubbish and stuck it in the other one. Bugger for the wheelchair, though – got steps up, hasn't it? Expect we'll manage. You know, Blackie – I sometimes wonder what people think of us. When we're out and about, sort of thing.'

'Couldn't give a turquoise fuck what people think of us . . .'

'No, I know – but I do occasionally wonder how we sort of, you know – come across. Couple of old queers, shouldn't wonder.'

'Not, though. Are we?'

'Wouldn't have said so. Hardly. No sex for starters.'

'Hm. Although at our age – my age, anyway – there probably isn't much, is there? Any more. Even queers, they can't fancy old men, surely? It'd be more – companionship, I should hazard. Marriage being what you make it, sort of style.'

'Here, Blackie – sudden thought. How about this? "A woman is only a woman, but a good old boy is a *bloke*." What do you think? Could've put that into one of my fortune cookies, in the bad old days. Oh dear me . . . I am, you know – really quite tired. Weary. Go up, will we? Oh by the way – don't know if I told you. The man that Susan went off with? Wasn't the boy after all. Someone else. Married.'

'Ah. Well aren't we all, one way or another. Yes – I think

439

I will, you know. Call it a day. No, don't trouble – I can get myself over to the lift. Night, old man.'

'Goodnight, Blackie. Sleep well. I'll be up too in a minute.'

Just damp down the fire, turn out the lights . . . then make sure the door's locked. Because you need to these days, don't you? Know you're safe.